## LAST CHANCE

*Rachel McKenna shocked the gossips of Last Chance, Montana, when she agreed to dance with Lane Cassidy, her former student—now a legendary gunfighter. But for two lonely hearts haunted by the past, it was a last chance for happiness . . .*

"Readers who loved *After All* . . . will be overjoyed with this first-rate spinoff."

—*Publishers Weekly*

## AFTER ALL

*The passionate and moving story of a dance-hall girl trying to change her life in the town of Last Chance, Montana. Gruff rancher Chase Cassidy didn't think Eva had what it took to be housekeeper for a bunch of ranch hands. But he was in for a big surprise—when she captured his heart. . . .*

"Historical romance at its very best—a combination of high adventure and the magic of love."

—*Publishers Weekly*

## UNTIL TOMORROW

*Cara James was a backwoods beauty who passed the time making rag dolls. Then a soldier returning home from the Civil War showed her that every dream is possible—even the dream of love. . . .*

"Landis does what she does best by creating characters of great dimension, compassion, and strength."

—*Publishers Weekly*

"Four stars . . . a delicious delight."

—*Affaire de Coeur*

## PAST PROMISES

*She was a brilliant paleontologist who came west in search of dinosaurs. But a rugged cowboy poet was determined to unearth the beauty and passion behind her bookish spectacles . . .*

"Warmth, charm and appeal . . . *Past Promises* is guaranteed to satisfy romance readers everywhere."
—Amanda Quick

"An incredibly poignant and humorous story . . . *Past Promises* shimmers with vitality . . . a love story of grand proportions!"
—*Romantic Times*


## COME SPRING
Winner of the "Best Romance Novel of the Year" Award

*Snowbound in a mountain man's cabin, beautiful Annika tried to resist his hungry glances—but learned that unexpected love can grow as surely as the seasons change . . .*

"A beautiful love story."
—Julie Garwood

"A world-class novel . . . It's fabulous!"
—Linda Lael Miller

"A winner."
—Dorothy Garlock

# JADE

*Her exotic beauty captured the heart of a rugged rancher. But could he forget the past—and love again?*

"Guaranteed to enthrall . . . an unusual, fast-paced love story."

—*Romantic Times*

# ROSE

*Across the golden frontier, her passionate heart dared to dream . . .*

"A gentle romance that will warm your soul."

—*Heartland Critiques*

# WILDFLOWER

*Amidst the untamed beauty of the Rocky Mountains, two daring hearts forged a perilous passion . . .*

"A delight from start to finish!"

—*Rendezvous*

# SUNFLOWER
### Winner of the Romance Writers of America's "Golden Medallion for Best Historical Romance"

Jill Marie Landis's stunning debut novel, this sweeping love story astonished critics, earning glowing reviews including a FIVE STAR rating from *Affaire de Coeur*.

"A truly fabulous read! The story comes vibrantly alive, making you laugh and cry . . ."

—*Affaire de Coeur*

*Titles by Jill Marie Landis*

DAY DREAMER
LAST CHANCE
AFTER ALL
UNTIL TOMORROW
PAST PROMISES
COME SPRING
JADE
ROSE
WILDFLOWER
SUNFLOWER

# DAY DREAMER

# JILL MARIE LANDIS

JOVE BOOKS, NEW YORK

DAY DREAMER

A Jove Book / published by arrangement with
the author

PRINTING HISTORY
Jove edition / June 1996

The Putnam Berkley World Wide Web site address is
http://www.berkley.com

Jill Marie Landis's World Wide Web site address is
http://www.nettrends.com/jillmarielandis

ISBN: 0-515-11948-2

A JOVE BOOK®
Jove Books are published by The Berkley Publishing Group,
200 Madison Avenue, New York, New York 10016.
JOVE and the "J" design are trademarks
belonging to Jove Publications, Inc.

PRINTED IN THE UNITED STATES OF AMERICA

10  9  8  7  6  5  4  3  2  1

*Day Dreamer* is dedicated to
Patricia Teal and John D. Diamond,
and everyone at The Berkley Publishing Group,
with many sincere thanks and good wishes.

Dear Reader:

*Day Dreamer* is a story I've wanted to write for quite
some time. Celine Winters, the heroine, is compelled to
exchange places with a stranger in order to save her life.
From the moment she steps into a dark carriage on a
stormy night in New Orleans, Celine finds herself on a
grand adventure.

From the colorful streets of New Orleans, a mansion
on the banks of the Mississippi, a voyage to the West
Indies, and a sugar plantation on a tropic island, Celine
is unable to escape her past—or her future.

Destiny has sent Celine to Cord Moreau, a man with a
dark, embittered soul who has lost everyone he ever
loved. He may be bound by an agreement between families to marry Celine, even though he has never laid eyes
on her, but he is determined not to love her. What he
doesn't count on is Celine's deep belief in the power of
love and her ability to bring his heart back to life.

So sit back, put your feet up and slip into Celine and
Cord's romantic adventure and, for a while at least, you
can be a *Day Dreamer*, too.

Enjoy!

*Jill Marie Landis*

# DAY DREAMER

# One

## NEW ORLEANS 1816

*I*t was late afternoon in the brick, market building as Celine Winters moved amid the other shoppers—Creole aristocrats, slaves and common folk like herself—crowded together in the compact stalls. She paused to gently palm and squeeze one of the last tomatoes of the season, found it too soft for her taste and carefully set it back atop the small pile that remained.

"Nothing today, Celine?"

Old Marcel, a familiar, gap-toothed vegetable vendor who reminded her very much of a gnome, winked up at her. His hands roamed over the tomatoes, restacking them by touch as he kept his roving eyes and his smile fixed on her.

"Not today, Marcel. I have all I need." She touched the basket that dangled from her arm then glanced down to be certain. A bag of rice, French beans, sweet potatoes. A bottle of beer for Persa and salt fish for both of them. All together more than enough for two.

"Cabbage?" Marcel tried again.

Celine started to decline and then changed her mind. Cabbage would keep a while.

"Yes." She nodded. "I think so."

As Marcel picked out a fine head of cabbage with his knotted, dirt-stained hands, Celine paused to glance around the market. From one of the vendor's carts near the pillars, the heady scent of coffee almost tempted her to linger a while longer, but it was time to get back and start the evening meal. If she kept Persa waiting too long, her guardian would worry.

"How is the old fortune-teller today? I don't see much of her anymore." Marcel asked as he wrapped the head of cabbage in thick paper and carefully set it in Celine's basket.

"Her hip bothers her more every day. She doesn't leave home very often now." After Celine paid him in coin, Marcel surprised her with a bunch of violets.

"Lagniappe," he said as he pressed them into her hand. Like the other merchants, Marcel often included a little "something extra" free of charge to favored customers. "You tell Persa that Marcel sends his regards, eh?"

"*Merci*," she said with a smile. "See you tomorrow."

With her basket swinging at her side she took a deep breath and headed through the Vieux Carre to the *briquete entre poteaux*, brick and post cottage near rue de Rampart, the only home she had known since she and Persa arrived in New Orleans fourteen years ago.

She strolled out of the long brick market structure and

walked along rue de la Levée toward the open square known as the Place d'Armes. There was rain in the air and the slightest touch of fall that no one but a native would have noticed. Celine took a deep breath and smiled.

No matter what the season, she loved every facet of New Orleans. She took great pleasure in walking along the same streets where slaves and freemen mingled with haughty Creoles, newly arrived immigrants and the bold, brash Americans who had been flooding in since statehood. As she strolled along, she paused to admire the grace and charm of an elegantly dressed octoroon, the not-so-secret mistress of one of New Orleans' wealthiest gentlemen.

Born in London, Celine spoke English, of course, and now French like a Creole. She liked to think of New Orleans as a fortunate orphan, like herself, for the city had been much loved by its Spanish, French and American guardians, just as she had been coddled and loved by Persa, the gypsy fortune-teller.

At the corner of Chartres and St. Ann, she glanced over St. Louis Cathedral while she waited for a passing cart to rattle by. Incense still tainted the air after afternoon services. Long shadows filled the muddy street. Careful to stay on the walkway to avoid the oozing quagmire, she passed beneath an iron-railed balcony suspended over a narrow wooden banquette. Water splashed in a courtyard fountain behind a rusting garden grille in the wall that fronted the street.

A carriage rumbled past, the driver pushing the horse at a gallop, far faster than the city laws allowed. Daydreaming as usual, lost in the sights and sounds around her, Celine almost failed to recognize Jean Perot, one of Persa's younger, more frequent clients, hurrying along the opposite side of the street. He was nineteen, a year younger than she.

"Good afternoon, Jean," she called out, drawing his attention.

She saw him pause and look startled to see her there on the sidewalk.

"I'm so glad I have run into you, Celine." Tension unraveled his tone as he hurried toward her.

The Creole dandy's dark gaze darted everywhere but failed to meet her eyes. Although the weather did not warrant it, his upper lip was slick with sweat. He was usually haughty, far too conceited for someone with the looks of a ferret. She had never really cared for Jean Perot, the spoiled only son of a well-known family, but he always had plenty of coin to spend when he sought Persa's advice, so Celine made a habit of treating him with courtesy.

He paused before her, glanced over his shoulder and then said, "I just went to see Persa, but . . . she was not in the shop and I—"

"Are you certain? Did you go in? Did you call out?" Unsettled and a bit alarmed, Celine started walking again. Jean quickly fell into step beside her.

"I went inside, but she wasn't there. The man next door said he thought she went across the street for coffee, but I could not wait to find her." He was watching her closely and then, as if he had just made up his mind about something he quickly added, "I went to Persa for advice, Celine, but perhaps you can help me. I'm willing to pay you handsomely."

Jean dogged her steps as Celine paid him no heed and continued to hurry home. Persa rarely left the cottage now. Almost sixty, the fortune-teller had begun to limp so badly over the past two years that she could barely walk. Her eyesight was no longer what it once was either. Celine worried about her constantly.

The Durels, a young couple to whom Celine had once sold one of Persa's love potions, strolled by arm in arm. A slave followed them carrying a lantern. When they stopped to cordially greet her and Jean both, Celine was forced to halt again. As briefly as she could without seeming rude, she asked after their health and that of their two children. Moments later, when the Durels finally bid them good evening, Celine hurried on, with Jean close beside her.

"I am willing to pay you double, even *triple* the usual amount for your advice. Are you listening to me, Celine?" Perot stopped abruptly, blocking her path.

"Not really. I am concerned about where Persa might be."

"She is probably gossiping over *latte* . . ."

"I doubt—"

"Please, Celine."

There was a thread of undisguised desperation in his tone that gave her pause. She held her basket's handle in both hands, dangling it in front of her, balancing the heavy load as she studied him carefully.

There was nothing alarming about his appearance. He was meticulously attired in a double breasted jacket, a tall beaver hat with a smartly curled brim and fitted trousers strapped beneath the arch of his short leather boots. His dark hair was carefully oiled and combed, his clothing perfectly pressed and impeccably clean. Aside from the beads of sweat on his upper lip, he was the picture of ease and composure. Still, something about him made her nervous.

"I'm sure that Persa is there by now. Come with me and we'll find her." To appease him further she quickly added, "You are one of her most valued clients, Jean."

"Which is exactly why you should be willing to help me right now, Celine. We're only a block from my apartment. You'll be on your way in less than an hour."

"But, you know I don't have Persa's talents. I rarely read fortunes . . ."

"Anything you can tell me will help."

Persa had taught Celine early on that the gift of sight could be either a treasure or a curse. Whenever Celine opened herself up to another's thoughts, she saw the past, not the future, and it was the rare client who wanted to be reminded of the past. But once in a great while, when Persa had been too ill to keep an appointment, she had asked Celine to do the reading and use what she gleaned from old memories to make a prediction for the future.

Celine stepped back. "Jean, really . . ."

He suddenly looked so distraught that she found herself having second thoughts. Jean had spent a small fortune consulting Persa over the past few months. Her guardian would be furious if she offended him.

As Jean hastily ran his fingers over his hair, smoothing it down even further, she noticed that his hand trembled. She had never had a reason to be afraid of him before, but this afternoon he seemed so agitated, so very unsettled, that his demeanor gave her cause for alarm. He reached into the pocket of his striped waistcoat and pulled out two gold pieces.

"Here. Please." He thrust them at her.

She stared at the gold. So easily won. It was hard to believe anyone would pay so much for something accomplished with so little effort. Celine thought of her mother and what she had endured to keep them barely fed in London. By the time she was five years old, Celine had already known the meaning of the word *whore*.

The image of Jane Winters's face might have grown dim, but she would always vividly recall the moaning and panting, the squealing and thrashing, the sight of so many different men touching her mother in so many intimate ways.

The gold glittered in Jean's palm. It was more money than Celine would see in a year of selling Persa's potions. Before she could change her mind, she grabbed the coins and slipped them into her bodice. Returning home with a pocket full of coins would effectively cool Persa's temper if she was a few minutes late.

"All right, Jean, since you insist. I will help you this once, but I can't tarry."

Although he had rushed her along the street in a hurry to get her to his apartment, once they finally arrived there, Jean insisted she sit and have chocolate while he quickly attended to some business downstairs. She guardedly agreed, but only after he assured her that he would return in a few moments.

Celine waited in the cozy sitting room, with its polished tabletops, thick carpets and plush upholstered furnishings. Within minutes of Jean's departure, a house slave brought her a pot of chocolate and then disappeared.

Sipping hot cocoa, Celine passed the time trying to imagine what her life would be like were she mistress of a fine home like this one. Chances were remote that she would ever know. Without a dowry or an old family name to her credit it was unlikely anyone of significance would ever ask for her hand. She had no male relations to arrange a marriage for her, but she had long ago decided that was just as well, for she could not imagine what it would be like to marry a man she hardly knew and certainly did not love.

Lost in her thoughts, Celine suddenly realized that twilight had dulled to dusk. A steady rain had begun by the time she began to pace the upper sitting room of Jean Perot's apartment. She could not wait any longer.

She put down her empty cup and walked to the long, narrow French doors. Staring into the walled garden below, she wondered what was keeping him. Lamplight reflected on paving stones slick with rain. More than impatient with Jean, she decided to leave at once, before the gentle mist became a downpour.

As she bent to collect the basket of produce she had left near the door, Jean rushed in, even more frantic than before. Yet for one so flustered, his lips were set in a firm, determined line. His hat was gone. His hair no longer in place, it stuck out around his head at odd angles. The wide padded shoulders of his coat were damp, his shirtfront wrinkled.

"I have to leave, Jean." Celine announced firmly.

"No!"

The reaction was so fierce, so immediate, that she nearly dropped the basket. Recovering quickly, she was instantly thankful she was armed with the small knife she carried in a sheath tied to her thigh. She was unable to mask her annoyance and a rapid tattoo echoed off the toe of her right shoe as she tapped it against the floorboards.

"Get out of my way, Jean." She spoke softly, her hand creeping along her outer thigh. "I swear I'll call for help."

"Please, Celine. I'm sorry to have taken so long. I'm ready now. You must stay. Please."

She put her basket down beside the door once again.

Jean led her back to the settee beside the small table that held the empty Limoges cup and matching chocolate pot. He waited until she sat down and then joined her.

"You have no crystal," he said, looking startled.

Celine licked her lips and shifted her skirt.

"I don't need one." She didn't relish touching him, but in order to delve into his mind, she had to make some physical contact.

"Give me your hand," she said.

When he touched her, it was all she could do to keep from springing from the settee and racing for the door. She thought of the coins and forced herself to remain still, to close her eyes and let herself fall into a trance. She felt the familiar dizziness and nausea that always preceded a vision. She let herself go, slipped in further and became weak and light-headed. Her mouth went dry.

"What do you see? Tell me . . ."

At first there was only darkness. When she finally became lost in his memory, she saw images as if through his eyes. She eased in further and could not speak.

*The shop. Her cottage. Shelves lined with vials. Potions. Persa's crystal ball. Faded velvet. Persa. Backing up. Backing away. A table crashes. Glass breaks. Horror in Persa's eyes. Her mouth wide and screaming. Screaming until it is too late. Too late. Persa's lips all blue. Choking. Gasping.*

*Overwhelming rage. Hatred. Panic. Desperation.*

Celine's mind shut down as she fought for air and blocked the visions as Persa had taught her. The malevolent aura surrounding Jean Perot was too much for her. Her eyes flew open and she focused on him, but the depth of emotion she had experienced—*his* emotions—still frightened her deeply. She buried her face in her hands.

Too late she realized her reaction would give away what she had seen.

"What is it?" Jean's voice became low and calm as death itself.

She dropped her hands to her lap and shook her head, but the simple motion did not clear her mind of what she had just seen and felt.

"N-nothing." She barely managed to stammer the word. She raised her hand to her brow. "I'm sorry . . . I must be getting ill. I—"

Celine got to her feet but he was there, blocking her way.

"What did you see? What's wrong?"

"Nothing. It was so upsetting . . . to see absolutely nothing like that. This has never happened before. I'm sorry, Jean . . ."

She knew she was babbling, just as she knew she had to escape. She braced herself, ready to scream if need be. She had to convince him she was ill. She had to reach the courtyard, to race out onto the street.

"I must go." She had to get home, hoping against hope that her vision had been false and Persa would be there waiting for her. She had to get away from this man who may, indeed, have done her guardian harm.

He let her get as far as the door. When she stepped outside onto the *galerie*, her confidence soared. She would escape him after all.

"Wait," he commanded.

Celine froze, one hand on the iron railing outside.

"You forgot your basket."

She *had* forgotten. It seemed days ago that she had been at the market. He offered her the basket. She reached out, careful not to touch his hand as she took it from him.

She turned without thanks and hurried on, Jean close on her heels. A few more feet and she would enter the dark brick stairwell that led to the courtyard. They would be out of sight of anyone in the house.

But darkness, which might have been her enemy, afforded her protection as well. She whipped up the hem of her skirt and grabbed the knife as she pounded down the stairs with Jean right behind her. By the time she reached the bottom, she had the knife hilt firmly in one hand, the weapon hidden in the folds of her skirt.

She was panting from fear and exertion, poised to throw the basket at him should he attempt to stop her. Her low heeled slipper hit wet stone and she nearly fell back against the wall. The basket flew up and out of her hand then went crashing down and sent a shower of food splaying at her feet.

Furious, Jean grabbed her by the arm, hauled her up, then threw her back against the courtyard wall so hard that it nearly knocked her breathless.

"Let me go!" she gasped.

"What did you see?" All pretense of politeness had vanished. He was pressing into her now, leering into her face with fevered eyes full of loathing and his own dark fear.

Celine struggled. Ready to strike, she clutched the knife in her free hand. "I'm warning you. Let me go, Jean. Now."

"Tell me what you saw."

"Someone! Help!" Her cries echoed off the walls in the narrow, confined space.

"No one is here. I gave them the evening off. Those black devils are no doubt on Congo Square parading up and down, aping their betters. They won't be back until curfew."

"Which won't be long now." She tried to squirm out of his hold.

"I'm sorry, Celine—"

"For what? Let me go or you'll be sorry."

"It's too late. I had to find out if, like the old woman, you knew too much. When I saw you on the street, I realized you might be able to touch her and immediately know what happened. Your gift is much stronger than the old woman's, even though you only see the past. Like her, you know what I have done, so alas, now I'll have to kill you, too."

*The old woman? Kill you, too? Too?*

"What do you mean? What have you done?" Her heart was racing. "Did you kill Persa? Why? Why, Jean?"

"As I said, like you, she knew too much."

It was too horrible. She couldn't believe him, refused to accept what the visions had revealed—until she felt his hands slip around her throat. His fingers tightened on her windpipe and she knew the terrible truth. She had to get home.

Before she blacked out, she pulled her right arm back and drove the knife between his ribs. Perot gasped and let go of her as he fought for breath. Celine watched in horror as he staggered back, his hands flailing at the knife hilt that protruded from his side.

Too paralyzed to run, she stood numb with shock. Jean slipped and stumbled back, falling against a small fountain where a marble figurine of a nude cherub rode astride a spitting dolphin.

Jean reached out, trying to right himself. His blood-smeared hand slid down the damp marble. Rich dark blood, Creole blood, oozed from his wound. It pooled in the puddles on the stones.

His head bounced once against the paving stones and then he lay perfectly still. Celine glanced up at the house. Every room except the one she had occupied was dark. The kitchen and slave quarters on the ground floor were deserted. She gathered up her skirt hem and began to run, through the porte cochere, past the gateway grille, along the deserted street. Her slippers were quickly coated with mud, the gown of her skirt and the petticoat beneath it sodden and heavy.

She had to get home, desperately hoping she was not too late to help Persa. The bells of the cathedral marked the hour, the sound echoing ominously through the shadowed streets.

She darted around the lamplighter on the corner. The light reflected rain falling in steady sheets driven by the wind off the river. She stepped off the banquette without looking and wound up calf-deep in filthy gutter waste. But she did not allow the discomfort to slow her down.

There was no city guard in sight as she rounded the last corner and headed toward the old cottage. Single-story, small and cramped, it was still home.

Celine raced through the close-board fence and small garden, ran across the low porch. Her breath caught. The front door was ajar.

"Persa?" She crossed the threshold into the shop. It was too dark and still. Something was definitely wrong. She felt her way through the familiar room.

The table where Persa conducted her readings was overturned, its velvet cloth, worn and shiny, pooled on the floor. Amid the folds, glittering shards and spears of shattered crystal reflected what little light filtered in from the streetlamp outside.

Celine rounded the table and nearly fell over Persa's body. Her guardian lay stretched out on the cypress floor amid the crumbs of soft brick she had just that morning carefully sprinkled about to absorb moisture and dirt.

She knelt down and reached for Persa's hand. It was as cold and lifeless as the broken crystal ball. She recoiled in shock and horror. The scene was just as she had envisioned.

Celine didn't think her legs would hold her, but somehow she made her way to the shelf where they kept the sulfur matches. Her hands shook so hard it took many tries to light the lamp. Afraid of sloshing the lamp oil and burning the place down, she set the lamp on the floor. The flame was reflected in the countless crystal splinters. She knelt over Persa again.

Her beloved guardian's lips were indeed blue, just as Celine had seen in the vision. Persa's face was stark and horrifying, her expression was paralyzed into one of abject terror. Celine reached out and lovingly closed the eyes of the patient, caring old woman who had been both mother and father to her for so very long.

Then she leaned back on her heels and covered her face with her hands. Celine could not recall the last time she had cried. There had been no reason to until now.

Her first rush of soul-wrenching tears were spent in a matter of moments. There would be time to mourn after she saw justice done. Determined to find a policeman and lead him back to Perot's, she stood and shoved her hair back off her tear-streaked face.

The curfew cannon boomed on the square marking eight o'clock, the hour when slaves, sailors and soldiers were to clear the streets. Perot's slaves would soon return to find him lying in his own blood, the hilt of her knife protruding from his ribs.

They would know it was she who had stabbed him. His house slave would surely recall serving her chocolate. The Durels had spoken to both Perot and her on the street.

Perhaps a hue and cry had already gone out and the police were on their way to question her. As Celine stood up, she nervously brushed at her damp skirt and glanced around the room. She had nothing to fear. Jean Perot was the murderer. Why, then, did she feel so frightened? Why did she feel such a strong urge to flee?

She had killed in self-defense. She would show them Persa's body, show them what Jean had done. She had seen it all in her vision—

In her vision.

Would they believe her?

She paced the room with her hands clasped, her fingers as cold as ice, as cold as Persa's. Shivers ran up and down her spine. She was nearly soaked through to the skin and could not get warm. A light weight cloak of forest green was hanging on a nearby peg. She quickly drew it around her shoulders and tied the cord at her neck. Still she shivered, as her mounting panic chipped away at reason.

The Perot family was one of the oldest, most revered in the city. The elder Perot, a banker, had served as a legislator. She was no one. She was a fortune-teller's ward. She raised her fists to her forehead and closed her eyes. The gold coins in her bodice pressed against her breasts.

*Think, Celine.*

It would be her word against the Perots'. Her word against that of a rich Creole family with a pedigree a mile long. They could afford the best legal counsel. She could not afford to keep herself out of the old prison in the Cabildo for more than a day. Besides, who would care about finding the murderer of an old fortune-teller when there was the murder of a wealthy Creole to solve? Celine quickly realized that all she had on her side was the truth—and everyone knew money always spoke louder than the truth.

All she could do was tell the authorities about her vision of Persa's murder, about the way Jean tried to attack her and how she stabbed him in self-defense. She would tell the truth and quite possibly meet with ridicule. If everyone had believed in the gift of second sight, Persa would have been a wealthy woman.

Her only defense was the truth.

And no one would believe her.

# *Two*

## MOREAU PLANTATION, OUTSIDE NEW ORLEANS

The house held no secrets, yet a perpetual sadness hovered over it, shrouding the *grand maison* like the spongy Spanish moss draped over the oak trees on the lawn of the estate. The house was constructed in West Indian style, two stories of wood, brick and stucco surrounded by deep galleries shaded by a long, sloping roof. Two stories filled with silence, antagonism and vengeful wrath.

Alone on the wide, second-story gallery overlooking the crushed shell drive, Cord Moreau lifted a crystal goblet in a silent toast to a young woman he had never seen and hoped never to lay eyes on.

Senses dulled by over indulgence in his grandfather's finest Bordeaux, Cord stared beyond the light that escaped the windows to shimmer on a curtain of steadily falling rain.

Prayer was not a habit he cultivated. He was content to rely on luck alone and for most of his life, his luck had been nothing but bad. But now, with every passing moment that his intended bride failed to appear, he became increasingly optimistic that his luck was about to change.

Cord stepped up to the wooden railing, the sound of his boot heels muffled by the rain that streamed from the eaves of the wide *galerie*. With the wavering precision at which drunkards excel, he set his goblet atop the rail then clasped the water-slicked wood with both hands. Leaning forward, he welcomed the mist carried on the strengthening wind as it bathed his face.

In front of the house, the wide, well-tended acreage covered with oak, pecan and magnolia trees swept toward River Road and the levee that held the Mississippi at bay for most of the year. At the waterfront landing, he could see pitch torches that defied the rain. Cord closed his eyes against the night, the rain, the sight of the dancing torchlight and wished to God he could as easily shut out the ache lodged inside him—an ache that echoed louder with every heartbeat.

Tonight was to have been Alexandre's wedding night, not his. It was *Alex* Moreau, his cousin, who had been entitled to have it all: the bride, the greatest portion of the Moreau inheritance, the plantation. Alex *deserved* it all. But the dashing, confidant Alex—the much beloved heir to Henre Moreau's fortune—was dead.

And Henre Moreau, their grandfather, intended to make Cord pay.

The memory of Alex as Cord had last seen him would haunt him forever. They had been in residence at the

Moreau town house on rue Royal, the threat of yellow fever that swept the city with the summer heat was over.

Cord arose late that day, two weeks ago, his habit after a night of gambling and drinking in the Vieux Carré. Foster, his servant since childhood, had come knocking frantically on his door and then rushed in.

Foster Arnold had been Cordero's mother's servant. Foster and his companion Edward Lang had never quite accomplished the polish required of servants of the aristocracy, so they were sent to the West Indies with their mistress when she left England. The men had accompanied Cord from his island home fourteen years earlier.

Cord had never before seen the spry, carefully groomed Englishman as upset as he was that morning. Foster stood in the middle of the room wringing his hands. He would begin to talk, open his mouth to speak, and then snap it shut.

Cord would never forget any of the details of that morning, no matter how minute. He recalled the tension coiling in the pit of his stomach as he drew back the sheets and the mosquito netting and swung his legs out of bed. He sat there, the end of the sheet trailing over his nude body as he rubbed his eyes, aware of the need to concentrate on what Foster was trying—with so little success—to tell him.

"What's going on?" Had it not been an emergency he would have been disturbed, for he was not an early riser under the best of circumstances. With his head pounding from a memorable hangover, he was at his worst.

Foster merely shook his head and kept his hands clasped at his waist. Unshed tears shimmered in his eyes.

Cord's sense of dread heightened. "What's this all about, Foster? Usually Edward is the one who engages in all the hysterics. Has something happened to Edward?''

Foster held his hands wide, as if in apology and unceremoniously blurted, ''It's Alex!''

For a moment longer, the servant stood there numb, all color drained from his face, then he rushed from the room.

An unspoken, unmentionable fear welled up in Cord. His head pounding from a night of debauchery, his hands had shook as he shoved into his pants.

Bare to the waist, he raced after Foster, out of the room and down the stairs to the second floor, where the main living rooms were located.

On the second floor, he burst through the wide doors that opened onto another *galerie*. Surrounded by pots of fragrant rosemary, sage, and lemon verbena, he glanced over the wrought-iron railing. An unfamiliar carriage painted a glossy black stood in the courtyard near the fountain.

The door of the carriage had been thrown wide and left open. Cord raced to the end of the *galerie* and lunged down the stairs. At the bottom of the stairwell, he was met by a solemn entourage which had almost reached the kitchen on the ground floor.

Three men crowded in the narrow passageway, jostling Alex's lifeless body between them. Alex's once-flashing dark eyes were closed, his brilliant smile dimmed. There had been no attempt made to hide the wide crimson smear that stained the front of Alex's finely tailored shirt.

Cord stepped back as the men cleared the doorway and proceeded into the kitchen. The startled cook, her eyes wide with terror, hastily cleared the table in the center of the room. Without a word, Alex's grim bearers laid him on the table. Cord recognized Dr. Samuel Jacobs.

"What happened?" Sick at heart, feeling as if time was standing still, Cord stared at the doctor.

Jacobs ignored him. The other men contemptuously stared at him, their expressions cloaked, their eyes, when they met his at all, silently accusing him of some dark sin he could not fathom. He was used to slights, but not such an undisguised show of utter disgust.

"What in the *hell* is going on? Why are you looking at me that way?"

No one answered. Cord pressed. "For Christ's sake, tell me what happened to him."

By now, Foster and Edward and all of Henre Moreau's house slaves had gathered. They stared at Alex's lifeless body in wide-eyed grief and shock. As Cord stood on the cold stone floor in his bare feet, suspenders hanging uselessly from his waistband, his heart raced. He fought off a terrible wave of dizziness that threatened to bring him down.

In desperation, he turned to Foster and Edward. "Where's Grandfather?"

Edward Lang, the shorter of the Englishmen, his face streaked with tears, his fair complexion blotched, managed to whisper, " 'E don't know yet. 'E's still sleeping."

One of the older slaves hurried out of the room. The doctor hesitated, staring gravely at Cord.

"Help him, for Christ's sake," Cord demanded. "Do something before he bleeds to death."

"It's too late for that. I'm afraid he's already gone."

A surge of wild fury welled up in Cord as he stood there staring down at Alex and the crimson stain on his shirtfront. His cousin's bleached skin was shockingly white against his black hair and sideburns.

"He was killed at dawn in a duel in the Garden of St. Antoine near the Blue Ribbon dance hall," Dr. Jacobs told him.

Cord stared at Alex's body in disbelief, expecting his cousin to jump up at any moment and laugh it all off as a grand joke. He would embrace Cord and ask his forgiveness for carrying things a bit too far. But the ashen pallor of Alex's face told Cord that would never happen.

"What happened? Who called him out? Was it over Juliette?"

"No, monsieur." Dr. Jacobs cleared his throat and looked away.

"Tell me."

Cord appealed to the two other gentlemen standing nearby. He wished like hell that he could recall their names, wished for once that he had Alex's flair for social niceties. The taller of the two turned and left the room, then his companion followed close on his heels.

Cord lashed out at the doctor, grabbing him by the wide lapels of his cutaway coat and almost yanking him off the stone floor.

"Who is responsible for this?"

"You are, monsieur. Alexandre answered a challenge that was issued to you."

Cord felt as if he had been run through with a rapier. He let go of the doctor and stumbled back against the wall. Wrapping his arms around his waist as if he had suffered a physical blow, he mumbled, "I don't understand . . ."

"You were called out last night, monsieur, but rumor has it you were too drunk to walk. Alexandre saw that you were sent home. He knew you would not be capable of meeting anyone at dawn, so he appeared in your stead. I was summoned to attend, as were the two witnesses who just left here. It was a fair fight. Unfortunately, your cousin lost.''

On the heels of the terse explanation, Henre Moreau, followed by the house slave who'd summoned him, entered the kitchen, leaning heavily on the ever present silver headed cane he carried as a result of a riding accident a few years earlier. His starched white shirt shone beneath a satin dressing gown. His full head of silver hair was perfectly combed, his posture erect and commanding as always.

He glanced once at Alex's body and then never, ever looked at it again. The old man's voice did not waver as he addressed the doctor in the cold efficient tone he used with all underlings.

''If I heard you correctly as I entered, you said my grandson is dead, that he died in Cordero's stead?''

The doctor nodded. ''Alexandre took up a challenge issued to Cordero, yes.''

''What exactly was said?'' Henre asked.

The doctor cleared his throat. ''That your younger grandson is a drunkard. I am told Cordero merely laughed it off and said that he knew it, but that if the challenger insisted, he'd meet him at dawn. Cordero then proceeded to become so inebriated he could not walk. Alexandre sent him home and took his place beneath the oaks.''

Henre's eyes were iced with bitterness and rage that Cord could see even though his own were so filled with tears that his vision was blurred.

''You may leave us now,'' Henre said.

Henre turned his back on Alex's body, on the weeping slaves and Cord's personal servants, on the pall of death that hung in the humid confines of the kitchen.

"Come with me, Cordero," he demanded as he strode from the room.

Instead, Cord, ignoring his grandfather, pushed away from the damp brick wall and stumbled over to Alex's body. He knelt beside the table and stared at his cousin. Not until Alex had come to live there four years ago had this mausoleum been anything close to a home. Alex had accepted him for what he was, laughed at his debauchery and assured Cord that someday, when he met the right woman, he would settle down. Alex had never judged him, as so many others had.

Now Alex would never laugh again. Never smile that broad, ready smile he had for everyone. Never gift Cord with his acceptance and love.

"*I've always wanted a brother,*" Alex had said the day he arrived to live at the plantation. "*Come, let's be brothers.*"

By that time Cord had already come to accept Henre's lack of love and had hardened his heart against all others. He had been so lost and alone that it had been nearly impossible for him to reach out for the hand Alex had offered. But he *had* reached out, and they had become friends and brothers. Only Alex had ever loved him, in spite of his faults.

Kneeling on the floor beside Alex's body, Cord felt as alone as he'd been before Alex had arrived in New Orleans. He stared at his cousin's hand, more terrified to reach out than he'd been on the day Alex offered him friendship and brotherhood. But he could not let Alex go without reaffirming that bond.

Filled with dispair, Cord reached for his cousin's hand. It was cold. Alex was already gone.

Cord looked at the pale hand he held in his own and

was hit by the utter hopelessness of the truth. It was all his fault.

*I should be dead. I should be the one lying there.*

He buried his face against the back of his cousin's hand, hardly aware of Foster's gentle efforts to help.

"Stand up, Cordero. Your grandfather is waiting in the library. You don't want 'im to see you like this."

Numb with shock, Cord walked through the lower level and up the stairs to the library. He stood before the desk his grandfather used as effectively as a fortress wall between himself and those he summoned into this, his private lair. The old man was seated behind the desk, his cane propped nearby. A study in chilling hauteur, Henre gave no outward indication that his favorite grandson had just lost his life.

"Your behavior has cost me dearly, Cordero, to say the least. Just like your father before you, you have dishonored our name." Henre never looked up at Cord as he shuffled through a sheaf of papers on his desk. His hands were steady. He showed no outward sign of grief, but his rage simmered almost visibly.

"As you are aware, Alex was to have married in two weeks time. Now you will have to fulfill the bargain . . ."

"Impossible. I am leaving New Orleans for good." With Alex gone, he had no reason to stay in this place he hated. He would leave, sail home to the West Indies and, as a tribute to Alex's memory, try to make something of the land he had inherited from his mother.

"You are penniless. Where will you go?"

"Home to St. Stephen. On the first available ship." As soon as the words were out, a sense of relief swept through him that felt as strong and sure as the West

Indian trade winds. It was time to reclaim his life.

"So you intend to flee like the coward you are and live on that run-down plantation your mother left you?"

"Exactly."

"I have signed a contract with Thomas O'Hurley. His daughter is to wed my heir in two weeks' time. Unlike you, Cordero, I am a man of honor. I will see my word upheld."

"Marry her yourself. I don't want your money. I never did. I did not come here of my own accord, remember? I should have left four years ago . . ."

"But then Alex arrived."

"Yes. Alex arrived. I had expected him to treat me with the same disdain you have always shown me, Grandfather, but I was wrong. Alex befriended me. He made my life here somewhat tolerable."

Henre Moreau finally looked up. If Cord had expected him to have been moved, he was wrong. He should have remembered that the old man used information to strike where it would hurt the most.

"You say you loved Alexandre? If you did, you would do the honorable thing and marry this girl in his stead. Alex never balked at the notion of this marriage, not even as he professed undying love for his little mulatto mistress, the mother of his children."

"Her name is Juliette."

"I don't care what her name is. It is nothing to me. I should have known you would be too selfish, too much a coward to do the honorable thing."

"Think what you will."

"You will need money to reestablish that plantation on St. Stephen."

Cord shrugged. "Who knows? I may just sit there in the jungle and drink rum with the Caribs."

"I don't doubt it. But then, I don't really care what you do after you marry the O'Hurley girl. What I do care about is my good name, and Alex's." The only indication of the depth of his loss came when Henre's voice broke on Alex's name. It was a moment before he could add, "I will not have our honor besmirched."

Cord remembered closing his eyes as he stood before his grandfather recalling Alex's laugh, a joyous sound that could fill a room and lighten every heart in it. *Honor?* Cord had never once in his life done anything honorable. Not for himself, and certainly not for this man who had made his life miserable since he was eight years old.

But could he do the honorable thing, even for Alex?

"Well?" Henre waited. Eyes as fathomless as midnight stared at Cord. The old man, so adept at showing no emotion had leashed his temper, stowed his grief.

Cord let out a deep sigh. "For Alex. I will marry the girl—because Alex would have done so. Then I will sail to St. Stephen, with or without her. The choice will be hers."

As memories of the past now faded into the mist of what was supposed to have been his rainy wedding night, Cord wondered what the O'Hurley girl would say when she learned that he intended to sail on the noon tide? That is, if she ever arrived.

All was quiet downstairs where he had left the only invited wedding guests, his two distant cousins Stephen and Anton Caldwell and Father Perez, the Jesuit priest. Cord knew the twins were no doubt fortifying themselves with wine and that Father Perez was stuffing himself with beignets. The priest had been a permanent resident for over two weeks now, summoned first to preside over Alex's funeral, then bribed with Henre's full pantry and a cook at his disposal to stay on until he saw Cord well and truly wed.

Cord was thankful they had all seen fit to leave him to his liquor. He hoped by the time his bride arrived he would be in enough of a stupor to greatly repulse her, not to mention further infuriate his grandfather.

He would uphold his cousin's promise and claim the rich American merchant's daughter and her dowry. Her father had paid for a Moreau heir, and so she would have one, but little else. By midday tomorrow, his bride would learn that *this* Moreau heir intended to walk away from the inheritance and sail home to the West Indies.

If she wanted to remain his wife, she would have to sail with him.

He turned away from the railing, nearly stumbled, and righted himself. He grabbed the wine bottle by the neck and hoisted it to his lips, then felt the warm wine rush down too quickly. Before he could contain it, the burgundy liquid spattered like blood over his shirtfront. When he tried to survey the damage, the stains wavered and blurred.

The door to his bedroom suite opened. From where he stood on the balcony, Cord could look through the room and watch as one of the twins walked in without knocking, glanced quickly around and then looked toward the open jalousies. Stephen walked into the room and closed the door behind him when he saw Cord. Cord moved up as far as the open double doors and stopped there, edging his shoulder into the door frame for support.

Stephen Caldwell was barely eighteen, but he and his identical twin, Anton, could have easily passed for twenty. Six feet tall and still growing, the broad-shouldered, golden haired Adonis was one of a pair, the products of Henre's only cousin, Mariette, and her husband, a brash American naval officer who had died in battle at sea, following his wife in death shortly after she gave birth to the twins late in life.

Cord focused on Stephen, who was casually seated on the footboard of the massive tester bed, eyeing him thoughtfully.

"I see you're still standing," Stephen said, looking down long enough to straighten the fine linen cuff that extended exactly the right length beyond the sleeve of his coat.

"Not for long, I hope." Cord took another swig of wine.

"Is this any way to greet your intended?"

Cord spread his arms wide, the contents of the bottle perilously close to sloshing out and over the white-washed balcony floor. "This *is* the way I plan to greet my intended. If and when she decides to show up."

Cord didn't like the way Stephen's hazel eyes darkened as he stared at him thoughtfully. "Marriage might be the best thing for you, Cousin."

Cord's hand tightened on the neck of the wine bottle. "Turning traitor?"

Stephen shook his head. "No. But at the rate you're going, you'll kill yourself before too long."

"And you think a *wife* will be able to stop me?"

"Perhaps. If she is the right woman."

"Then you still hold women in far greater esteem than I do. No doubt it's because—"

"Of my American upbringing," Stephen finished for him. The twins had been reared in the East by their father's kin and had only recently returned to New Orleans. Moving in Creole society, they had embraced the casual elegance, the endless pursuit of happiness and the comforts of wealth that they had inherited from their mother.

Henre's own wealth and influence had opened every door for the two young Caldwell men until Cord's last and most grievous fall from grace had temporarily closed them. Cord reckoned it was for their own good more than his that the Caldwells wanted to see him quickly settled and gone.

The realization hurt. Cord took another swallow and continued to lean half in and half out of the room.

"She might be beautiful," Stephen mused.

"If I could, I would relinquish her to you."

"Her father parted with a small fortune in dowry money to see her wed the heir of one of the oldest, most established families in New Orleans. You do realize, of course, that you are the Moreau heir now."

"A fact I would just as soon forget."

Cord closed his eyes for a fraction of a second and felt a surge of satisfaction when the room began to swim. Thankfully, he would soon be incoherent, which was how he preferred to spend his days and nights lately. It was so much easier than facing the truth. He slowly opened his eyes again. Stephen still perched on the foot-board like an overgrown cherub, his light eyes and hair the exact opposite of Cord's dark features.

"O'Hurley thought his daughter was going to marry the most upstanding member of the family, not the black sheep. Perhaps she's heard Alex is dead and has changed her mind," Cord told him.

At the mention of Alex's name, and the fact of his death, Stephen's expression immediately sobered. They were all still hurting, Cord reminded himself. All of them.

Cord pushed away from the wall and strode back out

onto the balcony. A ladder-back chair stood near the wall. He sat down, tipped back and balanced the chair on two legs. Resting his head against the wall, Cord upended the bottle and drained it dry.

A slight noise drew his attention to the door. Stephen had followed him outside.

"I don't need a watchdog," Cord said, refusing to mask the bitterness in his tone. He let go of the bottle. It dropped to the floor with a hollow sound and rolled a foot away. "Why don't you go downstairs and play with Tony? Help keep Father Perez in beignets and claret?"

"Are you planning to drink yourself to death?"

Cord didn't know which he hated more, the genuine concern in Stephen's eyes or the undisguised pity in his tone. Ignoring both, he held his silence, and Stephen soon retreated along the *galerie* to his own room.

The rain was coming down harder now, falling in sheets of liquid color that reflected arcing prisms cast by lamplight. In the distance, fewer torches were visible.

*Are you planning to drink yourself to death?*

His cousin's parting thrust haunted him.

"I wish it were that simple," Cord said in a whisper that was lost to the rain-swept night.

He was too much a coward to drink himself to death when there was no guarantee that his nightmares would not follow him all the way to hell.

# Three

Celine had only attended mass once or twice in her life, so she felt like an imposter as she took refuge in the deep shadows outside St. Louis Cathedral, praying to God to help her escape the city. She drew the edges of her cloak together and tried to catch her breath. Her hair was tangled and damp beneath her hood, her shoes were soaked through, and her skirt was splattered with mud. The only thing she carried with her were the coins hidden in her bodice. There had been no time to take anything more. She had paused to linger near the church for a few seconds, long enough to get her bearings and ease the stitch in her side.

As she leaned against the corner of the building, a carriage pulled up directly in front of it. She stepped back, careful to stay in the shadows, where she watched a coachman climb down off the box. He stood in the street arguing with the unseen occupant, and then finally, after a brief discussion, he shook his head, spat and climbed back up onto the driver's seat. The carriage door opened with such force that it banged against the vehicle's side.

Celine watched a woman in a dark-hooded cloak step out of the carriage. A gold clasp at her throat glittered in the lamplight. She held her hem out of the mud and quickly made her way toward the door of the church. Too late, Celine realized the woman would have to pass within inches of her hiding place.

She sucked in her breath and waited, hoping to blend into the shadows. The heels of the woman's shoes rang out against the wet banquette. The image wavered as the cloaked figure ran through the curtain of rain. Celine was tempted to close her eyes and hold her breath as the woman passed by.

Just when she thought she would escape unnoticed, Celine was startled half out of her wits as the woman grabbed her wrist. Celine fought the urge to cry out, struggling to break free as the other woman flung open the door to the vestibule and jerked her inside.

A tall taper had been lit near the collection box for the poor. The flame nearly went out when the door swung shut behind them. The scent of lingering incense stung her eyes as Celine whipped around to protest. She found herself face-to-face with a young woman very near her own age. The girl was her exact opposite, as different from Celine as the moon from the midnight sky, with round blue eyes, fair skin and curly blond hair.

The girl shoved back the hood of her cloak and carefully eyed Celine up and down. Then she broke into a wide smile. When twin dimples appeared in the girl's cheeks, Celine thought she was surely gazing at an angel.

"I can't believe it. God finally answered one of my prayers, and just in the nick of time, too. I was beginning to give up." The beautiful stranger unfastened the gold clasp at the throat of her cloak.

She whipped off the expensive cloak and held it out to Celine. "Here, take it and be quick. And I'll need yours."

"What are you talking about?" Celine felt as if she had just walked into the pages of a book.

"I don't have all night." The girl glanced at the door and then shook the cloak at Celine. "Take it and give me yours."

"But—"

"Look, I know there's some reason you were hiding out there all alone at this time of night, and my guess is that you are on the run. Am I right?"

The hushed whisper was resoundingly loud in the deserted vestibule. Celine glanced around, refusing to answer.

"Please, I'm begging you. You have to help me," the girl whispered. The cloak hung forgotten in her hand. "I'm trying to get away, too."

"I'm in no position to help anyone," Celine said, intrigued by the girl's quick assessment of her situation. "And you're right: I am in a hurry to get away from here."

"Good. Give me your cloak."

Celine glanced into the dark recesses of the church. Votive candles shimmered at the side altars like golden tongues flickering in a constant prayer vigil. There seemed nothing sinister about the girl as she stood waiting impatiently for her to decide. Finally, Celine untied the plain cord that held her cloak closed.

"Why are you so willing to help me?" Celine asked.

"I'm offering you a way out of here in exchange for my own freedom."

Celine held out her worn cloak and they traded. Donning the fine, ruby-colored, velvet cape, her fingers trembled on the gold clasp as she snapped it closed. She waited in silence while the other girl adjusted the green cloak.

When the blond girl smiled at her again, Celine was certain God had sent one of his angels down to rescue her. Celine pulled the hood over her wet black hair.

The girl pushed her toward the door. "Keep the hood up, run across the street and get into the carriage."

"But the driver—"

"He can't wait to be rid of me. You, that is. Just don't let him see your hair or your face. He's a lout who won't even bother to help you aboard. Just climb in and slam the door."

"Surely I could never pass as you . . ."

"Where you are headed, no one has ever laid eyes on me. You will have a whole new life, if you decide to take it. By the time they find out you're not me, it'll be too late to do anything about it, and I'll have gotten away."

"Will I be safe?" Celine could not believe she was actually considering this outrageous plan.

"I would never send anyone into danger. So, you will do it?"

The girl had her hand on the door handle. She opened it a few inches and urged Celine out into the rain. The carriage was waiting. The driver sat hunched over on the box. Celine could not leave before she asked one last question.

"If I take your place tonight, what will you do?"

She would not have thought it possible, but the girl's dimples deepened.

"I will fulfill my wildest dream. I want to be a nun."

The girl was furtively watching the driver through the opening in the door. He glanced over at the church and placed one hand on the seat, about to climb down.

"Hurry! Before he sees us together. Keep the hood over your face." She placed her hand in the small of Celine's back and shoved.

"But—"

"Go!"

Celine raised the hood and pulled it close to her face. The girl gave her another shove and Celine felt herself propelled out into the rain. She took a deep breath and hurried across the street. If God had sent the angelic blond girl to save her, she was not about to turn down such a gift.

Just as the girl had predicted, the driver paid no attention when she ran up to the carriage. He settled back and let Celine open the door and climb into the dark interior. Before she had time to settle herself squarely on the seat, she was nearly tossed to the floor.

The damp cloak offered her warmth, but she continued to tremble from more than the dampness. The carriage turned right at the corner and headed for the levee road. When one of the back wheels hit a mud hole, Celine nearly flew through the roof before she came down again with a sharp thud. She braced herself on the cold, hard seat, too drained to do anything but slump against the wall.

It was a while before she realized tears were flowing down her face. She wiped them away with the back of her hand and then shrank into the corner of the seat and leaned her head back.

There was no relief from her sorrow. She felt as weak as a kitten now, but earlier she had somehow found the strength to move Persa's body to the small bedroom in the back of the house, lay her out on the bed and gently cover her.

Before she left the room, Celine said a hurried prayer, hoping to speed Persa's soul on to wherever it might be bound. Then, just as she was about to begin packing, she had heard the loud sound of men's voices as they shouted to each other in the street. A glance out the front window told her it was the police pounding up the walk. She had raced out the back door.

There had been nothing left to do but run. She had been intent on escaping New Orleans, whether by flatboat or with travelers going up the Natchez Trace, when she'd paused at the cathedral. And then the blond angel of mercy had appeared.

The carriage had by now left the city behind, traveling at what Celine considered breakneck speed. She could not recall ever having ridden in a carriage before, but if this were the norm, she was thankful she had missed the experience. Every so often she heard the whip crack over the horses' heads. There was a wild sway and bounce whenever the carriage hit a mud hole as they bowled down River Road and along the levee.

Praying that she had not exchanged one horrible situation for another, she was thankful that at least she was putting miles between herself and the city. While she was bouncing along, she decided that when she reached her unknown destination she would explain that her mysterious benefactor could not make the trip, then ask for shelter and employment.

She would not refuse any opportunity. She would willingly work alongside house slaves for room and board just to have a place to hide until she could be certain she was not wanted in the death of Jean Perot.

The carriage rumbled on for what seemed like hours. Lightning flashed. One loud clap of thunder forced her to cup her hands over her ears.

Just as she was certain the carriage was about to tip over, she realized the vehicle was merely turning right. She pulled back the leather window shade. They were moving up a long, oak-lined drive toward a grand house, whitewashed and ghostlike, that was barely visible through the moss hanging from the trees.

Even after the carriage wheels ground to a halt, Celine had the sensation that she was rocking. She fought back nausea, started to open the door, then put off revealing herself to the driver for as long as possible. She drew the hood of the cloak around her face and waited, perched on the edge of the seat with her hands pressed together between her quaking knees.

Rain beat down on the roof of the carriage. Above the din she could hear the driver as he dragged something heavy off the roof. She recognized the sound of a door knocker and waited, listening intently. She heard voices, but it was impossible to make out the conversation over the rain. Then, without warning, the carriage door flew open. The driver, whose features were barely visible between his hat brim and his coat collar, reached in without looking at her and offered his hand. With her face averted, Celine took it and climbed down. He let go of her as soon as her foot hit the ground.

She clutched the edges of her hood close to her face as the driver walked beside her. A balding, portly man stood waiting at the front door, permanent worry lines etched on his brow. He wore the clothing of a servant.

"Come in, Miss O'Hurley. Do come in out o' the

rain. What a night, eh? We'll have you right and tight in a minute, though, won't we? By the way, I'm Edward Lang.''

As he ushered her into the hall, Celine looked around to see who "we" might be, but the room was empty.

Her driver, a lumbering dolt if she ever saw one, hovered somewhere behind her for a moment or two and then walked out. When he came back a few seconds later, he shoved a huge leather trunk inside the front door. Celine kept her back to him and the hood of the cloak up over her head.

The worried servant glanced at the driver. "If you need to stay the night . . .''

The other man waved off the offer. "I was paid to deliver the goods and see that she didn't pull any stunts along the way. I'll be heading back to town before the road's flooded. You can keep this blasted bog.''

Undeterred, Edward turned back to Celine as soon as the door closed. He was eyeing her speculatively, circling her, taking in everything: the ruby-colored velvet cloak and gold clasp, her filthy, waterlogged shoes, the uneven hem of her muddy skirt. Celine choose her words carefully.

"I realize I'm not what you expected, but I can explain . . .''

"No need to apologize, mum. It's a 'ellish night out there. We'd all look like somethin' the cat dragged in after bein' out in that storm. The driver should 'ave taken more care to see that you didn't get so wet.''

Before she could explain that she was not the expected Miss O'Hurley or make mention of employment, three more men came strolling along the wide hall from the back of the house. Two of them, obviously gentlemen, were tall, blond, young and uncommonly handsome. They halted just inside in the doorway and stared at her curiously. As if that weren't bad enough, a priest walked in behind them with a glass of red wine in one hand and the last bite of a beignet in the other. He, too, stared.

Celine stared back at all three of them.

Edward politely made introductions. "Miss, may I present Stephen and Anton Caldwell? And of course, Father Perez."

"Bless you, my dear. Bless you," the priest said, then washed down the sugared treat with a swallow of wine and belched.

One of the twins nudged the other with his elbow and whispered. "Go get Cord. I can't wait to watch his face when he sees this."

Celine stiffened and avoided looking at either of the cocky young men. They might be American, but like most of the Creoles she knew, they appeared never to have done a day's labor in their lives. Good looks meant nothing to her. She had learned that lesson very young, when she had seen the cruelty of some of the handsome men who had paid for her mother's services. Some of the best-looking had been the most perverse.

Edward must have sensed her discomfort. "I'll see you to a room where you can freshen up and change before the ceremony."

"*What* ceremony?"

"This is going to be good," one of the twins said. He crossed his arms and lounged in the doorway, watching the proceedings with such a sarcastic twist to his lips that Celine wanted to slap it off him.

His identical match was more sober. "Maybe someone should get Grandfather."

"I sent Foster after him," Edward informed them.

Celine, wondering who Foster might be, quickly assessed her surroundings. The hall, lined with doors, ran the length of the house. It was toward one of these doors that Edward now led her, the others trailing behind.

"I would really like to explain," Celine tried again.

"I'll take your cloak, Miss O'Hurley." Edward paused just inside the door of what appeared to be a grand sitting room.

"Thank you, no. I'll keep it for a while if you don't mind."

Celine clutched the cloak tighter. It was of far more worth than what she wore beneath it, far more appropriate to the elegant surroundings.

She became more uncomfortable when the young gentlemen and the priest joined them in the sitting room. One of the twins took a chair near a rose-colored marble fireplace. The other was content to stand and watch her. The priest looked for a place to set his empty wineglass.

"I should explain to all of you that I'm not Miss O'Hurley," she began.

"Is this the girl?"

Celine whirled around at the sound of an unfamiliar voice and came face-to-face with a gray-haired older gentleman leaning on an ebony cane. He was dressed entirely in black. His piercing, hawkish, dark eyes were set deep beneath straight black brows.

"I'm Henre Moreau. I take it you are Thomas O'Hurley's daughter?" When he looked her up and down as if she were a prime racehorse, Celine hugged the cloak tighter.

"No, I'm not, but I'd be happy to explain. She couldn't be here, but when she found out I was longing to leave New Orleans, she insisted I take her carriage. I hoped to find employment outside the city."

She tossed a worried glanced in the direction of the priest and then looked up at the silver-haired gentleman again.

"I'm glad your father warned me ahead of time not to believe a word you said," Moreau told her curtly. Dismissing her, he turned to Edward. "See that she's cleaned up and back here in a quarter of an hour."

"But, sir, it will take at least—"

"Fifteen minutes, Edward. Call on Foster for help." Taking command of everyone in the room, Henre turned to the twin nearest him. "Stephen, go get Cordero. I want him down here immediately. We have put this off long enough. I want to get to bed. And you, Father Perez," he said, turning to the priest, "should gather up your Bible and candles and whatever ceremonial trinkets you need. While you are at it, you might want to brush the sugar off your cassock."

Father Perez stared down at the front of his black cassock. It was dusted with sugar and beignet crumbs. He left the room brushing furiously at them.

"This way, Miss O'Hurley," Edward said again.

Celine refused to budge. "I'm not going anywhere and I'm *not* Miss O'Hurley." She turned to the old man. "I came here to seek employment. If there is no hope of such, please tell me and I'll gladly leave."

"You really are very good at this, you know. Quite convincing, my dear. Jemma, isn't it? Your father warned me when I signed the marriage agreement that you were a consummate liar. I see he was right."

"Marriage?" She felt a swirl of panic. "But I'm *not* Jemma O'Hurley!"

"Did you or did you not arrive in the O'Hurley carriage, delivered by the O'Hurley driver? And is that not Jemma O'Hurley's trunk I saw in the hallway?"

"I did, and it probably is, but I assure you, I'm not the girl who should be taking part in this marriage to some . . . some . . ."

If Jemma O'Hurley was escaping marriage to this forbidding man, Celine was happy she'd helped her escape.

"To my grandson, Cordero," he said.

Henre Moreau appeared sullen, reluctant even to utter the groom's name. Celine was too panicked to feel relieved that this ogre was not trying to claim her as his own bride.

"Take her, Edward, and dry her off or something." He turned away, leaning heavily on the silver-handled cane, and limped slowly toward the windows.

"Anton," Henre said to the remaining twin, who had watched the scene in silence, "go see what is keeping Stephen. He may need help with Cordero."

*Help with Cordero?* Could Miss O'Hurley's intended be an imbecile? Was he insane or diminished in some way? What manner of man were they trying to wed to the angelic Jemma O'Hurley, a woman whose heart was set on becoming a nun?

"Miss, this way, *please.*"

The distress in Edward's voice was unmistakable. Hoping that once out of the room she might find a way to escape and eager to get away from the older man's icy stare, Celine obliged and followed Edward.

He led her along the corridor to a comfortably appointed ladies' parlor. A low, cheery fire lit to fight off the dampness burned in the fireplace, although the windows were open. She longed for nothing more than to collapse in one of the deep, upholstered chairs and sleep, but her mind was racing as fast as her pulse.

Edward stood by expectantly. "Is there anything I can get from the trunk, miss? Your wedding gown? I can beg time and 'ave one of the women iron it. You'll want to wear it for the ceremony.''

"I'm *not* getting married.''

"I'm afraid you are, miss, an' if I might be so bold as to say it, Cordero ain't all bad. Known him since the day he was born. It was Foster and I wot raised him 'fore we came to Louisiana. Given 'alf a chance, he could be as fine a gentleman as any—''

"I don't care what he's like. I won't be staying long enough to find out. I can't go through with this.''

"But you won't have to stay here," he said. A smile lit his face, erasing some of the worry lines. "We're sailing for the West Indies by midday tomorrow, miss. You, Cordero, Foster and me.''

Celine started to protest, and then the meaning behind his words registered. *Sailing for the West Indies. Tomorrow.* She snapped her mouth shut, waited a second more and then said, "Cordero, the groom, is leaving Louisiana tomorrow?''

Edward's smile faded. He began to wring his hands and cast worried glances in the direction of the door.

"It's true. Cordero's made up 'is mind to leave old 'enre's house for good. Leavin' it all behind. Now, I know your father expected you t' marry an' settle down 'ere, but I can assure you, I think this'll be best for all concerned. As I said, given 'alf a chance—''

Celine had to be sure she had heard him correctly. "The bride and groom are sailing tomorrow?''

"That's right, miss. To St. Stephen Island in the West Indies. If I might say so, miss, you'll never be free to run this place like a real lady of the house as long as ol' Henre is alive. Leavin' would be the only way. That's 'tween you and me, now, y' 'ear?''

Marry Cordero Moreau and she would soon be so far

away that the Perots would never find her. All she had to do was stand in for Jemma O'Hurley and marry some mad, moronic idiot that no one else would have and then sail over the horizon. Tomorrow. If the situation proved too miserable, she could disappear as soon as they reached the islands.

"I really am *not* Jemma O'Hurley," she assured Edward again.

"Whatever you say, miss."

"I didn't come here to get married."

"No indeed, miss."

The door opened and Celine half expected to see Henre Moreau standing on the threshold glaring at her. Instead, a spry, carefully groomed servant with light brown, thinning hair stepped into the room and closed the door behind him.

"I came as soon as I could," he said in an excited, hushed voice. He crossed the room and stood close to Edward, who quickly introduced him.

"This is Foster Arnold, Miss Jemma, Cordero's other personal servant. Also from St. Stephen, by way of England."

She nodded. "Hello, Foster. I'm not Jemma O'Hurley."

Foster glanced over at his fellow servant, who merely pursed his lips and rolled his eyes. "It's worse than we 'eard," Edward said.

Foster looked back at her and asked in a condescending tone one might use with a child, "Then who *are* you, miss?"

"My name is unimportant. I took Miss O'Hurley's place in the carriage with the intent of getting hired on here."

Foster turned to Edward. "At least we were warned."

"I'm not lying," she said. She was beginning to wonder exactly what it was they had heard about Jemma O'Hurley.

The two men eyed her pityingly.

"Cordero's not so bad, miss," Foster said.

"I tried to tell her that," Edward assured him.

"I don't care if he has two heads. I must be losing my mind, but I am thinking of consenting to this marriage. But it's definitely *not* because I am Jemma O'Hurley. I just wanted you both to know, I'll not do it under false pretenses."

"She'll do it!" Edward clasped his hands over his heart and beamed at Foster.

Foster took Celine's hand. "Thank you, Miss O'Hurley. And you'll see. He's not all bad."

"I'm *not* Miss O'Hurley," Celine repeated with a sigh.

"Whatever you say, miss," Foster said.

The men took her in hand. They found a coral silk gown carefully laid out on top of the clothes folded in the trunk. They held the gown up, shook it out and, after admiring every bow and stitch, insisted she *must* wear it, that it would be a crime not to. They hovered over her, giving advice and encouragement as one of the house slaves towel-dried her hair before the fire and then carefully fashioned it into an upswept style they all assured her complemented her eyes.

Celine changed out of her faded serge garment into the gown the Englishmen had chosen, careful to keep her coins hidden. It was the loveliest gown she had ever seen, made of coral silk with sleeves puffed at the shoulders and fitted to her wrists. Although it was trimmed with an embroidered satin bow that tied beneath her breasts, Jemma O'Hurley's gown was a good two sizes too large across the bodice.

"It's a shame it wasn't properly tailored," Foster commented.

"It's not my dress," Celine explained.

Foster and Edward looked at each other and shrugged. There was a moment of confusion when none of the shoes in the trunk fit either, and then, after trying in vain to clean the shoes Celine had arrived in, the men hurried her out of the room.

Twenty minutes later, the two servants entered the large sitting room where Henre Moreau sat scowling like an irritated potentate who'd been kept waiting far too long. Except for the priest, he was alone in the room.

"Monsieur Moreau," Foster said, casting a proud glance in Celine's direction, "she's ready." With a flourish, he made a courtly bow and presented Celine, who stepped into the room, forced to stand inspection once again.

Without comment or compliment, Henre Moreau motioned her to step closer. She crossed the floor.

"You don't look Irish," he said.

"I'm not. I'm English on my mother's side. She told me that my father was a dark-eyed gypsy she met one night when—"

"Your father is Thomas O'Hurley and is as Irish as they come. I've met him, don't forget."

Celine sighed. "I'm not—"

He quickly cut her off. "You have already become tedious, my dear. Cordero will have to put up with this behavior, but I don't need to suffer it."

He gazed over her head, toward the door. "We can begin at last."

Suddenly Celine found herself standing alone in the

middle of the room in a dress that was not hers, about
to wed a groom who was not hers. Doubt and fear
snaked up her spine. She was terrified to see what manner of man she was willing to wed to escape the hangman's noose.

The sound of footfalls and the scrape of a heavy shuf-
fle echoed off the walls of the sparsely furnished room.
She slowly faced the doorway.

The twins had already entered the room, half guiding,
half carrying a man between them. Severely attired, he
wore knee-high boots of black leather, black trousers
and black coat. The only white on him was a linen shirt
that was stained, open at the neck and unbuttoned halfway down his chest.

As he shuffled between the handsome twins, he raised
his head for a moment. His vacant gaze swept the room.
Like the twins, he was blessed with finely drawn features, clear skin and a strong jaw. His hair was fathomless ebony, shoulder-length and tied with a thin black
ribbon.

Blindness, Celine reasoned, would account for the
emptiness in his sky blue eyes, startling in contrast to
his dark hair and olive complexion. The poor soul, she
noticed, barely possessed the strength to stand. He staggered between the twins as they led him the rest of the
way across the room. When Cordero was almost beside
her, Henre Moreau stood up.

"Over here, Miss O'Hurley," he said. He did not take
her arm, merely leaned heavily on his cane.

She joined Henre and they stood before Father Perez,
who was waiting patiently behind a table draped with an
altar cloth adorned with a silver chalice and two tall
tapers burning in sterling candlesticks. Outside, the rain
continued to pour. The long windows behind the priest

were shuttered to keep the wind from blowing out the candles but air still seeped through the shutters, ruffling the altar cloth, fluttering the candle flames.

One of the Caldwell twins stepped aside and one remained to support the groom. Celine took a deep breath and prayed for God's forgiveness. She would atone for killing Jean Perot by wedding the blind and stumbling Cordero in Jemma O'Hurley's stead, sincere in the hope that in doing so, the Irish girl would be free to serve God. She only hoped that He would overlook her saving her own neck in the bargain.

She turned to look at her future husband, prepared to treat him kindly until they parted ways in the West Indies. She was ready and willing to be his helpmate throughout the voyage, bound and determined to do whatever she could to make the trip easier for the poor creature.

She was prepared for anything and everything but the rank odor of red wine that tainted the very air around Cordero Moreau. On closer inspection, she could see that his shirtfront was stained with enough wine to drown a rat.

"He's drunk!" she blurted.

"Not quite 'nuf," the groom mumbled. " 'M still standin'."

Henre Moreau stood to her left. To her right weaved her groom and beside Cordero stood Stephen—or perhaps Anton; she wasn't certain.

"Please begin, Father Perez." Henre's command brooked no argument.

The priest's bald head glistened with a light sheen of perspiration. Father Perez buried his nose in the open missal in his hands and intoned the words of the wedding ceremony in Latin.

Lost in lingering panic and the utter absurdity of the situation, Celine did not pay close attention until Father Perez put a question to her in English. She hadn't realized they'd all been awaiting a response.

"Miss O'Hurley?" Henre prodded.

"What?" She glanced around. They were all watching her expectantly. All of them except the groom. Cordero Moreau was hanging on his cousin's arm, bent double, apparently staring at his boots.

"I'm not Miss O'Hurley," she reminded them one last time. The effort was in vain.

Father Perez cleared his throat and tried again. "Do you take Cordero Moreau for your wedded husband?"

"Yes. I do." For a while at least.

"Do you, Cordero Moreau, take—"

Father Perez halted and stared at her, then at Cordero. His gaze shot to Henre Moreau, who was glaring at him. The priest's cheeks were blotched, either from embarrassment or too much drink. From somewhere inside his cassock he withdrew a handkerchief, wiped his brow, then mopped his bald head. He continued.

"Do you, Cordero Moreau, take . . . this woman . . . to be your wife?"

When Cordero failed to answer, the twin nudged him hard enough to send the groom reeling into Celine. With his eyelids half shuttered, Cordero Moreau righted himself but did not answer.

"Do you?" the twin shouted in his ear.

"Sure," Cordero mumbled.

"The ring?" Father Perez asked. "Does he have one?"

The twin elbowed Cordero again. "Ring?"

"No. No ring."

She closed her eyes. It was not the wedding that

dreams were made of. There was no grand cathedral, no orange blossom bouquet or flowing white veil. No family to wish her well. No love.

There was only a drunken groom and an uncomfortable silence that stretched on and on until Henre Moreau impatiently tapped his cane on the floor.

"I now pronounce you man and wife." Father Perez snapped the missal shut and waved his hand in the age-old sign of the cross, blessing them.

As an afterthought he mumbled, "God be with you."

# Four

"The girl's got spirit. You can say that for her."
Edward Lang slipped out of his coat and hung it in the standing closet on the side wall of the room he shared with Foster Arnold. Years ago, when they had first arrived with their young charge, Henre Moreau had banished them to one of the former slave quarters in an outbuilding that housed the kitchen. A second room was shared by Peony, the old slave who oversaw the cooking, and her daughter. Moreau obviously thought the two servants would be dismayed by the cramped quarters and lack of privacy. They found the arrangement perfect.

"I think she may be just the wife our Cordero needs." Foster took off his coat and handed it to Edward, who began to meticulously brush lint off the wool fabric.

Foster had liked the girl on sight, taken as he was by her bohemian looks and spirited quality. He thought the way she kept insisting she was not Jemma O'Hurley was quite humorous, really. She was certainly not at all like any of the fashionable Creole women old Henre might have chosen for his grandson. Miss Jemma O'Hurley, Foster felt, just might provide Cord the challenge he needed to put the past behind him, pull himself together and set his life to rights.

He walked to a small table covered with a white linen cloth on which a cold supper was laid out, along with two glasses and a bottle of wine, and waited for Edward to stop fussing over the coats and join him. Two candles were lit in the center of the table. Between them, a sprig of dogwood in a chipped piece of crockery added a touch of color to the simple setting. When they were both seated, Foster filled the glasses and then raised his in a toast.

"To Cord and Jemma. To a long and happy life together." They each took a sip and then he added, "And to us. 'Ere's to doing everything in our power to make this marriage work."

Edward nodded. "Cord certainly don't need another disappointment in 'is life." He took another sip of the red claret and held the glass up to let the candlelight shimmer through the wine.

Foster reached for a roll and broke it apart.

" 'E'll hardly be disappointed if this marriage don't work. I think 'is performance tonight were to scare 'er off entirely."

"She didn't much object to leavin' Louisiana." Edward tucked his napkin beneath his chin and lifted his knife and fork.

"No, she didn't, did she?" Foster picked at a cold

chicken breast with his fork, thinking about what his companion had just said.

"I'm beginnin' to wonder if she really *ain't* O'Hurley's daughter."

"Who else would she be? Besides, I for one don't care who she is. I like her, Eddie. There's something in her eyes . . . did you notice?"

"No. But I will say she seemed to be thinkin' of somethin' b'sides the wedding. Why'd she kept claimin' not to be Jemma O'Hurley but then agreed to get on with it? Don't make sense, if you ask me."

"Her father told old Henre not to believe a word she said about anything," Foster reminded him. "O'Hurley paid good money to see his daughter married right and tight to a Creole, 'oping it would 'elp his new business 'ere in New Orleans."

"I thought you wasn't going to listen outside o' closed doors anymore. It ain't dignified." Edward slathered butter on warm roll.

They continued to eat in silence, the only sounds in the room that of flatware against china and the rain pouring off the hip roof and splashing in puddles around the perimeter of the building.

"What if he don't take to her?" Edward wanted to know. "You can lead a horse to water . . ."

"We'll just have to do what we can in that area." Foster smiled.

"That might be 'ard to do on a ship," Edward speculated.

"You know I've always wanted to play Cupid," Foster admitted.

Edward smiled at his friend and filled the glasses again.

" 'Ere's to the newlyweds."

Foster joined in the toast. "And 'ere's to a swift voyage home."

Celine sat in an uncomfortable, straight-backed chair in Cordero Moreau's bedroom. She hugged her knees to her breasts, her legs hidden beneath the silk skirt of her borrowed wedding gown. Her toes were curled over the edge of her seat, the dress hem tucked beneath them. Under the chair lay her discarded, water-stained slippers.

Across the room, Cordero Moreau lay dead to the world, stretched out in breeches and shirt. His feet hung over the side of the bed. She studied the way his pant stirrups cut across his arches, black slashes against white stockings beneath. Foster, Edward and the twins had escorted them to the room after the ceremony. After depositing the groom on the bed, the devilish twins had offered smug smiles and speculating looks.

Edward and Foster had efficiently removed Cordero's boots and divested him of his jacket. Then they'd carefully put his things into a large, open trunk, one of two that stood ready for departure in the corner, and asked Celine if she wanted a lady's maid sent up. When she'd declined, Foster had told her that they would come back in the morning to escort them to the wedding breakfast, and she'd wondered if her new husband was capable of getting anywhere on his own.

A candle in a single candelabra threw shadows against the walls. She sat in the unfamiliar surroundings listening to this new husband of hers snore. Sorrow enveloped her the moment the servants exited the room. She had entered into a marriage with a stranger who according to law could treat her as chattel should he so choose. One glance at him assured her that she could not count on him for protection. More than likely she would have to look out for him.

She sighed and stood up, unaccustomed to the hushed whisper of silk that followed her every movement. Fingering the coral material as she walked toward the *galerie* for a breath of fresh air, she silently approved of Jemma O'Hurley's choice of gown. Celine stepped out onto the wide balcony that ran the length of the upper story and felt the kiss of a gentle mist. The storm had subsided, the downpour now just a drizzle. Through the mist and foliage she could see torches burning near the river's edge.

A horde of unanswered questions crowded her mind as Celine lingered outside and watched the torches flicker. But one question stood out from the rest: Why had Jean Perot killed Persa? What had the old woman done to incur his wrath?

Exhausted, she rubbed her eyes and then her temples. For a fleeting moment she thought of making an attempt to use the shadows of the night to creep out of the house and escape the web of deception she had spun, but the steady mist and the murky darkness, not to mention the threat of predators, human and animal, held her there.

When she turned to leave the *galerie*, she noticed two wine bottles, one standing, the other fallen beside it. She tried to imagine Cordero Moreau—her husband—tipping the wine bottles to his lips and draining them, one after another. What drove him to befuddle his mind with drink?

Celine walked back into the room and closed the jalousies behind her. The cypress floors were cool against her bare feet. The air was permeated with lingering dampness and the fecund scent of the fertile soil carried by the swollen river. She paused at the foot of the bed to stare at her unconscious groom.

Despite her past, she had dreamed that someday she might meet her heart's desire and fill a hope chest for her wedding day. But she had never pined for just any husband. She had never doubted that she would know him on sight, just as he would know her. Theirs would be a love that would last forever.

For her mother, there had been no such thing as love, merely self-preservation. According to Jane Winters, her father had been a dark-eyed gypsy, a master with horses and women who had charmed his way into Jane's bed for free and then, after almost a month of monogamy, had disappeared forever.

Cloistered in the shop, Celine had never had close dealings with men, except for Persa's clients. In a way, Persa used men just as she did women—for profit. She told their fortunes, sold them her potions, played upon their insecurities and desires until they were addicted to the advice she dispensed like opium. They would return again and again, desperate men like Jean Perot, hoping to use the knowledge she gave them to alter fate.

What none of them had known was that most of Persa's predictions came from her cunning knowledge of human nature and a very fertile imagination. Perhaps Jean Perot had suspected Persa of cheating him out of copious funds and then killed the old woman in a rage.

Celine stared at her new husband from the foot of the bed. Dead to the world, Cordero Moreau had not stirred. She was tempted to know more about him, and the only way to do that was to touch him. She hesitated, let her hand hover over him, but then drew it back. He was unconscious and would never know the difference, but she would know, and now that her initial panic had subsided, she did not feel desperate enough to steal into his past.

She stretched, aching all over from the jolting carriage ride. The bed looked all too inviting, with plenty of space for her to lie beside Cordero without touching him at all. Celine lowered herself gingerly to the edge of the bed. She waited, half expecting him to at least shift positions, but aside from a sigh, he didn't react. Slowly, cautiously, she stretched out and lowered her head to an herb-scented pillow.

Before she closed her eyes, she gathered the silk gown close and tucked it around her so that no part of it came in contact with him. Then, determined to awaken before him, she let herself relax and drift off to sleep.

His mouth tasted like he had rinsed it with New Orleans gutter water.

The bell which summoned the slaves to morning prayer rang twice more and then thankfully stopped before the sound split his head in two. Cord lay with his eyes closed, reluctant to increase the torture of what promised to be one of his more memorable hangovers. As he tried to piece together the events of the previous evening—the wedding he wanted to forget, the bride he had sought to outrage—his only recollections were of Stephen hauling him about and yelling in his ear and a pair of haunting amethyst eyes. The rest was a blur.

His head hurt like hell. Cord rolled to his side and opened his eyes to discover he wasn't alone. He stared curiously at the young woman stretched out beside him. When he'd agreed to do the honorable thing and marry the girl in his cousin's stead, Cord had never expected Jemma O'Hurley to be beautiful.

For a man who with no expectations at all, he found

himself wedded—and, it seemed, bedded—to a rare beauty. Perfectly still, she lay like a fallen angel with a riotous mass of long ebony curls that framed her face and draped across her breasts. Her eyes were closed, her dark lashes glossy half-moons against her cheeks. Her lips were full, lush and tempting.

Slowly, so as not to set his head throbbing harder than it already was, Cord raised himself on an elbow to better study her. The coral gown enhanced the golden tone of her skin. Beneath the low neckline and ill-fitting bodice, her shapely breasts rose and fell with each breath. Her hands were perfectly cast, her fingers tapered. One hand, palm up and open, rested above her head on the pillow. He was tempted to stretch across the space that separated them and touch the vulnerable underside of her wrist.

For the moment it was easy to forget that he did not want this marriage. It was easy to forget the world outside his door, and the real reason why he had agreed to marry her. All he could picture, and with the utmost clarity, was what a true bridegroom would be doing the morning after his wedding.

Without warning, she opened her eyes. For an instant she stared at the ceiling, then she blinked and slowly turned her head in his direction. The strange, near-violet eyes he recalled so vividly from the night before stared directly into his. He felt as if she could see into his very dark soul.

As if bewildered by his presence, she frowned.

"Good morning, *wife*." He managed a smile, although it pained him.

Her gaze never wavered. "I think you're still drunk."

"But you're still here. I'm surprised."

He was content to study her. She appeared much younger than he had first suspected, not more than eigh-

teen or nineteen years. Her skin was clear, almost glowing. Her thick curls were glossy and black. If she was
nervous, if being alone with him frightened her in the
least, it didn't show. She possessed the confidence of a
much older woman.

She traced a swirling pattern on the coverlet.

"I hoped you might find my condition last night so
offensive you would renege on the marriage agreement," he admitted coolly, testing her mettle.

She mirrored him by raising on an elbow and prop-
ping her head in her hand. "I did find your condition
offensive."

"But not enough to beg off." When she failed to
comment he tried shock. "Did we fuck?"

She blinked. Twice. "We did not. You passed out
shortly after the ceremony."

"But it did take place?"

"It did."

"And are we married, Miss O'Hurley?"

"We are married. But I'm not Miss O'Hurley."

"That's right. You are Mrs. Cordero Moreau now."

She looped a tendril of hair behind her ear. "I'm not
Jemma . . . O'Hurley or Moreau."

"Then who are you?"

He fought back the ridiculous need to reach out and
touch her again to be certain she was real. She was staring back at him with her incredible eyes. Her gaze
touched his hair, his eyes, his mouth, the open front of
his shirt.

There was a quick knock at the door. Without taking
his eyes off her, Cord called, "Come in. And for
Christ's sake, don't slam the door."

He recognized the timid knock as Edward's. No doubt

he had come to summon them to the accursed wedding breakfast.

The girl bolted up and stood awkwardly beside the bed. He almost found himself wishing he were Edward when he saw her acknowledge his servant with a shy smile.

It cost him dearly to roll over and sit up. The throbbing pain at his temples forced him forward. He grasped his head in his hands until the world stopped spinning.

"Good morning, miss. Morning, sir," Edward said.

Cord could not respond. He had known and loved Edward all of his life, but at the moment he found the man's chipper tone grating.

"Good morning, Edward," the girl said.

Her bright greeting rattled the pain in Cord's head.

"Do you have to shout?" he groaned.

Edward chattered with the girl as if Cord had not spoken.

"Did you sleep well, ma'am?"

"All things considered, I did, thank you, Edward."

"Foster 'as your trunk waitin' in the room next door. One of the women is there to 'elp you. Breakfast'll be served at 'alf past the 'our in the dinin' room."

"When do we sail?"

Cord's head snapped up. He regretted the move, but couldn't help but stare at her. "Are you planning to sail with us?"

"Of course."

"You actually *want* to go?"

"I'm looking forward to it."

That brought him to his feet. "Why?"

"Why not?" She glanced once more at Edward and then back at him, appearing a bit nervous. "You are my husband now. I go where you go."

Edward made a choking sound and busied himself near Cord's open trunk.

"The room next door, did you say, Edward?" she asked.

"To the right, miss."

Cord watched her walk around the end of the bed, pause beside a chair and pick up a pair of water-stained shoes. He saw her bare toes beneath the coral silk. She paused in front of him, hesitant, her confidence diminished.

"What is it?" he asked, realizing as he spoke that his words sounded unnecessarily harsh.

"You look as if you need some time to pull yourself together. If I were you, I'd start now."

Cord waited until she was out of the room before he looked at Edward. The servant was wringing his hands.

Cord sighed. "I'm still cursed."

"What do you mean, sir?" Edward wore his worried expression, the one that made him appear as if he had just bitten into a lemon.

"It seems I've married a nag."

# Five

The black silk pumps were too wide but they provided ample room for Celine to vent her nervousness, so she furiously wriggled her toes. It was not until she had taken her place at the delicacy-laden table that she recalled she had hardly eaten a morsel the previous day.

The house slaves in attendance moved around the dining table in the mute steps of a familiar routine as they served mouthwatering items with long-practiced unobtrusiveness. The air was tainted with the tempting scent of strong coffee laced with warm milk and steaming hot chocolate that hinted of cinnamon.

The *calas*—golden brown, deep-fried balls of rice, flour, nutmeg and sugar—smelled too luscious to resist. Tears threatened when she was reminded of Sunday mornings on the Vieux Carre when she and Persa would

buy the treats hot and steaming from a vendor who sang,
*"Bella Cala, Tout Chaud!"*

Her stomach felt edgy, her nervousness spawned by
uncertainty, but the tender white fish poached in tomato
and lemon, the veal rissolés, the fresh pineapple—all of
it tempted her beyond reason.

A short while later, as she stood beside her new husband, closeted in private audience with Henre Moreau,
it was too late to regret her overindulgence. She tried to
dismiss her discomfort and the fear that she might lose
the contents of her stomach over the well-oiled surface
of Henre Moreau's cherry-wood desk. Instead she concentrated on what the old man seated in the chair behind
the desk was telling Cordero.

"You realize that the moment you walk out of here
you will be cut off from our family and all you might
have inherited from me," Henre warned.

When Cordero made no comment at all, Celine cast
a sidelong glance at him. He was cold and aloof, returning his grandfather's bitter stare just as he had all
through breakfast. She could feel the tension radiating
from him.

After an uncomfortable silence he finally replied.
"What family? You? If you mean Stephen and Anton,
they won't be here long. Not once the novelty of New
Orleans wears off and you begin your overbearing brand
of rehabilitation on them. There is no need to worry,
Grandfather. Once I'm gone I'll never ask you for anything or darken your door again."

Celine stared up at Cordero's profile. When he felt
her gaze upon him, he looked down at her and suddenly
flashed a smile. Taken in by the radiance of it, she did
not realize it was calculated until he whipped his attention back to his grandfather.

"What about her dowry? I married her. I want it now."

Henre leaned back in his chair. "It is a sizeable amount." He unlocked a drawer in his desk, removed a false bottom, and withdrew a felt bag, heavy and bulging with coins, and handed it to Cordero.

"How long will it take you to drink and gamble it away, do you think?" Henre asked.

"I have a small stipend from my mother's estate, as well as whatever the plantation earns." Cordero dangled the bag at his side.

"For what little good that will do you. There have been no funds from the crop on that place in years. You are just like your father. You will never amount to anything. You are doomed to fail."

"A prediction you have made with unfailing regularity for the last fourteen years," Cordero said.

"Why should you suddenly change overnight into a conscientious planter? You have never taken an interest here, never even balanced a column of accounts. You have been foolish enough to declare that slavery disgusts you. Most likely you will free your slaves, only to have them slit your throat some night."

"It's none of your concern what I do with my property or the people who toil there, is it?"

"Thankfully, no."

The hatred between the men was so palpable she could almost see it. Both men were as rigid as swamp cypress. Unnerved by the harsh exchange of words, she smoothed her palms down the front of her borrowed finery, an emerald traveling gown that Edward and Foster insisted looked perfect on her. Once buttoned, the jacket almost fit. Her slight movement drew Henre's attention. She fought the urge to squirm.

"So, you intend to sail with Cordero?" Henre asked.

"Yes." She wanted to be on her way as soon as possible, so she kept her response brief. "I do."

He was watching her with open distrust. "Last night you tried to back out of the wedding and then suddenly changed your mind. Why did you go through with it?"

"That's what I asked her earlier," Cordero said. "I think she just wanted to bed me."

"Nothing could be further from the truth," she countered.

"That remains to be seen." Cordero was toying with the heavy bag of gold, bouncing it up and down on his open palm. He said to Henre, "We need to be on our way. Is there anything else?"

Henre picked up a document and handed it to him.

"Since you were incapable of this last night, you'll need to sign the marriage certificate. It has already been witnessed by Father Perez and the twins."

"How convenient," Cord said.

Henre set a bottle of ink near the edge of the desk. Cordero paused as he dipped a quill in the ink pot. He leaned close to Celine.

"This is your last chance to back out," he offered.

She was tempted, but could think of no easier avenue of escape from Louisiana. Her palms felt cold and clammy. She was still uncomfortably full from breakfast. She swallowed, took a deep breath and shook her head.

"I won't change my mind."

"I can't be sure of what we'll find on St. Stephen. In a few months I could be virtually penniless," he said softly.

It was the first hint of compassion she had seen in him. She wondered what it had cost him to admit the truth, especially in front of his grandfather.

"I will sign," she said.

Cordero signed the certificate first, then handed the pen to Celine. She quickly scrawled a signature across the bottom of the parchment. She hoped that if anyone ever tried to decipher the letters of her true name, it would be long after they had sailed.

She held her breath until Henre blotted the signatures without looking at them and then rolled the parchment and slipped a blood red ribbon around it.

"The carriage is waiting." Cordero took firm hold of her arm above the elbow and began to usher her out of the library.

Celine drew up short a few feet outside the door, and Cord paused to look down at her, a question in his eyes. Before she spoke, she shook off his hand.

"He is family. This might be the last time you ever see him." She thought of Persa and the abrupt, senseless act of brutality that tore them apart forever without even the chance to say good-bye. "Won't you at least bid him farewell?"

When she looked up, she saw a flash of hatred in her husband's eyes that made her want to flinch and draw away. Sober, he was no man to be toyed with. It suddenly occurred to her that deserting him might not be as easy as she had first reckoned.

Cordero looked at the library door. His eyes narrowed and his full lips thinned to a hard line.

"The only thing I would like to tell him is to go straight to hell."

The carriage ride back to New Orleans was nothing like her journey to the plantation. They traveled in two conveyances, Foster and Edward and the baggage in one, she and Cordero in the other. The dark ominous weather of the previous night had given way to smiling blue skies and sunshine. Celine noted that the weather did little to brighten Cordero's mood.

They rode in silence, careful not to touch, seated opposite each other like wary adversaries. Cordero was preoccupied, staring out at the passing landscape. Celine tried to control her anxiety over their brief return to the city. She would not feel safe until they had set sail.

"Why did you do it?" she asked him, trying to focus on anything but the possibility of her arrest.

He started, looking hesitant to answer, even wary.

"Why did I do what?"

"Agree to this marriage. Was it for the dowry?"

"No." There was a flash of pain in his arresting eyes. He looked away.

"Then why?"

"I owed someone a great debt. And you, Jemma?"

"I am not Jemma O'Hurley."

He sat forward, concentrating on a wagon loaded down with vegetables that they had overtaken and were now passing. "You're not Jemma O'Hurley. You expect me to believe that?"

"Yes, because it's true. I was at the cathedral last night praying for a way out of New Orleans when she came rushing up to me. She wanted out of the marriage, wanted to be a nun, not a wife, and persuaded me to take her place in the carriage. I did so hoping to gain employment when the carriage reached its destination."

"This is rich. Are you telling me I married the wrong woman?"

"It looks that way, doesn't it?"

"No. It doesn't, because I know what you're up to, Jemma. Edward and Foster tried to warn me that you might try something like this. They said you protested the wedding last night and that my grandfather had already been forewarned by your father that you had a— now how did Foster put it?—that you had 'a chronic ability to stretch the truth.' ''

They were at the outskirts of the city. Celine felt her heartbeat quicken and leaned back away from the window. She would not tell him her name until they were well away from New Orleans.

''Believe what you will.''

His lips curved into a slight smile. ''Alex was used to a docile woman. I wonder what he would have made of you.''

''Who is Alex? And how do you know I'm not docile?''

''Alex was my cousin. He was to have been your husband, but he died. I felt compelled to take his place. He would have done as much for me. More.'' He leaned forward, staring up at her as he propped his elbows on his knees. ''You have very strange eyes.''

''There are not many people with eyes this color, I suppose.''

''It's more than that,'' he said.

''What do you find so strange about them?'' The close perusal was making her fidget.

''I feel as if you can see right through me. If you can, I'm sure that by now you have discovered there is nothing inside.'' He picked up the hat lying beside him on the seat and dismissed the disturbing discussion. ''We're here.''

Celine looked through the window and panicked. They were not at the wharf, but on a street, drawn up before a whitewashed mud house on Rampart. It appeared old but well tended, not unlike Persa's cottage.

She recognized the area, too. It was a quiet, well-manicured street where Creole gentlemen housed their Negro mistresses. Had Cordero come to collect his before sailing?

"This isn't the levee. I thought we were going directly there. Where is the other carriage?"

"They went on ahead. I have one stop to make first. Are you coming or do you prefer to wait here?" he asked.

She could try and hide in the confines of the carriage, she knew, but feared that some curious passerby would spot her. By now her description might have been posted all over the city. She would be safer inside the house. He was outside the carriage now, standing with one hand on the handle of the mud-splattered door, impatiently scanning the street while he waited for her to decide.

Hastily she pulled up the hood of her cloak and slid forward on the leather seat. "I'll go with you."

"It's getting warm," he said when he noticed she had donned the cape over her traveling outfit and covered her head with the hood.

Celine pressed her fingertips against the gold clasp at her throat. "I may have taken a chill last night in the rain."

Cordero led the way up a narrow walk to the front of the house. They stood beneath a wide overhang that shaded the porch as he knocked on a door draped in black crepe and quickly turned his back to it. A middle-aged, exotically beautiful mulatto woman answered the summons. She was dressed entirely in black, her eyes red-rimmed and swollen from crying.

When she recognized Cord she let out a sharp cry and tears streamed anew from her almond-shaped eyes.

"Please, come in, Monsieur Moreau," she whispered. "Come in."

Cordero waited until Celine entered before him and then stepped in behind her. The woman closed the door. Somewhere in the back of the house, a child was sobbing. The sound tore at Celine's heart. Surely, she thought, someone should see to the child's pain.

Cordero seemed as uncomfortable as she felt as he introduced the woeful woman to her as Madam Latrobe. He reached into his coat and withdrew a money bag not unlike the one which had held the dowry money. It was half the size, but stuffed full. He held it out to the woman.

"This is for Juliette. It should be enough to last her a good many years. The house has been paid for. Alex would have wanted me to see to her future and that of the children. Perhaps she could buy a small business, a millinery—"

"But monsieur!"

Cordero seemed as uncomfortable in this house of tears as Celine. He took a step toward the door.

"Tell her I have gone back to St. Stephen but that—"

Madam Latrobe shook her head back and forth and began to weep, sobbing openly, her shoulders shuddering. "My Juliette is dead, monsieur. I thought you knew."

Cordero appeared so devastated by the news that Celine was tempted to reach out and take his hand.

"How? When?" It was all he could manage. His eyes shimmered suspiciously. Celine looked away.

"She hanged herself four days ago. We buried her yesterday. I sent word to Monsieur Moreau . . ."

Cordero's expression iced. "The bastard did not tell me or I would have come sooner."

When Madam Latrobe suddenly appeared on the verge of collapse, Cordero surprised Celine by leading the woman to a nearby table. He pulled out a chair and gently helped her to sit. Celine hurried to a side room which housed a small kitchen. She poured a glass of water from a delicate china pitcher and carried it back into the sitting room.

She and Cordero exchanged a quick glance over the woman's head as Celine set the water on the table beside her.

"What about the children?" Cordero asked. His color had faded to an ashen hue.

Madam Latrobe continued to wipe away tears but could not stem the flow. "They are as one would expect of two little lambs who have lost both their father and mother in a little over two weeks."

"May I see them?"

She nodded and tried to rise, but her legs would not hold her.

"I'll get them," Celine volunteered, anxious to afford Cordero and Madam Latrobe some privacy. Following the soft, tormented sound of crying, she walked to the back of the house and paused in the doorway to one of the bedrooms. A girl, who was maybe ten years old, was comforting a little boy with a headful of glossy black curls. He was lying with his face buried in her lap, crying as if his broken heart would never mend. The lovely girl looked up and noticed Celine hovering there.

"Can you come with me? Cordero Moreau has come to see you," Celine said softly. She was taken aback by the resemblance to Cord that she saw in the little boy's face when he stopped sobbing long enough to look up at her.

"Uncle is here?" he said, brightening.

Celine nodded. Swiping at his tears with the back of his hand, the child scooted off the bed and darted past her as he ran to the sitting room. The girl stood up, straightened her skirt and tossed her long, dark curls over her shoulder. Her haughty movements belied the deep shadows of grief dwelling in her eyes. If Celine didn't know better, she would have thought the beautiful girl standing before her was pure French Creole and not of mixed blood. As did the boy, the girl had the Moreau look about her.

"I'm Celine," she told the girl.

"I'm Liliane Moreau. My brother is Alan."

"Your uncle wishes to see you," Celine said. At least, she told himself, Alex Moreau had acknowledged his two bastard children by his mistress.

She followed Liliane back to the sitting room, where she found Cordero hunkered down with the boy who was resting against his knee. He cradled the child against him, smoothing back Alan's tousled hair. Her first impressions of Cordero had not prepared her for the sight, and she had to admit to herself that she was deeply moved.

"Perhaps someday you can come to see me, but your *grand-mère* needs you much more right now," Cordero was saying.

"That's right, *cher*," Madam Latrobe said softly. "You are the man of the house."

Cordero noticed Liliane beside Celine and reached out for her. She moved into his embrace and he gently kissed her cheek, then laid her head on his shoulder. "I have left enough money with your *grand-mère* for both of you to be well taken care of. If you need anything at all, write to me and see that the letter is sent aboard a ship bound for the island of St. Stephen.''

"Papa always said you would take care of us, Uncle Cord." A single, pitiful tear slid down Liliane's cheek, a testament to her grief. She slipped her arms around Cord and buried her face against his neck.

"Your papa was like a brother to me, and so you are like my own."

*Like my own.* Celine had an instant vision of Persa and felt tears well up again. She turned away, pulled the cloak close around her and walked over to the window, where she saw the Moreau driver and carriage waiting in the street. Behind her, Cord continued to hold tight to the children as they clung to him.

"I don't want you to go, Uncle Cord," Alan told him.

"I would be happy to take you both with me, but your *grand-mère* needs you."

"They are all I have, *monsieur*," Madam Latrobe said softly.

Celine heard the thread of fear laced through the woman's tone and then heard Cordero tell the children, "I don't want to leave you, but I have to. When you're older, you can come to visit me. I'll show you the island and teach you to swim. Would you like that?"

Alan shook his head no. "I want you to stay."

"I'm afraid that's impossible now."

Celine waited until he bid his niece and nephew farewell one last time and kissed them both. He asked them to be good and to take care of their grandmother. When Celine turned around, he was standing by the door waiting for her, his eyes shining suspiciously again as he watched little Alan climb upon his grandmother's lap and turn away.

Celine hurried to Cordero's side, raised the hood of her cloak and then preceded him out of the house. She looked neither right nor left, but kept her eyes on the open door of the carriage, praying that they would reach the levee without notice.

She glanced over at Cordero. He was preoccupied as they pulled away from the house on *rue de Rampart*. He was staring out the window, his thoughts far away. The gentle, caring man she had seen in the Latrobe house was not the hardened cynic who had stood beside her in his grandfather's library. What manner of man had she married after all?

"Alex loved them so much," he whispered.

She knew he had been thinking aloud when he turned around to see if she had heard.

"And yet he would have gone through with the arranged marriage," she said.

Cordero frowned. "He always did what he perceived to be the honorable thing. For him, there was nothing wrong with following the Creole tradition of fathering children with both his mistress and his wife."

"And for you?"

"I have no mistress, if that's what you're asking. No children that I know of, either."

"Perhaps you should have made arrangements to bring the children to St. Stephen."

The look he shot her could have melted iron. "Are you mad? What would a reprobate like me do with two children? They're better off here with their grand-mother."

"As you were with your grandfather? They might fare better with you."

"It's out of the question."

"You claim to be a drunk and a wastrel, but I have yet to see you take a drink today. Besides, the man I saw back there was not a heartless sot. He was a loving, caring uncle.''

He smiled slowly, crossed his arms and leaned back against the seat.

"We've been in each other's company less than a full day. Don't even begin to think you know me, wife.''

When she didn't rise to the bait, he dangled more.

"I doubt you will be around long enough to know me at all. Wait until you find yourself living in dire straits on the island. You will be more than ready to run back to your rich papa and the luxuries to which you are no doubt accustomed.''

She met his gaze and tried to mirror the cool smile that did not reach his eyes.

"Don't even begin to think you know *me*, husband.''

They were among the last passengers to board. Long-forgotten sights and sounds came back to Celine as she stepped from the gangway onto the main deck of the *Adelaide*. She was instantly reminded of the unremitting noise aboard a sailing vessel. Sailors shouted to each other from every corner and from atop every mast. The wood ship creaked and squealed, each joint and timber sounding a complaint. The clamor would grow even worse, she knew, once it was coupled with the roar of the open sea.

All manner of livestock which would be served up at meals were housed in cages on deck. The fowl clucked, the pigs grunted, the sheep bayed. At least their fate was predetermined. The passengers faced endless days of boredom and confinement, close quarters shared with strangers, and the ever-present dangers of shipwreck, disease and fire.

"Are you all right?'' Cordero stood beside her,

watching her with a fair amount of grudging concern.

How could she be "all right" when her mind was suddenly full of faded memories filled with blood and death? The last time she had been aboard a ship, her mother had caught yellow fever and died trying to take Celine to a better place. Had it not been for Persa's agreeing to adopt her, she would have ended up in an orphanage in New Orleans.

Now all she could think of was the stark image of her mother's shrouded body as it slipped into the cold Atlantic waters. That and the sight of Persa lying dead on the floor. And Jean Perot in a pool of blood. No, she was not all right. She was definitely not all right.

She longed to tell him that she might never be "all right" again. Instead she nodded slightly and turned to look back at the city.

New Orleans lay pressed against the river like a lover. The open square called the Place d'Armes where couples strolled, families picnicked and the condemned were hanged. The market where Marcel the vendor hawked vegetables. The maze of narrow streets and alleyways she knew so well. The courtyards, the fountains, the rumble of carts and carriages that blended with the shouts of drivers. The city pulsed with its own lifeblood, and that pulse had drummed in her veins for too long to deny it.

Tall ships' masts stood like a forest of leafless trees along the waterfront. Crates and barrels, trunks and carriages all vied for space on the docks. Sweat-sheened, heavily muscled men with skin of darkest ebony rolled hogsheads and hefted bales of cotton and other goods along the wooden wharf. Fat, well-dressed merchants argued with sea captains over the price of their cargoes. A tea-colored woman with a burnt orange chignon wound around her hair walked through the crowd balancing a basket tray upon her head.

Celine could not conceive of loving any place as much as she loved New Orleans. She was tempted to leave Cordero Moreau to himself and his journey and run back to the small little house on rue de St. Ann. She wanted to know that someone had taken care of Persa. She couldn't bear the thought of her beloved guardian lying cold, alone and abandoned in death. She almost screamed with the pain of having to bear it all in silence as she slipped away like one of the rats that hid aboard the cargo ships.

He touched her hand in that unguarded, vulnerable moment when her mind was occupied with sights and sounds and sorrows and she had dropped her guard. Skin to skin, the connection was made, and dizziness raged through her. She felt her head begin to whirl and her hands go clammy. Darkness clouded her vision until images from Cordero's past, as seen through his eyes, flitted through her mind.

*New Orleans long ago. The streets less crowded than now. The wharf throbs with life. The crowd ebbs and flows around him. Foster and Edward stand beside him. Waiting. Henre Moreau appears. He marches toward Cord with four ebony slaves, his expression hard and set. Grim determination fills his eyes.*

*Terror is lodged deep in Cord's heart. Anxiety. Abandonment. Anticipation. Loss and betrayal. Utter desolation that fear only heightens. All of them swarm like a maelstrom inside him.*

Even after Cordero released her, the residual despair that had seeped from his past into her mind continued to rock Celine to the core. She stared up at him, searching his eyes for some trace of the deep-seated hurt he had experienced—pain which had been replaced by cynicism and cool detachment.

This time when he placed his hand at the small of her back, she was ready for the contact. To protect herself, she created a filter of rose light, the way Persa had taught her so long ago. She felt only the touch of his hand this time, warm even through her clothes, and possessive.

"You *are* ill," he said.

"No. Just a bit melancholy. I'll miss this place."

"I thought you and your father just moved here from Boston."

Celine sighed, too distressed to argue the facts; besides, it was still to early to explain. "What are our accommodations?"

"We have two cabins in the stern."

"With windows," Foster added. The servants had come aboard and directed the stevedores hefting all their trunks and boxes, and now joined Cord and Celine.

"Windows?" Edward voiced his worry aloud. "What if they leak? What if water seeps in during a gale?" He frowned so hard his brow became a solid, wrinkled hood above his eyes.

Neither Cordero nor Foster bothered to reassure him.

*Two cabins.* The underlying worry of how she was to avoid intimacy with Cordero over the journey began to gnaw at Celine anew. From here on she would have to rely on a quick wit—and perhaps, if she could get the ingredients, one of Persa's sleeping potions. The thought of that option lightened her step as they made their way toward the passenger cabins where those who could afford the price traveled in greater comfort.

She had spent most of the daylight hours on the long voyage from England roaming the deck with the other emigrant children. Along with their families, they had been crowded together in steerage, sleeping in narrow, open berths arranged like so many shelves in a pantry, forced to cook, eat, give birth, relieve themselves and even die—as her mother had—in a common area with barely enough room to turn around.

On good days, their meals had consisted of salt beef and barreled pork. She could recall her mother, and then Persa, offering her a handful of raisins on the days when only flour, suet and raisins were doled out to them for pudding.

The moment she and Cordero reached the stern where the first-class passenger cabins were located, Celine knew her experience this voyage would be far different from her last. They passed through a saloon with a dining table in the center of an otherwise bare room. Then Cordero moved to one of the many doors that lined the saloon and opened it. He stood aside to let her pass.

Celine stepped inside the confined space of the cabin, which proved to be nothing more than a very large closet. The doors and walls were paneled in wood, polished to a high shine. Her gaze flew to the bunk against the sea wall. The shelf, barely wide enough for two, took up most of the floor space.

Jemma O'Hurley's trunk had already been delivered. It stood in the middle of the floor alongside two others, one small, one a bit larger.

She pointed to the other two trunks. "Those were delivered to the wrong cabin. Are they yours?"

Cordero walked to the small window, bent to allow for his height and peered outside. "You can see downriver."

"I said, your trunks somehow wound up in my cabin." She started for the door to seek out Foster and

Edward. "I'll get one of your men to remove them."

"Why? This is my cabin, too."

"You said we have two cabins."

"We do. Foster and Edward have one. I'll not have them in steerage."

Celine would not condemn a dog to the 'tween deck, let alone these two men who had been so kind to her. That hadn't been what she meant.

"Why can't the three of you share a cabin? Certainly a cot could be arranged . . ."

"That's impossible." The corners of his lips twitched.

"Why?"

Cordero threw his hands up and shook his head. "Why? Why? Because I say so. I haven't been married a day and already you are nagging me to death. Is this shrewishness something that girls learn at an early age or some mystical metamorphosis that takes place an hour after vows are exchanged?"

"I wouldn't exactly call what passed between us last night an *exchange* of vows. You were barely lucid."

"Lucky for you."

"Nothing about this situation is lucky, if you ask me."

"We haven't weighed anchor. There's still time to back out of this."

She realized what he was up to. It was her last chance. She could leave him now if she chose, walk down the gangway and out of this dark comedy of errors.

But she knew she might just as well fashion a hangman's noose for herself.

Celine took a deep breath. She looked at the bunk that was just wide enough for two. At least she had a few hours left before she had to face that dilemma, she consoled herself.

She forced herself to smile. "As much as you'd like me to leave, I'm staying. We're merely having our first disagreement."

"The first of many." He crossed his arms and leaned against the doorjamb.

"I'm sure," she said.

"It's going to be a long voyage, Jemma."

"It will be if you insist on calling me that. I've told you time and again, that's not my name."

"But you've given me no alternative. What should I call you?"

There was no doubt that he was only humoring her. She glanced out the porthole at the city and took a deep breath. "Celine. That's not too much to ask, is it?"

He nodded. She didn't like the way he was watching her from beneath half-lowered lids. She didn't like it at all.

"Celine, then. If you insist. An interesting choice."

"It's my name. I prefer you use it."

"Whatever you say. Just don't nag." His stare had grown quite intense and lingered on her lips so long that it made her nervous.

Somewhere the crew was weighing anchor with much shouting and an earsplitting rattling of chains. Celine walked to the window and watched the muddy water of the Mississippi rush past. The ship began to swing out away from the dock and take up the motion of the current.

"How should I address you?" she asked.

"Cord will do," he said after a pause.

She nodded, wishing he would leave her alone. The thin walls of the cabin had already begun to grow confining. The room was barely large enough for one, let alone two. Privacy would be impossible. Celine grasped the window frame. The air in the cabin suddenly seemed humid and stagnant.

"Would you like to go up on deck?" Cord asked.

She could not hide her relief. "It is stuffy in here."

He walked over to the door and stood aside. "After you, Jemma."

Celine turned on him, ready to launch into protest, but then noticed the teasing glint in his eyes and figured it was better than having him glower at her.

Cordero raised his hands in surrender. "Cecilia. Ceylon. Celine. I'll call you anything you like if it will stop your nagging."

Celine refused to rise to the bait again.

With a tall glass of whiskey in hand, Cord comfortably lounged in a chair beneath an awning raised on the poop deck. He stretched out, crossed his legs and studied his new bride as she stood at the rail, observing their passage downriver. She had finally abandoned the hooded cape she had insisted upon wearing earlier despite the fall heat. Her slender hands lay upon the varnished rail, her tapered fingers curved over the rich wood surface. With her dark hair lifted on the breeze and her face turned to the sun, he grudgingly admitted to himself that she was more than lovely. He couldn't help but wonder how Alex would have felt about her.

By nineteen, Alex had met Juliette, fallen in love and fathered his first child. Because the two could never marry, Alex had been content to remain a bachelor, but he was prepared to eventually align himself with someone acceptable, preferably another Creole whose bloodlines were well-known so that the family name would remain untainted. It was a rare Creole bride who went into marriage unaware that nearly every husband had two families, one secret and one recognized.

But this woman he had married was Irish American. Her father had recently moved to New Orleans from Boston. At the Latrobe house, Celine had expressed sympathy for the children, but how long, Cord wondered, would she have approved of Alex's continued allegiance to Juliette, Liliane and Alan, had she married him?

When Cord thought of little Alan and the broken, hopeless look in Liliane's eyes, he was reminded all too well of his own childhood. He knew what it was to have one's life turned upside down because of the death of both parents.

He took another drink. The alluring woman beside the rail, his wife, had begun to stroll along the upper deck. The entire poop deck had been set aside for their pleasure, for there were no other first-class travelers. Cord watched Celine walk slowly along the rail and then pause in the stern and look back before turning her attention to the two sailors manning the wheel. The helmsman rang the bell marking ship's time and another bell in the bow above the sailors' quarters immediately echoed it.

The sailors smiled at her and before she proceeded on her way, Celine smiled back. The breeze off the river molded her gown against her, outlining firm breasts and shapely legs. Cord could see that the sailors were admiring her form just as he was and felt an unexpected surge of anger and a tug of possessiveness.

Finishing off the last of his drink, he realized that even though she might have been meant for Alex, this Jemma-Celine O'Hurley was now his. And in that stunning instant, Cord decided there was no reason why he should not take full advantage of his marital rights.

He stood up, empty glass in hand, and headed toward Celine, adjusting his stride to the motion of the ship. They were nearing the open sea. He felt a curious anticipation and was surprised, for any emotion other than anger had been foreign to him for so long. He did not know if he was more excited at the thought of returning to St. Stephen or of bedding his new bride.

Celine was leaning against the rail, intently watching a sailor climb the rigging with the agility of a monkey. Cord took a place beside her.

She glanced over at him, at the empty glass in his hand, and then looked away again. "I see you have taken up your favorite pastime."

"I see you are still a nag."

He could also see that she was fighting a smile. "Have you sailed before?" he asked.

"When I was a child."

"Did it agree with you?"

She nodded. "For the most part it did. There were some bad days, though. I remember spending them in bed."

"Then I'll pray for rough weather."

Her gaze flashed in his direction and locked with his. "What do you mean by that?" she asked.

"Just that I'd be content to spend the entire voyage getting to know you—as my wife."

She stiffened and looked away. Her fingers tightened on the rail. "How do you mean?"

"I think you know exactly what I mean, Jemma."

"Celine."

Cord edged closer until they were shoulder to shoulder. If she was frightened by him, she didn't show it by trying to scoot away. Instead, she pretended to ignore him, but the stiffness in her back and shoulders told him she was all too aware of his nearness.

"We are husband and wife. Our wedding night might have been a disappointment, but you can rest assured I intend to make up for that tonight."

"Don't go to any lengths on my account," she said softly, content to stare ahead and avoid his gaze.

Cord reached out and, half expecting her to pull away, looped a wayward strand of dark hair behind her ear. He traced his thumb along her cheek, down her throat, over her collarbone. She shivered.

"Why did you agree to this marriage?"

She turned toward him. She bit her lip and frowned, searched his eyes and then said, "I wanted to get out of New Orleans. I did not marry you because I wanted a husband."

He felt an odd sort of relief. "At least neither of us suffers from delusions of love."

In the center of the main deck below them, three sailors put their backs into rotating the capstan to raise more sail. Yards and yards of canvas snapped full and billowed as the ship cleared the final shoals. Freed by the wind, the *Adelaide* split the water as they headed into the open sea.

Cord watched Celine push back from the rail, extend her arms before her and stretch. She turned to him with a slight smile.

"Since both of us had reasons other than love for entering into this arrangement, then you must agree that it would be absurd to assume we should sleep together."

"I wasn't talking about sleeping," he assured her.

"You know very well what I meant. I do not know you at all."

"That is probably to your advantage. Besides, what does that have to do with marriage? Don't tell me you believe in all that hogwash about romantic love?''

She blushed.

''You do,'' he said, appalled.

She was watching him closely, looking up into his eyes, searching them as if she were trying to see into his soul. Cord felt a twinge of discomfort.

''In Louisiana arranged marriages are an everyday occurrence. Few Creoles marry for love.''

''But I'm sure the participants have at least met before the wedding,'' she argued.

''Probably,'' he admitted grudgingly.

''We never laid eyes on each other before last night.''

''Correct.''

''I had hoped you would grant me some time before expecting me to perform my . . . my wifely duties.''

Cord turned around and found her staring at him in wide-eyed horror. He leaned back with his elbows on the rail and smiled. He tried to imagine trade winds carrying the scent of the tropical waters as he closed his eyes and tipped his face toward the afternoon sun.

''I will grant you some time,'' he conceded.

''Thank you.''

She sounded so relieved that he tilted his head toward her and raised his eyelids just enough to see her reaction. ''You can rest assured I won't press you until tonight.''

# Six

By late afternoon the Louisiana coastline had disappeared. The swells increased with every passing hour, but the *Adelaide* sailed valiantly over each crest and climbed every trough. Celine remained at the rail long after Cord left her, trying to acquaint herself with the pitch and roll of the ship. She stared off at the far horizon, wondering what was in store for her.

One word played itself over and over in her mind.

*Tonight.*

Tonight Cord would expect her to perform her conjugal duty. The very idea of it filled her with dread—not because of ignorance of the act itself, for she knew far more about that than most girls her age, but because too many firsthand recollections of her mother plying her trade had been burned into her memory. The groaning, the panting and sweating, the feigned cries and whimpers of false passion were all elements of sordid scenes she never would forget.

Persa had once told her that Jane Winters had shared far too much with a curious five-year-old.

*"Your mother, rest her soul, was a whore,"* Persa had said. *"And by the grace of God, you will never become one."*

*"Then what will I do?"* Celine had asked.

*"First, you will learn to survive on your own, and then—but only if you desire it—you will marry. A woman should have the right to choose. Some women, for one reason or another, are not suited for marriage."*

Persa's eyes had misted, and Celine recalled how the old woman had absently rubbed her crippled hip.

*"Remember this well, Celine: I will see to it that you never have to whore like your mother."*

She was only five when Persa had taken over her care, and from that day on Celine's life had changed forever. There had been no more squalid rooms in back alleys. No more fear of hunger. Nothing remained of the sordid life her real mother had led. Persa had seen to it that Celine's was a life of pleasant routine. The old gypsy understood her better than anyone. Persa had never made fun of Celine's gift or recoiled in fear of her touch.

Fate had thrown them together, Persa had always said, because Celine needed to learn when to use her gift and how to close her mind to the visions, how to guard her touch and use her second sight only when needed.

True to her word, Persa had taught her to survive. Before she was old enough to work in their shop selling potions, Celine had hired out as a companion to an old woman down the street. She knew the pride of counting the coins she had earned from long hours of work.

Thanks to Persa's training, she was able to get the most for her money at the market. She learned how to save and knew the difference between things she needed and things she merely wanted.

But nothing she had learned about the men who visited Persa's shop had prepared her for marriage. She knew with certainty what a good whore did in bed, but not what a good wife did.

Tonight, by law, she would have to give herself to Cord. Without love, would she be any better than her mother? Any better than a whore?

The ship's bell sounded, forcing her to set aside her dark thoughts. She had but a quarter hour to freshen up before dinner. Two members of the crew were in the saloon as she passed through to get to her cabin. They were bustling in and out of the open pantry, tending the covered pots of food that had been carried from the galley in the bow of the ship. All of the cabin doors were closed save for one that belonged to Josiah Campbell, the ship's surgeon superintendent. He was a spry, thin-faced gentleman with white hair and deep smile lines that bracketed his mouth and creased the corners of his eyes. Dr. Campbell acted as go-between for the captain and the crew and passengers. Since there was far from a full complement of travelers this voyage, the doctor had time on his hands.

He was seated on a cane chair just inside his cabin door studying the pages of a book in his lap. He paused long enough to look up and smile as Celine made her way across the saloon. She nodded and then gently knocked on the door to her cabin. She didn't relish walking in on Cordero unannounced, and catch him unawares.

The door to the adjoining cabin opened and Foster,

dressed far more like a gentleman than a servant, poked his head out and smiled.

"Can I be of 'elp, ma'am?"

"I was just going to freshen up and I wondered if . . . if my husband was inside."

Foster shook his head. " 'E's in the captain's cabin. Said to tell you 'e'll join you for dinner. I've taken the liberty of laying out a gown for you."

Celine looked down at the traveling outfit she was wearing and wondered why he expected her to change. She was still uncomfortable wearing Jemma O'Hurley's clothes. It was one thing to take a woman's unwanted fiancé, but quite another to wear out her clothes.

An hour later she was seated on a bench at the long dining table, wedged between her new husband and the captain's mate, both of whom seemed content to do little more than stare down the gaping front of yet another ill-fitting bodice. Celine was so nervous she was not certain she could manage at all. Aside from the fact that her husband had insisted he would claim his rights later this evening, she was the only woman in the presence of Cord, the mate, the surgeon superintendent and Captain Isaac Thompson. She had been disappointed when she'd learned that Foster and Edward would be taking their meals with the steerage passengers, where they would apparently feel more comfortable. When she'd protested, Cord had assured her it was their choice and not his.

A set of fiddle rails ran the length of the table to keep the china from sliding off onto the floor. The sea had become so rough that the plates slid from side to side between the rails. The table and benches were bolted to the floor.

"Are you finding your accommodations to your liking, Mrs. Moreau?"

It wasn't until Cord nudged her that Celine realized the captain was addressing her. The man seemed to be totally oblivious to the fact that the ship was groaning and straining at every seam. Isaac Thompson was a congenial sort who looked to be in his midforties, with brown hair and eyes and the beginnings of a paunch at his waistline.

Celine watched as a halo of light from the lamp swinging above the center of the table momentarily highlighted his features, then answered, "The cabin is fine, thank you."

"I understand you are newly wed." He smiled over at Cord. "My congratulations to you both."

When the captain lifted his wineglass in a toast, Celine watched the cabernet slosh with the motion of the ship. Its rhythm matched that of the lanterns swaying above them. She tried to concentrate on the man's smile rather than the constant rolling motion of the ship.

Cord acknowledged the toast with a nod and drained his wine. Celine wondered if it would help to match him glass for glass. She might very well pass out and he would be forced to wait to press her into doing her wifely duty. She took a gulp of wine, came up sputtering and decided she would leave overindulgence to her husband.

Captain Thompson signaled one of the sailors in the nearby pantry to refill his plate with mutton and boiled potatoes. Celine glanced down at her food, which she had barely touched, and felt faintly nauseous. She swallowed and tried to concentrate on what the captain was saying.

"Seeing you two together reminds me of my wife. She comes along whenever she can, but she's near the end of her confinement and had to stay at home."

He forked a slice of mutton, piled potatoes on top of it and lifted the concoction to his lips. Celine looked away as he shoveled the food into his mouth. Cord had eaten one helping of everything and seemed now to be content with just wine. He did not comment on the captain's statement.

"Is this your first child?" she asked.

The captain washed down his food with another hearty swallow of wine and shook his head. "Got five already. You would think that would be enough, but my wife loves babies. About the time we've got the last walking, she's after having another."

He cut another piece of lamb and paused with his fork halfway to his lips. Winking at Cord, he said, "I can't say as I mind having to oblige."

Celine dropped her fork, which clattered against her plate. She set down her knife and folded her hands together in her lap.

"Where do you make your home, Captain? In the West Indies?" she asked, trying to change the subject.

"No. Heavens, no. My wife hates the islands. Too hot, too humid, still too uncivilized for her," he said, laughing. "I understand your husband is returning after a long absence, but have you ever been there, Mrs. Moreau?"

Celine grabbed the stem of her wineglass to prevent it from tipping over. "No. I've not had the pleasure."

Cord deftly took the glass from her. The blood red cabernet sloshed near the lip, threatening to spill. He leaned close and murmured in her ear, "You should drink this. It'll take the edge off."

She ignored him, but her heart began to beat double-time. He drank the wine for her.

Dr. Campbell had finished his dinner and appeared to

be asleep, but suddenly he spoke up. "The islands aren't for everyone, that's for certain. Some people don't take to the tropical heat, especially Englishwomen. I've seen some who cover themselves completely, head to toe, kerchiefs tied about their heads and faces, hiding under parasols to keep every bit of sun off their fair skin. Don't go out at all during the day; they say it's—"

Cord cut him off effectively. "My mother was English. She never even wore a hat."

"I'd say she defied convention," Captain Thompson said.

"You might say that," Cord replied. Then so softly that he was almost speaking to himself, he added, "She liked to dance beneath the stars, too."

Celine reminded herself to ask him more about his mother.

The doctor looked over at Celine. "You're not English, I take it, Mrs. Moreau?"

"She's Irish," Cord volunteered.

"I'm not," she said. "Actually, I am English. I was born in London."

"Quite exotic features for an Englishwoman," Dr. Campbell noted to no one in particular.

The ship lurched, and Celine nearly fell off the bench. When Cord reached out to steady her, she quickly righted herself.

"My father was a gypsy," she said, hoping to shock Cord. With his Creole background, she doubted he wanted a wife whose blood was tainted in any way. She hoped the disclosure would keep him from wanting to bed her. But when she glanced up at him, she could see that her admission had not disturbed him in the least.

"You'll stand the heat better than a fair-skinned woman. Extreme heat doesn't bother the slaves, they say,'' the doctor noted sagely.

"That's merely an argument made in favor of keeping them toiling in the hot sun during the heat of the day,'' Cord told him. "It's been my experience that they drop from the heat just like anyone else.''

The first mate, a redheaded man, younger than the others by far and even younger than Cord, had been silent up to now. He tore his gaze away from Celine's breasts long enough to comment.

"Are you against slavery, then, sir, if you see them as men? If so, you are going to meet opposition on St. Stephen.''

Cord let the captain fill his wineglass again and took a sip before he answered. "I have no idea what awaits me on St. Stephen.''

"But you have land there?''

Celine listened with interest.

"Dunstain Place. A plantation of nearly two hundred and fifty acres.''

"I assume that, as an absentee owner, you have an overseer?'' the captain asked.

"A manager,'' Cord replied.

"Do you intend to grow sugar? That requires quite a labor force. You may have to change your views on slavery.''

"I'm not sure what condition the plantation is in at this point. There were fields and fields of sugar when my father was alive. I'll have to see what it will take to put the place back into production. *Most* of my plans are still quite indefinite, in fact. I live one day at a time.''

When Cord looked down at Celine and smiled, she knew that he was subtly letting her know that his plans for tonight were quite definite. She shivered despite the closeness of the quarters and the heat from the warming stove in the pantry.

Celine traced the floral design on the rim of her dinner plate as the mate entered into quiet conversation with the doctor. The idea that if she chose to remain with Cord she would have to take her rightful place as mistress of well over two hundred acres of land and an estate filled her with dread. Along with running the household, all responsibility for the health and welfare of any slaves he might own or acquire would fall to her. It was one thing to learn to be self-sufficient in a small shop in New Orleans, but she had no idea how to cope with the role of mistress of a sugar plantation.

The captain had emptied another plate of food. He signaled one of the men waiting in the pantry and the sailor began to clear the table.

The scent of lamb and onions lingered in the saloon, and Celine longed to go back on deck. Captain Thompson wiped his mouth with a napkin and then said, "I hope you don't mind being the only woman aboard, Mrs. Moreau."

"Not at all." It wouldn't matter if she were one of one *hundred* women aboard, she thought ruefully. She was the one Cord wanted tonight.

"We usually carry quite a few passengers, but the weather can be so unpredictable this time of year that not many want to make the journey. We're well into hurricane season."

She had not known. Now that she did, she realized she'd not only have to deal with Cordero Moreau, but with the possibility of a hurricane.

By the time the table was cleared the *Adelaide* was bouncing like a cork in a washtub. Celine excused herself, performed a precarious walk across the saloon and left the men to their port and cigars. A shuttered door was all that separated her from their loud conversation and the pungent, nauseating scent of their cigars. But the odor managed to filter into the small cabin.

She locked the doors to both the saloon and to Foster and Edward's adjoining cabin and prepared to change out of the pale peach gown. Jemma O'Hurley's trunk was wedged in the corner near the bunk, its lid raised so that she might have easy access to the wardrobe inside. One of Cord's servants had carefully spread a white lawn nightgown across the bunk. Steadying herself with one hand, Celine quickly wriggled out of her evening gown and tossed it toward the trunk. The sight of the bed gave her pause. It looked far too small for two.

A particularly violent swell sent the room tilting at a sharp angle, forcing her to wait to slip into the nightgown. When she did, the gaping scooped neckline drooped off her shoulders. She tugged up the left side, only to have the right sag until it exposed nearly all of her breast. Finally, after much wriggling and adjusting, she gave up. She put her evening gown away and gingerly sat down on the edge of the bunk with her hands folded in her lap and her knees pressed tight together. She couldn't take her eyes off the door.

As another rough swell hit the ship, a wave of discomfort forced her to lie down and draw her legs up. Curled up on her side, she tucked the hem of the nightgown over her toes and stared at the wall. The wool blanket felt rough beneath her cheek. She wished she could put off the inevitable, wished that Persa were still alive and they were both safe at home in their little cottage. She longed to wish away the ship's incessant rocking, the disconcerting sound of creaking timbers and the cloying odor of cigars. Most of all, she wished she were on solid ground and that Cordero Moreau were miles away instead of lurking just outside the door.

At ease with the pitch and roll of the ship beneath him, Cord sat in silence at the dining table, staring up at the darkened skylight above it. Captain Thompson and the other men had long since left him to dwell on his future—not to mention his bride—alone. He had tired of wondering what to expect when they reached Dunstain Place. Nor did he particularly want to think about what he would do once he arrived on St. Stephen. His thoughts were occupied with his dark-haired beauty of a wife, who now claimed to have gypsy blood. If nothing else, she was proving to be highly entertaining. His gaze strayed to the door directly opposite his place at the table. Was she waiting inside with anticipation or dread?

There was only one way to find out.

Cord stood and stepped over the long bench. When he reached the door, he tried the knob and found it locked. He knocked softly. When there was no response, he scanned the saloon. All of the adjoining doors were closed and there was no one in sight.

"Celine. Open the door," he whispered.

Still no response. He tried again, louder this time, his anger piqued. "Celine?"

Cord heard a slight sound on the other side of the door, and then the bolt snapped. The door swung inward to reveal his bride standing there with one bare foot atop the other, staring up at him with a pained expression on her lovely face. Her hair was in wild disarray, her nightgown drooping off one shoulder. He reached out and pulled the gown up. The opposite shoulder immediately fell.

Celine batted his hand away, reached up and grabbed both sides of the gown's neckline. A wave of nausea hit her. She wanted nothing more than to lie down again, but with Cord framed in the doorway, his ice blue eyes assessing her as if she were a ripe peach ready for the picking, she decided against it.

"Are you going to let me in or not?" He thought she might be rooted to the spot, capable of little but staring.

Still clinging to the gown, she stepped back. As he moved past her, she was careful to keep her bare toes away from his heavy boots. He glanced at the bed and saw that it was still made up.

"I see you waited up for me," he said.

She held on to the doorknob for dear life.

The ship listed to one side and quickly righted itself again.

"Are we going to sink?" she whimpered, not caring if he saw her fear. The recollection of her mother's body disappearing beneath the waves flashed through her mind.

"Not before morning."

Her face blanched. When he realized his answer had truly frightened her, Cord reached out for one of her thick, ebony curls and rubbed it between his fingers.

"I'm only teasing. We are in no danger of sinking."

"How do you know that for certain?"

He let go and watched the curl tease the flesh over her collarbone.

"The captain has gone to bed. If there was any real problem, I'm sure he would be up on deck having the men bail water or something," he said.

He shifted his weight with the roll of the ship, walked over to the bunk and sat down. Cord patted the blanket beside him.

"Come here."

Celine took a step toward him. As she attempted to take another, the ship rocked, the floor went out from under her and she ended up sprawled across his lap. The nightgown gaped precariously low, giving him a tempting view of her breasts.

"I didn't mean for you to throw yourself at me." Cord righted her gently until she was seated beside him.

"When will it stop?" she moaned.

"We haven't gotten started yet."

"I meant the motion of the ship. Surely this isn't normal." She shook her head. "I don't remember anything like this . . ."

"How old were you when you sailed before?" he managed to ask despite the inspiring view of her breasts which the ill-fitting gown afforded him.

"Five."

"Then you were too young to remember exactly what that voyage was like, weren't you."

Celine pressed her palm to her forehead. "I don't think I would have forgotten something this . . . *What* are you doing?"

While she was worrying about capsizing, Cord had slipped his hand into the gaping neckline and cupped a breast. When he did not withdraw his hand, Celine slapped it away.

He crossed his arms and watched her gather the front of the gown into a tight wad and then try to tie it in a knot. When the attempt failed, she pressed her fist between her breasts to hold the material there, effectively cutting off his view, then glared up at him.

"Do you intend to deny me my rights?"

"I really think I should lie down," she said.

There was no way she could refuse him, not when the

law declared a husband could resort to force if he had to.

"Don't think you can get away with lying here with your eyes closed and your fists clinched like a virgin sacrifice—"

"I'm not thinking anything of the sort right now. I *need* to lie down."

He stood up and began to pace the cabin. Three strides found him nose to nose with one wall. Cord started back the other way. By the stubborn set of her shoulders, he could see this was not going to be as easy as he had hoped.

"Go ahead and lie down then," he snapped.

She was not doing a damned thing to arouse him, yet he found himself fully aroused. He probably had the damned oversized gown and the enticing view of her breasts to thank for that. After all, he *had* been celibate of late.

It didn't help knowing that she was a virgin . . .

"You *are* a virgin, aren't you?"

The startled look she shot him said more than words.

No help for it then, he thought. What a pity Alexandre was dead. Cord knew his cousin would have known exactly how to woo the girl, how to put her at ease, skillfully deflower her and even have her thinking it had been her idea. Alex had been faithful to his Juliette all those years, but he had also been a consummate flirt well adored by the ladies.

Cord couldn't help but wonder now if it wouldn't have been better for all concerned to have done the less honorable thing and to have refused to fulfill the marriage contract in the first place.

Celine lay down on the bunk and curled in on herself. From the moment Cord had walked into the cabin, the room seemed to have shrunk three times. He filled the place with his very maleness. Even now he stood there bigger than life, the top of his head nearly grazing the ceiling, his feet planted wide, his hands fisted on his hips as he stared down at her, his expression waffling between contempt and desire.

The ship creaked; the timbers groaned. Cord began to unbutton his jacket and strip it off. She quickly closed her eyes.

''Don't fall asleep,'' he warned.

He quickly unbuttoned the neck and first few buttons of his shirt, then pulled it over his head and tossed it aside.

''As if I could,'' Celine mumbled to herself, certain that the next swell would send her rolling off the edge of the bunk.


''What's going on now?'' Edward whispered. He stood with one hand on his companion's shoulder while Foster pressed his ear against the door to the adjoining room.

''They're still talkin','' Foster whispered back. ''Cordero seems to be moving around. I can 'ear 'is footsteps.''

''You think they'll do it?''

Foster put his finger to his lips and shook his head. Cord was moving closer to the door. Both men held their breath until they heard him walk away again.

''I noticed the miss was in a panic when she came in to change for dinner.''

''Oh, no,'' Edward said. Behind him the cabin was crowded nearly floor to ceiling with their trunks plus some of Cord's. ''Do you think she'll refuse 'im?''

''I don't know. So far she's everything 'er father warned ol' 'Enre about.''

"What if she plans to run off once we reach St. Stephen? What if that's why she agreed to leave New Orleans? It'd be a way to get away from 'er father. Is that window *leaking*?" Edward ended on a squeak.

Foster glanced at the window. "No. Now calm down, Eddie. We don't need an imagined crisis when a real one might be 'appenin' in the very next room."

"I think they should 'ave separate cabins. I'd be just as happy to bunk on the 'tween deck, but I don't like the way the bosun's been lookin' at me. He looks as if he'd like nothin' better than to—"

"Would you please stop imaginin' the worst? We 'ave to keep our wits about us. It's best they been thrown together like this."

There was a distinct thud on the other side of the door, and Edward's hand tightened on Foster's shoulder. "What was that?"

"A boot hittin' the floor."

There was a second, identical sound.

"Other boot. Good. Now we're gettin' someplace." Foster rubbed his palms together.

"We can only 'ope. Wot if she does refuse?"

"They 'ave to consummate. Otherwise she can get 'erself an annulment."

Edward sighed. "Cordero needs someone in 'is life. I'll never forget 'ow much his father loved our Miss Alyce."

"Cord don't need just anyone, though," Foster reminded him. " 'E needs someone who'll shower 'im with all the love 'e deserves."

"Everyone the poor lad ever loved 'as died or abandoned 'im."

"Everyone but us, Eddie." Foster shifted and pressed his ear closer to the door. "Damn. I don't 'ear anythin' now. Maybe I should have opened a bottle of wine and 'ad it ready for them.''

Edward smiled. ''You're such a bloomin' romantic, Fos.''

Cord stared down at Celine, certain there had never been a less enthusiastic bride. She wasn't even looking at him. She was lying so damn still he thought she might have actually fallen asleep.

He felt like a fool standing there naked as the day he was born, fully aroused, debating what to do next. He could awaken her with gentle kisses, undress her, coax her with tenderness. He could whisper sweet words of love that he did not mean but knew most women loved to hear.

Or he could shake her awake, rip off her gown, ravage her and have done with it—but then Alex would probably haunt him forever. Besides, ravaging would require too much effort, especially if she put up a fight—one which everyone on board would undoubtedly hear.

As he stood there debating, the ship slammed down a swell.

The *Adelaide* shuddered. Celine's eyes flew open. She shoved herself to a sitting position. The only lamp in the cabin was violently swinging from a hook on the wall. Cord stood in the wavering ring of light, hovering over her, buck naked.

''Oh, my God!'' Celine slapped her palm across her mouth and held it there. Her eyes began to water.

''Look, there's no need to get hysterical.'' Cord's erection started to wilt under the uninspiring look of sheer panic in the wide, beautiful eyes staring at him over an outstretched hand.

She shook her head violently.

He reached toward her. "Just calm down. I've already decided against ravaging you."

She moaned behind her hand.

"Get ahold of yourself. You're my wife, Celine. I have every right, you know."

Celine pulled her hand away from her mouth and took a deep breath. She swallowed twice.

"I'm going to throw up."

Before he could move, she grasped the edge of the bunk and vomited all over his bare feet.

"What's going on now?" Edward said, nudging Foster between the ribs.

"I don't—" Before he could finish, the bolt popped and the adjoining door flew open so hard it smacked into the wall. The support gone, Foster fell into Cord's cabin, with Edward right behind him. Foster quickly regained his balance and found himself face-to-face with Cord, who appeared to be wearing nothing but vomit where his stockings should have been.

Foster adjusted the collar of his nightshirt and straightened his spine. "May I be of 'elp, sir?"

Edward reached up and smoothed the few wisps of hair left atop his bald head. "Ready to serve, sir."

"I'm afraid, gentlemen," Cord said with as much dignity as he could muster, "that my wife has exploded."

# Seven

Looking at her now, he thought she might up and die and leave him a widower. Cord hadn't seen Celine for twelve hours, so it came as a shock to find her lying in her bunk in the same position in which he had last seen her. Her face was the color of watery split-pea soup.

"You look like death warmed over." Unable to think of anything more encouraging to say, he stood there waiting for her to open her eyes.

She didn't move, but did finally manage to croak, "Get out."

Cord stayed as far away from her as he could in the confining space. He shoved his hands through his hair and then settled them on his hips. She looked like hell. Her hair was matted, the delicate skin beneath her eyes shadowed. Foster had expressed concern that she would become dehydrated and had instructed Cord to see that she took something.

"Do you want anything to eat or drink?"

She moaned and rolled over to face the wall, presenting her back to him. As he stood rigid and at a complete loss, she mumbled, "What are you doing here? Have you come to torture me for last night? Surely you don't expect me to . . . you know."

"Edward has also taken ill and Foster is too busy seeing to him to tend to you."

Cord had found it a bit suspicious that Edward professed to be ill, since the servant had not once suffered from seasickness on the voyage to New Orleans years ago. He had gone to see for himself and found Edward in his new bunk on the 'tween deck, refusing food, refusing to do anything but lie there with the covers up to his chin. Celine looked far worse than Edward. At least his servant was not the color of sheets tinged green.

Cord tried again. "If you're hungry, I'm sure the cook still has some nice gray gruel left from breakfast."

"Please stop."

He almost smiled. The way she looked at the moment and the memory of last night made verbal torture far more appealing than the thought of bedding her.

"If that's not to your liking there's liver and onions."

She rolled over and glared up at him with a jaundiced eye.

"I know what you're trying to do. You married out of some twisted sense of honor and now you find yourself stuck with a wife you never really wanted, so you've decided to slowly torture me to death. Why don't you just shoot me and get it over with?"

"You know me too well already, I see. Actually, putting you out of your misery is not a bad idea. I can't say I'm looking forward to another night like the last.''

"Where did you sleep?''

"Did you long for me in the middle of the night?''

"Of course not.''

"I took Edward and Foster's cabin. I'll be staying there from now on. They have moved to the 'tween deck.''

"They were very kind to me last night, which is more than I can say for you. I'm sorry they were put out.''

"It's their job to be kind. But it's not mine, especially when I'm forced to wear used dinner. You need not worry about them, however. I'm not so heartless that I would make them stay in less than desirable accommodations. There are only three other passengers down there this trip. Aside from Edward's sudden illness, they seem quite comfortable.''

"I wish I could say the same,'' she said.

He sat down near her feet at the edge of the bunk.

"What are you doing?'' She tried to see what he was up to.

"You don't need to worry. Your virtue is quite safe for now. The way you look, I don't think you could even tempt a shipwrecked sailor.''

"Thank you.'' She wished he had not chosen this particular morning to find a sense of humor. "The motion seems to have lessened.''

"Becalmed.''

"I am calm.''

"The ship is becalmed. The winds have died.''

"So we're forced to bob like a cork at the mercy of the wind?''

"I'm afraid so. Unless you can commune with nature.

Are you sure you won't even take a little water? Foster thinks you should.''

"If Foster had my stomach, he might think differently.''

He watched her try to swallow and grew concerned when he thought her eyes were about to roll up into her head.

"Celine?''

"At least you finally have the name right.'' She closed her eyes and flopped back on the pillow.

Aside from frequent hangovers, he couldn't recall ever being sick. Henre wouldn't have allowed it. Cord had no idea how to deal with any ailing individual, let alone an ailing wife. He stood up and poured her a cup of water from a flask in a cupboard beneath the basin. When he was beside the bunk again, he held the water out to her.

"Here. Drink this.''

She gazed up at him as he stood holding the cup at arm's length, very careful to keep his shining boots away from the bed.

"Your bedside manner is terrible,'' she said.

"Let's just say I'm far better *in* bed than standing alongside it.'' Cord sat down beside her again, watching her closely so that he could jump out of the way if the need arose. He reached out and slipped his hand beneath her head, cradled her gently and held the cup of water to her lips.

"Drink it slowly,'' he warned. "Just a few drops at a time.''

Celine did as he asked: took a sip of water, let the blessed moisture roll over her tongue and then swallowed. She waited until she was certain her stomach was not about to react violently and then took another sip.

"Better?" he asked when she had swallowed a few more drops.

"No. But not as miserable as before."

"Would you like to try standing? Maybe a walk in the fresh air?"

"I would like to get off this boat."

"Impossible."

"Will it be much longer, do you think?"

"Not if the wind picks up and holds steady. Forever if it doesn't." He looked down and found her watching him closely. He hadn't moved from her side, hadn't even taken his arm from around her. When he realized he was still cradling her like a babe, he gently laid her back down.

"You seem to have acquired a sense of humor," she noted.

"I am looking forward to going home."

He was as happy as he dared let himself feel about anything. Home to St. Stephen. It had been a dream for so long that he knew he wouldn't really believe it until he was standing on island soil. He never dreamed he would be returning with a wife, though. It was still too foreign a concept to consider for more than a few moments at a time, so when she shut her eyes, he began to dwell upon her looks instead.

She appeared younger, more vulnerable with her dark, wild hair spread out on the pillow. She seemed to have shrunk inside the lawn nightgown. It drooped off one of the smooth shoulders visible above the edge of the sheet. Her skin was soft as silk, and far too tempting a reminder that she was his to do with as he pleased.

"Are you feeling any better?"

She opened her eyes again and followed the direction of his gaze. He was staring at her bare shoulder. When their eyes met, she shook her head.

"If I said I thought I was feeling better, what would you say?"

"After last night I'd want to be very, very sure first."

There was a shout from above and the sound of many footsteps running on the poop deck.

"What is it?" She took advantage of the opportunity to tug the sheet up to her neck.

Cord stood up and stretched. "Probably sighted another ship. I'll come back later on and see if you're ready for some food or a walk on the deck."

He watched her flop back down on the bunk and cover her eyes with the crook of her arm. "Just ask Captain Thompson to get us there with as little movement as possible," she requested.

The shouting had intensified. He hadn't thought of taking a gun on deck, but by the time Cord had cleared the doorway and was standing on the main deck beneath the maze of sails and tangle of rigging, he wished he had. He found himself in the middle of a small invasion. A rugged schooner flying a flag he failed to recognize had come alongside and the ill-prepared crew of the *Adelaide* was engaged in hand-to-hand combat with a shipload of unsavory-looking characters. Pandemonium had broken out everywhere.

He ducked back inside the double doors to the saloon and returned on the run to Celine's cabin.

"We're being attacked by pirates. Lock the door and for God's sake, don't be an idiot and go out on deck." He raced through the adjoining door to his new cabin, slammed it behind him and pulled a pistol out of a small trunk. In less than three minutes he was back on deck.

Foster, armed with a pistol and a paring knife, was

just clearing the ladder from 'tween decks. Edward, apparently having made a miraculous recovery, brandished an antique-looking pistol.

"This way!" Cord called out to them as he threaded his way around the masts and through the melee, pausing once to dispatch a pirate with his fist as he headed up the ladder to the poop deck, where the first mate was locked in hand-to-hand combat with a giant, toothless invader.

*"Pirates?"*

The noise overhead had become thunderous with shots and shouts and the unmistakable thud of men falling against the wooden deck. Celine jumped to her feet and shoved her hair out of her eyes.

*Lock the door?* Was he mad? Did he think a locked door would keep out a band of brigands?

She heard a gun fire and spun around, leaned over the bunk and tried to see out of the minuscule porthole. Mile upon mile of water and the ever-shifting horizon were all she saw. When she felt her stomach quiver, she deemed it better not to look. The sounds overhead appeared to be dying out. She was not going to wait like one of the chickens in those cages on the deck to see who came to get her.

Celine cracked open the door and peered around the saloon. It was empty. The ship was no longer rocking, but blessedly still. All of the doors to the adjoining cabins were closed save the one to the pantry. She could see the tall cabinets against the wall and decided the room probably held nothing of value to a passel of pirates. She dashed across the saloon, opened the door to a lower cabinet, hurriedly pulled out three huge soup pots, set them on the shelf opposite and then climbed into the empty space.

Curled up with her arms locked around her knees, Celine pressed against the back of the cupboard, closed her eyes and listened, trying to distinguish Cord's voice in the shouting overhead.

The confrontation was over.

Captain Thompson, being of sound mind and determined to live to see his precious wife again, surrendered before there was any loss of life on his side. Cord was of another mind as he stood alongside the crew of the *Adelaide* and his fellow passengers, all of whom were bound and lined up at the rail.

A burly, bearded fellow called Cookie, whose girth attested to his culinary skill, stood three men down from Cord. Before the truce he had been wielding a deadly-looking knife as well as a skillet. "We could have taken 'em," the cook grumbled. "Now there'll be hell to pay."

Cord followed the man's gaze. Across the deck, most of the motley pirate crew had gathered around a fallen comrade while the remaining four stood guard over the prisoners.

As Cord watched, their leader knelt down, felt for a pulse in the wounded man's neck and then stood up. The pirate captain was no more than five foot three at the most, nearly as wide as he was tall and garbed in a mismatched assortment of clothing. He wore an oversized saffron shirt, an undersized brocade waistcoat, purple satin trousers cut off just below the knees and shoes that had absorbed so much saltwater in their day that the color was indistinguishable and the toes curled upward. A half dozen gold chains hung about his neck and two emerald earbobs dangled from one lobe. A saber was sheathed at his side.

The outlandish character shook his head. "Jimmy's done for," he said in a voice as rough as gravel beneath a buggy wheel. "May the Lord bless his soul. Now toss him overboard."

Without a backward glance, the pirate marched across the deck, heading toward his captives. Each stride took him no more than a foot forward. His short arms and squarish hands swung back and forth at his sides with such purpose that he looked like a mechanical toy.

He walked up to Captain Thompson, forced by his diminutive height to crane his neck to stare up at the taller man.

"I see you're a sensible man, Cap'n, surrenderin' like that afore we were forced to cut all of your miserable throats." He took a deep, sweeping bow. "They call me Captain Dundee. I'm sure you've heard of me."

Someone near Cord choked back a laugh.

"Although I haven't had occasion to hear of you, sir, we are at your mercy nonetheless." Thompson spoke in such a humble, ingratiating tone that Cord wanted to close the captain's mouth for him.

Thompson continued on in the same bent. "We've nothing of value aboard save food stores and household goods bound for St. Stephen. You're welcome to take whatever you like in exchange for the life of my passengers and crew."

Cord was relieved Thompson made no mention of Celine.

Captain Dundee puffed out his chest, which only added to his considerable girth. He squinted up at Thompson with a barking laugh.

"It don't seem to me you be in a position to make

any kind of a bargain with me, Captain. First thing we got to settle is the matter of poor Jimmy's murder. His dear old mother was dependin' upon me to keep him safe and now he's dead. I can't go back without assuring her someone paid for what happened to him. An eye for an eye, so to speak.''

He began to stroll past the line of prisoners, his head twisted back on his thick neck so that he could eye each of them. Cord didn't even try to hide his contempt when Dundee halted in front of him.

''There something you got to say to me?'' With his hands locked behind him, the pirate rocked up onto his toes and down again, waiting for Cord to answer.

Cord wanted to spit in his eye and tell Captain Dundee he was a poor excuse for a pirate. He had just begun to enjoy the recent skirmish when Thompson had waved a flag of surrender, and now he was spoiling for a fight. After the events of the past few weeks, some serious bloodletting was just what he needed, but it was hard to ignore Edward quaking on one side of him and Foster standing stubborn and proud, willing to die for him if necessary, on the other. And he was forced to remind himself that he had a wife hidden away in the main cabin.

''I've nothing to say.'' He looked over the man's head, concentrating on the horizon. After another long pause, the pirate moved on.

When Captain Dundee reached the end of the line of prisoners, he started back in the same manner, strutting like a peacock until he reached Thompson again. ''I ain't the most patient of men. Jimmy's dead and one of you is going to pay. Who's gonna own up to the deed?''

Not one of the prisoners moved. Cord was afraid Edward had stopped breathing and for want of air would pitch face forward.

"One of you did it," Dundee shouted, pacing back along the grim assemblage. "One of you is going to die for it."

"This is uncalled for, sir," Thompson said. "Your man died in a fair fight after you attacked us. We have surrendered."

Dundee whirled around, strutted back to the captain of the *Adelaide* and barked, "Shut up. I'm in charge here."

Cord wondered how Dundee had won control over the rest of his rough-looking crew. All of them were taller, if not broader, than Dundee, all were more sinister in appearance, and yet all of them stood with pistols and cutlasses at the ready, waiting to move on his orders.

Dundee stopped in front of Cord once more.

"You . . ."

"Are you talking to me?" Cord looked down his nose at the man. It was a considerable distance.

"I don't like your looks . . ."

"I don't like the way you smell," Cord said without hesitation. "And your wardrobe leaves a lot to be desired."

"Take him," Dundee said, pointing at Cord. Before Cord could draw another breath, a pirate with flaming red hair that hung past his shoulder blades and biceps as thick as smoked hams was hauling him across the deck.

Celine was certain that if she didn't crawl out of the cupboard in the next few minutes she might never walk again. It had been deathly quiet for a while now, the ruckus having died down just after she pulled the cupboard door shut behind her. There was no sound but shifting timbers and waves lapping against the hull. The ship did not seem to be moving at all. Everyone had gone silent—or they were all dead.

She took a deep breath, then slowly opened the cupboard door. With a bit of awkward maneuvering, she pulled her head and shoulders out by resting her weight on her hands, palms down on the deck. She could see through the open pantry door that the saloon was empty.

Celine walked her hands along the floor until she finally extracted herself from the cupboard, stifling a groan as she stretched out her cramped legs. By the time she got to her knees she was certain she would never walk again, but a moment or two later she was on her feet, stumbling through the door. She stood beside the dining table long enough to let her legs become reaccustomed to her weight.

She was sure she could hear someone shouting from somewhere near the fore castle. Her feet were bare, she was still wearing the none-too-fresh nightgown and her hair stuck out a foot around her head, snarled beyond any quick repair. She headed out the double doors and onto the main deck.

The sun was so bright she had to squint and shield her eyes with her hand as she stepped out of the saloon. She nearly stumbled headlong over a coil of rope, righted herself and then gaped at the scene before her.

Captain Thompson and his crew, Foster and Edward and three other gentlemen she had seen strolling the main deck were lined up against the starboard rail like so many trussed ducks at the market. Standing guard over them was a band of disreputable-looking, scroungy men.

She realized with a start that Cord had not been in error when he said the ship was under *pirate* attack. Although pirates had once frequently strolled the streets of New Orleans, she had personally never seen one before; still, there was no doubt in her mind that each and every one of the assorted brigands standing guard over the passengers and crew of the *Adelaide* aptly fit the description. Not only were they brandishing all manner of frightening weapons, but they sported an abundance of tattoos, gold rings and beards.

It soon became abundantly clear that each and every one of them had witnessed her untimely appearance. They all stared at her as if seeing an apparition, and a few of them even crossed themselves. As she started to back away, intent on taking refuge in the saloon again, a shout came from near the forward mast.

"Kujo. Get her!"

Celine's attention was immediately drawn to the man who had bellowed. He was short, far shorter than she, outlandishly outfitted in brilliant yellow silk and purple satin. Sunlight glinted off gold chains layered around his neck. He was pointing at her and glaring, his jowls aquiver, his complexion mottled with a hue close to that of his pants.

As Celine stood frozen to the spot, a bare-chested black pirate in a crimson turban with a matching cummerbund around his waist was making his way toward her. She looked left and right. With no alternative but to jump into the sea, she decided she would rather see what fate had in store for her here.

The black pirate's long legs ate up the deck. She braced herself, ready to run, half expecting him to grab her and bind her hands as the pirates had those of the other prisoners. He did nothing of the sort; indeed, he

made a point of not touching her at all. He stood over
her with his arms folded across his chest and indicated
with a nod that she walk toward the squat pirate, who
was now shaking with rage.

To give them less of a spectacle, she was forced to
clutch her nightgown in place. It wasn't until she was
halfway across the deck that she noticed Cord standing
not far away from the little man who was shouting com-
mands. Cord's hands were tied behind his back and a
noose was settled around his neck, but neither of these
encumbrances prevented him from glaring furiously at
her.

For a man who was about to die, he appeared more
intent on finding a way to murder her than on saving
himself.

"It weren't wise not to tell me you had a woman
aboard, Thompson," the pirate captain yelled at Isaac
Thompson as Celine drew near.

"You never asked, Captain Dundee," Thompson
shouted back.

Celine never took her eyes off Cord.

"I thought I told you to stay below." Cord ground
out the words, ignoring everyone around them, friend
and foe alike.

"Who is she?" Captain Dundee demanded. Without
waiting for an answer, he shouted at Celine, "Who are
you?"

Before she could answer, the black pirate spoke up in
a kind of pidgin English. "Not good fo' you, dis one.
Dis be de one will curse you."

"Shut up!" Dundee ordered.

If Kujo was affected at all by Dundee's fury, he gave
no sign. "She got the looks of a *jumbie* about her. Dem
eyes. See trew you. See trew me, trew time and back.

*Jumbie,* she is, dat sure.'' Kujo crossed his arms over his chest and kept his distance from her.

His words startled Celine. This African, who undoubtedly possessed some mysterious talent of his own, had somehow divined that she had a gift.

His words did more than startle Captain Dundee— they struck terror in him. The pirate leader was now standing stock still, staring at Celine as if he were facing the very jaws of hell.

Cord struggled against the rope around his wrists but could not so much as budge his hands. He had resigned himself to his fate, certain that his life had been cursed from beginning to end. He was never going to see St. Stephen again, never going to get home to walk along the shore or dive beneath the turquoise waves. He would not live long enough to find one moment of peace or to forgive himself for Alex's death. He was not even going to have time to bed his wife.

Those had been his thoughts before Celine had stumbled on deck, her skin a ghastly greenish white, her hair sticking out like a dozen hummingbird's nests pressed together, her eyes wild. She looked for all the world exactly like a ghost—the *jumbie* the pirate Kujo claimed she was. The sight of her had nearly scared the purple satin pants off Captain Dundee. Cord was close enough to discern that the man was trembling more from fear than anger. Fear had a distinct smell about it.

Tied up like a goose on the way to Christmas dinner, Cord knew that any attempt to help Celine was out of the question. All he could do was watch as Dundee questioned her.

The pirate's voice had gone up a good octave. ''What are you doing aboard this ship?''

"Traveling to St. Stephen." She faced him squarely. Even she was forced to look down at the man. The only outward sign of her nervousness was the way she kept her hands clamped tight on the neckline of her night-gown. She did not so much as glance in Cord's direc-tion, nor did she give any indication that they were in any way connected.

Across the bow Captain Thompson protested, but no one paid any attention. Celine lost her footing, lurched forward and grabbed Dundee for support. As she clutched the man's upper arm, her color faded until she was white as one of the sails luffing overhead. She ap-peared to fall into a trance. Her eyes were unfocused, as if she were gazing at something no one else saw. Dundee sputtered and clawed her loose, shoved her back and put a good three feet between them. He was sweating pro-fusely, the thick coils of his plump neck ringed with dirt that streaked his collar.

"Stay away from me . . ."

"I'm the one." Celine spoke so softly Cord had to strain to hear. "I'm the one you have feared for half a lifetime."

Dundee shook more violently, fighting to maintain control. His gaze whipped about the ship. Cord was afraid Dundee was going to lash out at Celine, and strug-gled with his bonds.

She continued speaking softly, furtively to Dundee. "Long ago, a fortune-teller told you a woman would be your downfall, that you would die because you would wrong her and she would then curse you. Your whole life you have held yourself away from women because she told you that one day you would meet a woman who would call a dreaded curse upon your head. *I* am that woman."

The way Celine was staring at Dundee frightened even Cord. He half expected the pirate captain to run screaming over the side. Even the forbidding Kujo shifted nervously and cautiously backed farther away from Celine.

"Take her! Throw her to the sharks!" Dundee screeched in panic while Celine continued to stare through him. Cord was wringing wet with sweat. She had pushed too far. He would be forced to stand by helplessly while she was tossed overboard and drowned. Beside him, Edward whimpered.

"You have wronged me, Captain Dundee, and now you'll pay." There was strength and fury in her voice. "This man"—Celine pointed at Cord—"is my husband. You were about to hang him, were you not?"

"Cut him loose!" Dundee ordered. "For the love of Christ, somebody cut him loose!" When no one moved to obey, Dundee pulled a long saber out of the scabbard at his side, stretched up on tiptoe and sliced the rope above Cord's head.

For the first time since Alex's death Cord found himself glad to be alive.

"You think that will appease me?" Celine threw back her head, grabbed her hair with both hands and laughed the wild haunted laugh of one demented. Then she pointed at Dundee.

"You are cursed, Captain Dundee, cursed to die a wretched death more terrible than any mind can conjure. You will die at sea in a terrible storm. Your bloated corpse will be fish bait."

"No! No!" Dundee was no longer shouting. He stared unseeing at Celine and shook his head from side to side. The emerald earbob in his left ear glinted in the sunlight. He continued to clutch the deadly saber. Celine had pushed Dundee too far. She was within range of his saber and, much to Cord's dismay and disbelief, she would not shut up.

"You will meet your fate this very day . . ."

"No!"

"Yes! There is nothing that can be done to save you . . ."

Cord watched Dundee flinch, saw his eyes narrow into slits in his round face. Overwhelming fear was about to become anger fueled by a sense of inevitability. Cord had to warn her that the man believed he had nothing to lose.

"Celine . . . ," he tried.

She never glanced Cord's way. "Nothing will save you now, Captain."

Dundee raised his saber.

Celine raised her voice. "Unless . . ."

Dundee hesitated, watching her closely. His fear was back, but it was coupled with desperation.

"What would you have me do?"

"Take your crew and leave this ship and everyone aboard it unharmed."

"And you'll remove the curse?" He held the saber at the ready.

Celine shrugged and shook her head. "Even I cannot change what fate has decreed. Only you can do that, Captain Dundee. Only you."

"How?"

"Give up your pirate's life and do only good."

"I don't want to die," he moaned.

She closed her eyes, took a deep breath. Her tone held a note of resignation and inevitability.

"We all die, Dundee. But you won't die today, nor will your death be as miserable as the one you'll deserve if you continue down this path of murder and mayhem.''

His hands still bound, Cord watched helplessly as Dundee stared at Celine and alternately clenched and unclenched the hilt of his saber. Celine still looked more like an apparition than a seasick young woman, but she stood calm in the face of the pirate's deliberation.

''You say I've got to change?''

''Definitely.''

This idea seemed to pain him more than the threat of death. He cast aside his fear to question her. ''How do I know you speak the truth?''

''Because I know things about you no one else could possibly know.''

He cocked his head. ''Prove it.''

Celine stared up at the sky. As if she had summoned the wind, the sagging sails luffed. The ships, anchored and lashed together, strained against one another. The slight breeze ruffled the streaming ends of her hair. The hem of her gown billowed around her slim ankles. She used the change in the elements to heighten the drama. Holding her hands stretched out before her, she let the breeze thread through her fingers.

''One day, when you were a small child, your mother took you to a county fair in Cornwall. You ate a pasty that had gone bad and nearly died. You had a puppy you loved dearly. You called him King. Your mother's name was . . . Mary. There's not another living soul on this side of the sea who knows these things.''

Dundee's hand was shaking so badly he nearly dropped his saber.

''Change your ways, Dundee, from this moment on, or everything I've told you will come to pass before sundown.''

He sheathed the saber, turned away from the sight of

her and began barking orders.

"Kujo, bring the men."

"And Dundee . . ." Celine called after him.

He paused just as he was about to swing over the rail. When he looked back, fear still kindled his eyes.

"What is it now, you she-witch?"

"Get yourself some new clothes."

# Eight

As soon as the crew of the *Adelaide* was released and the last pirate had swung over the side, Edward and Foster rushed over to Cord and Celine. Flustered, Foster began sawing at Cord's bonds with the paring knife until Captain Thompson nudged him aside and had Cord free almost instantly.

"God damn it, Thompson, we could have all been killed." Cord said, letting loose the fury that had been consuming him.

"I suppose you think we should have fought it out armed with paring knives and skillets?" Thompson argued.

Cord refused to back down. "It wasn't *your* neck in that noose."

Celine stepped between them, laid her hand on Cord's

arm and said, "I think I need to lie down."

He shook off her hold, then grabbed her arm and shoved her toward the saloon. Edward and Foster followed in their wake.

"What in the hell was that performance all about?" Cord shouted.

Exhausted, Celine did not try to answer until the four of them were crowded together in her cabin. Edward and Foster hovered behind Cord, who stood over her like an avenging angel, demanding an explanation.

"You should thank me for saving your neck instead of hollering at me." She sat down on the bunk, folded her arms beneath her breasts and met his glare with one she hoped was just as intense.

He anchored his hands on his hips, intent on bullying her, but she refused to let him. "If that idiot Dundee didn't frighten me, what makes you think you do?"

His eyes darkened. His lips thinned. He turned to Foster and Edward, who were trying to disappear into the woodwork.

"Leave us," Cord told them.

The servants left.

"Now. I want to know why you left the safety of the cabin when I expressly told you not to. I want to know how you were able to scare the hell out of Dundee. Do you know him?"

The brief respite of calm had ended and they were under sail again.

"May I lie down, your royal highness?" she asked.

Cord quickly stepped away from the bunk. "Are you going to be sick?"

"Not if I lie down."

"Then by all means." He waited until she was settled before he pressed. "Start talking, Celine."

"First of all, I left the cabin despite your orders because I wanted to. Everything was too quiet. For all I knew, all of you might have been killed and I was alone on a ghost ship. Secondly, I have never laid eyes on Captain Dundee before today."

"Then how did you know those things about him?"

"Let me finish." Stalling for time while she tried to think of a plausible explanation, Celine draped her arm over her eyes and said weakly, "I'd like some water, please."

She could tell from his pause that he was about to refuse, but then she heard him move. Celine's mind raced. She could not tell him the truth—he would think her mad if she tried to explain her ability to read the past. It would be easier to let him think that she had known Dundee, but how could she make him believe she'd had an association with such an unsavory character?

By the time Cord had handed her a cup of water and she'd slowly drained it and given the empty cup back to him, she had her answer.

"Every English child has gone to at least one county fair and I'd wager that every one of them has gotten sick on a bad pasty at one time or another. I simply made an accurate guess."

"How would you know about English fairs? I thought you were from Boston."

She sighed. "I lived in England as a child."

"I suppose it was a lucky guess that he was from Cornwall, too?"

"Dundee's accent gave that away," she said.

"What about his mother's name?" Now, he thought, he had her.

"Mary is one of the most common names in England."

"And the dog named King?"

"I guessed at the name. Every boy has a puppy." She looked him square in the eye.

"I had a monkey."

"Which jumped to your tune, I'm sure."

Cord shook his head. "I can't believe you had the gall to brazen it out."

"I didn't have much choice, did I?"

"What if it hadn't worked? What if he'd never gotten sick over a pasty or lived in Cornwall?"

She couldn't very well tell Cord that she had actually feigned stumbling so she could purposely touch the pirate in order to learn something of his past. She had experienced the vivid scene where Dundee's mother took him to the fair and he became ill, an incident lodged in his earliest memories.

Nor could she tell him that her powers had enabled her to divine that years ago some fortune-teller had predicted that Captain Dundee would one day be cursed by a woman, a curse that would ultimately be connected to his death. The prediction had greatly influenced Dundee's life. Celine merely coupled the information she had channeled with the drama she had often witnessed during Persa's finest fortune-telling performances.

"Answer me, Celine. What if it hadn't worked?"

She shrugged. "Then you would have hung and I would probably have been ravaged by the entire pirate crew, chopped up and fed bit by bit to the sharks." She propped herself on an elbow and smiled up at him. "Then again, you told me earlier I wouldn't tempt a shipwrecked sailor, so I probably had nothing to fear in the way of ravaging. Now the crew is safe and so are you."

She shot him a questioning glance and looked away before adding, "I suppose there is still a chance that I'm in danger of being ravaged when and if this godforsaken crate ever reaches your island."

A hint of a smile teased his lips.

"A very slim chance," he told her. He let out a pent-up sigh and tried to relax. "You are insane, you know that, don't you? Any other woman would have been cowering beneath the bunk, but there you were, in nothing more than that damned flopping nightgown, toe to toe with a cutthroat maniac—"

"Dressed in satin, don't forget."

"In purple and yellow satin." His slight smile broadened.

"You look better when you're not frowning so." She had not thought he could be any more handsome.

"Was that meant to be a compliment?"

Cord walked over and sat down beside her, so close that his backside pressed against her hip. In a move that surprised her, for it bordered on tenderness, he reached out and attempted to arrange her tangled hair. He gave up almost instantly.

"It appears I owe you my thanks," he said.

"Actually you owe me your neck, but I will settle for a little kindness."

"You are a strange woman, Celine."

"You are far from a model husband."

"That's exactly what I was thinking while I was standing there on deck trussed up like a turkey." His expression darkened again. "I should have stayed with you, protected you during the attack—it would have been the honorable thing."

She shoved her hair out of her eyes and watched him closely. He was frowning now, no doubt going over the whole incident in his mind.

"Some might think the honorable thing would have been to put a bullet in my brain as soon as it looked like all was lost."

"That entered my mind. It gave me something to think about while I was waiting to hang—wondering what they would do when they found you, hoping they would be merciful, knowing they wouldn't. Killing you first would have been the honorable thing to do."

"Then I'm glad you aren't one to rush to do the honorable thing."

"That's how we ended up married, you know. For once in my life I did the honorable thing." He turned around to look at her. "Why did you do it, Celine? Why did you go through with this marriage?"

"My guardian . . . died very suddenly. I wanted to get away, to change my life. I told you how I came to be at your grandfather's home that night." It wasn't exactly a lie.

"We make quite a pair."

He had said the words to himself, but she heard them. Unlike last night when she was trying to fight off sea-sickness, she used his being lost in thought as an opportunity to study him closely.

Cordero was exceedingly handsome, of that there was no doubt. He had the suntanned, rugged look of a man who spent much time out of doors. Unlike many wealthy planters' sons, he did not appear unaccustomed to physical labor. His shoulders were broad beneath his white shirt, and his hands were strong. He had a firm jaw. Far too often for her liking, his eyes had a far-off, brooding look about them.

She wondered what it would take to make a man like this truly happy. Was there a woman alive with enough love to give to heal the hurt and anger he carried inside?

Before she was aware of what she was doing, she reached out and gently touched the back of his hand, compelled to learn more, to know why he always seemed so lost, so closed off from the world.

Cord looked at her in question, then at her hand where it lay over his. She thought he might draw away, but he did not move. Celine felt the familiar dizziness, felt herself slide into a dreamlike state as she slipped into his mind.

*A beautiful woman in an outmoded gown danced in a luminous froth of waves on a silver sliver of sand beneath a starry sky.*

A wave of overwhelming love hidden somewhere in the deep shadows of his memory poured through Celine, but the haunting image and joyous feeling vanished like smoke as a rapid pounding on the cabin door shook her from her dream state. Cord had no time to ask the question she read in his eyes.

He called out and Edward rushed in. The servant stopped short in the middle of the cabin, wringing his hands. His expression bordered on sheer terror.

"What is it now?" Cord demanded. "Don't tell me Dundee is back?"

"Worse. There's a storm brewing. A big one. Cap'n Thompson sent me to tell you to keep to the cabin. Later on there'll be a cold supper, if cook can manage it. The cap'n don't want any fires in the galley 'cause it's bound to get rough, 'e says."

Edward was practically hopping from foot to foot, fretfully glancing at the porthole over Celine's bunk as if he expected the sea to burst through.

Celine groaned. "It's going to get rough?"

"A real blow, 'e says, ma'am. Told the hands to batten down the hatches."

"Calm down, Edward," Cord told him. "If you stay this worked up you're liable to have a heart attack."

"Better than drownin', if you don't mind me sayin' so."

"I do," Celine said.

Last night's bout of seasickness had been bad enough; there had even been a few hours when she was certain she was going to die. Now she would have to weather a fierce tropical storm, possibly even a hurricane.

She glanced up and found Cord watching her closely while Edward busied himself closing her trunks, securing things around the tight quarters.

"I'm afraid it'll be much worse than last night," Cord said.

"My mother was buried at sea," she told him, unable to keep the fear out of her voice.

Over in the corner, Edward overheard. He stiffened like a marionette, cast one desperate glance at them and raced from the room.

Cord watched his servant flee. He looked down at Celine and sighed. "I need a drink."

It was one of the worst storms he had ever experienced.

Through pelting rain and mountains of water that crashed over the side with each swell, Cord mounted the ladder that led from the 'tween deck to the main, intent upon making it back to the saloon without ending up washed over the side. He had gone below to see to Edward, who was cowering in his bunk. Foster had resorted to tying him down to keep his companion from rolling onto the floor. Both men looked the worse for wear, but

Foster was doing his best to hide his fear. Edward, on the other hand, sobbed and clutched the four-inch rails on either side of his bunk.

An accountant named Alfonse Pennyworth, two bunks over, was content with alternately spewing vomit into and around a bucket and promising the good Lord he would never transgress again. As Cord passed him on the way to the stairs, he wondered what the whey-faced young man might consider a transgression. Forgetting to use a napkin?

Although he had much worse to be forgiven for, Cord was not ready to make God any promises or to beg for mercy. The only God he had ever learned about was of an unforgiving nature, a God who set shrubbery ablaze when He wasn't hurling fire and brimstone. Cord decided long ago that he would prefer a trip to hell. The company would no doubt be more to his liking.

He was exhausted, having done his fair share to help the crew batten down the hatches and stand storm watch. He didn't know how the exhausted sailors were able to stay on their feet, but when Thompson told him to go below and see to his wife, Cord realized how thankful he was to be a passenger and to have that right.

As his head and shoulders cleared the stairwell to the main deck, a wave washed over him. Water cascaded down the ladder. He wiped his eyes and stepped outside. There was no difference between the color of the sea and the leaden sky. The world appeared shrouded in seething gray clouds, lashing rain and undulating swells. He waited until the *Adelaide* was climbing up a wave before he made a dash for the saloon doors. Forced to walk on a water-slicked floor, he intended to make it to the cabin door unharmed.

When the ship plunged through one particularly deep

trough, he reeled into the dining table, unable to right himself before smacking his hip on the edge of the table hard enough to knock the wind out of him. He staggered to Celine's cabin door. Thankfully, it was unlocked, but when he opened it, another lurch of the ship jerked the knob out of his hand and sent the door slamming back into the wall.

He glanced first at the porthole over Celine's bunk. It was seeping water, and he thought immediately of Edward. He looked down at her bunk and thought the weak light was playing tricks on him. She wasn't there. Nor was she on the floor by the bunk. His throat tightened with fear. It had been hours since he had seen her last. Cord spun around and opened the connecting door to his cabin. The porthole there was not leaking, but the bunk was empty.

"Celine!" he called over the tremendous roar of the sea and the groan of protesting timbers. There was no answer.

The ship was tilting at a forty-five-degree angle. He grabbed hold of the doorjamb between the two rooms and hung on. As he stood there straddling the line between the rooms, he noticed Celine in her cabin, crouched behind a barricade of shifting trunks and boxes. With her face hidden in the crook of her arm, all that was visible of her was the top of her head and her very bare shoulders.

He cursed and lunged for her, forced to grab her bunk to keep himself from sliding back into his room when they dove down a wave. He shoved the trunks aside. A small, barrel-shaped carrying case rolled past him and rumbled all the way to the far end of the other cabin, where it hit the wall and popped open. His personal possessions went flying.

"Celine?"

He took her by the shoulders. Her skin was cold and clammy. Cord shook her. When she looked up at him, he saw nothing to relieve his anxiety. The light in her eyes had been extinguished by fear.

"I'm dying," she whispered.

He was able to read the prediction on her lips.

"I should be so lucky," he jested.

She didn't smile. He waited until the ship righted itself between onslaughts and then stood, pulling her up against him. She was trembling so hard she could not stand on her own.

He held her alongside him as he struggled into his cabin. There, at least, the bed was dry. He whipped back the bedding and urged her down.

"Take off your gown," he yelled.

She looked up at him and shook her head forlornly. "Not now, Cord. Please."

"Don't be absurd. Take off your gown. You're soaked through."

"Will it matter once we've capsized and I'm drowning?"

"You aren't going to drown."

"My mother—"

"Your mother was buried at sea. Spare me the details." Cord reached out and grabbed the front of her gown. It was so sodden it had nearly slipped all the way off her on its own. Rather than waste time struggling with it, he gave a quick tug and ripped it off.

She did not protest at all.

"You're worse off than I thought," he mumbled.

She had black-and-blue marks all over her shoulders, breasts and ribs. As he whipped the wool blanket from his bunk, he shouted, "What in the hell happened?"

"I kept falling off the bunk," she said, taking no notice as he wrapped her in the wool cocoon. "I gave up being tossed around and barricaded myself behind the trunks. I'm so tired. Are you tired?"

"Lie down," he said, gently pushing her back onto the bunk and sliding her up against the wall. He was too tall to stretch out comfortably in the small space, but now his height served him well, as he braced his boots against the wall at one end of the bed and his shoulders against the other. Wrapped around her, he could hold her against the sea wall so that she would not go flying off the bunk.

He felt her trembling against him and found it hard to believe that this was the same woman who'd been brave enough to face down a pirate crew. To calm and reassure her, Cord began to stroke her head. Within minutes he found his own anxiety beginning to seep away.

"Tell me about St. Stephen," she whispered against his ear. "I want to imagine what it will be like if we get there."

"We'll get there," he promised.

Her breath was warm. It teased his neck. Cord found himself nuzzling her cheek before he realized what he was doing, and immediately stopped. He closed his eyes and let his mind drift back. All the years he was in Louisiana, he'd never spoken of his island to anyone. No one had ever cared enough to ask. Not even Alex.

"Sunshine and rainbows," he began. "The air is warm and balmy, perfumed with the scent of flowers." He smiled to himself in remembrance. "I never wore a pair of shoes before I was eight.

"We lived charmed lives, island lives. My mother was English. She had inherited the Dunstain land on St.

Stephen from a childless aunt and uncle. She met my father and fell in love with him. My father ran things and kept mother happy. They lived like the other landed gentry, but he was always considered an outsider and less than they because he was only a Creole from New Orleans, while they were a titled set. It never bothered him. He didn't really care what any of them thought, only that my mother was happy.''

Cord braced himself when the ship shuddered after a particularly hard hit. Celine slipped her arms free of the blanket and wrapped them tight around his ribs. He glanced down. Her eyes were closed. Her cheek was pressed against his heart. It was strange, this new sensation, this need to protect and to comfort her.

"The house," she whispered. "Tell me about the house."

"It isn't like any plantation house in Louisiana. It's as large, but not all that grand. My mother's gardens are filled with plants that bloom every color of the rainbow. There is fruit ripe for the picking anytime you want it. On the hillside below the main house there is a sugar mill and distillery. The slave village is nearby. The hills and valleys are covered by acres and acres of sugar cane, a waving sea of rich emerald green.''

Celine lay with her arms wrapped tight around him, her mind capturing not only the sights and sounds he painted with words but those that swirled and eddied about him like a mist of tangled dreams. Since childhood, she had never clung to another living soul. Drifting between sleep and wakefulness, pressed full length against him, her unguarded mind feasted at a banquet stocked with a cornucopia of memories.

No place on earth, she thought, could be as beautiful as the visions of the island locked forever in Cord's mind. She saw the tableau as he set the stage for her, and she could see the players as well.

*Foster and Edward. Younger. Caring for the young boy and his family. Alyce Dunstain Moreau. Cord's beautiful mother. The lady who danced by starlight.*

*A sudden chill. A rush of anguish. Hurt and betrayal. Black crepe. A man who looks like Cordero. A view from the foot of the bed. Half his head swathed in bandages. Terror and loss. Cord listening, paralyzed with grief. Too numb to cry anymore.*

*"Your mother died in the accident. She's never coming back. Eight-year-olds are too old to cry. You will be leaving tomorrow—"*

The dark pain was suddenly cut off. Somehow, Cord had managed to force the feelings into some place inaccessible to both of them. Celine stirred. She realized how deeply Cord had buried his pain, how strong a will he must have created in himself to do so. He had perfected hiding the hurt, even from himself, over many, many years. She hurt for him, and closed her eyes again.

The island was safe for him; that was why he went there so often in memory. She saw the place again the way he had seen it last. She walked with him along a shore with sparkling pink sand, dove beneath foaming sea green waves.

She let his thoughts and the words he whispered against her hair slowly allay her fear of the roaring wind and pounding sea. She let herself take refuge in his arms and felt safe for the first time since she had run from the sight of Jean Perot's blood pooling on the cobblestones in his courtyard.

She let herself dare to hope that the horror of that night was truly behind her. She swore to the Infinite Power behind all life that if they should come through the storm alive, she would do everything she could to be a good wife to Cord. She would offer unconditionally the one thing he had never been able to hold on to: She would offer him love. She would give him her loyalty. She would make him believe in life again.

She felt his arms tighten around her as he braced himself in the bunk. The warmth of his strong, hard body seeped into her. The slow, steady beat of his heart against her ear lulled her to sleep.

Cord knew the minute Celine fell asleep. She was too exhausted to fight her fear any longer. At the same time, almost imperceptibly, the storm had started to weaken. The ship no longer shuddered down every swell, the timbers no longer screamed with every gust of wind. He let himself relax, but remained alert in case the gale picked up again.

With one arm tight around Celine, he continued to stroke her glossy black hair. Holding her close had been an act meant to comfort her, but slowly it had become something else. A pervasive calm had settled over him from the moment he had taken her into his arms.

When she had asked him to describe St. Stephen, he had almost denied her innocent request, fearing the pain lodged with the memories. But once he'd begun the telling, sharing it with her had seemed natural. He'd no longer been alone with his pain.

He gently worked the tangles out of her hair until it slipped like ebony silk between his fingers. He pressed his body closer to hers. He was fully aroused, and had been for too long to deny it. It was a stolen pleasure. He smiled as he imagined what Celine would say if she knew.

From the moment he had laid eyes on her, she had

surprised him at every turn. Her outrageous confrontation with Dundee had not only scared the hell out of him, but had amazed him as well. Her quick humor amused him more than anything had in a long while. They had been bound only by an agreement made between two old men, but she had trusted him enough to fall asleep in his arms.

He felt something inside of him tighten, a stirring he had not allowed himself in years. He warned himself not to care for her, not to become attached to this slip of a girl who kept denying her true identity, who kept claiming to be part gypsy.

Everyone he had ever let himself love had abandoned him. Why would she prove any different? If the situation at the plantation proved impossible, and Celine was miserable, he would let her go.

If she chose to stay, perhaps in time they could at least learn to give each other mutual satisfaction. It wasn't an impossible idea. Most of the men he knew had wed through arranged marriages, and many had made the most of it. Chances of finding a love match like his mother and father's were one in a million.

There was absolutely no need to risk falling in love with Celine. He could not allow her to walk off with whatever remained of his heart.

It was bad enough that she had already made him realize there might be a bit of it left after all.

# Nine

eline knelt on her bunk at the porthole watching glittering moonlight kiss West Indian waters. The moon seemed close enough to touch. She never slept well during a full moon, and tonight was no exception. The *Adelaide* sliced through the calm sea, her sails proudly billowed and straining, as if the ship itself, as much as her passengers and crew, anticipated reaching St. Stephen on the morrow.

Celine slipped a mint green day dress over the shift which had doubled as a nightgown ever since Cord had destroyed the other. As she smoothed down her skirt and opened the cabin door, she was surprised not to find Cord in the saloon. After the way he had been drinking at dinner, she decided he must surely have passed out at the table.

He had been drinking heavily since the night of the storm, and in part she blamed herself. If she had not asked him to describe St. Stephen, he would not have tapped into the past he kept locked so deep inside.

Celine left the saloon and walked along the rail of the main deck, grateful to be up and about. Now that there were only a few hours of the voyage left, she had finally found her sea legs. She reached up to brush a stray lock of hair behind her ear and then paused to lean against the rail and stare out at the midnight blue water. Moonglow backlit the clouds an eerie blue-white. The breeze was balmy, tinted with a hint of fragrant blossoms. Somewhere out over the water a seagull cried. Land was near.

A sailor carrying a heavy coil of rope passed without a glance in her direction. The crew had given her a wide berth since she had pretended to curse Captain Dundee. Foster told her that the sailors half believed she truly had put a curse on Dundee. They were a superstitious, uneducated lot, he said, and it served them right if they wanted to think that a slip of a girl like his mistress was capable of black magic.

She had seen more of Edward and Foster since the storm than she had of Cord. His visits to her cabin had been restricted to quick, carefully polite inquiries about her health. When they reached calm waters, she had half expected him to approach her with his original request, but he never again demanded she sleep with him. Nor did he ever show the level of caring he had during the storm. He was reserved, almost cautious in her presence, watching her when he thought she was not aware.

As she stood alone in the dark, she quickly discovered there was a magical quality about the ship at night, with its green and red lanterns mounted as running lights along the port and starboard sides. The slick teak rail felt as cool and smooth as glass beneath her palms.

Celine raised her face to the heavy moon, shook out her long hair and let it sway against her back. She took a deep breath of the salt air. It was good to finally be free of the stifling four walls of the cabin. She would be glad to touch land.

As she stared at the ribbon of moonlight playing on the water, she recalled the image of Cord's mother, Alyce, as she danced beneath the night sky. His love for the beautiful woman was only one of the memories she had stolen from him during the storm. Still unsettled, Celine left the rail and strolled back to the ladder that led to the poop deck. She had expected to see a helmsman at the wheel, but it came as a surprise when she found Cord on the deck as well. He stood alone at the upper rail, an imposing figure cast in moonlight and shadow, staring down at the water. His full-sleeved shirt billowed as blue-white as the clouds. His arms were spread wide and his hands gripped the rail.

She walked up behind him, the rush of the water and the crack of billowing sails masking the sound of her steps.

"Do you feel like dancing beneath the moon?" The moment she asked, she realized she had made reference to a secret memory of his mother.

He started, then looked down at her. "I came out to watch for the first sign of light from the island."

"In the water?"

"Come look."

She stepped up beside him and leaned against the rail. The water foamed in a spectacular phosphorescent display against the hull. It was like nothing she had ever seen. "It looks like lightning beneath the water."

"Sort of."

"You must be very excited about tomorrow." She sensed his anticipation.

"No."

She knew he was lying, that he simply would not let himself admit he could not wait to reach the island he called home, just as she couldn't wait to see if the island was half as splendid as his memory of it.

"I am excited," she said.

"Don't be," he warned. "You leave yourself open to disappointment."

"But you made it all sound so wonderful."

"I was trying to humor you, to take your mind off the storm. Nothing more."

"You succeeded."

He ignored her for a time, even though she stood so close their shoulders touched. A comfortable silence stretched between them. Finally he said, "You seem to have found your sea legs."

"That's what Foster said earlier." When Cord continued to stare across the sparkling water, she asked, "Do you mind me standing here?"

"Suit yourself."

Celine wished she could touch the glowing water. "You drank so much wine at dinner that I thought you might have fallen overboard."

"How much or how little I drink is no concern of yours." He stared down at her with his unreadable blue eyes. "Are you nagging again?"

"No." She looked away to hide a smile.

He leaned back against the rail, studying her so closely that she finally glanced up. She found his look unsettling.

He was staring at her mouth.

Somewhere inside her, something melted. It was the same heady sensation she had experienced once before in her life—the night Cordero had held her in his arms. At the time she thought she must have been dreaming, but now it was happening again. She felt hot and cold at once, struck by a sudden inexplicable yearning she could not define. Without thought, she took an involuntary step toward him and felt her face flush with color when she realized what she had done. Thankfully, the moonlight masked her discomfort.

Cord wished he could make her nervous enough to hike up her skirts and run back to her cabin. He had avoided her as much as possible over the past few days, attempting to take little notice of her at meals, trying to drown his growing need in the captain's expensive liquor. But his efforts had seemed to have the opposite effect on him. Instead of thinking of her less, he had become obsessed with her.

The moonlight shimmered off her dark hair, turned her skin to a creamy ivory. Her lips were full, dark and tempting. He could not forget the way she had felt in his arms, the way his blood had raced and his loins tightened as he'd held her close during the storm. They had fit together perfectly. It was easy to imagine how well they would suit in bed.

For a split second he almost broached the subject to her again, but then decided that if she did not outright object, she would only concede because she had no other option. He suddenly realized that it was important for Celine to come to him because she wanted what he could give her, not because she felt obliged to do so.

He let himself caress her with his eyes as he gazed down at her tempting mouth, her soft cheeks, her dark lashes. He drew his sight along her throat, to the vulnerable pulse point there, then to the gentle slope of her shoulders. In the semidarkness he could not be certain of the color of her gown, but it was something pale and soft, like her skin in moonlight. The neckline scooped low, revealing enough of a tantalizing peek of her bosom to make his blood pound. The gown fell gracefully from where it gathered just below her breasts, the style emphasizing them even more. The wind played its part in seducing him by molding the pliant material of her skirt against her thighs.

Cord swallowed and turned around again, bracing his hands against the rail. He gulped deep drafts of tangy salt air. The phosphorescent water did indeed look as if it were streaked with lightning. The foam sparkled as it rose and then melted into the surrounding water. A school of flying fish raced beside them, sailing up, skimming over the water, then disappearing like silver darts in the iridescence.

"Oh, no!"

He spun around at her cry. Celine was kneeling on the deck, trying to scoop up one of the slippery flying fish until it lay there on its side, its wing-shaped fins forever stilled, one sightless black eye reflecting the moon.

"Dead," he pronounced without emotion.

"Oh, it can't be." Celine carried the fish over to the rail. She leaned over and let it slip out of her hands into the water. The silver scales were reflected in the moonlight for an instant before the lifeless fish floated off in the ship's wake.

"How sad," she said softly.

"It's a fish, Celine. With a brain the size of a pea."

"Is it hard for you to act so callous all the time?"

"Are you upset because I won't mourn a flying fish?"

"Just because I allow myself to have feelings is no excuse for you to make sport of me."

"What do you mean by that?"

She stared up at him, as if weighing her words carefully. "Why do you run from your feelings, Cordero? Why do you hide your pain in liquor?"

She was so accurate in her description that he was momentarily silenced.

"I'm beginning to think you really are a witch." He shoved off the rail and took a step toward her.

With her long, unbound hair blowing in the wind, her perfect features highlighted by the moonlight, he almost believed she possessed powers beyond those of a mortal woman. He definitely felt as if she had cast a spell over him.

He expected her to step out of his reach. Instead she didn't move, merely watched him close the gap between them. Reason bid him stop. Lust urged him on.

When he took her in his arms and covered her mouth with his, it was not the gentle first kiss of a suitor trying to woo a virgin, but the bold, demanding exchange of a man hungering for all a woman had to give. His lips slashed across her tender, pouting mouth as he tangled his fingers in her hair and cupped her head in his hands. His tongue slipped between her teeth, delved the warm, sweet recesses of her mouth in imitation of what he wanted to do to her body. She moaned and pressed against him. As if swimming through deep, uncharted waters, Cord reacted more powerfully to her than he ever had to any woman. It scared the hell out of him. So much so that he instantly let her go.

Celine fell limply against the rail and tried to recover her senses. She stared up at Cord. The kiss left her mind filled with no more substance than that of the clouds that drifted across the moonbeams. A few moments ago she had suspected he was going to kiss her, but nothing on earth could have prepared her for what he had just done.

Her senses had never felt so alive. The sound of the ship, the hum of the water beneath the hull, the scent of the sea and the fragrant hint of distant island flowers overlaid and threaded through the sensation of Cord's hands entangled in her hair, the biting taste of rum on his soft lips and searing tongue. He smelled of sunshine and salt and bay rum. Nothing had prepared her for the demand he had communicated with his kiss. Not only the sensations it evoked, but also the powerful need that drove him, shocked her to her toes.

"That was nice," she said without thinking. It had been more than nice. It had been something she could not even put into words.

He looked none too pleased with the compliment. "It's late," he said abruptly.

He glanced over his shoulder, and Celine followed the direction of his gaze. The helmsman was still at the wheel near the stern, but he didn't seem to be paying them any mind.

"Yes, it's late." It was an inane response, but all she could manage with her heart in her throat.

"You can stand out here all night, but I'm going in."

With that, he walked away without a word or touch, his shoulders rigid. He reminded her of Henre Moreau.

She watched him climb down the ladder to the main deck, wondering what had set him off, until she realized that perhaps he had just experienced the same startling, blood-stirring reaction.

It must have come as a great shock for a man who worked so hard to feel nothing.

\* \* \*

St. Stephen was alive with sights and sounds and colors Celine had never seen before. As she stood beside the pile of trunks and crates—hers, Cord's, Foster's and Edward's—she tried to take it all in at once. They had sailed into the bay on waters as clear and turquoise as the sky above them. Like the wharf at New Orleans on a much smaller scale, Baytowne was the island's major port and as such, the hub of activity. Schooners scheduled to be careened and to have their hulls scraped and painted were docked there. Warehouses lined one side of the wharf. In the shops and stalls, natives and merchants who hocked their wares vied for space with potters bent over their wheels as they fashioned various pieces out of yellow clay.

Through the shifting crowd she saw a large town square where a small rock church proudly stood. Its bell tower and spire reached toward the heavens. Behind a stone fence beside the church, moss-covered stone crosses marked the graves of St. Stephen's most prominent citizens. Ancient banyans with roots large enough to house a child and massive tangles of vines shaded each corner of the square.

The humid air was heavy with floral musk. The hillsides surrounding the bay were covered in a profusion of foliage dotted with the bright colors of hundreds of species of flowering trees and plants. Brilliant white sand blanketed the beach where the waters of the bay met the land.

As she tried to take in everything at once, a heady sense of excitement swept through her. She shifted from foot to foot, beginning to wilt in the heat. Using one of the trunks for a seat, she sat down to wait for the men. She could feel her cheeks and nose beginning to burn. Cord had disappeared without a word about where he was going. Edward and Foster, who had gone off to procure a carriage and a wagon to carry them all to Dunstain Place, had promised to return shortly. Obviously, their idea of the word *shortly* was not the same as her own.

A well-dressed gentleman almost passed her by, but when she glanced up at him and smiled, he abruptly stopped. He looked to be in his early fifties, still handsome, with a full head of silver-gray hair. He assessed her and the assembled baggage as if she were a commodity rather than a person.

She had watched her mother ply her trade on the London streets. There had been an unforgettable, undeniable look of lust in men's eyes when they'd propositioned her. The gentleman staring down at her now had that very same look. When he addressed her, it was with a decidedly cultured English accent.

"A lovely lady such as yourself shouldn't be out here alone. I would be happy to accompany you to one of the local establishments to see that you are comfortable."

"That won't be necessary, sir. I'm awaiting my husband and his servants, who have just gone to hire a carriage to take us to his home."

She raised her chin a notch higher and watched his expression of lust cool to one of intense curiosity.

"Allow me to introduce myself. I'm Collin Ray, assistant to His Royal Highness's appointed governor of St. Stephen, my brother, the Honorable Sir Simon Ray."

In her mind, Collin Ray had already insulted her, so her estimation of his person did not rise after the introduction. Her first inclination was to send him packing, but thinking of Cord's need to establish a place among the island community, she held her temper.

"I'm pleased to make your acquaintance. My name is Celine Moreau. My husband, Cordero Moreau, is—"

"Moreau?" His eyes widened and he drew back in surprise. "Not Auguste Moreau's son?"

"I suppose, if he is the former owner of Dunstain Place. Cordero has come home to take over."

"Oh, he has, has he? That should prove interesting." Collin Ray's brow arched. He leaned back and folded his arms.

"I'm sorry. I don't understand."

He looked down upon her pityingly. She couldn't decide which she hated more, his earlier, lascivious perusal or his mock sympathy.

"Your husband has his work cut out for him. Dunstain Place is in a shambles, as you'll find out soon enough. Auguste committed suicide after his wife's death and his manager left shortly thereafter. I suppose there are a few slaves left up there, but from what I hear the plantation has fallen into ruin."

Celine's heart broke for Cord. He had lost not only his mother, but his father shortly thereafter. Now even his dream of returning to run the plantation was tarnished. If he had not yet heard the news, she knew she would have to find the courage to tell him.

"Have you been to Dunstain Place?" she asked.

"No. Neither has anyone I know. It's remotely located, high in the hills almost across the island."

He infuriated her by causing her to feel he was speaking to her breasts, not her. "Perhaps it is not as bad as you say, Mr. Ray."

"It's probably worse." He brushed a speck of lint from the cuff of his expensive coat before he looked her over again, this time without emotion, much the way a buyer would inspect a prime piece of horseflesh.

"I doubt your servants will find a conveyance to hire today, what with the festival going on."

"Festival?"

"The unveiling and dedication of the bronze of Wellington that will grace the square. Governors and dignitaries from the other islands as well as colonists of note have come to St. Stephen for the occasion. Which reminds me, I must keep a pressing appointment."

He tipped his beaver hat to her and bowed. "It was nice meeting you, Mrs. Moreau."

"Thank you, sir."

He started off, then paused and turned back. "By the way, after you have seen the miserable place your husband has brought you to, if you should happen to find yourself unable to suffer the situation, please remember that I would consider it an honor to offer you my protection."

With a sly smile and a nod, Collin Ray turned and walked away.

Speechless, Celine jumped to her feet, her hands fisted in the folds of her skirt. She glanced back toward the ship, wondering if she should go back and wait on board. When she turned around again, she was relieved to see Foster hurrying toward her. Two black men wearing nothing but ragged pants cut off above the knee were following close behind. Foster's usually unreadable expression was clouded.

"I'm sorry to have taken so long, miss, but we've had the devil's own time finding lodging. It'll be impossible to leave for Dunstain Place before tomorrow. There's a celebration going on here in Baytowne."

"So I've already heard." Still troubled by Collin Ray's insulting demeanor, she didn't go on to explain how she knew, but waited for Foster to direct the porters to carry the trunks to an inn on the far side of the dock. As he followed close behind the two men, Celine hurried to keep up with him.

"Have you seen Cord?" She wished she could be with him when he heard about the conditions at Dunstain Place.

Foster glanced over at her, unable to hide his embarrassment. "Not since I saw him go into a grog shop down the way."

She had grown closer to both servants over the voyage, but it wasn't until this moment that she realized how highly Foster regarded her. He did not try to make excuses for Cord out of loyalty, but treated her with a respect equal to that he paid his master. They trailed after the two porters, who toted the heavy trunks with little effort.

The inn was run-down. The paint was peeling; the sign above the door sported a barely recognizable, faded painting of a frothing mug of ale and a smoking pipe; the stairs to the rooms on the second floor were worn by the many feet that had trod them over the years. When Foster profusely apologized for the accommodations, she wanted to tell him she had once lived in far, far worse.

They found Edward in the room appointed to her and Cord. He had already stripped and changed the bed and had the pillows airing in the sunlight on the balcony. When they walked in he was in the process of dusting a scarred bedside table. As Celine cleared the threshold, he stopped and hurried over to her.

"Oh, miss. I don't know what to say 'cept we're sorry. There ain't a decent room nor carriage to be had, not a wagon, not a cart, not a mule because of—"

"The dedication of the statue," she finished for him.

"I know." She glanced around the drab little room, with its lumpy bed and its dingy mosquito netting, which sported holes big enough to admit a horde of ravenous insects. "This place doesn't disturb me as much as what I just learned on the dock."

She immediately had their full attention. Celine waited until Foster paid the silent porters and the two blacks left the room. Then she looked at Foster and Edward in turn.

"I need your advice," she said.

"Whatever we can do, miss." Edward's whole face drooped. He couldn't disguise his worry.

"We're here to 'elp." Foster took a step closer to Edward.

She was warmed by their response. "While I was waiting on the dock, a man introduced himself as Collin Ray and offered me his . . . assistance."

"He didn't make advances toward you, did 'e, miss? If 'e did, I say we tell Cordero right off and—"

Celine dismissed Foster's suggestion with a wave of her hand. "I'd rather we not get into that. What disturbed me was what he said about Dunstain Place. He claims the plantation has fallen into ruin and that the manager left years ago."

Edward plopped down on the edge of the bed. Obviously not thinking clearly, he pressed the dirty dust rag to his temple. Foster frowned and shook his head. "That can't be. I know for a fact that Cordero has continued to get his monthly stipend from the estate, because our pay comes out of it."

Celine paced over to the open French doors on the balcony, thinking out loud. "Ray claims the place is in ruins. What if Cord is penniless?"

"Beggin' your pardon, miss, but Henre Moreau

would have turned us out long ago if all Cordero's money 'ad dried up. We're provided for by Miss Alyce's will, from the monies in the estate that come from England. What the Dunstain Place plantation earns, if anything, I wouldn't know.''

Celine frowned as she observed the bustling scene on the docks.

''What should we do? If he hasn't already heard it, do you think we should tell Cord?''

''What if it ain't all that bad?'' Edward asked. But his uncharacteristic burst of optimism soon faded. ''Then again, what if it's worse?''

''I can't bear to think what this might do to him,'' Celine said.

''There's no better place to pick up information than in a tavern.'' Foster shoved his hands in his jacket pockets.

''No better place to get drunk, either,'' Celine muttered.

''Now, miss, we know he ain't perfect,'' Edward said.

''He's probably just trying to get the lay of the land,'' Foster added.

''No doubt,'' Celine muttered with a sinking feeling of loss. She was not some innocent who did not know what a wide variety of entertainment a gentleman could procure at a tavern.

Before they could discuss the matter further, the distinct sound of footsteps sounded in the hall. In a moment Cord was in the doorway, leaning a shoulder against the jamb. His face was flushed from more than heat, his blue eyes glassy. He held a package tied up with paper and twine beneath one arm and a half-empty bottle of rum in his hand.

"I'd come in, but the room's too small to hold one more," he said.

Foster smoothed his shirtfront. Edward gave the dust rag one last flick over the dull tabletop. Then both men hurried toward the door. They were abandoning Celine before she had made a decision. Cord stepped aside to let them pass, then walked into the room and tossed the parcel on the unmade bed.

"How was the tavern?"

She had not meant to sound like a nagging harpy, but seeing him standing there so nonchalant, so handsome, and holding himself at a cool distance set her nerves on edge.

"The tavern was fine. I learned something very interesting there." He was staring at the bed.

"I was afraid you might. Just remember things aren't always as bad as they seem."

"No. I suppose if I were to think hard on it, there might be some sort of benefit in having a wife who has become legendary as a bona fide witch."

"After all, many people start with nothing and have—" Celine stopped pacing and stared at him. "What did you just say?"

"Maybe I should ask what *you* are talking about?"

Far from relieved, she said quickly, "Never mind. What do you mean, I'm legendary as a witch?"

"Well, I wasn't just referring to your temperament. I happened to be seated at a table beside some sailors who had just reached port. A week ago they came across a shipwreck on an inexcessible section of the west coast of Barbados. Among the other bodies there happened to be one they could identify . . ."

"Oh no." She covered her mouth with her hands.

"Everyone agreed it was none other than Captain Dundee."

She gasped.

Cord sat on the footboard of the bed and crossed his arms. "Dundee was lashed to the ship's wheel. There was enough purple and saffron satin left on his body to see that it was really him. That and the fact that the dead man had been shorter than most women."

"Drowned?"

"Drowned and picked over by vultures of both land and sea. It wasn't a very pretty sight. No telling how long he might have floated tied to the wheel before he died—a horrible death, they say."

He was watching her closely. She could see that he might just believe she had truly cursed Dundee.

"Did all hands die? How was my name connected?" she whispered, afraid to hear the answer.

"They later found some surviving crewmen on the beach who were only too willing to relate the tale of Dundee's confrontation with a witch aboard the *Adelaide* who had cursed him just before he died. The witch, of course, was you, wife."

"What does this mean?" She walked to the balcony, stepped outside and lifted her hand to shield her eyes from the sun. She knew nothing of the customs of the island. Within minutes she might be on the run again. "Do they still burn witches at the stake here?"

Cord laughed. "No. But I doubt we'll be able to keep any slaves once they get wind of this. They believe in all manner of beings—ghosts they call *jumbies* or *duppies*, witches, sorcerers." He tipped his head and eyed her speculatively. "Then again, the slaves still respect supernatural powers. You might be quite an asset."

"You don't believe it, do you?" Celine paced back

to the bed and sat down beside him without thinking. He watched her closely.

"No, I don't believe it. Should I?"

"You shouldn't even have to ask. I had nothing to do with Dundee's death. Nothing. Good God. I would never hurt anyone—"

She stopped abruptly. She had killed Perot, although not intentionally. Now Dundee was dead. Even though she was not responsible, she'd have to carry another soul on her conscience. She was thankful, at least, that Cord did not believe this nonsense. She wasn't certain she could stand up to the gossip alone.

Her head was splitting from the combination of sun and lack of food. Celine cupped her face in her hands. Suddenly she felt Cord's hand on her shoulder, rubbing it gently. Surprised by the unexpected show of tenderness, she looked into his eyes.

"I don't believe any of it, Celine. I know you were only bluffing to play on his fear."

"Thank you for believing in me," she said.

Her heart tripped as he returned her gaze. She wished she saw more in his eyes than reassurance. She wished she saw trust, coupled with just a hint of affection. But that, she knew was asking the impossible. Cordero Moreau had taught himself not to feel anything that could not be drowned by a night's drink.

"You have no reason to lie," he said.

Guilt hit her square on. She had never claimed to be Jemma O'Hurley, but she had not told him the full truth about the murder or exactly why she'd left New Orleans. She would be living a lie until she felt safe enough to tell him everything—which meant that she might well be living a lie for a long while to come.

She glanced down at the hand on her shoulder. As if

he suddenly realized what he had done, Cord quickly stood and moved to the foot of the bed. With a heavy heart, she thought of what Ray had told her.

"Is that all you heard at the tavern? I suppose you were busy drinking and whatever they call it here . . . wenching?"

"I'll admit to having had a rum or two, but I've had no wench yet."

She looked at the bottle. "More than a rum or two, I'd say."

"Nag." He almost smiled.

"Cord, there's something I need to tell you, something that needs to be said." She linked her fingers and took a deep breath. There was no easy way to break the news.

Cord could see that she was as nervous as a guilty defendant in a witness box. The longer he watched her fidget with the mint green ribbon beneath the bodice of her gown, the more he was certain that she had changed her mind and wanted to get out of the marriage before it was too late.

Who could blame her? He looked around at the squalid room, at the filthy mattress, torn curtains and ruined mosquito netting. He was not a man given to making excuses or pleading his cause. And besides, of late he'd found himself thinking of her far too often. Maybe it would be safer for both of them if she left before he could no longer control himself, before she could steal the bit of his heart she hadn't yet managed to.

If she wanted out of the marriage, so be it.

"Get on with it, Celine. I've places to go."

"Such as back to the tavern?"

"Maybe."

"You were certainly gone long enough last time."

One of his thick brows hooked. "Damn, but you are a nag. You were about to say—?"

"You aren't going to like it."

"I'll be the judge of that." She was leaving him. Good riddance. At least she wouldn't be around to torture him any longer. He would go straight to the nearest whorehouse and treat himself to the most expensive whore there. One with large bosoms, preferably a very leggy blond. It didn't matter what she looked like as long as she was not a petite, raven-haired, amethyst-eyed little witch who had the power to haunt his dreams.

"Spit it out, Celine." He almost told her he knew what she was about to say, but if she wanted out, she would have to suffer through telling him so. She was obviously distraught. She looked close to throwing up again, even if they were on dry land.

He watched her blink twice, rub her hands together in a manner reminiscent of Edward, then take a deep breath.

"You're ruined," she blurted. "I mean, the plantation is in ruins."

# Ten

"What are you talking about?" He let the mask that hid his feelings drop into place with well-practiced ease. She was up now, pacing the confines of the small room.

"While I was waiting at the dock, a gentleman introduced himself to me. When he inquired to see if I needed any help, I told him no, that I was waiting for my husband."

"Celine, for God's sake, stand still. You're making me dizzy."

She continued pacing. "The rum is making you dizzy, Cord. Anyway, this man recognized your name and acted quite surprised that you were planning on taking up residence at Dunstain Place. That's when he told me . . ."

She paused long enough to infuriate him, casting a pitying glance in his direction.

"Get on with it."

"He said the place had gone to ruin. He claims the manager left years ago and the slaves ran off." She looked down at her folded hands and then back up at him, waiting for him to say something.

"He was a wealth of information, I see." His hand curled into a fist at his side. It was the only show of emotion he allowed himself.

"I've been thinking . . ." She stopped pacing.

"A frightening thought in itself," he mumbled.

"I wonder if perhaps he might not be exaggerating."

"Who was he, this bearer of bad tidings?"

"His name is Collin Ray. His brother is a local magistrate or something. He seemed quite enamored of himself."

She was standing so close he saw the faint smattering of freckles that an hour in the sun had drawn over the bridge of her nose. He forced himself to study each and every one of them carefully. It kept him from giving in to his rage.

"Say something," she prodded.

He walked over to the table where he had left the rum bottle, uncorked it and looked down at the rich brown liquor inside. "There's not much to say, is there, Celine?"

He took a long pull on the bottle and welcomed the feel of the rum burning its way down his throat. It wouldn't be long before the liquor numbed his pain.

"You could find out if anyone else knows what has been happening at Dunstain Place over the past eighteen years." She reached out and put her hand on his forearm, stopping the bottle halfway to his lips. "You could do a lot more than pour rum down your throat.''

"But rum is the most immediate remedy.''

"And it's far easier than facing your feelings or finding out whether or not you'll have to put the plantation back on its feet.'' She watched him a moment longer. "I know you must be devastated.''

He slammed the near-empty bottle on the table, which rocked back and forth on its wobbly legs with the force of the blow.

"I'm nothing of the kind. My grandfather warned me I was probably coming back to nothing.''

"You still get your monthly stipend—''

"What do you know about that?'' Hating the pity he read in her eyes, he stepped away from her.

"I . . . Foster and Edward told me about it when I informed them what I had heard from Collin Ray.''

He ran his hands through his hair and headed for the door. "So, all of you held a gabfest in my absence? Was it enjoyable, all of you sitting around here like a trio of clucking hens?''

"They sincerely care about you.''

"I don't need anyone to care about me. I don't *want* anyone to care about me.''

"You need someone to care about you worse than anyone I've ever known.''

"Stay out of my life, Celine.'' What right did she have to tell him what he felt or what he needed?

"Of course. You'd like that, wouldn't you? You should be *allowed* to stomp around and glare, to close yourself off from the world. I know you love this island, I know you love Dunstain Place—''

"And what makes you so sure of that, Miss All-Knowing One?''

"The way you talked about it the night of the storm.''

He had to get out. This time he would keep going.

"It would be better if you forget all about that night, Celine."

"Have you?"

Her question surprised him.

"Of course," he lied "There wasn't one memorable thing about it."

She looked crushed. He stepped over the threshold. He had to get away from this room and the bruised expression in her eyes. Baytowne was celebrating. He would find a way to take his mind off Dunstain Place. There was plenty of rum to be had, plenty of wenches to sport with. In an hour he wouldn't care about the state of the plantation. He wouldn't even care that his nagging, meddling wife had just looked at him with suspiciously misty eyes, as if she'd been blinking back tears.

As an afterthought, he turned around—although still poised in the open doorway, ready to walk out—and said, "This is the perfect opportunity for you to leave, Celine. Since we haven't fucked yet, the marriage can still be annulled."

She stood there mute, staring up at him as if she realized he had just tried his damnedest to shock her.

"Is that a no?"

She didn't answer, simply stared back, waiting for something he couldn't give, waiting for him to soften, to tell her he had not meant the harsh word, to ask her to forgive him for it. She was waiting for him to do what he was incapable of, and it made him feel like a heartless bastard.

"That's for you," he said, pointing to the package on the bed. He turned away from the haunted look in her eyes and left her standing there.

Celine didn't move until she heard his footsteps fade

down the hall. The overpowering scent of garlic and grease from the dining room below made the air heavy and nauseating. Cord had tried to anger and shock her, had tried to force her to take the easy way out, but Cordero Moreau didn't know what she was made of. A little vulgarity was not going to scare her off.

She walked over to the bed, picked up the brown paper parcel and slipped off the string. The paper crackled as she opened it to reveal a frothy white lawn nightgown. It was much like the one he had ruined.

The gown had a deep flounce around the skirt, but instead of having long sleeves, it had been adapted to island wear, cut like an undergarment, sleeveless, with a row of tiny pearl buttons up the bodice. When she held it up to herself, she could see that, unlike the other, this one was a perfect fit. Not all of his time alone that morning, she realized, had been spent in a tavern.

The man who tried so hard to convince everyone that he had no feelings had taken the time to replace her nightgown with one that was not only her size, but of far better quality than the one he had ruined.

Burying her face in the soft folds of the white fabric, Celine closed her eyes and made herself a promise. Fate had sent her to Cordero Moreau for a reason—and if that reason was to bring his battered heart to life, she would do it.

Foster halted in the shadows of the stairwell and motioned to Edward, who quickly sidled up to him. "What is it?"

"I've Miss Celine's supper arranged. She's to eat in a private dining room with an older gent, a bookseller from Barbados. I'm going up to collect her now," Foster said.

"Where's Cordero?"

"I ain't seen him since she tol' him about Dunstain Place. I've a feeling we won't be seein' 'im 'til mornin'."

Edward cast a troubled glance up the darkened stairwell. "I think the sooner we can get 'im to Dunstain Place the better. There's bound t' be too much temptation for Cordero 'ere in town, what with the bad news an' all . . ."

"It just don't seem possible the place has gone to wrack and ruin. I'll 'ave to see it with my own eyes first."

"Poor miss. It ain't like she's had the greatest time of it, what with 'er bein' sick on the voyage an' all, an' now this. I'm surprised she ain't up and demanded to be sent back 'ome." Edward shook his head forlornly.

"She's surprised me all the way around." Foster ran his fingers beneath his collar. His skin was sticky from the close, humid air. "I would have thought a rich merchant's daughter wouldn't 'ave stepped one foot into that room upstairs, but she took it in stride. You think there might be anything to that story she tried to sell us in Louisiana? You think she really *was* going to try to hire on as a servant at ol' Henre's place?"

Edward fanned his face with both hands. The heat from the first story rose up the close confines of the stairwell. "I don't know what to think anymore." He frowned and looked over at Foster. "I still think they make a fine pair."

"They just don't know it yet," Foster said.

"It's up to us to make 'em see the light."

Foster propped his chin on his thumb. "Sharin' a

cabin on the ship didn't seem to work too much in favor of intimacy.''

"And there are eight bedrooms at Dunstain Place." Edward sighed forlornly.

"Then we'll just 'ave to see to it that they end up in one together . . . or at least in rooms that are side by side." Foster grabbed the handrail. "I'll go on up and bring 'er down for supper. You 'ave something in the taproom. I'll join you there, and after we eat we'll start lookin' for Cordero."

Edward shook his head and started down the stairs again. "I've a feelin' we'll be gettin' reacquainted with the seamy side o' Baytowne tonight."

It was too humid to eat. After the first few bites of sautéed fish in hot pepper sauce, Celine didn't even make an attempt to have more as she sat at a small table in a closet that passed as a private dining room in the Tavern Inn. Her dinner companion was a lean, older gentleman with ruddy skin, thinning hair the color of burnt nutmeg and sharp blue eyes. The bookseller had come to St. Stephen for the statue dedication.

Although at first she wished she'd been dining alone, she soon found Mr. Howard Wells to be a gentleman, well-spoken and entertaining. After commiserating with Celine about her seasickness, he had launched into a long soliloquy detailing the hazards of sea travel in general. Finally, he paused long enough to drain his mug of ale and leaned back in his chair.

"You said your husband has returned to St. Stephen after years of absence?"

"Yes, that's right." She paused while a round of boisterous laughter echoed through the taproom next door. "He was raised in New Orleans."

"That explains it."

He appeared so sympathetic she had to ask, "Explains what?"

"Your lack of invitation to stay elsewhere. Obviously your husband has no connections here in Baytowne. No family?"

She shook her head. "Not that I know of."

A young, buxom waitress walked in and took their plates, promising to bring Celine coffee and Mr. Wells another mug of ale.

"The planters here in the English islands are a close-knit group, and have been since the first aristocrats among the colonists banded together and excluded everyone else. Had your husband's family been well friended, you would not have had to suffer this place tonight, but would be the guests of someone here in Baytowne. With the dedication festival in progress, there are numerous parties and soirees going on tonight and through the week."

"I'm sure that once word is out that my husband has come back, he will be included."

"You say he was born here?" Mr. Wells asked.

"He was. His mother's family owned the plantation Cordero has inherited. His father was a Creole from New Orleans."

"And you?"

"I'm from New Orleans also."

Celine had more than enough to concern her; she didn't need to worry about not having been invited to rub elbows with the landed gentry. The serving girl brought her coffee, heavily laced with chocolate as Celine had requested. She stirred the steaming brew and waited for it to cool. As they sat in companionable silence, Celine's thoughts drifted to the matter she had been pondering all evening—was there any way she could help Cord make Dunstain Place profitable again?

"Mr. Wells, do you know anything at all about raising sugar?"

"Anyone who's spent his lifetime on Barbados can't help but know something about raising sugar. Why do you ask?"

"I'm afraid I don't know a thing about it, and I'm about to set off to live on a sugar plantation. I'd like to be of some help when we get there."

He looked at her as if she were some new species. "Now there's a novel idea. A planter's wife actually wanting to become involved?"

"Is that so outrageous?"

"From the one's I've met it's highly unusual."

"That may be, but then again, I've always been a bit on the unusual side, Mr. Wells." It was an understatement, she knew.

He smiled at that. "What do you want to know?"

"Does it take much money to get a plantation up and running?"

"A small fortune in slaves. Not so much for equipment, though—that is, if you already have a mill, a boiling house, a curing house, a distillery and a contract with a storehouse."

Celine wondered how Cord would ever come up with the money to get Dunstain Place producing again.

Howard Wells continued. "The slaves need to be fed and housed and clothed, and a doctor must be provided for them, along with a seamstress, a carpenter, a smith, a mason, coopers to make casks and barrels, food . . ." He paused and then said, "My dear, you are looking quite befuddled."

"I don't know how Cord will do it all."

"One step at a time, I'd imagine. He can start with obtaining credit, as most planters do."

"But the debt . . ."

"Debt is the foundation of the sugar industry. Everyone is in debt to someone. Only the inept planter loses money, even in the worst of times. With any luck, the land won't be worn out." He held his mug in his lap as he stared up at the ceiling. "There are a few perils involved. There's yellow blast, an insect that bores into the roots of the sugarcane and saps the life out of it. Or there's black blast, a swarm of insects that ruin the crop. There are hurricanes, too much or too little rain, rats . . ."

Celine propped her elbows on the table and her chin on her hands. There'd be no stopping Howard Wells now.

"Your mill roller could break, the furnace hearth could crack, boiling coppers might burn out or cistern pipes snap. Any of those disasters could spoil a year's worth of output. If you delay the cane processing by a day or two, that's all it takes for the juice to deteriorate, and the sugar crop is lost."

"It all sounds overwhelming."

"I'm sure your husband knows what he's facing."

She knew Cord probably did know what he was facing and had most likely decided he wasn't up to it. His grandfather had made certain he had no faith in himself. In the face of everything Cord just might do what he had threatened—sit beneath a palm and drink rum with the Caribs all day.

"Well, my dear, I'm an old man and must be away to my bed, such as it is. Might I see you upstairs so that you won't have to walk through the taproom alone?"

"Thank you. I'm afraid our servants have found other

duties to attend to,'' she said.

Foster had assured her that they would be back as soon as they had found Cordero and made certain he was all right. Obviously, they had not had much luck.

She let Howard Wells accompany her through the crowded taproom. As they climbed the precariously sagging stairwell, she tried to converse over the noise that echoed around them. The hallway was dingy and dark, the wooden floor scuffed and marred, the paint peeling from the walls. There were rust-colored stains in the plaster where rain had seeped in.

He saw her to her door and bid her good night. Hoping Cord would not object, she extended an invitation to Mr. Wells to visit them at Dunstain Place if he found the time. He assured her it would be a pleasure and wished her luck.

Celine walked into her room and closed the door. Leaving the lamp dark, she moved to the open balcony and stood at the rail, watching the boats in the harbor sway at anchor. The *Adelaide* was still docked across the wharf, a solitary seaman walking its deck. Only one or two of the ship's running lights were lit. The naked masts rose against a starless sky draped with low-hanging clouds.

A gentle rain began to fall, sending her back to the shelter of the open doorway. She listened to the rain as it began to stream off the tile roof, the atmosphere a painful reminder of hot summer nights in New Orleans.

Celine gazed though the rain, past the masts and rigging of the ships in the harbor toward the dark horizon. She knew that the memories of her years with Persa would be forever written on her heart. She could only hope that her past would stand her in good stead in the days to come.

\*　　\*　　\*

"Go ahead and knock." Edward nudged Foster with his elbow as they stood together in the dimly lit hallway of the island's most renowned whorehouse, Madam Felicity's Hotel.

"I don't see any way around it, do you?" Foster asked for the third time, as if repetition would somehow change his friend's answer.

"No, I don't. If we're going to get 'im back to the inn and Miss Celine, there's no other way. Knock."

Foster looked over his shoulder and glanced down the hall. There was no one in sight. A loud giggle followed by a squeal of delight issued from the room next door. Edward pursed his lips, grimaced and shook his head in disgust. Foster delivered a short, rapid burst of knocks.

"Are you sure it's the right room?"

"Twenty-four." Edward pointed to the gold numerals painted on the bright fuchsia door.

"No one answers." Foster was ready to turn away when Edward reached past him and knocked again.

Suddenly the door flew open to reveal a frowsy blond in her early thirties. She stood a good head taller than either man. Her hair frizzed out in a wild nimbus. Her breasts were quite unforgettable—if one was interested in such things. Her legs, of which there was far too much showing, in the servants' opinion, were long and shapely. Her expression revealed her impatience.

"What is it?" The woman demanded.

"We've . . . that is, you see . . . we thought . . ." Edward couldn't find the words.

Foster stepped up and took charge. "We need to see Cordero Moreau. We were told he was here."

They could both quite clearly see the object of their search holding a glass of amber liquid, reclining fully clothed across a bed that nearly filled the small room. But the amazon stood between them and Cord, who acted as if he were stone deaf.

"Nobody's supposed to give out the room numbers," she complained.

"Madam Felicity herself told us 'e was 'ere," Foster said, not bothering to explain that for a hefty bribe, Madam Felicity, a mountainous black woman swathed in yard upon yard of crimson silk and Belgian lace, had been more than willing to give up Cordero's room number. She would have given up much more had he been at all interested.

"Let them in, Bonnie," Cord called out. "And do say hello to my two consciences. I'm lucky—most men have only one."

When they stepped into the room, Cord raised a glass and toasted them.

"Gentlemen. What brings you here on this muggy, rainy night looking so harried and slightly conniving? Nothing urgent, I hope."

"I think you know, sir," Foster said.

"On the contrary, I have no idea what you want."

"We just think, sir—"

"You two aren't paid to think . . . but I would be interested in hearing what you have to say."

"We don't think it's safe for Celine to be alone at the inn."

Cord polished off the rum left in his glass, looked down into the bottom of the tumbler to be certain he had drained every drop, then stared up at Foster.

"If you hadn't left her, she wouldn't be there alone, would she?" Cord frowned. "Did you see that she had supper?"

"Yes, sir."

"Good. Then why don't you go back and take turns guarding her door or whatever it is you feel should be done until I get back tomorrow."

"Tomorrow?" Edward cast a wary glance in the direction of the whore, who stood with her hands planted on her ample hips, waiting impatiently for them to leave.

"I'll be back tomorrow morning and not a minute before. And don't start in on me. You know as well as I that this marriage wasn't my idea."

While Edward stood mute, looking crestfallen, Foster could not let the subject go without one more comment. "It weren't her idea either, if you don't mind myself sayin' so. She told us what she 'eard about Dunstain Place. We're as upset as you are about it—"

"I'm not upset about it. I half expected it. Now get out. I'll see you two in the morning." As Cord watched the men leave, Bonnie walked toward him, swinging her hips provocatively. When she reached the side of the bed, she knelt down beside him, took his empty glass and set it on the table, then began unbuttoning the front of his linen shirt.

"I take it this Celine they spoke of is your wife?" She leaned forward and placed a kiss on the pulse point just above his collarbone.

"In name only," Cord said, as he wrapped his arm around her waist and drew her to him. She was a good armful, not a petite package like Celine. When he had walked into the bordello he had told Madam Felicity that he required her tallest, most robust whore. She had to have blond hair and he didn't care what color eyes she had as long as they weren't amethyst. He'd paid for the entire evening.

As he lay back and let Bonnie strip off his shirt, Cord cursed Edward and Foster for bringing Celine to mind just when he'd thought there might be a glimmer of hope of shutting her out of his thoughts for a few hours.

He had insulted her in the hotel, and lied in trying to convince her that rum would numb the hurt he'd felt when she'd told him what she'd heard. He hadn't lied to his servants—he had half expected the plantation to be in ruin—but hearing it confirmed had been a blow that hit him almost as hard as if Henre had delivered it himself.

Since he'd walked out of the hotel his head had been reeling with the ramifications of what lay before him. He had Celine's dowry—which was half gone already, and certainly not enough to get a sugar plantation up and running—and the monthly stipend from his mother's estate, which would barely cover living expenses for himself, Foster and Edward, not to mention a wife. Women needed *things* . . .

"Your wife must be half crazy not to let a man like you into her bed," Bonnie mumbled as her lips trailed down his bare chest.

"Only half?"

"Entirely crazy . . ."

Cord stared down at the blonde laboring so ardently over his pectorals. What she was doing with her tongue and lips should have made him forget all about Celine and Dunstain Place, he said to himself. It should have made him hard as a rock, and have him conjuring up all the other delicious things she would do to him, instead of picturing Celine alone at the inn wearing the demure nightgown he had bought for her earlier. It infuriated him to realize that the luscious and expensive Bonnie, with her long legs, memorable breasts and talented tongue, paled in comparison to that image.

"Why don't you get me some more rum?" Cord said

sharply, as angry at himself for his lack of response as he was at Celine.

Bonnie drew away, unable to hide her irritation. As she tried to smooth her frizzy hair back out of her eyes, she told him, "I'm not a bleedin' waitress."

"I paid for you to be anything I want you to be tonight."

The rum was on the floor on Cord's side of the bed. She stretched out across him, provocatively rubbing her breasts against his thighs as she reached down for the bottle, then taking her time backing across him until she drew herself up to sit on her heels. She grabbed the glass off the bedside table.

"Here you go, your highness." Bonnie tipped the bottle and poured rum into his glass. When the tumbler was full, she held the bottle against her breasts and stared down at his crotch. She knit her brow and then pursed her lips in a way most men would have found kittenish and quite provocative.

"Maybe you had something a little more stimulating in mind," she said.

"Actually, what I have in mind is fairly boring. I'd like to finish off this rum and go to sleep."

"*Sleep*? You mean, as in close your eyes and snore?"

"If you like to think of it that way."

She shook her head, incredulous. "Sleep? That's it?"

"Sleep. I paid for an entire night with you, but I wouldn't even mind if you wanted to go downstairs and solicit another customer, as long as you stay out of here and leave me in peace."

"But—"

"If this is a problem, I'll talk to Felicity. She seemed an accommodating sort."

"No," she said quickly. Bonnie sat back and watched

him closely, as if he had just sprouted two heads and she was trying to comprehend exactly how he had done it.

"Now that I think about it, getting paid for a night of beauty sleep might not be a bad idea. It's a novel one, I'll give you that." She filled his glass to the top and put the empty bottle on the floor, then scooted to the opposite side of the bed and stretched out on her side, facing him.

Cord polished off the glassful of rum in a series of long swallows. He looked down at the woman smiling up at him. It would take more than a night of sleep to restore any real beauty she might ever have possessed.

"You want me to hold you or anything? I could pretend I was your nanny. Maybe coo to you like you were a babe?" She reached out and ran her fingers through his hair and pushed it back off his forehead.

"What I want," Cord said, stretching out half clothed and crossing his ankles, "is to get some sleep. You can stay here and do the same—just do it on your own side of the bed."

"You don't prefer boys, do you? Felicity just got hold of a little chap who was a cabin boy for a—"

"No, thank you."

"How about a duck that—"

He almost laughed. "Not tonight."

Before closing his eyes, he noticed that Bonnie was still frowning in thought, lying on her back and chewing on her thumbnail. He couldn't tell if she was disappointed in her seduction skills or perplexed about his request to be left alone. He didn't really care what she thought. He was more disturbed over his lack of enthusiasm than he was about what she might think of him.

When he did finally close his eyes, he was treated to

a haunting vision of his wife's amethyst eyes.

"Witch," he mumbled. He felt Bonnie bolt to a sitting position beside him.

"Witch? Would you like me to cackle and pretend I'm riding a broomstick instead of your—"

"Blow out the light and then go to sleep, or get out."

# Eleven

The heat was close and stifling. Thick tropical growth crowded in on itself, creating a barrier that blocked the trade winds as effectively as a solid wall. Celine wondered if the interior of the dormant volcano that created St. Stephen was any hotter than she felt right now.

For too many hours to count she had been traveling across the width of the island in the back of a rickety wagon—the only conveyance they could find—crowded with Foster and Edward and all of the luggage and supplies. Her skin was slick with a fine sheen of perspiration. The humidity made every movement an effort. Her arms and legs felt as if they were full of sand.

Except for the sweat stains on their clothes, Foster and Edward appeared unaffected. They were so anxious to see Dunstain Place again that they somehow managed to ignore their discomfort. The hired driver, a grizzled, toothless man with tufts of white hair growing above his ears, had not spoken a word the entire journey. He barely moved as he sat hunched over the reins, staring at a point in the pockmarked road somewhere between the draft animals' ears.

Earlier, before they had passed through open fields and entered the tropical forest, Celine had hoped the trees would provide relief, but the tangle of dense foliage on either side of the road blocked what little breeze there was and gave the sensation that the forest was closing in on them.

She was staring at a stand of banana trees when the wagon hit a particularly deep rut in the road. Celine grabbed the side of the wagon and hung on. She wondered if anyone would even notice if she was pitched over the rail. Edward dozed. Foster leaned against the side of the wagon and watched the dappled sunlight stream through the treetops.

In a foul mood since he'd met them at the inn that morning, Cord had chosen to travel on the new horse he had purchased in town—ostensibly so that he could ride ahead and report on the condition of the road. So far he had not returned to report on anything. Celine had not had more than a glimpse of him since they left Bay-towne. If the shuttered expression he wore when he rode away was any indication, he was fighting not only child-hood memories, but anxiety over what lay ahead as well.

When he'd returned to the inn for breakfast, he had offered no explanation for his whereabouts last night, nor had she expected any. But whatever he had done had earned him Foster and Edward's silent condemnation, and they had been tight-lipped and cool toward him all morning.

When raucous chattering and sharp, chiding squeals echoed in the branches above them, Edward awoke with a start.

"What is that?" Celine asked, scanning the trees as a shiver slipped down her spine. The screams were enough to have raised the hair on her arms.

"Green monkeys. They can be quite destructive to the crops," Edward told her. "The planters kill off as many of the poor things as they can, but it's a constant battle."

The white-faced, exotic animals scolding them from high in the treetops jumped from limb to limb, Celine experiencing them as playful now rather than ominous. But the creatures' merry antics could not lighten Celine's mood, especially now that she knew that some of them would be hunted down. Turning her gaze to the road, she noticed Cord riding toward them on the powerful white gelding. The trail was so overgrown that he seemed to have materialized out of the dense forest vegetation.

There was no denying that he rode as if he had been born on horseback. He wore no coat. A wide-brimmed hat shaded his face from the sun. His white linen shirt was open at the throat, the sleeves rolled up to reveal his muscular forearms. His dark hair shimmered with hints of sunshine. Usually careful to hide his feelings, his eyes were alive with anticipation.

"We're almost there." He drew up alongside and kept pace with the wagon.

"I hope so," she sighed, moving with the sway of the uncomfortable vehicle.

"The heat is bothering you," he observed.

She blew at a stray lock of hair hanging over one eye

and knew she must look perfectly bedraggled. She tugged at the collar of the traveling suit, which was far too heavy for the tropical weather. "I'm not exactly dressed for it," she said.

"We'll have to find you something cooler to wear."

She glanced over at Edward and Foster and lowered her voice. "Be careful—someone might just find out you aren't as uncaring as you like to appear," she warned.

"You certainly seem out of sorts today."

She could not help but notice that he held the reins expertly.

"No more than you," she said, refusing to be taken in by his devastating good looks.

"Already regretting your decision to come along?"

The wagon hit another rut in the road. Celine tightened her grip on the vehicle and stared without comment.

"You can always go back to Baytowne with the driver," he suggested.

"You would like that, wouldn't you?"

"I don't really care." He was watching the road again.

"You made that quite obvious last night."

He whipped his head around, his attention entirely focused on her. "Don't try and tell me you expected me to warm *your* bed last night."

She felt her face burn with color. "I was quite warm enough last night, thank you."

His gaze left her as he scanned the tropical forest around them. "Just as I thought," he muttered. "You can see the top of the house from here."

She followed the direction of his gaze and finally noticed a long, unbroken roofline through the trees at the top of a rise. "Dunstain Place," she said softly.

Cord nodded.

"Do you want to ride ahead? I know how anxious you are to arrive," she said.

He held the horse to a walk. "No."

Celine knew he was nervous. She knew, too, that there was nothing she could do or say to ease his anxiety. She turned her attention to the road, waiting for her first glimpse of what was to be her home, at least for the present. They turned down a side lane and suddenly more of the house became visible as flashes of white through the trees. A row of traveler's palms fanned out to create a natural barrier along the drive to the house. In the undergrowth around the palms, hibiscus and wild tamarind vied for space. They were going ever higher up the hillside, and she had begun to feel the blessed trade winds off the sea.

It appeared someone had made a halfhearted attempt to hold the encroaching jungle at bay. Piles of cuttings dried to a crisp brown lay next to the road. Amid the tangle of wild growth along the drive, a few vibrant hibiscus blooms had survived the onslaught of forest. The cries of the monkeys mingled with the sound of palm fronds rustling in the breeze.

Finally the house came into full view. The structure reminded Celine of an old woman in need of a fancy new gown. The paint was faded and peeling in spots. There were large patches of mildew beneath the eaves. The roof of the overhang above the veranda was decayed, ferns sprouting here and there in the debris between the shingles. The long jalousies stood open, some lopsided and sagging, the hinges broken or rusted away.

Despite her irritation, Celine could not help but wonder about Cord's reaction. As she watched him closely, her heart went out to him. He uttered not a word as they pulled up before the dilapidated structure and he smoothly dismounted. She expected him to stride immediately toward the house, but he surprised her by waiting to help her down, stalling the inevitable a moment longer.

Celine looked into his eyes and knew that he was wrestling with deep, desperate emotions. She longed to help him, but there was only one way she knew how.

As she gathered her skirt and reached for his hand, she opened her senses to his touch. The tropical mountain forest around them dimmed as she experienced the familiar, light-headed sensation that always came when she was open to visions of the past.

On a wave of images, she saw the plantation house as he had known it last, not as the sad, shabby relic it was now.

*The garden pruned and trimmed. The shutters and window frames bright green. A woman singing. Soft melodious sounds of an angelic voice. Footsteps on floorboards. The scrape of a chair. The smell of burnt sugar and citrus. A lovely, fair-haired woman. "Come, Cordero, sweetheart. Mama loves you, you know that, don't you?" She reaches for his hand. Walking through the garden. "I've planted something new."*

*Her hand is soft. Comforting. Her smile is filled with love.*

*Love and security. Contentment and peace.*

"Are you all right?" Cord withdrew his hand long enough to place it on her shoulder.

The sound of his voice snapped the link between his past and her present. Celine fought down a wave of dizziness that came with the abrupt uncoupling of her mind from his memory.

"I'm fine. It must be the heat."

As they turned toward the house, he dropped his hand from her shoulder but continued to walk along at her pace. Celine drew his attention by touching his sleeve, and Cordero glanced down at her.

"The gardens look as if they were once well tended."

"They were my mother's pride and joy."

She tried a smile. "I would be willing to bet that *you* were her pride and joy."

His eyes were haunted by the lingering sadness that comes with loss that lasts a lifetime. He quickly looked straight ahead, toward the house.

"Do you think she would be happy that you have come home?" she asked.

He stopped dead still. "Do you have to keep this up?"

"I was just thinking out loud."

"I would appreciate it if you didn't think at all," he said.

"No doubt that's true, but I can't oblige you. Looking at this place, thinking about how beautiful it must have been and how lovely it can be again, I know your mother would be pleased."

"Unlike you, I have other things to think about."

Safe things, she thought. Things that did not involve emotions. They walked up the stone path to the edge of the veranda. She could see the tension in his jaw, the way his eyes missed nothing, not a single broken shutter or sagging step.

Foster and Edward climbed out of the wagon and stood side by side on the path staring up at the two-story house, at its wide verandas and windows that looked out onto the sea.

"Oh, my," Edward said. Celine glanced back and

thought he might burst into tears.

"It's not so bad." Foster's tone was glum. "Everything will be fine. You'll see, once we have time to put things to right again." He looked around full circle. "A bit of pruning, some paint . . ."

"It's too much. I need to lie down," Edward mumbled.

The driver had already begun unloading the wagon, setting trunks and boxes on the ground. Celine saw Jemma O'Hurley's grand trunk among the others. Not many pieces inside were suited to the intense heat.

"Are you ready?" Celine said, looking up at Cord. She and the others saw no reason to move until he could face going in.

Cord knew all three of them were watching him closely. Foster and Edward hadn't given a damn what he did all morning. Why now, he wondered ruefully, when their solicitous concern only added to his guilt over his curt dismissal of them last night? And then there was Celine, staring up at him with her haunting eyes, trying to see inside his very soul. Crusading, for reasons known only to her, to make him dredge up the past.

She stood there steadfastly by his side, staring up at what had become a shambles. Her unwarranted, unwanted show of support made him uncomfortable. What was even worse, for some inexplicable, irritating reason, it made him feel better to have her beside him.

"You don't all have to treat me like an invalid. It's my *house* that's fallen apart, not me," he lied. He felt crippled, unable to move. He could not yet face going inside and stepping into the past, especially with Celine and her understanding gaze walking beside him. He hated his cowardice.

Abruptly, he barked instructions to the driver and then Foster and Edward.

"Let's get these things inside before the afternoon rain begins. Unpack the provisions, set up the kitchen and get as organized as you can. I'm going to survey the property and see if there's anyone about."

When he looked at his wife, he found Celine staring at him as if she had never seen him before.

"Did you think all I was capable of was imbibing cheap rum?"

"No, but I was convinced that's what *you* thought."

"I made a promise to Alex's memory that I would try to make what I can of this place. I intend to keep that promise." Before Celine could say anything, they were interrupted by the sound of a shrill voice inside the shadowed interior of the house.

"Oh, just look! We have callers, Gunnie! Put on the tea." The words were accompanied by the sound of rapidly approaching footsteps.

Celine glanced over at Cord, waiting for an explanation he could not give. He did not recognize the voice at all, nor had he ever laid eyes on the cheerful matron bustling across the veranda toward them. She was portly, with bright blue eyes in a plump, smiling face. Her features were barely lined, but her hair, which was almost entirely gray except for a hint of faded brown here and there, attested to her age. She wore thick braids coiled around her head. Her once royal blue gown was faded, its crocheted collar and cuffs tattered. She and the house appeared to have aged together.

"Welcome to Dunstain Place," she trilled. "It's so very nice to have callers. Of course, I wasn't expecting anyone—"

When she spied their trunks and bags she exclaimed,

"Oh, my! You've come to visit a while. This is such a welcome surprise." Without pause she called over her shoulder, "Gunnie! There will be guests for dinner."

"I ain't stayin'," the driver grumbled as he unloaded the last box and climbed aboard the wagon seat again. Edward walked to the back of the wagon to untie the reins of Cord's horse. As the driver managed to negotiate the team and wagon back around in the direction from which they had come, Cord stared at the woman on the veranda.

"Who are you?" he asked bluntly.

"Why, I'm Ada Dunstain. Who are you, sir?"

"Cordero Moreau."

"Cordero!" The woman's eyes instantly flooded with tears.

With surprising agility, Ada Dunstain nearly flew down the steps and ran over to Cord. She threw her arms around him, pinning his to his sides. He was helpless to do anything more than stare at the top of her head as Ada pressed her cheek against his chest and held on tight.

"Cordero, I'm your aunt Ada. Do your recall your mother ever speaking of me?" She pulled back, his greater height forcing her to crane her neck to look up at him.

He was so stunned by this cherub-cheeked woman's clinging to him with so much unabashed adoration that he was rendered speechless. When she finally released him, Foster and Edward caught her eye.

"Why, if it isn't Arnold and Lang," she said, using their surnames. "The last time I saw you was the day Father sent you two off to live with Alyce here on St. Stephen."

Edward and Foster smiled in acknowledgment of her

recognition and told her how pleased they were to see her.

"How long have you been here, Aunt Ada?" Cord asked.

"Why, I don't know. Nearly eleven years, I suppose."

"Eleven *years*?" Cord glanced over at Celine. His wife was watching Ada Dunstain with as much curiosity as he.

"And who is this exquisite young woman?" Ada asked turning toward Celine.

"This is Celine . . . my wife." Cord glanced over at Celine as he introduced her. She seemed almost relieved by Ada's appearance. "You said you've been here eleven years, Aunt Ada . . . ," he remarked.

"I see there is a lot to explain. If you'll bring your things in before it starts to rain, I'll have Gunnie set out a cold buffet and we can talk."

Ada whirled around and started up the stairs, the hem of her full skirt carefully gathered in her hands, the lacy hem of her petticoat showing beneath. She nearly tripped on the top wooden step, which was swollen and crumbling with dry rot, but she caught herself in time.

With a laugh, Ada paused on the veranda and called out over her shoulder, "This old place needs a bit more care than I've been able to give it." She looked at Celine again and then smiled. "Cordero's wife. Alyce will be so pleased." She instantly sobered, as if she had said too much, and hurried inside before anyone could question her.

"Do you think she meant your mother?" Celine asked Cord.

"My mother is dead."

Standing here in this place where his mother had

loved and laughed and filled his young life with so much joy, Cord found it excruciating to say the words aloud.

"I'm sure she said Alyce *will* be so pleased ...," Celine said softly.

"I'm not so certain that woman isn't more than a bit addlepated."

"Always was," Foster told them as he started toward the steps with a piece of luggage.

"Good to have a *nice* surprise, for a change," Edward added as he followed Foster into the house.

Cord glanced down at Celine. There was no putting it off any longer. Sooner or later he would have to go into the house. Aunt Ada was waiting. Celine needed to get out of the heat. He held out his arm for her before he realized what he had done. As if it were the most natural thing in the world, she let him lead her up the dilapidated steps.

There was no going back now. He had come home.

Situated on the crest of the hill, the house was constructed so that every room faced the turquoise sea. Inside, the wall coverings were faded and water-stained where rain, driven by tropical storms, had seeped in around the window frames. The furnishings were in need of upholstery, the drapes fit for the rag bag. Edward was so upset that Foster had sent him to his room. But Celine easily imagined the place as it could be with a little hard work.

Ada had insisted they go directly to the dining room, where the housekeeper had gathered together a ratoon supper. Celine thought the array of leftovers—named for the ratoon sugarcane cuttings left in the fields to sprout again—was both interesting and exotic. The sideboard was piled with an assortment of cold vegetable dishes and a platter of sliced ham. There were bowls of golden-orange sliced papaws, sweet pineapples, melons and juicy mangoes. The silver serving pieces were tarnished and salt-pitted, the surface of the sideboard scarred with signs of age and long use without care.

The legs of the dining table and sideboard were standing in small dishes of water. When Celine asked Ada why, the woman shrugged and explained quite offhandedly, "A necessary precaution, dear. The centipedes are quite poisonous. The water keeps them from climbing up the table legs. We have them under the bed legs, too." Celine shivered and tried not to think of climbing into bed and finding a poisonous many-legged creature between the sheets.

A steady, refreshing, salt-scented breeze blew in off the sea. It lightened Celine's spirit and renewed her vigor. While she ate in silence, she was able to watch Cord deal with his aunt.

Although Ada kept up a steady stream of rambling conversation that seemed to have no point to it at all, Cord appeared to relax more and more the longer he lingered at the dining table. His gaze often wandered to the long windows, which opened onto a view of the aquamarine water.

"Aunt Ada?" Cord interrupted his aunt in the middle of a long, convoluted recitation of a concoction of corn-meal, okra and seasoning.

Ada blinked as if someone had just shaken her awake. "Why, yes, Cordero. What is it, dear?"

"Tell me about Dunstain Place."

"Where would you like me to start?"

"What was it like when you arrived? I thought my father's manager was still in charge of the place."

Ada carefully wiped her mouth with her napkin before

she answered. "A horrible man, I must say. He and I didn't agree on anything. In fact, I don't think I was here three days before I fired him."

Ada shifted so that she could address Gunnie, a slender black woman who had come into the room to clear the empty platters from the sideboard. The woman was rail-thin, her hair cropped close to her head. Her clothing was plain, well-worn navy blue Osnaburg that looked able to withstand hard labor.

"Was it three days, Gunnie? Or did he last a little longer?" Ada asked.

"Tree days only." Her head high, her arms full of plates, Gunnie left the room without acknowledging anyone except Ada.

"That's what I thought. His name was Philpot, I think, and he was a terrible taskmaster. Very intolerant, Cordero. You would have been appalled at the way he ran things, I'm sure."

"What happened after he left?"

"Why, nothing, dear."

Cord cleared his throat and shifted in his chair. "You hired someone to replace him?"

"No . . ."

"With no overseer, who sees to the slaves, who runs the plantation?"

Ada blinked her wide blue eyes. Her brow puckered in a slight frown. She shook her head, a gesture which set her second chin quivering. "A few of them ran off. It was so long ago, it's hard to recall how many exactly, but not many. I suppose you would say I am in charge, but Bobo helps."

"Bobo?"

"Yes. He seemed the most capable. Came to me and told me not to worry, that he would help to keep things running smoothly. I never had any reason to doubt him.''

"And the others?'' Cord crossed his arms over his chest, took a long, deep breath and sighed.

"They still live in the village down below the mill.''

Celine watched and listened as Cord questioned his aunt. She could see him straining to hold his temper. This innocent, somewhat vague woman seemed to have single-handedly ruined a once thriving sugar plantation.

"What do you live on, Aunt?''

"Oh, I have a very small inheritance from the Dunstain estate. Don't ever think I have spent the sugar money, dear. Your father's solicitor still handles that, but he is away just now. Gone to England, I think. His wife's family—''

"You're still growing sugar?'' Cord effectively cut her off, the only way to get Ada's attention.

Ada frowned. "Why, of course we grow sugar. Dunstain Place is a sugar plantation, isn't it?''

"But we heard in Baytowne—''

"Posh." She waved away the notion. "What do they know? I don't have anything to do with anyone down there.''

"Are you saying you've been running this place alone and that it's still producing sugar?'' Unable to hide his impatience any longer, Cord shoved away from the table and stalked over to the open windows, where he stood staring out to sea. Celine knew him well enough to know that he was at the end of his rope.

When Ada glanced over in a silent appeal for help, Celine was forced to come to the gentle woman's aid.

"I'm sure your aunt did what she thought best . . .''

Cord turned his attention to Celine.

"My aunt fired the manager. She hasn't hired another

in all these years. You expect me to believe that she arrived from England—a maiden lady—with the capability of running a sugar plantation? Can you honestly tell me you believe that? You've seen the state of this house and the grounds.''

"It's true that I never married . . . ,'' Ada said softly, apologetically, twisting her napkin in her hands.

Celine stood up and walked around the table until she stood behind Ada's chair. "Don't you think a woman is capable of running a plantation as well as a man?''

"Do you?'' he countered.

Celine crossed her arms and raised her chin a notch. "Of course I do.''

Ada tried to appeal to Cord. "Please. I don't want to be the cause of an argument between you two . . .''

"We don't need you to provide cause,'' Cord assured her without taking his eyes off Celine. "My wife and I find enough to argue about on our own.''

Both women were watching him now. Ada's eyes were filled with unshed tears. Celine's flared with anger. The two of them were driving him insane, but in vastly different ways. Ada's vague answers and her admission that she had been running Dunstain Place alone raised his ire, but the last hour in Celine's constant presence had raised more than that. He was aware of every move she made, every time she looked his way. He was constantly aroused by her. She was driving him mad.

When he'd walked into the dining room she had already been seated at the table, and he'd caught her licking sweet mango juice off her lips. She had paused to look up at him and had smiled in greeting. He'd tried scowling very hard, which put an end to that.

She'd taken the time to change into the low-necked coral gown she had worn aboard ship. Her breasts should have paled in comparison to the whore Bonnie's, but although Celine's were not overly large, there was something ultimately more seductive about the tantalizing glimpse of the ripe firmness of her silken skin. It would have been difficult not to notice the way her skin glistened or the way her midnight hair clung in curling wisps around her damp hairline.

Each time Celine shifted in her chair, he was aware of it. Each time she leaned forward to reach for her wineglass and gave him another view of her cleavage, he imagined what it would be like to bury his face in her breasts. He watched her slender hands move, watched her fingers grasp the wine stem. Each time she ran her tongue over her lips or touched her napkin to them, he felt a quickening in his loins and was forced to look away.

Each and every time he looked at Celine he wanted her. He felt like an idiot. He wanted his own wife so badly that he was hard pressed not to leap over the table and take her amid the mangoes.

He wanted to take her in his arms, to make her cry out with the same need she so unwittingly compelled him to feel. He wanted her over him, beneath him, around him. He ached for her. He wanted her with the fiercest need he had ever felt for another living soul. His need scared the holy hell out of him.

"I have to get out of here," he said to no one in particular as he shoved his hand through his hair and pulled at the collar of his shirt. He was nearly choking with frustration.

Ada was near tears again. "I'm sorry, Cordero. I fired Philpot so long ago. I truly meant to hire another manager."

"I'm sorry too, Aunt. I'm not angry with you." He

felt guilty as hell about the anxious, apologetic look on Ada's face, but he couldn't think past escape, even if Celine would probably see it as another attempt to run from his feelings.

*And this time she'd be right*, he realized. But as far as he was concerned, she could think whatever she wanted.

He stalked out of the room, unaware that Celine had followed him until he was nearly through the huge, open beamed sitting room at the front of the house where a portrait of his mother still hung above the fireplace mantel. She grabbed his arm just as he was about to step out onto the veranda.

"Cord, how can you upset her like that and simply storm off?"

He stared pointedly at her hand, where she had gathered a fistful of shirtsleeve and was holding tight. She let go.

"You hurt that dear lady for no reason," Celine said.

"I asked a few questions and stated my opinion. If she chose to be hurt by that, it's her prerogative."

"It's too bad no one ever taught you that what you give comes back to you, Cordero."

"Is it really that simple for you, Celine?"

"Yes, because I believe it. It could be for you, too, if you would ever let yourself feel anything but anger."

He started off again.

"Where are you going?" she wanted to know.

"What do you care as long as I'm not pressing you for favors you are not willing to grant?"

His question had the desired effect. Her anger was immediately replaced with shock.

She was standing too close. He picked up the floral scent of her hair. He saw every facet of her eyes and became incapable of moving toward her or away. He felt threatened, as if he were hovering on a precipice where one step in either direction would send him to his doom.

But threats of doom had never set well with him.

Cord reached out with lightning swiftness. Before he could change his mind he slipped one hand around the back of her neck and his other arm around her waist. He pulled her up against him, hard and fast, and covered her lips with his.

The feel of her in his arms, the taste of her sweet lips rocked him and stoked his need. He felt shock and surprise reverberate through her, followed by a weak attempt to hold him at bay. He continued to press her, forced her to open up to him. He slipped his tongue between her teeth and heard her moan, whether in stifled protest or pleasurable surprise he could not tell. He delved deep, teasing her with his tongue. She tasted of mango and honey and the promise of a sweetness he had never savored. His hand cupped one of her breasts, his fingers traced the swell of bosom above the low neckline of her gown. He heard her gasp, felt her press her breast against his palm.

He finally tore his mouth from hers. With his hands on her shoulders, he stood there breathing hard, staring down into deep violet eyes wide with shock. He had to get away before he took her there on the threshold.

At the hitching rail, his horse whinnied. The sound was just enough to break the spell. He let go of her and walked away without a word.

Celine watched Cord stride off. His footsteps pounded so heavily over the veranda's rotted floorboards that she thought it might give way. He cleared the steps and jerked his horse's reins free of the hitching post. Without pausing to glance back, he mounted the white horse and rode off down the lane.

Still trembling in the aftermath of the shocking sensual assault, she reached up to trace her lips, then pressed her hands over her frantically beating heart. Her flesh burned where his fingers had touched her. She knew a frightening hunger that pulsed through her, flooding her with longing. He did not love her. If she gave herself to him, if she went to his bed, would he open a Pandora's box of desire that might never be closed? Would he awaken in her whatever need had driven her mother to ply her trade?

Cord had not said a word, but there was no mistaking the message behind his kiss—he wanted to do much more than plunder her mouth, he wanted to touch more than just her breast.

She closed her eyes and tried to pretend she had no knowledge of carnal acts between a man and a woman, tried to forget the tarnished memories of her mother with her lovers.

She tried to dismiss the abandoned way Cord had just kissed her, but it was as impossible as trying to forget to breathe. His touch, his scent, his taste were still upon her. Not to mention his spell.

Celine could not move. She could not think beyond the moment. The road that disappeared into the thick foliage was deserted, but in her mind she saw Cordero riding away. She closed her eyes and saw him standing over her, brash and naked in the small cabin aboard the *Adelaide*. She experienced him as caring enough to hold her throughout the storm, bold enough to take her in his arms and kiss her senseless.

She was willing to give herself to him as wife. But thinking of him now, all too aware of how easily her body had responded to his touch, she realized for the first time that giving herself to Cord would put her in danger of losing her heart to a man who might never learn how to love in return.

# Twelve

ord stood in the shade of a stand of banana trees watching the inhabitants of the slave village go about the business of life. Although none of them paused to stare at him directly, he could feel their eyes watching him—the eyes of those he owned through a mere circumstance of birth.

Overhead, the tattered leaves of the banana trees whispered on the trades as naked children of dusky hues played in the dirt among the cluster of crude shacks gathered near the sugar mill. The children spoke in a mixed patois of African words long ago corrupted by English and Carib. Cord could not help but call to mind other words that bespoke the origins of the slaves—Ashanti, Fanti, Dahoman—names of languages and tribes intermingled and mistakenly used by slavers to identify people brought to these islands in chains.

From where he stood, Cord could see women tilling the soil in gardens of corn, sweet potatoes and cassava planted behind their homes. In a lean-to not far away, three women sat on a grass mat weaving baskets while a man beside them fashioned a length of rope.

His grandfather, Cord knew, would never understand the Caribbean planters' custom of giving their slaves house plots on which to grow their own cash crops and raise small livestock and poultry. On Sundays the slaves were allowed to move freely about the island, to take their extra produce to the marketplace to sell or barter for clothes, rum or cash. Nor would Henre understand his need to draw up the paperwork to set these people free as soon as his father's solicitor returned.

Cord moved out of the shade and crossed the open space before the mill. The main house was visible at the crest of the hill behind him, but out of necessity, he put it and Celine out of his mind for the moment. A few of the children stopped playing and ran over to him, while others stood shyly watching from afar. Within a few seconds, he saw a tall, well-built man in his early thirties duck below the doorjamb of a shack and begin walking toward him.

The man was dressed in blue, coarse canvas pants cut short at the knee. Although some of the men wore shirts on Sunday, this one was bare-chested. He was thick-necked, with powerful shoulders and arms. There was mild curiosity on his face, but no greeting smile.

"You are Moreau, owner of Dunstain Place," he said. It was not a question.

"I am," Cord replied.

"I am Bobo. Chief gang boss and boiler."

"My aunt says that since the manager left you have

been overseeing things here.'' Cord watched Bobo carefully. He wanted to be accepted without upsetting the workings of the place. His success depended upon how he dealt with this man.

"Miss Ada been runnin' dis place."

Cord could not fathom any such thing, but for the moment he was content to go along with what Bobo said.

"How many slaves are still here?"

Bobo looked up at a passing cloud that stood out in white relief against the azure sky.

"Maybe one twenty. Broke in tree gangs. Some workin' sugar, some in the tobac and corn, some wid the animals. One work in the house for Miss Ada. Gunnie be her name." Bobo sized up Cord, his deep-set ebony eyes studying the newcomer intently.

"Tobacco and corn, you say?"

Bobo nodded. "An' cattle. Some horses."

Cord folded his arms and glanced at his horse, grazing on the hillside. "You mean to tell me my aunt has diversified?"

"I don' know 'bout dat. I mean to tell you de truth, is all."

"There's been no outside help?"

Bobo shook his head without hesitation. "Nobody help."

"I heard in Baytowne the slaves had all run off."

"A few mebbe. Half dozen. Long time ago now." Bobo added with a shrug, "Mos' like to stay on de place where dey born, de place dey kin buried. Dis an island, mon. Where dey go?"

"I'd like you to show me around the place. I'd like to see what . . . my aunt . . . has accomplished."

Bobo proceeded to show him the mill where the sugarcane was ground between a set of three huge, cogged rollers. It was exactly as Cord remembered it, down to the deep furrows worn in the earth by the plodding cattle that powered the mill.

During production, dark brown cane juice flowed into the trough between the rollers. Piped through a cistern to the boiling house, it was clarified and evaporated into crystallized sugar. Bobo's task as a boiler was to ladle freshly extracted juice from a cistern into the first copper, skim off the impurities that rose to the surface and then ladle the remaining liquid between copper pots graduated in size.

As the juice passed into progressively smaller, hotter coppers, with constant skimming and evaporation, it became thick and ropy, dark brown in color. A gallon of juice contracted into a pound of *muscovado*, or crude sugar, which then had to be refined.

As the complicated and dangerous skimming and pouring continued until the sugar crystallized, the boiler had to be not only an expert but somewhat of an artist. Not only did he endure suffocating heat and the stench of scalded sugar, he had to avoid being scalded himself. The boiling sugar had cost many slaves a limb or a life.

A planter's fortune depended not only on his field hands, but on his millers and boilers. Cord knew that Bobo must have earned his way into his position of authority. Cord also knew that ultimately, the sugar had to be warehoused and sold. And he knew that times had not changed so much that the warehouse merchants would welcome conducting business dealings with a slave.

"Does my aunt handle the sale of the sugar and rum?"

Cord felt as if he were moving through an intricate

dance around the truth. Bobo obviously knew the steps well.

Bobo's brow knit. He rubbed his hand over his hair, scratched his head and then shrugged. "De neighbor, de man over de next place, he store and sell sugar for her."

"And this neighbor, do you know his name?"

Bobo rubbed the bridge of his nose with one finger. "Reynolds."

"Reynolds."

"His name be Roger Reynolds. But he nevah dere," he added quickly.

Although he hated to be beholden to any man, Cord was thankful that there had been someone to oversee his property. Most of the island's land was tired, worn out as year after year sugar was planted in overworked soil. Dunstain Place could boast of still fertile land that had not been burned and rutted with troughs for cane. Here tobacco, cattle and sugar all thrived.

"So my aunt is not really in charge, is she?"

Bobo was hesitant to admit anything, but finally he nodded. "She been tink so for years. Now you de boss."

"I'm not sure I'll be any better at it than Ada Dunstain." He wanted to try, though. God knew he wanted to succeed, and not only for himself or to spite his grandfather. Cord had promised to dedicate his efforts to Alex, and it was mainly for Alex that he wanted to succeed.

Within an hour she had fallen in love with the old house.

Because the breeze rose above the trees, the place was cooler on the second floor than on the first. Almost a dozen bedrooms opened onto a long hall on one side and a wide balcony that connected them all on the other.

Although in need of paint, new fabrics and many personal touches here and there, the room she chose for herself was nearly as large as the entire house she had shared with Persa. Double doors opened onto the *galerie* that overlooked the sea. The view beckoned her so profoundly that Celine found herself continually walking back to the open doors and staring out to sea.

"Miss?"

She recognized Foster's voice and found him standing on the threshold. Edward hovered behind him, looking anxious.

"Come in," she said, turning her back on the view. She waited while they carried in a heavy trunk and set it in the middle of the floor. "What's this?" She walked around the old, rolled-top trunk. They had already unpacked the clothing she'd inherited in Jemma O'Hurley's trunk.

"Some of Cord's mother's things. We thought there might be something in here more suited to the climate that you might like to wear," Foster told her.

Celine watched while he knelt before the trunk and opened it. Edward hovered nearby and when Foster lifted the lid, he clasped his hands over his heart and sighed.

"There's that wonderful sky blue gown she always loved so." Edward reached out to touch the lightweight gown. "It matched her eyes to perfection."

Foster and Edward leaned over the trunk, exclaiming in remembrance as they pulled out gown after gown along with matching hats and shoes that gave off the musty scent of time.

"Everything is so beautiful," Celine said as she ran her fingers over the blue silk dress Foster had just handed her.

"Some of them are a bit old-fashioned, but we'll air and press the ones you might like to wear," Foster told her. "I can see your feet are much smaller than Miss Alyce's were," he added as he began to reverently re-pack the shoes in the bottom of the trunk.

Celine held the dress up to her shoulders and swayed from side to side. "It will certainly be much cooler than anything I have with me," she agreed.

At that moment, Ada stepped into the room. The absent look on her face turned to one of confusion as she stared at Celine and the gown she held up to herself.

"Alyce?" Ada whispered. "What have you done to your hair?"

"No, Aunt Ada, it's Celine. Cordero's wife." Concerned, Celine handed the dress to Foster and stepped toward Ada. The older woman had perched herself on the bed, which was covered in a faded spread of tropical flowers worked in crewel embroidery.

Ada shook her head and smiled. "Of course you are, dear. But for a moment there I thought you were Alyce and that you had done something to change the color of your hair. Although, come to think of it, I've never spoken to her in this particular room."

Celine glanced at Foster and Edward. The taller man appeared merely puzzled, but Edward's eyes went wide and he pressed his fingertips to his lips. Both men waited expectantly to hear more.

Celine had a niggling feeling that Ada would have an explanation. The logic would be apparent only to herself.

"She always slept in the master suite with Auguste. They were very much in love, you see. What I should have said was that I've never heard her spirit speak to me in this room. Of course, I'm not in here very often, as there are so many things to see to in the house."

Edward stepped just to the right of Foster's shoulder.

They were both looking expectantly to Celine.

"Her spirit?" Celine said.

Ada tried to fluff her hair, which was limp from the humidity. "Alyce's ghost, I suppose. The slaves call her a *duppie* . . ."

"Is that the same thing as a *jumbie*?" Celine wanted to know.

"I believe so. Such wonderful words, don't you think?"

"You've spoken to Alyce in this house?"

"Oh, yes, and in the gardens." Ada looked toward the open doors and the sea beyond. "She loved the gardens so. I've tried to keep them up the way she would have liked, but it's too much for one person and the slaves always seem to be so very busy with the crops and their own gardens that I'm hesitant to ask them for help."

So, a ghost walked the halls of a house where the mistress of over ten years was afraid to bother the slaves. It was all too curious. Celine walked over to the bed and sat down. Foster and Edward didn't even pretend to be working as they stood there waiting for the exchange to continue.

"Do you hear her often?" Celine asked, hoping the voice of Alyce Moreau was nothing more than a figment of Ada's imagination. If the spirits of the dead *could* roam the earth, it might mean that Jean Perot's—not to mention Captain Dundee's—might find her here on St. Stephen.

Ada shook her head. A smile twinkled in her eyes. "Only when I need someone to talk to."

"Does she talk back?" Edward could hardly contain himself. He was practically quaking with fear.

"Of course."

"Oh, my," he said.

"Obviously Alyce's presence means no harm," Celine said, more for Edward's reassurance than her own. She had more to fear in her present situation than Alyce Moreau's ghost.

"That's exactly what I told the obeah man, but he didn't care to listen." Ada's smile faded. She shook her head.

"The obeah man?" Celine asked.

"An old man the slaves believe is some sort of a magician or sorcerer. He holds a very powerful position among them. I've seen him try to cure the sick by waving a bone rattle around and throwing vile-smelling potions into a fire. When I first arrived, I couldn't get anyone to work in the house. The place had been closed since poor Alyce died and Auguste committed suicide at sea. The slaves were convinced the house was cursed. Finally, I think because he was afraid of a slave insurrection, Bobo convinced me to let the obeah man come in and impart some incantations. But Alyce is still here." Ada's beatific smile showed her joy.

Edward whimpered.

"You've no need to worry, Lang. Alyce always liked you," Ada assured him. "Besides, I'm the only one she talks to."

Celine brushed off her skirt, then pushed her hair back and fanned her hands to cool her face.

"Now, I came up here for a reason. What was it?" Ada muttered to herself, then snapped her fingers. "You don't intend to sleep in here, do you Celine, dear? If Cordero is anything at all like his father he will be very upset when he finds you have set up camp, so to speak, in this room. Why don't you have Lang and Arnold take your things into the master suite?"

Celine colored immediately and looked at Foster and Edward.

"I think she's right. Don't you?" Foster nudged Edward.

"About the ghost?" Edward still appeared chagrined.

"No, about moving into Cordero's suite," Foster explained, a bit impatiently.

"Ah. Yes. Much better idea." Edward nodded vigorously.

"I'm staying right here in this room," Celine said in a tone that she hoped sounded convincing. "Cordero will be busy with the duties of running this place and adhering to a schedule. I'm sure he won't mind in the least if I prefer not to be disturbed."

Ada stared at her with a look of shock.

"But you're newly married. Don't you want to . . ."

"Of course you do! So we'll just move this trunk—" Foster began, hastily starting to toss the gowns back inside.

"Stop! Please." Celine held up her hand. Foster quit tossing the gowns into the trunk. "I've already made up my mind. This is the room I've chosen, and I would appreciate it if you would all abide by my decision."

Foster began pulling the dresses out again and draping them over Edward's arms. Ada frowned, trying to understand. Then she brightened.

"At least Cord will be close by."

Celine felt her heartbeat escalate. "What do you mean?"

Ada pointed to the door in the wall opposite Celine's bed. "Why, the master suite is right through that connecting door."

*   *   *

Cord moved through the dark house, as familiar with the place as he had been as a child. The absence of light hid the shabbiness that had aged the once beautiful furnishings and wall hangings. He walked through the dining room, where memories loomed around him in the shadowed shapes and forms of the massive sideboard, the long dining table, the chandelier. He could almost hear his father's voice and his mother's answering laughter in this room where they had so often entertained.

A self-protective mechanism, an inner alarm kept him from dwelling on old memories, memories of times long gone that only brought him pain, the old deep-seated pain he refused to let himself feel. He had run from them earlier, just as he had run from Celine, but it was late now and there was no way to avoid the place.

He had spent the day with Bobo riding over the estate, from the sloping hillside covered in cane to the wide crescent beach below. He had taken his meals with Bobo, eating whenever and wherever food was offered—fruit from the trees or slave fare of corn, plantains, sweet potatoes, beans and salt fish. Bobo had seen to it that the slaves had been given their weekly rations of rum and molasses. Many had offered Cord more than a swig.

Surprisingly, Dunstain Place had thrived over the years in an unfettered way. A wide field of tobacco planted for slave use had expanded into a thriving second crop. The sugar crop had been staggered so that the sugar fields would ripen in succession from January to May, the driest and best months for harvest. A small herd of healthy cattle grazed in the coastal grasslands.

After a day of close inspection and discovery, Cord

was convinced that no one on the island realized that Dunstain Place had thrived under the direction of his addlepated aunt, a slave who worked as boiler and gang boss, and an often absent neighbor named Roger Rcynolds.

Tired but refreshed by a swim in his favorite pool, situated beneath a rushing waterfall, Cord crossed the sitting room. He paused at the bottom of the stairs and rested one hand on the cherry-wood pineapple atop the newel post. Beside him, a window was open to the stars and the night breeze. The rustle of palm fronds and the cry of green monkeys in the distant forest mingled with the cloying scent of night-blooming jasmine. He closed his eyes and took a deep breath. Beside the long, open windows, panels of lace, like gossamer phantoms, shifted with the breeze.

As he started up the stairs, he realized he had no clear notion of where he was headed. He recalled the room he had slept in as a child, but suspected Foster and Edward would have seen him ensconced in the master suite. A vision of Celine waiting for him in the bed his parents had so lovingly shared flickered through his thoughts. Then the cynical smile of a realist curved his lips. After this afternoon she had no doubt found a room as far from his as she could manage, then promptly barred the door.

He took the stairs two at a time and then strolled the length of the wide hallway, listening to the hollow sound of his solitary footsteps. The quiet, empty hall was totally different from the way it had been during his childhood, when it rang with laughter and gaiety. He wondered if Dunstain Place would ever know such joy again.

He found the door to the master suite ajar and lingered

for a moment in the hallway, steeling his emotions before he stepped inside. The last time he had been in this room, his father had been lying in bed staring out to sea, a beard of stubble shadowing the lower, unbandaged half of his face. His remaining eye was bleak, as if his soul had been snuffed out with Alyce's death. That was the day Auguste had told Cord that he was sending him away.

Propelled by the old anger, Cord shoved the door open. The room was darker than the night sky but even so, he could see that Celine was not there waiting for him. His anger quickly dissipated and was replaced by a rush of ancient loneliness.

He left the room bathed in darkness and walked to the foot of the bed. It was massive, set upon a raised dais and draped with yards of mosquito netting. Seeing it now, as a man, he could only imagine it as his parents' playground.

Unable to predict what his reaction to Celine might be right now, he remained determined not to seek her out. He unbuttoned and stripped off his shirt and tossed it over a nearby chair, where he then sat to remove his boots. He peeled off his socks, then stood and flexed his shoulders and biceps. Clasping his hands together, he stretched his arms high overhead. Riding across the property had left him sore but feeling more alive than he had in a long while.

He was still on edge, his mind crowded with all he had seen and learned today. He wanted a drink, but decided to step out on the balcony and listen to the pulsing sound of the sea rather than prowl the house in search of liquor. He crossed the balcony and walked to the railing. Far below the overgrown garden that bordered the house, past the sweeping hillside and the open grassland beyond, lay the sea, a black jewel shimmering beneath the scant light of a crescent moon. Starlight danced on the water. The surf pounded against the shoreline, the sound drifting up to him on the gentle wind.

Over the sound of the sea, he heard a swift intake of breath, a gasp of surprise. He turned. Framed in the open French doors of the room next to his, Celine stood poised on the threshold.

"I didn't know you were out here," she said softly, unable to hide the tremor in her voice.

The sleeveless white gown he had given her billowed about her bare ankles, brushed against the tapered arch of a foot. She reached up to sweep her hair off the side of her face, where the wind pressed it to her cheek.

"Not much of a witch after all, are you?"

He thought she would turn away. The acid drip of his tone should have sent her running into the shelter of her room, but she didn't move. Instead, she chose to stand there with the wind caressing her wild, midnight hair, tempting him with her innocence, her silence. With a concern and a caring he did not want or need.

Finally she spoke. "Why did you do it?"

"What have I done now?"

"Why did you kiss me like that today?"

He looked out across the sea again, unable to bear the sight, knowing she was naked save for a yard or two of sheer cotton, incapable of looking her way without wanting her.

"You live to torment me, don't you?" he said softly.

"Because you are so easily tormented. So willing to *revel* in your pain. Let it go, Cordero."

Cord crossed the balcony in two strides and stood

over her, afraid to touch her. Afraid it might prove too much. The spell she so easily wove around him angered Cord more than his inability to control his need.

"You're nothing but a pampered merchant's daughter who bought herself a husband with a fat purse. You play at life, concocting fantasies about a gypsy father and a life in London. What do you know of pain?"

"Enough," she whispered. "And I know enough not to hoard it and guard it like a miser's treasure the way you do."

"What would you have me do, wife?"

"Let go of it, Cord. Forget the past. You are here now. You have land and a home, faithful servants and an aunt who loves you. Be grateful for that. Let them love you, and love them in return. Choose what you want to believe about me, but never assume I know nothing of heartache just because I don't choose to wear it on my sleeve like a hard-won trophy."

She began to turn away, but before she could, he reached out and grabbed her by the shoulder. The warmth of her skin through the thin fabric snaked like a shock wave up his arm. His fingers tightened on her tender flesh and he felt her flinch, but he could not let go. He pulled her to him, slammed her against his bare chest and buried his face in her hair. He closed his eyes and breathed in the heady scent of her.

He slipped his hand down to her hips, cupped her buttocks and pressed her against him so that she might feel and be aware of his raging need.

Cord drew back slightly, framed her face with his hands and was once again reminded how small she was, how vulnerable. Starlight and hope and even fear shimmered in her eyes. She was breathing hard, as if running for her life. Her pounding heart echoed the beat of his own. His breath whispered against her ear. "I want you, Celine. I want you more than I've ever wanted anything on this earth. And I want you now."

## Thirteen

"*I want you now.*"

Starlight and the sound of the sea bathed them in silver and thunder. Cord's hands cupped her face. His intense gaze locked on her eyes. Celine was powerless to refuse him anything.

When he spoke of his need, when his heated touch communicated his desire, she experienced such a swift, aching longing of her own that to deny him would be to deny herself.

She spread her fingers and lay her hands on his bare ribs, guarding her touch so that images from his past were closed to her. She wanted no part of the past tonight, nor would she think of the future. This moment in time was all that was important now—the twinkling star-washed sky, the sound of the sea . . . and Cordero.

When she touched his ribs, he shuddered and closed his eyes. She heard him sigh before he lowered his head and touched his lips to hers. She thought the kiss he had pressed upon her that afternoon had been demanding, but it was nothing compared with the way he compelled her to open to him now. His tongue delved, warm and searching, arousing her with a suggestive imitation of a more intimate act.

He let go of her face and clasped her to him, pulling her up against his bare chest. His heart pounded against hers. His hands were everywhere at once. She gasped when he cupped her breast and she moaned when he took her peaked nipple between his thumb and forefinger and gently teased it through the fabric of her gown until she arched against his arm.

He dipped his head to her breast, took her nipple in his mouth and suckled through the thin layer of cotton. Celine clasped his head in her hands, ran her fingers through his dark, wavy hair and pressed him closer, demanding he take more, silently urging him to suckle harder until she cried out with the pleasurable pain of it.

She went nearly limp in his arms, panting, aching, wanting him. Longing she had never experienced before welled up inside her so violently that she did not think she could bear it another moment more. She clung to him, certain she would shatter into more pieces than there were stars in the Caribbean sky.

He pulled back to stare into her eyes. It was a long, searing look that spoke volumes. Then in one swift move he slipped one arm beneath her knees and carried her into her room.

As he drew aside the mosquito net and lay her across the bed, as he fanned her hair out across her pillow, his rough, man's hands were as gentle as a butterfly's kiss. Desire drove her to reach for his shoulders. She moaned in frustration when he pulled away to unbutton and slip off his pants. As Celine watched his every move, hungering for him to begin again, she tried to convince herself that she was not like her mother, that this was her husband, that she was no whore.

Unable to take her eyes off him, she watched Cord step up to the bed. He stood before her brash and bold, the moonlight illuminating the hard planes of his well-defined body, the tense, set line of his jaw, his erection. The moon revealed nothing soft or pliant, nothing warm or giving about him. He spoke no false promises of love or countless tomorrows, but his body gave silent testimony to his need for her.

He took the flounce of her nightgown in his hands and Celine raised her hips. Cord drew the fabric up along her thighs to her waist. He knelt beside her, then stretched out full length until she could feel his heated flesh pressed along her side. Reverently he placed his open palm in the hollow over her navel and began to slip it lower until he was stroking the soft mound between her thighs.

No one had ever touched her in this gentle, intimate way. She wanted to weep with the magic of it; she wanted to weep with the joy and heady sensation of it.

He dipped his head and kissed her navel as his hand and fingers continued to work their spell. She closed her eyes. Her hands kneaded his shoulders as he moved over her. He trailed kisses ever closer to that most secret spot hidden at the apex of her thighs. When she felt his tongue touch the bud hidden at the core of her melting, pulsing heat, Celine ceased to reason, to worry, even to wonder.

She gave herself to the frantic beat of her heart and the driving tempo that set her hips undulating beneath his mouth. Afraid she was coming apart, she reached out and grasped the headboard. She arched off the bed, giving herself to him, urging him to take more. Panting, moaning over and over, she strained for release. When it came, she cried out, a strangled scream that was lost on the wind, tangled in the sound of the pounding surf.

Cord wrapped his arms about her hips and lay his cheek atop the silken nest of curls. He waited until she stopped shuddering, waited until she sank back onto the pillow and he felt her fingers slide through his hair as she stroked his head. When she'd reached her climax and a cry of release was wrung from the depths of her soul, he had nearly spilled his seed. But now, as she lay replete, his desire was at a higher pitch than he would have ever thought possible. The scent and taste of her was driving him wild.

Cord released her, eased himself to his knees and slowly drew her nightgown off her breasts. Her eyes were closed. The trace of a teardrop along her cheek glistened in the moonlight. He kissed it away.

*I don't love her. I will not love her,* he reminded himself over and over as he gently lifted her shoulders so that he could draw the nightgown over her head. Careful not to tangle the fabric in her hair, he tossed the nightgown to the floor.

*She is my wife. We are bound by empty vows and an exchange of money, nothing more.*

He reached between her legs and found her warm and wet and ready for him. With a touch, he urged her to open her thighs. Bracing himself above her, Cord looked down at Celine. She was staring up at him in the darkness, watching him, waiting. He moved his hips until the tip of his member was poised to enter her. He lingered there, his goal within reach, willfully and gratefully enduring the sweet torture of self-restraint.

*She is my wife.*

He allowed himself a fraction more, sliding in smoothly, slowly, until the head of his shaft was buried inside of her. The welcome heat was too much. He knew he would go mad if he tarried longer. In one swift, sure plunge, he tore into her and buried himself to the hilt. She cried out. He grasped her hips and held her still. He knew he was hurting her, knew his fingers would brand bruises on her hips where he clung to her, but he wanted to be inside of her as long as he could—an eternity, if possible.

Celine thought his thrust would rip her apart when he filled her. His fingers bit into the tender flesh of her hips, imprisoning her beneath him. She tried to move, to break free of the tearing fullness, then slowly realized he was silently urging her to lie still. She closed her eyes against the ebbing pain and clung to him, afraid to move, afraid he would do something to make the searing pain begin again.

His rapid breath was hot against her ear. Chills ran down her spine, and she shivered. He groaned. He filled her. In her and above her, he was poised, taut as a bowstring.

She was his now, his wife in more than name and title. He was inside her, part of her, stretching her, filling her. She ran her hands down his smooth, well-muscled back, over his ribs, down to his hips. The idea that they were joined by flesh further aroused her. The pain was barely remembered. They lay as one, coupled on the crisp, cool sheets. The sea breeze caressed them. The mosquito net cascaded around them, a filmy cocoon.

Cord was afraid to release her hips, afraid she would move in an attempt to escape the pain and send him over the edge. He tried to gentle her with a kiss and trailed his tongue around her ear and down her neck.

He felt a honeyed warmth melt around him. He began to move inside her, slowly at first, hesitant to hurt her again. She went still, waiting, barely breathing as she continued to stroke his back with her fingertips. With agonizing slowness he withdrew until he had all but left her.

"No, please . . . stay," she whispered.

His control shattered. Cord threw back his head with a cry of release and drove himself into her over and over again, pouring his seed into her womb.

His pounding heartbeat slowed, and he held himself above her on his elbows and watched as she opened her eyes, then turned her gaze to the open balcony doors. He was happy to have been able to give her satisfaction earlier; he knew she had not peaked again when he did.

"You were a virgin," he said, feeling more awkward than he ever had in any moment of his life.

"You make it sound like a sin."

"It won't ever hurt like that again."

Her mouth was too tempting. He felt compelled to kiss her again, this time lingering over her lips, savoring the taste of them.

When he eased out and off of her, a momentary sense of loss settled over him. They lay naked, side by side, barely touching, savoring the cool breeze that wafted over their heated skin. Celine longed to ask him what he was feeling, desperate to know if she would ever again experience the soul-searing explosion of sensation that had come earlier when he had taken her over the edge. Had the same ultimate release caused him to cry out?

"What are you thinking?" Cord asked.

It sounded more like a demand than an idle thought.

"Is it always this way?"

"I told you it will not hurt again, unless you are forced against your will."

She turned her head on the pillow to look at him. "You would never force me."

Once more he was moved by her trust. She knew him better than he knew himself.

"I did not mean the pain," she said. "I meant the other, the . . ."

"The pleasure?"

"Yes."

Cord wondered how he could guarantee such satisfaction would come again when before tonight he had never felt such intense pleasure with a woman.

"It's always different, and yet the same."

She wished they were better friends; she might have asked him to try to explain. As it was, she was too embarrassed.

One thing was clear to her now: Her fears had been dispelled forever. She knew she was nothing like her mother—for it would be impossible for her to engage in an act of such sheer intimacy with strangers night after night, even for all the money on earth. She would starve first.

The mosquito net luffed and sagged as the trades calmed. In the quiet stillness there was no sound but the hum of frustrated, bloodthirsty insects hovering outside the net and the whisper of Cord's rhythmic breathing. She thought of what they had just shared. What would it have been like had theirs been a love match? How could it have possibly been any more intense?

"Don't expect me to love you, Celine. I don't have it to give."

If she hadn't known better, she would have thought he had read her mind.

"We all have love to give. It's just harder for some than others," she said.

He worked so very hard at keeping the barriers around his heart that she wanted to reach over and take his hand, wanted to assure him he was not alone. Instead she asked, "Would your cousin Alex have wanted you to close yourself off and cease loving? You said that he loved you. Would he want to see you live out your life with a heart of stone?"

"A heart of stone feels nothing, neither love nor pain. I have lost everyone I have ever loved."

"And so you would rather live without love than risk that again?"

He rolled over. "Why are you so damned desperate to help me?"

"I'm still naive enough to believe what I was taught by a very wise person," she said.

"And what is that?"

"That love cures all ills, heals all wounds."

"I'm not ill or wounded."

"But you are hurting all the same."

"Let it go, Celine."

Afraid he would go back to his room, she stopped pushing, but couldn't help adding, "I would be content to see you smile more often."

He ignored her comment and lay back down. Celine fluffed her pillow, smoothed it out, then reached down for the sheet and pulled it up to cover her nakedness.

"Are you finished wriggling?"

She settled back with a sigh and closed her eyes. "Yes."

Cord listened to her deep, even breathing. He had never slept through the night with a woman, and just because Celine was his wife, he saw no reason why he should start now, no reason save one—that he was loath to leave her.

The desire simply to lie there beside her infuriated him. She rolled toward him and snuggled closer in sleep. He reached out and pulled the sheet up over her shoulder.

*Love*. A waste of time and a source of great pain. Love was for fools and the foolhardy who were willing to be hurt.

She shifted in her sleep. Her hand slid across the sheet and came to rest against the wall of his chest. The touch was light, innocent, given unconsciously, yet to Cord it spoke volumes. They were connected now by more than vows. They had come together as man and woman, flesh to flesh, in an exchange as old as time.

They were man and wife. There was no harm in sleeping in her bed. Besides, here in this room there were no memories waiting to haunt him, as there were in the master suite. He would sleep with her, he decided, until just before dawn.

But he would not love her.

Foster and Edward, bare-legged, in nightshirts and shoes, crept down the hall each carrying a candlestick. As soon as they stopped outside the master suite, Edward pressed his ear to the door.

"I don't 'ear nothing," he whispered.

"Try the knob," Foster urged.

"Try it yerself, Fos." With a flourish, Edward blew out his candle, and then Foster did the same.

As far as they could tell from outside, the master suite was dark and silent. Foster reached around Edward and slowly turned the doorknob. The heavy door opened without a sound and swung inward. The two men tiptoed over the threshold and stared at the empty bed on the dais.

" 'E's not 'ere," Foster said, somewhat surprised.

"You don't suppose . . ." Edward sounded hopeful.

"Maybe we're in luck." Foster led the way to the connecting door to Celine's room.

"I don't 'ear nothing," Edward said again. This time he tried the knob himself.

Foster shifted behind him, pressing closer, eager for a look. The floorboards beneath their feet creaked in protest. Both men froze and held their breath. There was still no sound from within.

Edward gave the door a gentle push and opened it a crack.

"I can't see anything." Frustrated, Foster shifted so that he could see over Edward's shoulder. "Oh, my."

"What? Tell me." Edward was shaking with anticipation.

"There, on the floor—"

"I see 'em. Cordero's pants . . ."

"And a nightgown."

Foster whipped the door closed, at the last moment, remembering to shut it without a sound. He hurried to the middle of the master suite, glanced back once at Celine's door and tried to contain his joy.

"They did it, Eddie! They did it. There's 'ope now, real 'ope that this marriage will take."

Edward shook his head. "I was about to give up 'op-ing. It's been weeks now and they ain't so much as kissed, as far as I know. Oh, Fos, this is the best thing our Cordero ever done, ain't it? Maybe things'll be different for 'im now."

"We can only 'ope, but the moat 'as been crossed an' the fortress taken, so to speak."

Edward patted Foster on the arm. "You've a real way with words, Fos. Sheer poetry."

Celine had not expected to find Cord in bed with her when she awoke the next morning, but neither had she expected the sinking disappointment she experienced when she realized he was indeed already up and gone. She brushed aside the mosquito net and felt herself blush when she found her nightgown draped over a nearby chair. She picked it up and carried it over to the tall armoire in the far corner of the room.

All of the gowns that had belonged to Jemma were hanging there alongside two or three that had been Cordero's mother's. After choosing one of the old gowns and brushing her hair, Celine left the room, tempted by the delicious aroma of breakfast. Ill at ease with the thought of seeing Cord again, not knowing how to act after their intimate exchange, she decided to take her cue from him—if he was not already about his business.

She found him at the dining table, lounging with one arm draped over the back of the chair, staring into space. Ada was in the middle of what sounded like a recipe recitation.

"And then I take a little piece of toast—generally it's good to use toast points, but not entirely necessary—and I evenly spread the glazed—" Catching sight of Celine in the doorway, Ada looked up, blinked and smiled. "Why, good morning, my dear. We were hoping you'd be down before Cordero has to be on his way. It's such a thrill to have him take over for me. I don't know what I would have done if I had to see to all of this much longer. Why, I recall one year, just after the hurricane . . . When was the hurricane, Gunnie?''

''Eight, mebbe nine year ago now,'' Gunnie said without breaking stride as she brought out a plate for Celine. It was mounded high with enough food for three. The servant set the dish down at a place setting at the table and left the room.

When Ada paused to catch her breath, Cord stood up and held Celine's chair while she gathered her skirt and sat down. She could not stop the rush of heat that scalded her cheeks.

She dared to glance up at him over her shoulder, and found him frowning down at her.

''Is something wrong?'' she asked.

''Is that my mother's dress?''

Celine nodded. ''Foster and Edward thought that some of your mother's things would be cooler than the ones that I have.'' She started to rise again. ''If you don't want me to wear them—''

He waved her back down. ''Not at all. It's just that I thought I had seen it before. It's out of date,'' he added.

''I don't care about that. It's a lovely gown.''

''Speaking of Alyce,'' Ada interjected, ''she said she is so very happy both of you are here. She's glad I won't have to be so lonely anymore.''

''Is this a jest, Aunt Ada?'' Cord's tone was forbidding.

''Why no, dear, it's no jest. I thought you and Celine might have discussed this already.''

It was Celine's turn to be the recipient of Cord's demanding stare. She tried to smile.

''Discussed what?'' He stood tensed, his hands fisted at his sides, his forehead creased with a frown.

"Your aunt believes she is in communication with your mother's spirit," Celine said softly.

"I don't merely *believe* it," Ada clarified. "I *do* hear her."

Celine said gently, "I'm sure that you do, Aunt Ada."

"I'm sure that you don't." Cord was scowling so fiercely at his aunt that Celine reached out and took his hand.

Whatever anger was brewing in him passed like a summer squall at her touch. When he glanced down at Celine again he concentrated on her beautiful face.

"She thinks she talks to my mother and you believe her?"

"Who's to say it's not true?" Celine countered.

Cord looked at the two women and then threw his hands in the air. "I've not been around women for extended periods. I'm beginning to believe you are all addlepated." He walked back to his place at the head of the table.

"I don't want to discuss this again, Aunt, if you don't mind," he said once he was again seated.

"Tell us about what you learned yesterday," Celine encouraged him, as much to change the subject as to gratify her curiosity about the workings of the plantation.

As Celine ate, she listened to Cord give a detailed, businesslike account of all that he had seen and heard yesterday. He praised his aunt for her smooth management and gave equal credit to a slave named Bobo.

Celine watched him talk, intent upon the way his hands moved, the nonchalant way he shifted comfortably in his chair. She was reminded of the way his body had moved over and inside her last night. She could not help but recall everything he had done and made her feel.

She felt her color slowly rise again when she recalled crying out in wild abandon as he'd brought her to a climax. She could almost hear the way his voice had sounded when he'd reached his own release.

How could he seem so unaffected now? He gave no sign whatsoever that he'd been touched by what had passed between them.

"Are you all right, Celine?"

Cord was leaning toward her, watching her closely. She couldn't look away from the depths of his dark eyes. Nor could she find many words.

"I . . . why, I . . ."

"You're red as fire."

"I'm fine. Really." She looked down at her plate and began to mobilize a pile of peppers into a straight line.

"Did you get any sleep, dear?" Ada leaned forward, her hands resting on the edge of the table.

Celine felt herself grow even hotter. "Yes, certainly."

Cord, thankfully, did not comment, but when Celine glanced over at him, she saw a hint of a smile tickling his lips.

"What did you say you were going to do?" Celine asked, swiftly moving the topic away from herself.

Cord sobered. "I'm going to see how much more labor we'll need in order to maintain the house as well as the crops. Perhaps you can oversee the garden and housework gangs for me?"

Celine nodded, thrilled she'd have a part in bringing the house to life again. "Do you want it exactly the way it was?"

"We have no plans to go by."

It was more than apparent that he did care, but did not want to make it seem so. Celine was thankful she had the images from his memories to guide her.

"I can ask Alyce what the place looked like," Ada volunteered.

Cord massaged a point above the bridge of his nose and sighed.

"I'm going down to the mill," he told them. "I can't waste any more time talking about consulting ghosts." He pushed back his chair and stood up.

"Have I upset you, Cordero dear?" Ada was wringing her plump hands. There was a shimmer of tears in her eyes.

Cord had noticed, too, and rounded the corner of the table to hunker down beside his aunt's chair. He reached out and covered both her hands with one of his. As he smiled up at Ada, Celine made a significant discovery: This man who tried so hard not to show his vulnerability to anyone had a smile that could charm the hide off a goat.

"Aunt Ada, I'm not upset."

"But you don't believe me about Alyce, do you?"

"I'm afraid not."

Ada sighed. "Your mother's disappointed to hear that," she said.

Cord stood up and found Celine watching him closely. A knowing smile teased the corners of her mouth, the most delectable one he had ever tasted. Backlit by the windows, she sat with sunlight shimmering through her long, unbound hair. There was a smudge of jam on her lower lip and as he watched, the tip of her tongue peeked out to lick it away, removing the temptation for him to do it for her.

When she had walked into the room earlier, he'd felt himself quicken. Had it not been for his aunt's presence and his willpower, he would have pulled her up out of her chair and carried her back upstairs for another round in bed.

Having caught his stare, Celine studiously ignored him, her cheeks aflame and her head bowed over her plate as if she were more interested in food than anything else in the world. He walked around the table and stopped beside her chair and almost reached out for her hand the way he had his aunt's, but he stopped himself, determined to keep whatever intimacy they shared behind closed doors. It would do no good to let himself become dependent upon her nearness.

"I'm not sure when I'll return," he said.

She looked up, her cheeks on fire, her eyes sparkling with life and promise. Despite his resolve to see to the estate, he was ready to haul her into his arms, carry her up the stairs and lock them in a room for the rest of the day.

But before he could move, the door flew open without warning and Gunnie burst in. She started to address Ada, remembered Cord and turned to him.

"Obeah man be here. Trouble at de door." The fright in her eyes spoke volumes.

Celine set down her fork with a clatter. Ada stood and nervously began poking her fingers into her hair, trying to arrange it. Cord let Gunnie lead the way.

They found a group of nearly thirty slaves gathered at the back door between the building that housed the kitchen and the veranda. He had met many of them just yesterday. All of them had been curious; none of them had been as hostile as they appeared now.

The men were openly scowling, the women frightened. The children were ominously quiet, some clinging to their mother's skirts. In the center of the group stood a toothless, stooped old slave. In hands knotted with

arthritis, he clutched a walking staff—a rattle orna-
mented with cat's teeth and shells. A goat hide was
draped over his skeletal shoulders. Bobo, who towered
over the old man, stood beside him.

Celine put her arm around Ada's waist. Cord stepped
away from them and walked to the edge of the veranda.
Before he could say a word, Bobo addressed him.

"Some folks went to market yestiddy. Dey hear all
about a witch. Folks say she de one come here with you.
She make one ship go down. Obeah man he come see."

Cord glanced over his shoulder at Celine. She had lost
all color.

"Step up here beside me, Celine." He tried to keep
his voice calm and even, tried not to frighten her any
more than she already was. He wanted to be beside her
if she fainted.

When she moved to the edge of the veranda, a hushed
whisper rippled through the gathered slaves. Cord
slipped his hand around her waist and gave her a slight,
encouraging squeeze.

The obeah man took a step forward, craned his neck
to look at her and held his rattle extended before him in
protection.

Cord took her hand and addressed the crowd. "This
is my wife. She is a good witch. A very powerful good
witch." His voice was full of authority.

Celine gasped. "What are you saying?"

"Trust me," he whispered.

Celine stared up at him in disbelief and then looked
back at the crowd. Dark eyes filled with suspicion stared
back. The obeah man's eyes were the most fathomless
of all. One look told her that he possessed otherworldly
power, but whether he used it for good or evil, she could
not be certain. The power she saw in his eyes did not

extend to his body. He was bent and twisted with age, so much so that it pained Celine to watch him move. He stepped forward, his swollen, knobby knuckles protruding as he clutched the rattle tighter and fiercely shook it at her.

"I tro grabe durtty upon you!" he shouted.

"What is he saying?" Celine gripped Cord's hand tighter.

" 'I'll throw grave dirt on you.' It's a curse. If the guilty come in contact with grave dirt, they weaken and die. His obeah, or magic, can kill those who believe."

Celine stiffened. No magician was going to frighten her with false accusations.

"I suspect this is a bid to show he has more power than you," Cord whispered.

"That's ridiculous. I don't want to usurp his position," she whispered back. "Tell them I'm no witch."

"They have already heard otherwise and will never believe me. They need to know that you'll do them no harm, and so they have gone to him for protection. Magic fills the void in their lives. Their beliefs run very deep."

She nodded, let go of his hand and took a step toward the edge of the veranda so that she could speak directly to the slaves.

"You have been here much longer than I. This is your home as much as mine. I swear I will not harm any of you." She glanced up at Cord. "Neither will my husband."

Cord was proud of her courage in a situation where most other women would have swooned. Celine stood straight and proud as the trade winds lifted the ends of her hair and fanned it around her shoulders. She tried to make eye contact with each of the slaves in the throng.

When Cord stepped up beside her and took her hand again, she felt a rush of warmth and gratitude.

"I have come home to make this place better for all," he began. "My wife will help me. She—"

Suddenly a soul-shattering scream rent the air. A frantic woman darted through an opening in the overgrown shrubbery that surrounded the yard. Celine watched in startled fascination as the slave ran up to Bobo, clutched his hand and babbled uncontrollably between sobs.

"What's wrong? What is it?" Celine asked, tugging on Cord's hand.

The crowd no longer concentrated on Celine, but on the hysterically sobbing woman. All attention had been diverted from the obeah man and his challenge.

"She's Bobo's wife. Their little boy is missing." Cord ran down the stairs and Celine plunged after him, the crowd parting to let them move up beside the gang boss.

The obeah man stood forgotten on the edge of the crowd. The unveiled threat in his eyes chilled Celine to the bone.

Ada came up beside her. "What's happening? What is the trouble?"

"Bobo's child is missing." Celine's heart went out to the young, distraught mother, who stood beside her husband sobbing her heart out.

As Ada began to lament the disaster, Celine tried to ignore the obeah man's ominous glances. The slaves near her had stepped back a few paces, fear and distrust reflected in their eyes and postures.

Cord glanced around at the seventy or so people surrounding them and slipped his arm around her shoulder, drawing her to his side.

"The boy has been missing for almost two hours.

He's only six," he explained.

As she stared at the young mother who was not much older than herself, Celine felt plunged into conflict. There was a chance she could learn something of the child's past that might help divine his whereabouts, but it would put her in danger of escalating the slaves' fear. Still, as she looked at Bobo and his wife, she realized she could not turn her back on the situation to save herself. Persa had warned her that there could come a time she would be forced to use her gift to do what was right even though the cost to herself might be high.

"Trust me," she whispered to Cord. "Tell them I want to hold the girl's hand."

"What are you doing? This isn't the time for theatrics."

Celine knew that if the hard look in Cord's eyes was any indication, there would be no changing his mind. The huge gang boss was her only hope.

She turned to Bobo.

"If I could hold your wife's hand, I might be able to help find your boy."

When Bobo stared down at her as if he hadn't understood a word she'd said, she repeated her request slowly and then added, "I will not harm any of you, most especially the child."

Bobo stared at his distraught wife. Celine could see that he was riddled with fear and indecision.

"Please. There's no time to lose," she prodded.

Bobo grabbed his wife's arm and thrust her hand at Celine.

Celine took the young woman's hand in both of hers. She had to hold tight, for Bobo's wife was so frightened she tried to pull away.

"Tell her to relax and think of a place the child loves to play."

"Celine—" There was a warning note in Cord's tone.

"Tell her," Celine urged.

Bobo spoke to his woman in a rush.

Celine shut everyone else out and opened her mind to the slave girl's memories. At first she felt nothing, then her vision began to dim.

*The bowels of a ship. Below the 'tween decks. Row upon row of shelves. No, not shelves, beds. All of them filled with bodies, some half alive, others dead. Misery, filth and offal. The clank of chains. Moaning, lost souls, too weak to cry. Sickness. Death and fever. Fear coupled with terror.*

"Celine!"

She felt Cord's fingers dig into her shoulder. She had tapped into the wrong memory and was forced to open her eyes and wait for her vision to clear. Swallowing lungfuls of air, she tried to clear the horror of the slave ship out of her mind.

"What in the hell happened?" Cord sounded more afraid than angry.

"I'm fine. Tell her . . ." Celine brought herself to look at the girl, suddenly ashamed of her own place in a world that looked upon slavery as a necessary evil. "Tell her to think of the child, only the child, and of his favorite places."

"Stop this now."

She heard Cord's concern under the anger in his tone.

"I can't. Not when I might be able to save the boy," she said.

Cord glanced around the crowd. They had pressed in close, waiting and watching the white witch. Bobo spoke quickly to his wife and then nodded at Celine.

"Again. Try again," he said.

*A horse. Gray with a ragged mane. A bright, shiny pink shell. Bananas. Water, crystal clear and splashing. Not the sea. Clear water. Falling. Tumbling over rocks. Thundering into a pool. Sparkling like diamonds on moss and ferns. A waterfall. Overwhelming joy. A child scrambling up the slippery rocks. Pride and fear as she pulls him back. No! Do not go near the water. Too near. Do not fall!*

Celine tore her concentration away from the images, let go of Bobo's woman's hand and took a deep breath. When she felt steady again, she looked over at Cord. He was glaring at her.

"I think I know where the child might be," she said.

## Fourteen

"hat are you trying to do?" Cord ground the words out close to her ear. "Are you insane?"

"I'm trying to save a child."

"Or get yourself killed. Look." He nodded toward the old man.

She glanced over at the obeah man. One look at him convinced her that she should she speak out, she would make an enemy.

But with a child's life in danger, she had no choice except to act. Ignoring both Cord, who was furious, and the obeah man and his penetrating stare, Celine spoke directly to Bobo.

"Is there a waterfall nearby?"

Bobo backed away from her a step. She read dawning understanding and awe where an instant ago his dark eyes had only harbored suspicion.

Slowly he nodded, then tossed words at his woman that Celine could not understand. Together Bobo and his wife shoved their way through the crowd and quickly disappeared beyond the tangled hedge. The crowd slowly dispersed, some running after Bobo, a few gathering near the obeah man and casting wary glances in Celine's direction.

"Do you know of a waterfall nearby?" She laid her hand on Cord's sleeve.

"I want to know what you're up to—"

"There isn't time. Please, Cordero, I'll explain later."

"We'll take my horse."

The commotion had drawn Foster and Edward outside. They took up positions on either side of Celine and Ada while Cord unhitched the huge white horse tied near a trough filled with moss-covered water. He mounted up before he rode over to Celine, who waited expectantly until he held out his hand and pulled her up in front of him.

Once she was safely mounted, Cord deftly held the reins and urged the horse forward. They thundered past the obeah man and the few lingerers in the yard.

Celine heard Ada call after them to take care. After that, it was all she could do to concentrate on keeping her seat while Cord kicked his horse into a full-out run. Unaccustomed to the jarring motion and terrified that she would slip and fall beneath the great animal's flashing hooves, Celine held tight to the pommel on the leather saddle.

They passed the men and women running down the road, Bobo in the lead, and soon left them behind. The jungle undergrowth beside the road gave way as they ascended a bare hillside, then came down the other side.

Here the terrain was more rugged, the wind stronger as it swept unimpeded over the crest of the hill. The path they took wound its way through rugged volcanic rock and sunburned brush before it dipped down into a ravine filled with foliage.

The waterfall and the deep, fathomless pool below it had been one of Cord's favorite childhood spots. There had been many lonely days in Louisiana when he would dream of returning to St. Stephen and diving into the pool fed by a mountain spring.

The reality of this moment was quite different as he let his horse negotiate the rocky hillside down to the pool. The roar of the waterfall was thunderous. Mist drifted in the small, secluded glen. The bank around the pool and the stream that fell away from it were slick with moisture and rock. Cord was barely able to contain his fury as they rode into the glen.

"This is nothing but a wild-goose chase—"

"Look!"

His gaze shot in the direction in which Celine pointed. It took him a moment to make out the figure of the small, naked child against the black volcanic rock. The boy was perched halfway up the side of the waterfall on a narrow rock ledge, frozen with fear as he clung to a vine draped across the stones. His eyes were wide with terror as he pressed his back against the rock.

Celine scrambled out of the saddle. As soon as her feet hit the ground she was racing toward the pool. Cord knew every crevice and foothold and was running after her in an instant.

"Celine, wait. I'll get him." He sat down and began pulling off his boots, then his socks. He tore a button getting his shirt off.

She was at the side of the pool, staring down into the

dark water, when he walked up behind her. He touched her shoulder and she jumped.

"I'm going after the boy. Will you be all right?"

"Of course," she said. "Hurry, Cord. He's so close to the edge, one slip and he'll fall and hit the rocks."

He stood at the water's edge, prepared to dive in and cross the pool to where he would begin the climb.

"Cord!"

"What?"

"Be careful, please."

He sliced through the pool, unable to enjoy the cold shock of the mountain water. When he reached the other side he pulled himself out and without hesitation started to climb up the rocks next to the waterfall. Water roared beside him. There was a fine coat of mist hovering over everything. He had climbed these same rocks more times than he could count when he was not much older than the child clinging now to the slippery rock ledge.

He could hear the little boy whimpering. Now the child had to fear not only falling, but the strange white man climbing toward him. With his mind too much on the boy and not enough on his footing, Cord slipped. His foot shot out from under him and he banged his shin against the rock. He could feel blood trickle over the top of his foot, but he kept climbing until he was within an arm's reach of Bobo's son.

"Come over here and I'll help you down," he shouted over the water's din. "Don't be afraid."

The boy stared past Cord and down the face of the rock wall, gauging the distance to the pool below, and vigorously shook his head no.

"I'll take you down and you can see your mama again."

The little boy shook his head no again.

Cord pressed his forehead to the rock and sighed in frustration. He levered himself up until he was seated on the ledge beside the boy.

"How would you like to climb onto my back? You can ride down." Cord turned around, hoping the boy would decide to hop on his back. "Come on."

Bobo and his wife had arrived at the pool. They stood beside Celine, staring up at the tense scene, their voices drowned out by the pounding water.

"I won't let you fall," Cord told the boy. "I promise."

The boy glanced down at his father and mother and then gingerly moved over to Cord's side. He threw himself at Cord's back, slipped his arms around his neck and hung on tight enough to strangle him.

"Ease up a bit," Cord said, loosening the boy's hold. "That's it."

Just as he remembered, it was much harder climbing down than going up. One false handhold, one misstep, and he and the child would go hurtling down onto the rocks below.

Celine stood beside Bobo and his woman at the edge of the pool. Together they watched Cord make his descent, the boy clinging to his neck. She was shaking with fear and anxiety, and the palms of her hands were damp. The huge man beside her had slipped to his knees and was slowly rocking back and forth with his hands clutched together, watching Cord's every move down the treacherous rock. Sweat glistened on his ebony skin. The massive muscles of his shoulders and arms rippled as he held his clasped hands to the heavens.

The child's mother cried softly, her face buried in her hands, unable to watch Cord make his way down the rocks. Celine could not take her eyes off him. If he was worried at all, he did not show any signs of it. His progress was steady and sure as he slowly and carefully made his way down. Finally, when he reached the edge of the pool, he waved at Celine. It was an unguarded moment. She had never seen him so openly happy, so triumphant.

"They're safe!" she told Bobo. "Your son is safe."

Bobo's expression was one of a man coming out of a deep fog as he watched Cord swim the boy back to their side of the pool. The young woman snatched the child away from Cord, held him in her arms and buried her face against the boy's neck.

Cord watched, unable to look away from the joy and innate tenderness of their reunion. The young family had nothing save the clothes on their backs, and even those paltry items belonged to Cord, yet the happiness and love that shone in Bobo's eyes for his wife and child could never be bought or owned.

It was a luxury Cord could not afford, not at the risk of his sanity.

The slave looked over his wife's head, met Cord's eyes and slowly nodded in silent communication.

Celine ran up to him. Sweat dampened her hairline and the wind had made a hopeless tangle of her long mass of ebony curls. She held his shirt and boots in her arms, smiling at him with open admiration and something more, something he didn't wish to acknowledge, in her eyes. She presented quite a picture with the skirt of his mother's gown scooped up between her legs and knotted on both sides, exposing shapely calves. His wife, it seemed, was wearing no stockings, only her low-cut, square-heeled walking shoes.

"You were wonderful . . ."

The sound of the waterfall faded, but not the pounding

of his heart. Bobo's boy was safe, but now Celine would be even more suspect of witchery. Not only had the obeah man lost face, but his power had been greatly diminished when it was Celine and not he who had, somehow, divined the little boy's whereabouts.

"How did you know where the boy was? I'd like a straight answer this time, Celine. The truth. Not some of the hogwash you gave me on Dundee's ship."

She wiped a trickle of sweat from her temple and then pressed her palms to her sun-stained cheeks.

"Are you all right?" she asked, glancing down at the cut on his shin.

"It's nothing. I'm waiting for an answer."

"Is there somewhere cooler we could talk?"

"If this is a scheme to get me to forget about this . . ."

"I promise it isn't. I'll try to explain, but I'm so hot right now I can't think," she said.

Indeed, she did look like a wilted rose transplanted into the wrong soil.

"Let's get out of here."

When her smile faded, he felt as if he had just stepped on a rosebud, but all he could think of was getting her away from here before the others appeared.

He untied his horse and held it steady until Celine had mounted up and he had put on his shirt again. Then he tied his boots behind the saddle and swung up behind her without a word.

This time the pace was slow. She reached behind herself, ran her hands up the nape of her neck and gathered her hair in her hands. Deftly, with a skill Cord could not fathom, she was able to twist her hair into a knot that kept her hair off her neck. Her skin was soft, nearly translucent on the back of her neck, a vulnerable spot that belied her inner strength and stubbornness.

He rode along the open hilltop until they reached the cane fields that carpeted the hillside and swept down to the sea. Various openings signaled the beginning of a maze of pathways that provided passage through the fields. As the trail they were on began to wind back toward the house, he turned in the opposite direction and they began to ride between high walls of cane, heading toward the sea.

The field they passed through would ripen first and then be burned, bundled and hauled to the mill. Right now, he was too angry and confused by what Celine just had done to feel much excitement over the first harvest and milling he would witness as owner of Dunstain Place.

The air was close and dense with humidity between the cane rows. Above them the slender, feathery tips of the stalks whispered on the trades. He felt Celine shift against him and innocently bring him to arousal without any notion of her power over him. She wiped the back of her hand across her brow.

"We're almost there," he promised.

Within seconds they had cleared the edge of the cane field. Before them lay a crescent strip of white sand that bordered aquamarine waters as clear as a looking glass. Lazy, rippling waves teased the shoreline.

"It's so beautiful." Celine sat forward, trying to take the beach in all at once. It was an oasis, a private cove protected by the tall, waving cane and the azure sea.

He rode the white gelding to the edge of the water and stopped just out of reach of the foaming tide.

"Give me your shoes," he requested.

Celine looked over her shoulder, and realizing what he intended, a wide, guileless smile broke over her face. He had to remind himself that he was upset.

She pulled off her shoes and handed them to him without embarrassment. He reached back and tucked them into a saddlebag and then when he saw her beginning to dismount on her own, took her arm and helped her down.

With the abandonment of a child, her skirt still tied up almost to her knees, she walked into the water and began to drag first one foot and then the other through the foaming tide line.

"Now this," she announced with another grand smile, "is heaven."

Cord left her playing in the waves as he guided his horse to a spot where a banyan tree shaded the beach, its far-reaching branches extended over the sea. After he tied the reins to a protruding root, he rolled up his wet pant legs, then walked through the warm sand to join her. The breeze blowing off the sea felt degrees cooler than the stifling air in the thick cane.

As he walked up to her, she turned, her eyes shadowed, as if she did not know what to expect from him. And he could not blame her, for indeed he did not know how to deal with his wife.

Unconcerned with getting his pants any wetter, Cord moved past her and kept walking until he was almost hip-deep in water. He raised his arms over his head, sprang up and dove beneath the aquamarine waves.

Celine wished she could follow him in, but she didn't relish the thought of thoroughly soaking her clothing, or drowning. She watched Cord break the surface of the water. His wet hair was black and glistening as he shook droplets back into the sea. She could not take her eyes off his broad shoulders as he emerged from the water like some mythical sea god.

He walked out of the water not one bit mindful of his

soaked trousers and the way they revealed his anatomy. Passing close to her, he took her hand, walked another few steps until they cleared the tide line, sat in the sand and pulled her down beside him.

"You have some explaining to do," he said. "You told me you had no hand in Dundee's death. I believed you when you claimed it was only accurate guesses that allowed you to come up with things about Dundee's past, but there was more to it than that, wasn't there?"

He was waiting for a logical explanation, when all she had was the truth. Celine pulled her knees up to her chest and began brushing sand off her toes.

"Well?" Despite the heat, Cord felt a chill run though him. He had a feeling that whatever she told him would not bode well.

"Yes, there's more to it," she admitted softly. "But I don't know where to start."

When he did not comment right away, she looked over at him. He was frowning in concentration, watching her as if he believed she had actually cursed Dundee and wondered what else she was capable of.

"Why don't you start at the beginning?"

"I'm not certain when it all began, and I certainly don't know why or how. All I know is that from my earliest memory, I have always been able to see images of other people's pasts."

She glanced over at him. If she had just told him she had grown another head he couldn't have looked more skeptical.

"It's more or less like fortune-telling in reverse," she said, fighting hard to find words to explain. "When I was a little girl I realized the visions only came to me when I touched someone. Does that shock you?"

"Let's just say if I hadn't seen you use this . . . this

power with my own eyes, I'd be certain you were having sunstroke. But I heard what you told Dundee and I saw what happened this morning when you held Bobo's wife's hand.''

''And?''

''Does it happen every time you touch someone?'' Cord leaned on his elbows in the sand, his mind working, thinking back, racing ahead.

''It only happens when I will it, when I open my mind and let the images in. I rarely use my gift.''

''Gift?''

''My guardian, Persa, always called it that, although sometimes I wonder if it isn't really a curse. When I was little, I thought everyone was like me. My mother soon convinced me otherwise.''

''When you held that girl's hand today, I thought you were going to faint dead away. You lost all color. Does it cause you pain?''

''Only insofar as I can feel what the person who owns the images feels, although never as deeply as they did when the experience was new.''

''So you have the uncanny ability to eavesdrop on someone else's memories,'' His blue gaze was chilling. ''When I first laid eyes on you, I felt as if you could see into my soul. Have you used this . . . this *gift* on me?''

Celine looked out to the horizon, unable to meet his eyes.

''Yes,'' she finally admitted. ''I have.''

He sat up.

It was a nightmare. Cord tried to fathom her lurking in his memory, seeing all the things he had fought so hard to hide from himself. Did she know all of it? The trials and loss that had caused him such pain—pain he had tried to hide behind a wall of detachment, or drown in a bottle.

"You've looked into my past? Crawled into my mind?"

"It wasn't like that, Cord . . ."

He was visibly angry, more so than she had ever seen him. His cool-hearted detachment she could handle; this hard, angry man frightened her.

"When, Celine? When did you steal my memories?"

"When we went aboard the *Adelaide*, I wanted to know what manner of man I had married. And then the night of the storm at sea, when you held me in your arms . . . I hadn't meant for it to happen, it just did. I was so exhausted I was not on guard and—"

In one lithe movement he pushed up and loomed over her.

"What about last night? Did you creep into my mind last night when we were—"

"No! I did nothing of the sort." She hadn't thought he could get any angrier, but he surprised her.

"Why not? It seems the perfect opportunity. Here." He thrust his hand at her. "Touch me now and read my mind."

"Cord, please, don't do this—"

He whipped his hand back and indicated the emerald sugarcane field stretched out behind them. "I should have known things were too good to be true. The plantation is salvageable. I have a wife who pleases me in bed. I should have known by now that *I* never have this kind of luck. Is there anything else you have to tell me? Do you possess any more little secrets or hidden talents that I should know of?"

*Secrets?*

He was so furious that there was no way she could

tell him why she had so readily agreed to take Jemma O'Hurley's place, that she had married because she was afraid for her life and had to flee the police in New Orleans.

He didn't wait for a reply, but headed for his horse. He was scared he might kill her, and was afraid at the same time that he might take her in his arms and forgive her everything just to have her beneath him again.

Celine pushed herself out of the sand and shook off her skirt as she hurried to catch up to him. He paid her no mind, simply gathered up his boots and shirt. When he had buttoned his shirt up again, he tied his boots to the back of his saddle, then reached for the reins.

Celine grabbed his arm. When he jerked away from her touch as though it had scorched him, his blatant rejection wounded her deeply. She protectively crossed her arms at her waist and pressed her palms against her midriff.

Persa had warned her that there were those who would never trust her, those who would view her with suspicion if they knew she could glimpse the shadows of the past hidden in their minds. The anger and betrayal she had seen in Cord's eyes only confirmed Persa's predictions. But from anyone else the rejection would not have hurt so much.

She tried to tell herself that he would calm down. She even tried to tell herself that it shouldn't really matter what Cord thought since, no matter how much she might wish it were different, their marriage was not a love match. Why, then, did she feel as if she were coming apart inside?

She stared at his rigid stance, at the hard line of his jaw in profile. Then, when he slowly turned to stare down at her as if he had never laid eyes on her before,

Celine realized with sudden, blinding insight that somehow, someway, over the past few weeks, she had fallen in love with Cordero Moreau.

She had never intended to love him, but surely she must, she reasoned, for why else would it matter to her what he thought?

Why else would it hurt so much to think that he might never touch her again?

What would he do if he ever found out she had done the one thing he had warned her not to do?

She had fallen in love with him.

"Cord, please. I promise, I'll never open my mind to your memories again without your knowledge."

He reached out, almost grabbed her shoulders, checked himself, and then quickly dropped his hands. He ached to touch her, to pull her to him and tell her it was all right. The witch. She had him hard for her even now that he knew of her perfidy, of her deception—and surely it was a cruel deception to keep such a dark secret.

"How do I know I can trust you?"

"Because we can't go on like this for the rest of our lives," she said softly.

He could barely hear her words over the roar of the rolling waves as they ground into the sand. Unshed tears shimmered in her eyes. He read something deep inside them that he didn't want to acknowledge. She was looking up at him as if his forgiveness and trust truly mattered to her. It frightened him to know she cared.

He turned his back on her, intent on mounting up but knowing he would have to touch her, that he couldn't very well ride off without her.

He was about to put a foot in the stirrup when Celine realized she could not let this go any further without trying to break through his anger and stubborn pride.

She closed off that accursed portion of her mind that wandered through the embers of memories and reached for him just as he shoved his foot in the stirrup. She was stirred in another more primitive, sensual way by the contact with his heated skin through the fine chambray of his shirtsleeve.

"Cord, listen . . ."

At her touch, heat reverberated through him. He jerked his foot down, widened his stance and, throwing caution to the wind, clasped his hands on her shoulders.

Her head was thrown back, her eyes closed. A single tear leaked from beneath her dark lashes and spilled off the slope of her cheek to fall lost in the sand at their feet. The sea breeze played havoc with her waist-length hair.

This woman, this witch, this wife of his, Cord thought, had been slowly weaving her spell around his heart—through his mind.

"You're right, Celine," he said, tightening his hold on her shoulders, forcing her to open her eyes and see him. "We can't go on like this for the rest of our lives."

His driving need overrode his fear. He pulled her even closer, stared deep into the secret depths of her eyes, taunted her with his nearness as he dared her to take another glimpse into his soul.

"You want to be a voyeur into my past, go ahead, sweet Celine. If that is the price I have to pay to bury myself in you, then there's nothing for me to do but pay it."

He slipped an arm around her and held her imprisoned against him while he reached down with his other hand and began to unfasten his trousers. Half expecting her to struggle, he found her blessedly still, waiting, staring back into his eyes.

"I want you, Celine. Damn you, but I want you again."

She couldn't argue, not when she was experiencing her own mounting need. He went down on one knee and pulled her down into the shade of the banyan. The sand was surprisingly cool, nothing like it had felt out in the hot sun.

There was so much she wanted to say to him, so much she wished his stubborn heart and mind would hear and accept, but she already knew him well enough to know that soft words of love and promises would only become links in a chain that would weigh like a shackle around his heart that he had never wanted to bear.

He wanted her. She needed him. Giving herself to him freely was the only way she could communicate with him now. Letting him satisfy himself in her was the only way she could reach out to comfort him, to give him solace. Sharing her body with him was the only way she could offer him all the love that he resisted out of fear of abandonment and lack of trust.

He let her go and drew back long enough to rid himself of his pants and reach for her skirt. The knots in the hem gave him pause, but he soon had them loosened and tugged the fabric up past her hips.

"Wrap your arms around me, Celine. Close your eyes and slip into my mind, but know this: I'll only allow it when I can no longer deny myself the pleasures of your body." He lowered himself over her, throbbing and ready, aching with need and hating himself for it.

"No," she said, tossing her head from side to side even as she reached out for him. "I promise. I won't—"

He reached between them, found her wet and stretched

her gently, silencing her as he forced himself to put aside his anger for the moment. He had not always been an honorable man, but he had never physically harmed a woman.

He opened her wider, felt the slippery wetness between her thighs, picked up the rhythm of his fingers until she moaned and clung to him. With a thrust of her hips she told him without words that she wanted more, needed this as much as he did.

The breeze was tinted with salt and mist. The fragrance of frangipani wafted around them. Unable to wait, unwilling to weigh the consequences of his act, he buried his face in the curve of her neck and thrust himself into her. She was hot and tight and wholly his, at least for this one blissful moment in time.

She raised up to meet him when she felt him enter her, half expecting to feel the tearing, searing hurt of last night. But nothing of the sort happened. Just as he had promised, there was no physical pain, only the bittersweet knowledge that what he felt for her beyond his desire was worse than anger—it was nothing at all.

True to her promise, she did not slip into his mind, but concentrated instead on the sensations that he aroused in her. Cord began to move to a cadence set by the pounding surf, then, impatient with the slow, even tempo, he quickened his thrusts, reaching deeper with each powerful drive.

He was doing maddening things to her as he nipped at her neck and shoulder with his teeth. She could feel his warm breath against her neck, shivered as he traced his tongue around the pulse point in her throat.

She arched against him, wanting more, craving it all—his seed, his surrender, her own fulfillment. She called out his name, demanding he bring her release. Her cry was swallowed by the sound of the sea, carried away on the trade winds.

Fueled by her hunger, he couldn't stem his own. He thrust deep, felt her quicken and pulse around him. He could not hold back, could not tempt or tease her, and so reveled in the pleasure of his release as he poured himself into her again and again.

He didn't know if it was the surf he heard or the roaring of his own heartbeat. Forgetting his anger, he gathered Celine in his arms and held her close, smoothed her damp curls away from her face, felt the sand clinging to the back of her hair.

Then memory jolted him out of the idyllic moment. He let her go, rolled off her and sat up. He pulled his shirt over his head, tossed it aside and, buck naked, jogged across the sand and dove beneath the waves.

Celine sat up, unwilling to give in to the melancholy that threatened to settle over her. It was insane to grieve over the loss of something she'd never had and never intended to want. She got to her knees and pulled down her skirt, squinting against the sun as she watched Cord swim away from the shoreline with sure, steady strokes. His bare bottom flashed in the sunlight as he ducktailed up and then disappeared beneath the crystal blue water.

She envied him the freedom to escape into another realm, if only for a few minutes. She knew that as long as her memory was alive there was so much she could never really escape. But she also knew that it did little good to cry over the past—especially when an uncertain future was staring her in the face.

She stood up and hurried over the sand and then along the shoreline as Cord continued to swim with long, sure strokes, working out his frustration. She pulled up her skirt and waded through the waves at the edge of the beach. The water was warm but refreshingly cleansing as she walked in until it was nearly up to her waist. Juggling her skirt in one hand, she cupped water to splash over her face and neck, used it to tame her hair and then let it trickle between her breasts down the open neckline of the gown.

She could see Cord striding out of the water as if he did not have a care in the world. She waited until he had time to dress and then, regretting having to leave the water, she slowly waded out and walked down the beach to join him.

By the time she reached him, Cord thought he had his emotions under control. Still, he avoided looking at her, afraid he would be tempted by her pouting lips or her haunting eyes.

"It's time to go back," he said, holding his hand out to help her mount. She hesitated and then slipped her hand into his.

"Cord, I give you my word, I'll never again—"

"I would prefer you not speak of it," he said as coolly as he could. He didn't want her word. He wanted the whole maddening reality of her strange ability to go away until he was able to resolve it in his mind.

Once she was in the saddle, he mounted up behind her and headed back toward the cane road.

Celine was conscious of the way he held himself away from her, the control he used so as not to accidentally touch her as they worked their way across the fields. Thankfully, they were closer to the house than she realized. The cane soon gave way to the overgrown tropical forest and what had once been the garden. Once they were in the yard, Celine slipped off the saddle without waiting for Cord's help and hurried to the house.

He didn't call her name or try to stop her.

Cord watched Celine hurry away from him, her bare feet slapping against the stones that lined the overgrown path, her heels flashing. Her dark hair, still dusted with glittering sand, swayed back and forth at her waist. He wished he knew what to say to her, but he still felt so damned deceived. It was hard to reckon with all she had told him.

He had spent a lifetime shielding himself from memories that she could dredge up at will, her will, without his knowledge. Just when he'd thought all was not lost, that he would be able to make something of Dunstain Place and fulfill his promise to Alex, his desirable little wife had informed him she was capable of sneaking into his mind.

She was so beautiful, so desirable and so convincing that he had been tempted to take her in his arms and forgive her. He couldn't deny that it must have been painful for her to tell him the truth, to admit she was abnormal, but that didn't matter to him. What did matter was that he didn't know whether or not he could trust her not to sneak into his mind again.

Emotionally, he needed time to think things through.

Physically, he was addicted to her as if she were a drug.

Cord retrieved his boots and Celine's shoes before he handed his mount over to a waiting stable boy.

He was a few feet from the veranda when Ada bustled out of the house to greet them. Clad now in a gray watered silk gown with a wide lace collar and cuffs, she lingered in the doorway, eyeing Celine's disheveled appearance. Cord stepped up beside his wife and offered his aunt no more than a nod in greeting.

"However did you get your pants all wet, Cordero? Celine, you look in need of a bath. I'll have Edward fill you a cool tub.'' She started to turn away and then, as an afterthought, said, ''We heard about Bobo's little boy. I'm so glad he is safe and sound. What a hero you are, Cordero, and what a day we've had around here.''

Cord wanted nothing more than to slack his thirst and change into clean pants, but there were duties he could not dismiss lightly. ''No more trouble from the obeah man I hope?''

Ada fluttered a hand in the air. ''No, no. Nothing like that—it's just something so unexpected. At least, you didn't remind me to expect any houseguests . . .''

''Expect *who,* Aunt?''

''Why, the magistrate's own brother, Collin Ray, along with a bookseller from Barbados. A Mr. Wells, I believe he said. Howard Wells. Celine invited him to visit when they shared dinner in Baytowne. By the way, speaking of dinner, we will be dining in an hour,'' Ada said.

She ran her hand over the flyaway strands that escaped her braids and went on before Cord could comment. ''I have Foster overseeing a few special dishes while he works on the silver. One is a pudding with a bit of rum sprinkled into it as it cools. It only bakes for an hour, but sometimes if one isn't careful—''

''That sounds wonderful, Aunt Ada,'' Celine cut in, coming to Cord's rescue. ''Would you mind sending Edward up now?''

''There's just so much to do!'' Ada appeared thrilled to have so many details to see to. She bustled off toward the back of the house with a smile on her face and a spring in her step.

Cord waited for Celine to enter the house first and then followed her up the stairs. He paused outside her bedroom door and when she stepped inside he said, ''I didn't know you met anyone in Baytowne besides Ray. Now it seems you have two admirers under our very roof."

"Mr. Wells is old enough to be my father. He's a kindly gentleman, well-read and interesting. When you were not around to escort me to dinner that night, Foster and Edward chose him as a safe companion for me. I didn't think you would mind my extending an invitation. If you're worried that I might be tempted to steal into the guests' minds, rest assured I won't. You can trust me with them."

Cord watched her closely, weighing her words.

"We'll all have to trust you, won't we?"

# Fifteen

Thanks to the efforts of Edward and Foster, the Moreau silver glinted against a backdrop of freshly washed, starched and pressed table linens. Afternoon sunlight gilded the room with honey gold hues and streaks of butter yellow that gave even the faded floral wall covering new life. Celine had insisted that Ada reign at the end of the table at Cord's right hand. She, herself, sat beside Howard Wells, rather than Collin Ray.

The magistrate's brother sat stiffly beside Ada. His dress attested to his position as an island aristocrat, the heavy brocade vest, cutaway coat and laced cravat—a stark contrast to Cord's white, open-throated shirt, with its billowing, full-cut sleeves and buff-colored breeches.

From Ray's position, he could—and did—watch Celine unceasingly, lending only half an ear to Ada's detailed descriptions of the meal preparation. Celine found the man's speculative leer offending. Cord did not give any indication that he noticed the silent animosity that passed from her to Ray, but her husband only glanced her way infrequently.

As Celine attempted to ignore Collin Ray, she turned her attentions to Howard Wells. She found that gentleman's warm humor and ready smile comforting. She was about to ask him what he had read and enjoyed lately when Ray drew everyone's attention.

"There is talk in town that your wife is something of a witch, Moreau." Collin Ray lifted his wine goblet. As he took a sip of the blood-red wine, he stared at Celine over the crystal rim.

Celine put her fork down and folded her hands in her lap. She refused to back down and look away from the odious man. She wished she truly could wield a powerful curse now and again, for now was certainly the time.

"My wife is a nag, not a witch." Cord said. His closed expression suggested he did not favor such talk.

Celine was thankful he did not go into any explanation.

"You poor dear," Ada said, addressing Celine. "I don't understand all this talk about you being a witch. How ridiculous." She turned to Ray, obviously impressed by his dress and manner and willing to humor him. "This morning there was quite a scene here with the obeah man."

"A scene?" Ray took a sip of wine, easily leading the unsuspecting Ada into detailing the event.

"I doubt Mr. Ray is interested, Aunt," Cord said.

"Why, of course I am. Quite a scene, you say?" Ray took another sip of wine.

"The slaves were quite upset. Some of them heard the rumors in town and naturally, anything mysterious upsets them." Ada began to relate the details of the obeah man's confrontation with Celine and Cord.

"I wasn't aware that there were that many slaves left here on the estate." Ray's gaze flicked over Celine to Cord. "Now that you're back, do you plan to allow an obeah man to practice that mumbo jumbo here? Most planters believe those witch doctors are the fastest way to slave insurrection. If you know his identity, you should have him sold off the island."

"My father believed different, and so do I," Cord explained. "He knew how important it was to give the slaves some peace of mind. There is little basis for trust in their lives. Magic fills the void. You might call the obeah man's work mumbo jumbo, but if the slaves believe he is capable of curing their ills or meting out justice among them, what's the harm?"

"But it sounds as if your wife might be in jeopardy."

Cord drained his wineglass and waited while Edward stepped out of the shadows to refill it.

"My wife has proven she is not afraid to stand up to the obeah man. The slaves appreciate a show of strength. Besides, she saved the overseer's child."

"I wasn't aware you had an overseer up here."

"He's one of the slaves. Also the head boiler and gang boss. Why shouldn't he be in charge?"

"He's a slave, that's why. You have actually appointed him overseer?" Ray was stunned.

"No. He's more of a manager. Things were running quite smoothly with him in charge before I arrived and I've no wish to upset the apple cart." Cord drained his wineglass again.

Ray was unable to hide his contempt.

"I hope to God we don't find you all murdered in your beds."

Celine turned to Howard Wells, hoping he might provide a new topic of conversation, and found him smiling at Ada. Neither of them were paying any attention to the heated discussion. Cord's aunt was well aware of the man's perusal and was blushing coyly.

"Would you care for more *chocho*, Mr. Wells?"

"I would. It's delicious," Wells said of the mild green island squash.

Finding no help from that quarter, Celine carefully studied the spacious dining room, with its massive table and its bank of long, wide windows to the sea. Foster and Edward had already made great strides in overseeing the cleaning and refurbishing of the house and after only a day, the place had begun to glow with new life. Every prism dripping from the chandelier above the table had been washed. Candlelight reflected off the crystal droplets and was scattered over the walls.

Celine sipped her wine, lost in thought, wondering if Cord was still upset with her, wondering if he would set aside his anger when they climbed the stairs tonight.

"You intend to do *what*?" Collin Ray's incredulous shout startled her so much that she spilled her wine on the clean cloth. Edward slipped out of the room.

"I said I'm going to have emancipation papers drawn up for all the slaves at Dunstain Place as soon as my father's solicitor returns from England."

"You can't," sputtered Ray.

"Why not? There are already many freed slaves established in business here on St. Stephen. Besides, it's only a matter of time before slavery is abolished in the islands. I predict it will come much sooner than in America."

"Preposterous."

"I agree with Cordero," Wells said, and then beamed at Ada.

Cord startled Celine by asking, "What do you think? Am I mad to turn loose of so many assets?"

"No." She smiled over at him, and although it was not returned, she felt as if their animosity had been set aside for the moment. "In fact, I believe this is one of the few times since I laid eyes on you that I think you are perfectly sane."

By the time the meal ended, dusk had gathered and torches were lit around the perimeter of the house. Ada suggested she show Howard Wells the collection of books in the library. Uncomfortable without their diversionary conversation, Celine excused herself early, leaving Cord and Collin Ray to argue over brandy and cigars. She slipped out to the kitchen, where she found Foster and Edward helping to clean up the remains of the feast. Gunnie was up to her elbows in soapsuds.

"Thank you for a wonderful meal," Celine told the men. "I know most of it was your doing."

"Miss Ada 'as some wonderful recipes." Foster handed Edward a dry platter and the shorter man bent to place it carefully in a cabinet.

When Edward straightened he said, "It looks to be a beautiful sunset. Good time for a romantic stroll in the garden. I can go get Cordero and—"

"He is busy with Mr. Ray." She was certain a romantic stroll in the garden with her was the last thing on Cordero's mind.

On her way out the door, Celine paused to thank Gunnie for dinner, but the woman did not acknowledge her compliment. Celine slipped out the back door and

crossed the veranda. She made her way along the overgrown garden path to a terrace that had once provided
a panoramic vista of the sea. A stone bench near the far
edge of the terrace beckoned. What it lacked in comfort
it made up for with a view of the spectacular sunset.

A sense of peace and belonging imbued her as she sat
with her hands folded in her lap. She looked around,
wondering if perhaps Alyce's spirit might be with her
now, hovering protectively in her garden, enjoying the
sunset and the coming of night. She watched the sky
change from subtle peach to a brilliant orange and yellow.

If Cord didn't forget to spare a few laborers for the
task as he had promised, the garden would soon be returned to its former splendor. And Celine was not ad-
verse to rolling up her own sleeves to help.

The blissful moment fled instantly as Celine felt a
cold chill of warning settle over her like a damp cloak.
The sensation was strong enough to prompt her to turn
and gaze over her shoulder. When she saw a man sil-
houetted against the deep green foliage, she started to
smile, thinking it might be Cordero—until he stepped
out of the shadows. It was Collin Ray.

She immediately quit the bench, intent upon escaping
into the house, but Ray was far swifter than she imagined. He quickly crossed the terrace, effectively blocking
her way. When he stepped in front of her, she could not
help but be reminded of Jean Perot and the way he had
cornered her. She began to shiver uncontrollably.

"Are you cold or merely excited?" Ray asked, a
smile of smug satisfaction on his face.

"Let me pass. I'm needed inside."

"You're needed right here."

"I'm afraid I don't understand," she said, stalling, trying to edge around him.

"I'm sure you do. You recall our little meeting on the docks . . ."

"You make it sound like an assignation when it was absolutely nothing of the sort." She tried to sweep by him, lifted her skirt so that the fabric would not even touch him as she passed by.

He grabbed her arm above the elbow.

"Are you ready to accept my offer of protection?"

"What are you talking about? I'm married . . ."

"To a man who did not glance your way more than once at dinner. Surely you can't wish to remain here. The place is in a shambles. That old woman is senile. Moreau allows the presence of a witch doctor, who feels challenged by you, thanks to those idiotic rumors. Your life is in danger, Celine."

"It is not. You said yourself obeah magic is a farce. Dunstain Place is not the way you make it out to be, either. With very little effort, Cord will be able to make this place what it was before."

He pulled her closer. She winced at the pain and tossed back her head to glare up at him.

*"Let me go."* She struggled to get away from him.

He leaned close. She could smell the sour scent of onions and cigars on his breath. His ice blue eyes were cunning, full of greed and avarice.

"Do you know where your husband spent the night while he left you in Baytowne's worst excuse for an inn?"

"No, and I don't care." She didn't want to know. Didn't want to hear her suspicions confirmed.

"He was at Madam Felicity's, the most notorious whorehouse in the West Indies."

Ray's eyes roamed over her, the heat behind his gaze so intense she could feel it sear her breasts, her lips, her throat. She tried to break free.

"You are far too beautiful to waste away hidden up here with a husband who barely gives you the time of day. My offer of protection still stands."

"What makes you think my wife needs protection, Ray?"

Celine whirled around and found Cord crossing the veranda. Behind him, Foster and Edward hovered in the shadows. She blessed them for their meddling.

Cord was furious at what he had just witnessed. When he'd first come upon them, he'd been ready to blame Celine for tempting Ray under his very nose, but then he'd heard enough to know different and had seen Celine flinch away from Collin Ray in disgust. Now, as Cord strode across the paved terrace, his boot heels rang sharply against the stones.

"I could call you out for this, Ray."

Cord stepped up beside Celine. He gently took her arm and began rubbing his thumb over the place where Collin Ray's grip had surely left bruises. Although her show of confidence had been intended to belie her fear, he was not surprised to find her trembling.

Collin Ray straightened the lace on his cuffs. "I've merely made your beautiful wife a better offer."

"As your whore?"

"Face it. You won't deal well here, Moreau. You're just like your father. He ran with the underbelly of island society. No one will forget that."

"What do I care for your society? I'm not English, nor do I pretend to be like the rest of you island colonials who were born here and still refer to England as 'home.' I can take care of my wife, Ray, without help from you.

Now, get out before I have to throw you out. Don't ever come near my wife again or I'll have to kill you. I won't warn you again.''

"I only thought to offer myself to her because you obviously don't appreciate her, Moreau. I'll be happy to leave.'' Collin Ray made a formal bow to Celine. "Good night, madam.''

Thankful for Cord's hand riding her waist, Celine did not acknowledge Ray's departure. As soon as the man was out of the garden, she buried her face against Cord's shirtfront.

Uncertain, Cord stared down at her dark hair. Her cheek was pressed against his heart. Surprisingly, it pleased him to find she would turn to him for comfort. He slowly raised his hand and began to stroke her hair.

"I'm not afraid of much,'' she said softly, "but he frightens me.''

"I'm not always very kind either, Celine, and yet you are not afraid of me.''

"But you are not evil.'' She knew that whenever Cord was cold or hard, when his anger surfaced or he seemed indifferent, it was only because he so closely guarded any deeper, softer emotion.

Finally she felt composed enough to step away from him. Cord walked to the edge of the terrace to watch the sky purple and the stars take their places on the night's empty stage. He tried to blot out the sight of Ray's hands on her.

"Our marriage was a business agreement, not much different from the one Ray has offered you . . .''

"I am no whore.''

"I know that,'' he said without hesitation.

Celine tried to fight back the tears stinging her eyes. There came a slight breeze, a very faint lifting of leaves atop the hibiscus that had once been a neat hedge but was now a solid green, massive wall of leggy stems. The gentle breeze carried the scent of frangipani, and with it the feeling of peace and contentment she had known earlier. A sensation of calm settled over her.

Cord turned around and found her watching him closely. The juxtaposition of her innate stubbornness and her petite stature and vulnerability was alluring. What would she have done if Foster had not sent him out to join her? How long could she have held Ray off?

For the first time in his life, he felt the weight of being entirely responsible for someone else. And now, not only was there Celine to consider, but Ada and all of the others at Dunstain Place. Somehow he had become entangled in a tightly woven tapestry of emotional threads.

Cord sighed and, giving in to the unfamiliar need to protect, walked across the terrace to Celine.

"Don't worry about Ray. We're isolated from him and his kind up here. We don't need them," he said.

"You aren't invulnerable here, Cord. A snake often strikes without warning." They had made an enemy of a powerful man. She knew that nothing good could come of it.

"Did you read something sinister in his thoughts, Celine? I'm beginning to see where your odd talent may have its advantages."

"Persa always said there is no value in reading the past. I couldn't have discerned anything about Collin Ray's intentions even if I had wanted."

He stepped closer, drawn by a radiant loveliness in her that shone bright, even in the gathering twilight. As uncertain as he was about her promise not to slip into his mind, she was fast becoming irresistible to him. It was all the more reason to resist her, and yet touching her, burying himself in her again was all he could think of. When she was in his arms he could close himself off from the rest of the world, from his past and his future. When he was inside her, there were only the two of them. They were an island in and of themselves.

Collin Ray was less of a danger to him than were his own disturbing thoughts and intense longings. The last thing on earth he wanted was to put his battered heart into her keeping.

"Don't think about Ray," he told her, and then on impulse stepped back, certain that if he so much as touched her hand, he would need to take her to bed.

"It's late," he said, pausing on the low step before the veranda.

"Good night, Cordero," she whispered. Celine sensed his unease, read it in his stance, and looked away. The last hint of light had faded from the sky. The Milky Way was spattered across the inky blackness. When she turned to walk back to the veranda, Cord was gone.

The next morning, Celine experienced a wave of melancholy. Annoyed at her feelings, she again reminded herself that theirs was not a love match. And yet, when she allowed herself to remember their lovemaking, she could not help but wonder . . .

She dressed quickly and hurried downstairs, where she found Ada and Howard Wells just finishing breakfast.

"I'm sorry I overslept," she told them before she went to the sideboard, where a tray of sautéed fish barely tempted her. She had tossed and turned for hours thinking about the future, about Cordero and whether she was insane in wanting to try to teach him to tear down his defenses.

"Why, that's quite all right, my dear. Cordero told us earlier not to expect you anytime soon." Ada bestowed a misguided wink that made Celine blush and look away. "He said to tell you that there are three men at your disposal. They've already begun trimming the hedges around the terrace. Alyce is so pleased," she added before popping a spoonful of papaw into her mouth.

Celine sat down beside Howard Wells.

"I'm happy to see you didn't leave with Mr. Ray," she told him.

"Actually, I didn't even have the opportunity. He left quite suddenly, I hear." Howard turned to Ada, who blushed profusely for no apparent reason, then began folding and refolding her linen napkin.

"I've decided to accept Miss Dunstain's kind invitation to stay a few days and catalogue the library. I hope you don't mind?" he said.

Celine could not miss Ada's hopeful expression.

"I think that's a fine idea," she said. "If you find something you think I might like to read, please let me know."

"I'll do that." Mr. Wells's smile creased the skin around his eyes.

Celine ate a bit of the fish, which had been sautéed with peppers and scallions, but found it far too spicy. She left with a promise to Ada that she would not work in the hot sun too long.

After she had changed and was about to go out, Foster called out to her and quickly hurried to her side. Edward was not far behind.

"Is there anything you need?" Foster asked.

"Not at the moment. I'm on my way to the garden." She wondered why he looked so pleased with himself.

He cleared his throat, fidgeted with the buttons of his vest, then smoothed his hair away from his part.

"Do you have something you wanted to tell me, Foster?" Celine asked.

"I just wanted to tell you Cordero was out early, seein' to business," he said.

"And you had to 'ave noticed 'ow well he sits a horse?" Edward put in.

Celine knew what they were up to and tried not to smile.

"Yes, of course."

"Swims like a fish," Edward added.

"That he does," Celine agreed.

"Protected your honor last night when that man tried to accost you," Foster reminded her.

"We told you there was more to 'im than met the eye," Edward said.

"Told you 'e weren't as bad as 'e seemed," Foster added.

"He possesses many sterling qualities," she agreed. She had to give them credit for a campaign well fought.

Edward cleared his throat. "Did you notice he barely had anything to drink last night at dinner?"

"Or after." Foster was watching her closely. The man was practically gloating. "Might I be right in thinking you've a soft place in your 'eart for 'im despite 'is faults?" he asked.

Edward looked about to burst with curiosity.

Celine smiled at both of them.

"Let's just say my husband and I have come to an

understanding since we arrived here. We're taking things one day at a time.''

Edward clasped his hands over his heart and sighed.

"That's all any of us can ask for, ain't it?" Foster said. "One day at a time.''

# Sixteen

ours later Celine found herself thankful she had changed into an old gown that Foster had declared fit only for the rag bag. Her hands were filthy, her hair was in mad disarray, her face was streaked with dirt and sweat. As much as she had tried to maintain a proper demeanor as mistress of a plantation and to simply supervise the men Cord had left at her disposal, she had not been able to resist pulling weeds or slashing at the hedges with a long, lethal cane knife she had commandeered.

The air was thick with humidity. The sky was dense with clouds that had backed up over the island, a sure sign that it would not be long before the late-afternoon rains began. Hot and tired, she dismissed the slaves and sent them back to the village. Wiping her brow with the back of her arm, she started up the path that wound through the garden. She pulled up her hem and dabbed at the moisture at her throat and between her breasts.

Monkeys jabbered in the trees overhead, scolding her for intruding in their domain. Parrots joined in the clatter, their iridescent lime feathers making them nearly invisible against the backdrop of the forest. The air was heavy with the sweet scent of fallen guava. In short the tropical sanctuary was an enchanted world alive with sound and color.

Celine dropped her hem into place and straightened when she thought she saw Cord step through an opening in the trees. She waved and he waved back, but as he moved closer, she realized he was not Cord, but an equally handsome older version of her husband with raven black hair and a leather patch over his right eye.

The man was nearly as tall as Cord and moved with the same easy, confident stride. Nothing in his expression or manner caused her the prickly sense of alarm she had felt when she'd first laid eyes on Collin Ray, so she continued toward him.

Before she could speak, he took her hand and kissed it while performing a formal, courtly bow.

"I had heard Cordero returned with a beautiful new bride. I'm pleased to find the reports are true," he said.

His brilliant, open smile was charming, exactly what Cord's might have been, she mused, if his heart were free of its burdens. This man's manner was so disarming that she couldn't help but smile back.

"You are far more than beautiful. *Exquisite* is the word I would choose. You are Celine?"

"Yes. I'm Celine." She apologized for her filthy gown as she tried and failed to give some semblance of order to her snarled hair.

"You are Auguste Moreau," she said. There was no one else this man could be, unless Cord had failed to mention he had a handsome older brother.

"How did you surmise that, my dear, when all the world thinks me dead? You don't seem at all surprised to see a ghost standing here before you."

She cocked her head and studied him carefully.

"You are no more a ghost than I am. Where did you come from?"

"Off a ship anchored in a cove on the small plantation bordering this one. You might say the owner of the land is a close personal friend who welcomes my infrequent visits to the island. How do you know me?"

"I would know you anywhere. My husband is the exact image of you, except that he is taller and his eyes are blue and unfortunately do not hold the same sparkle I see in yours."

"And why is that?"

"Because of the way his life has unfolded since you sent him away."

He appeared surprised that she would so boldly discuss Cordero's disposition with a virtual stranger.

"I did what I thought best at the time."

"For him, or for you, monsieur?" She watched the laughter in his eyes dim.

"For him, I thought. I was a wastrel, a ne'er-do-well who married an heiress—not for her money, but because we were hopelessly in love. When Alyce died in a carriage accident that was all my fault, I thought my life was over. I could not help myself out of my grief. How could I have been any kind of a father to my son?"

She tried to put herself in his place, truly wishing she could understand.

"I intended to kill myself, but didn't want Cordero exposed to the scandal, so I sent him to my father in New Orleans."

"But, how could you have sent him to Henre Moreau when there was no love between you and your father? Didn't you stop to think that the man might take his anger and disappointment out on your son?"

"I couldn't think past my guilt, my grief. I hoped that where my father had failed with me, he would succeed with my son. And that seems to be the case, for I hear Cordero has come back to take over Dunstain Place."

"How did you find out? If you are still in contact with Ada, she keeps your secret well."

He shook his head. "She, like everyone else, thinks I'm dead. When I disappeared, it truly was with every intent of dying. I set out in a small sailboat without water or provisions, intending to let the sea take me. Instead I was found delirious and on the verge of death by an old pirate who taught me all he knew. As if I were resurrected to a new life, I left everything behind, changed my name to Roger Reynolds and became a privateer for many years. I have had one of my most trusted men overseeing things at Dunstain Place for years."

"Who?"

"Bobo."

"The slave?"

"Bobo is as free as you and I . . . if any man can ever truly be free in this life. He works for me, and believe me, he is well paid."

"Cord will be furious when you tell him. He already harbors an intense hatred for you for sending him away, but to let him think you were dead—"

True sorrow and regret darkened his expression. "In any case, I don't intend to walk back into my son's life.

It's enough to know that he has you, and that he has come home.''

"So you will abandon him again?'' She could not mask her anger any longer. Cord deserved to know the truth.

"He believes me dead. I would prefer to keep it that way.''

"Some privateer you must have been. You are a coward, monsieur.''

"I was the best of privateers, because I didn't care if I lived or died. That makes a man foolhardy enough to take many, many chances. But you are certainly right in one respect: I was too big a coward to raise my son.'' There was a deep sorrow in his tone. "Now, like his mother, he is lost to me.''

Too aware of Cordero's pain to be objective, she refused to back down, refused to let this man hide from what he did to his son. She reached for his arm, made him listen.

"It isn't too late to meet him, to let him know you're still alive. Surely you care for him enough to tell him why you sent him away? Don't let him go through life believing you threw him away simply because you didn't love him anymore. You can't know how haunted he is by your abandonment.''

"But I told you, I did not abandon him,'' Auguste cried out with undisguised anguish. "I have missed my son since the day I sent him away I would have sooner lost both eyes. But it is too late for regrets. He will only hate me more when he learns the truth.''

She could not stop her tears of frustration. When one slipped down her cheek she wiped it away and turned her back on him, unwilling to let him witness her dismay.

"I didn't mean to hurt you, Celine," he said. "I just wanted to meet the woman who will one day give my son a son of his own."

She felt his hand on her shoulder, but refused to turn around to face him.

"You didn't mean to hurt Cordero, either, but you did. Because of what you did, he is incapable of letting himself feel anything, of loving anyone . . ."

"Surely he loves you . . ."

She spun around, threw her head back and laughed. The bitter, anguished sound that threaded through her voice surprised her. She faced him and shook her head.

"No. He doesn't love me. He couldn't love me even if he wanted to, because he doesn't know how to love. He's never been taught to feel love—only how to lose it."

Alexandre's death, Henre's inability to give Cord any love—all of it was far too much for her to explain here in the garden. Afraid that Auguste would leave before she could persuade him to see Cord, she tried once more.

"Please, monsieur, I beg of you: Talk to him. Explain to him why you sent him away. Wouldn't your Alyce have wanted you to?"

Auguste reached out and gently wiped a tear from her cheek. He stared down at her, his expression one of regret weighed down by resignation. Finally, he sighed.

"It won't be easy."

Celine smoothed her palms on her skirt and took a deep breath before she admitted, "No, it won't be an easy meeting. I'm afraid Cord will be shocked and furious. Perhaps it would be better if I were to tell him first."

"Not yet. I need to get some of my affairs in order. I'll contact you again, through Bobo if need be. Until then, please keep my existence a secret a while longer.''

Cord wanted no secrets between them and except for Jean Perot's murder, she had told him everything. Now, Auguste Moreau was asking her to compromise that trust.

''But I can't lie to him.''

''You need not lie, just don't say anything yet.''

''Isn't that the same as lying?''

''Please, Celine. Keep my existence a secret for three more days.''

He smiled a smile that had no doubt broken many hearts on many islands. It was Cord's smile, she realized again, if he would ever allow himself one. She found it impossible to refuse.

''Three days, then.''

He took her hand and kissed it, and then with a wave he left the garden. She watched him make his way down the path and through the trees.

Hoping to reach the house before the clouds overhead opened up, she turned onto one of the newly cleared footpaths. Suddenly Gunnie appeared out of nowhere, running frantically toward her. Celine was afraid the slave had seen Auguste, until she noticed Gunnie had what appeared to be Cordero's coat clutched in her hands.

''Missus got to come!''

''What's happened? What's wrong?''

The slave was trembling. She thrust the coat at Celine, her eyes huge. Celine stared down at the wadded white fabric. A wide, red bloodstain had soaked into it.

''Where is Cordero? Has he been hurt?''

Gunnie swallowed and pointed along the path behind Celine.

''Went to see about de new field pas' the trees. He

been hurt. Bleedin' bad. Bobo, he say you better come now.''

Celine clutched the coat, ignoring the blood that was blending with the mud and dirt on the front of her gown. Cord was hurt—possibly mortally wounded, if the amount of blood on the coat was any indication. There was no time to lose.

She followed Gunnie down the path, tripped once on a newly exposed root and fell down onto her hands and knees, then got up and started running again.

Gunnie led her deep into the undergrowth of the tropical forest. In the inmost, shadowed interior, all she could see of the woman was a flash of white blouse as she sprinted through the trees. Celine reached out, trying to protect herself from the lash of tangled vines and low-hanging branches. Rain-soaked ground gave way to thick, oozing mud that sucked at her shoes, slowing her progress.

''Gunnie!'' Celine shouted, afraid she would lose the girl in the dense thicket. ''I think we took a wrong turn. I don't see any sign of the cane fields.''

She wished she had paid closer attention to Cord when he'd said he would be clearing new fields. She tried to recall anything he might have told her that would help her find him. The path had narrowed to a foot trail that was fast disappearing into swampland. Celine was beginning to doubt Gunnie's ability to find the place again.

Green monkeys swooped through the trees, mocking her stumbling progress. Sweat smeared the dirt on her face, matted her straggling hair against the back of her neck. Thunder rolled over the mountain. She could hear rain on the canopy of leaves overhead, but the first scattered raindrops had not yet penetrated the dense green tangle.

"Gunnie! Wait!" She couldn't see the slave girl at all now. Celine plunged on, frustrated and frightened, her heart pounding in her throat. Head down, with her gaze focused on the mire at her feet, she was not aware of anything but reaching Cord's side.

When Celine chanced to glance up again, she screamed and stopped just short of running headlong into the obeah man. He was standing in front of a casuarina pine, his body as gnarled as the tree's trunk. His eyes were alight with a triumphant glow.

She had fallen into a carefully laid trap.

Cord's coat had grown heavy, soaked as it was now with rain, mud and blood. So much blood. She clutched it to her breast.

"Where is my husband? Have you killed him, or is it just me you want?"

Celine took a step back, prepared to run. She found her way blocked by Gunnie and a young male slave she did not recognize. The youth had a long hemp rope slung over his shoulders. Gunnie's eyes were still wide with fright. The girl's gaze shifted uncertainly between Celine and the obeah man as she fought to catch her breath.

Celine whipped around, unwilling to take her eyes off the witch doctor. He raised a bone rattle, shook it with one hand and threw dirt on her with the other. Celine couldn't understand a word he said as he began to utter what sounded like a chant.

Gunnie and the boy moved up behind her and grabbed her arms. The obeah man's voice rose as his chant became frantic and furious. She knew without being told that he was conjuring dark images, calling on his gods to curse her, to strip her of her power. To destroy her.

She fought in vain. Her captors ripped Cord's coat from her hands and threw it into the mud. Even that token, all that might be left of him, had been taken from her, she thought ruefully. On the old man's signal, the other two led her deeper into the swamp. He followed them, chanting. The bone rattle clacked. The monkeys above them shrieked.

The rain was coming down in gusts, chasing away the close, intense heat and making her almost cold. Her hair and clothes were stuck to her skin. Mud was caked to her shoes and ankles.

She stumbled and called Cord's name at the top of her lungs, refusing to give up even though she was too far from the house or the fields for anyone to hear. They reached the bottom of the gully, where the ground was an oozing bog. Celine staggered and nearly fell. The young slave jerked her to her feet. She glared up at him, but unlike Gunnie, who would not meet her gaze, the youth stared back, fiercely defiant.

The old man paused where huge wild mango trees stood grouped together. While he shouted orders and curses, the young man dragged Celine over to one of the trees and forced her up against the rough bark. She didn't dare let herself think of the insects nesting in the decaying wood and fruit at her feet.

Celine struggled futilely against the slave's strong hold. She tried to kick, to scratch, to bite, but could not gain purchase. His muscles were well-defined from long hours spent working the cane fields. He easily maneuvered to hold her and dodge her attempted blows.

Gunnie forced Celine's arms wide and slipped the knotted rope over one of her wrists. She walked behind the tree, grabbed Celine's other wrist and looped the rope over it, strapping her to the tree trunk. Pain seared

Celine's wrists and echoed through her shoulders. The rope cut into her whenever she tried to wrench her hands and arms free.

The obeah man walked around the tree, chanting. Celine felt him tug on the rope to make certain it was tight. She tried to kick him when he passed in front of her. The young man cursed her. Celine caught Gunnie's eye as the girl hovered nearby, and tried to plead for help.

"Gunnie. Don't do this. I'll see that nothing happens to you if you let me go. Please. Tell them it isn't too late. Tell them Cordero will deal harshly with them if anything happens to me. Please, Gunnie!"

Gunnie turned her back and walked away. The obeah man smiled.

Celine faced him defiantly. Rain streamed down her face, into her eyes, matting her lashes.

"You haven't won yet," she yelled. "I haven't escaped the hangman's noose to die here in the mud at your hands."

She spat at him and had the small satisfaction of seeing him nearly fall in the mud as he lunged back.

Gunnie and the youth had disappeared, swallowed up by the forest. Helpless to free herself, Celine watched the old man hurry after them, their footsteps nearly obliterated by the pounding rain. Even the monkeys had taken shelter.

She was alone, at the mercy of the elements and the creatures of the night.

Cord straightened and pushed away from the table that he had commandeered as a desk in a small storeroom at the back of the distillery. He reached up to rub the back of his neck and stretch his aching shoulders. Near his elbow sat a tray of untouched food, long forgotten until now that his empty stomach had grumbled in protest.

He reached for a cold chicken leg and absently began gnawing on it while he looked over his father's old accounts. Incredibly, nothing had been recorded since Auguste's last year here. Cord caught himself staring at his father's neat signature at the bottom of a column of figures. How different things would have been had his mother not died. He wondered what it would have been like to have been raised here.

He put down the chicken bone and rubbed his eyes. It did no good to try to imagine what might have been, a practice he had never ascribed to and wasn't about to start now. It was bad enough he had married a woman with not only her own memories, but everyone else's literally at her fingertips.

Cord glanced out a small window above the table. Thoughts of his tempting wife had interfered with his work all afternoon, so much so that he'd had to fight the urge to return to the house, to Celine.

The rain had begun over two hours ago. When the clouds had finally broken, spilling a deluge typical of autumn, the tension in the atmosphere had seemed to be dispelled. He wished the rain could wash away his own anxiety.

"Damn witch."

He shook his head. Celine had crept into his thoughts countless times already today, and just as many times he had tried to put the thoughts aside, without success. Pushing back from the table, he stood and walked to the open doorway.

A small governess' cart that must have been stored somewhere since his childhood came barreling into the mill yard, drawn by a swaybacked dapple gray nag. Foster was futilely trying to control the animal. On small bench seats facing one another, Edward and Ada clung to each other, trying without luck to stay sheltered beneath a scrap of an umbrella now decorated with only a few remnants of torn lace about the edge. It provided scant protection from the rain, and Ada and Edward were as soaked as Foster.

"What brings you all out on such a fine afternoon?" Cord called without leaving the shelter of the mill.

Foster pulled back on the reins, hollering, "Whoa there! Whoa! Whoa! Whoa!" His voice held no conviction, and the stubborn nag knew it.

Cord hurried across the muddy yard and grabbed the old mare's bridle. He stood there while the three occupants of the cart all tried to talk at once.

"At first we weren't concerned—" Ada began.

"But then it began to pour and I went lookin'," Foster took over. "I couldn't find 'er anywhere."

"I insisted that 'fore any more time was lost we come 'ere straightaway and find you because somethin' terrible might 'ave 'appened and probably did." Edward was moaning by the time he stopped talking.

Cord stepped up to the side of the vehicle. He held out his hand to Ada. "Come in out of the rain."

"We can't. Cordero, you must come with us right now. We can't lose another moment," she said, her jowls quivering as fast as her lips.

With a feeling that bordered on dread, he read the panic and distress that their soaked clothing and plastered hair and the blinding rain had kept him from seeing until now. The hair on the back of his neck stood up.

"What's going on?" He was already nearly soaked through himself.

Ada reached out for his hand and clung to it. Her

urgency and desperation quickly communicated itself to him.

"It's Celine—" Ada said before she promptly burst into heart-wrenching sobs.

"She's missing," Foster told him.

Edward shook his head woefully. "Been hours since we seen 'er in the garden and now we can't find her anywhere. Miss Celine's gone missing."

# Seventeen

"What in the hell do you mean she's *missing?*"

Cord's thoughts raced back to the night before, to Celine and Collin Ray and the scene he had witnessed. Ray had taken Celine's refusal badly. Had the man been desperate enough to return and take her against her will?

Or had Celine played him false? She'd had enough time to mull over Ray's proposal and to stew about the revelation of his visit to the whorehouse in Baytowne. Perhaps, Cord reasoned, she had decided to take Ray up on his offer and had found someone willing to take her to town.

"We ain't seen her since she went out to oversee work on the garden," Foster shouted over the pouring rain.

"I went to look for her myself," Ada cried as she clung to the umbrella handle, "but she was nowhere near the house. I can't find Gunnie either."

"When *exactly* did any of you see Celine last?" Cord demanded.

"After breakfast," Edward said.

"Just before dinner when I went to see if she was coming in from the garden to join Miss Ada," Foster recalled. "She said there was a bit more she wanted to do and then she'd be in. When she didn't come in, I thought she got carried away with 'er work, so I set aside a covered plate."

Ada erupted again. "But she never came in, you see, even after it started to rain. Oh, my poor, poor Celine!"

There was no controlling Ada; Cord didn't even try. Realizing that the four of them were standing in the downpour like idiots, he came to a decision.

"All of you go back to the house. She may have returned by now. If you wait much longer, the road will be impassable. I'll get Bobo and the dogs and go back to the garden and start from there."

Cord did not wait to see them off. He ran back to the distillery, where Bobo was supervising a crew in coating rum barrels with wax to keep the rum white while it aged. When he approached the overseer, Bobo gave Cord his full attention.

"My wife is missing." It was all Cord had to say.

Bobo dropped the bellows he was using to stoke the fire below the wax pot and nodded. He pointed to two of the men.

"Good trackers," he explained. "Goat hunters."

"Get the hounds, too." Cord had already started out of the mill. The men dropped what they were doing and hurried after him.

*   *   *

It was nearly dark. The fetid sweet smell of rotted mangoes and guava was cloying without the cover of rain. Celine, soaked to the skin, shivered uncontrollably as the evening breeze eddied through the snarled branches above her.

Without the rain, mosquitoes swarmed her exposed skin, mercilessly stinging, retreating, then stinging again. Her bound hands allowed her no way to protect herself. At sunset, a chorus of bullfrogs had begun, and their scolding had soon reached a maddening din. She wanted to scream, but feared that once she started, she would not stop.

Battling to retain her sanity, Celine worked against the bonds that held her imprisoned. She felt the warm dampness of her blood on her hands. Convinced no one would ever find her this deep in the swamp, she struggled, trying to get loose and make her way out. She made a vow to not stop fighting until she had lost every drop of blood.

Had anyone at the house even missed her yet? She had not returned to the house for the midday meal. Surely Foster or Edward would have noticed if Ada had not.

And what of Cord? How long would it be before he realized she was missing? Would he care?

She closed her eyes against the darkness that crept through the swamp like a fog, threatening to steal any hope of rescue. She lifted her face to the dark heavens, opened her eyes and strained to catch sight of even one star through the jungle boughs. Desperately, she searched for one point of light, something to hold onto, some hope. She found none.

So this was her punishment for killing Jean Perot, she suddenly thought.

She had escaped the hangman's noose, and now God had taken his own revenge. Celine shook her head, fighting off the twisted logic. She had killed in self-defense, not out of anger or evil. Would God still choose to punish her?

Perhaps she should not have tempted fate, should have stayed in New Orleans, turned herself in to the police—

But then she would never have met Cordero. Never have married him or come to St. Stephen. Never have made love with him . . .

Would she take it all back now, even if she could?

The image of Cordero's eyes came to her, those wounded eyes that had so often sought hers and then shied away, unwilling to reveal any emotion. She wanted to give him back his laughter, make him believe in living, in love. By offering him love, she had hoped to heal his wounded heart. But she had not even begun to come close.

She cried out at the injustice of it.

Chills shook her. Cord's bloody jacket was lying somewhere in the mud at her feet. Was he already dead? Had the obeah man brought down his revenge on all of them?

She itched all over. Countless mosquitoes plagued her. She was going mad from stings that she could not scratch. Then, just when she thought things could not get worse, she suddenly felt the horrifying tickle of a hundred spidery legs on her thigh.

In a flash of memory, she saw the glass coasters filled with water beneath the furniture legs.

"*A necessary precaution, dear. The centipedes are quite poisonous.*"

She began flailing and kicking, but the creature continued to climb her thigh.

She jerked again. A piercing, excruciating pain near her groin forced Celine to double over. When she lunged forward and strained at the rope, the movement tightened the bonds on her wrists. Intense pain radiated up each arm, but it was nothing compared to the burning injection of venomous poison the centipede released.

A scream tore its way out of her throat. Just as she had feared, she did not stop screaming until everything went black.

Trailing mud, Cord paced the stone floor of the kitchen, pounding back and forth, giving vent to anger stoked by fear and frustration. For three hours, he and Bobo, the trackers and a pack of worthless hounds had scoured the fields and forest near the house. The rain had wiped out any sign of a trail.

Thoroughly frustrated, Cord had given up the search long enough to talk to the others, sending Bobo to question the slaves at the same time.

Ada was near collapse but holding up far better than Cord had expected. Ever calm, Foster had advised both Ada and Edward to take seats at the worktable in the center of the kitchen. Lying forgotten on the table's wooden surface were the makings of supper—cold ham, salt fish, a basket of fruit, some sliced pineapple.

Howard Wells, a silent but concerned observer of the proceedings, reached out for a pineapple slice and began to nibble on it.

"Try to get ahold of yourself, Edward Lang," Foster snapped.

Edward had buried his face in the crook of his arm on the table. His shoulders heaved with sobs.

"She's lost to us now. There's no telling what 'appened to 'er. Whoever carried 'er away probably done 'er in by now. Poor little miss. It ain't fair. Just when she an' Cordero were startin' to make sompin' of—''

Suddenly he stopped and raised his head to see if Cord had been listening. He earned a dark glance to add to his misery.

"This ain't the time to give out with that kind o' talk," Foster warned. "No need upsettin' everybody more than necessary."

"But this is *so* upsetting. What happened to her?" Ada wailed.

"Maybe that high-and-mighty gent wot was 'ere last night decided not to take no for an answer," Edward suddenly hiccuped a heartfelt but dramatic sob.

"What's he saying? What does he mean?" Ada asked, drying her tears with the hem of her gray gown.

Foster comforted the woman with a pat on the back, then shot a warning glance at Edward, silencing him.

"Celine has a good head on her shoulders," Wells interjected. "I'm sure wherever she is, if indeed she is a captive of that unscrupulous Collin Ray, she is plotting an escape."

"Shut up. All of you. Please just shut up." They were driving Cord mad. He couldn't think—not that he dared let his thoughts flow in the sorry direction theirs had taken.

His attention was drawn to the sound of voices outside the open door.

Forced to stoop to enter the kitchen door, Bobo shoved a lanky young male in ahead of him. With one meaty hand around the back of the boy's neck, he thrust the youth at Cord. The quaking boy kept his gaze focused on the stone floor at his feet.

Bobo did not let go of the youth. "Obeah man took de mistress. He went missin' a few hours now. Nobody talkin' 'bout him, but dey say dis one be wid obeah man 'fore he go."

Cord walked over to the boy and stood so close that the tip of his heavy riding boots was a fraction of an inch from the slave's muddy, bare toes.

"What's your name?" Cord demanded.

"Philip." The boy's thin shoulders turned in on themselves.

"Tell us what you know, Philip, and I want the truth. I'll know if you are lying."

The young slave remained mute.

"I said talk." Cord stifled the urge to beat the truth out of him.

"I kin make him talk," Bobo promised.

The boy started trembling more violently. He glanced up at Cord, then over at the hulking giant beside him. He chose the coward's way out. "Obeah man took de woman to the swamp. Say she bad magic. Gotta stop. Me an' Gunnie go wid him. Gunnie, she run off to the hills wid obeah man. Dey lef' me here and not comin' back, I tink—"

Cord reached for the half-naked boy. His hands tightened on the slave's sweaty skin. Already trembling, his eyes wide with fear, the youth whimpered.

"Don' kill me," he begged, writhing beneath Cord's hands.

"Believe me, I'm tempted, but I need you to lead me to my wife. Do that and we'll see about letting you live."

"Too dark." The boy's fear of the swamp at night was greater than any fear he had of Cord. He tried to squirm out of his hold.

Bobo swatted the boy on the head.

"Take him and don't let him out of your sight. Get the trackers and the dogs. We're not coming back without her," Cord told Bobo.

He wanted hot coffee and a change of clothes, but opted for only coffee. Foster, who knew Cord's wishes before he could voice them, handed him a steaming cup. Grateful, Cord nodded and deeply inhaled the rich aromatic brew. It was laced with brandy.

"Thank you, Foster," he said softly. "You've always been too good to me."

Taken aback by Cord's unexpected words of appreciation, Foster cleared his throat and looked away.

"Aunt Ada, see that Celine's room is ready and that there is plenty of hot water. I'm sure she'll want nothing more than to bathe and get into clean sheets," Cord told her, refusing to imagine any other outcome but Celine's safe return.

Ada nodded, pulled herself together and with newfound purpose bustled out of the room. Howard Wells started after her, then paused in the doorway.

"I'll select some reading material for her," he volunteered.

"I'll go see about some lavender to sprinkle on the linens," Edward sniffed. His eyes were red-rimmed, his complexion blotched. He walked out of the room, shoulders sagging, steps measured.

Only Foster remained. He watched Cord swallow the last of the coffee.

"You'll find her, sir, and bring 'er 'ome safe."

"What makes you so sure?"

"The two of you were meant to be together, else Miss Celine would never have come to you. Sometimes no matter how we try to fight it, fate wills things another way.''

"Things could go another way tonight," Cord said, fighting to shrug off the heaviness around his heart, wishing he could call back every harsh thing he had ever said to Celine, hoping it wasn't too late. Wishing they could start over.

"You'll find her, sir," Foster said again.

Cord could not let himself consider the alternative.

He choked down fear with every step. Holding his pitch torch aloft, hacking at the jungle with a lethally sharp cane knife, Cord followed Bobo, Philip and the dogs. The trackers had refused to go any farther once the search had led them into the maze of swampland.

At the first mention of the swamp, alarm had jolted Cord. As a child he had been lost once in a swamp, and even though the experience had lasted for no more than two hours, and it had been daylight, it was an ordeal he would not wish on anyone. He hoped Celine's usual pluck held firm and that she believed he would find her.

Then he realized how absurd that hope was. When had he ever given her a reason to believe in him?

He had so carefully cultivated his isolation, spent so much time rigorously guarding his heart, convincing everyone, including Celine, that he cared about nothing and no one, it wouldn't have surprised him if she held out no hope at all of anyone ever finding her.

As he raised the pitch torch higher, he began to shake. This was no time for his knees to buckle, he told himself as he crashed through the dense undergrowth.

The air was close and dank with the smell of rotted fruit and all manner of decay. In the inky darkness, the insects were unrelenting. Cord tried to speculate on how much protection Celine's clothing might afford her. He had not even seen her since he had so coldly bid her good night the evening before, so he had no notion of what she might have on.

There was a shout from Bobo, and a moment later the hounds sent up earsplitting howls. In his haste, Cord nearly tripped and fell headlong into the muck. They had paused in an almost undetectable clearing in the swamp. Illuminated by the glow of torchlight, bound to the trunk of a wild mango tree with her arms extended, Celine slumped forward. Her head hung down nearly to her waist. The ends of her long hair trailed in watery mud so deep her feet and shoes were buried.

Bobo was hesitant to approach her. Cord handed his torch to the man and waded over to Celine. His hands shook as he reached for her, searching for some sign of life.

His fingers connected with her skin. She was as cold as death, clammy. He pressed his fingertips gently against her throat and found a weak, thready pulse. A surge of relief almost brought him to his knees.

"Cut her down," he commanded Bobo.

The giant shoved the torch into the mud and stepped behind the tree, then sliced the rope with his cane knife. As Celine fell forward into Cord's arms, Bobo came around and started to lift her.

"She's my wife—I'll carry her," Cord said, tightening his hold.

"Should I kill him?" Bobo asked a moment later.

Cord looked over his shoulder. Bobo had his cane knife pressed up against the boy's thin neck. Philip sobbed silently, his eyes as wide as gold pieces.

Cord gave the boy a long hard look, considering Bobo's suggestion. Near death, Celine lay limp in his arms. It would be so easy to pronounce judgment on the boy, he thought, fully aware that most planters would not have hesitated to hang him. It was well within his rights to mete out justice on the plantation, but as he stared over at the quaking youth, Cord knew that snuffing out Philip's life would not save Celine's. Only God's mercy could do that.

And he was in no position to rankle God.

"Bring him with us," Cord commanded over his shoulder as he headed back. The boy broke down with relief and babbled deliriously.

Bobo's long strides soon led him past Cord. He held his torch aloft, lighting the way for Cord as they wound their way back along the newly cut path.

She was dying and she knew it. She was on fire. She was in hell. She was racked with chills.

Celine tried to speak, to cry out against the blinding pain that rippled through her in waves. She would welcome death. Anything. Anything would be better than this.

She felt as if she were moving, drifting through the dark swamp. Where were the stars? Even when she had been so miserable at sea, there had been stars to follow. Now there was only darkness.

She let her thoughts drift away from the pain, let herself settle into the warm arms that she imagined held her. Against the blinding red pain behind her eyes she saw New Orleans, the streets, St. Louis Cathedral, the marketplace. Old Marcel, the vegetable vendor. She silently thanked him for his smile.

Persa. Persa was there. Waiting in the little cottage on

rue de St. Ann. Waiting for her. Smiling. Extending her hand in welcome.

Persa would take care of her. She always had. Persa, who'd told her that her dreams of finding one true love were foolish daydreams. Persa had tried to teach her it was enough to be different. To have a gift. To hold love in her heart. She should have listened.

"Hold on, Celine. We're almost home."

Cord's voice came to her through the pain, found her through the red haze. She wanted to beg him to let her go. The pain was too great.

Cord, who had so much left to learn about life and love and laughter. There was so much she'd wanted to do to help him. Alyce's gardens were not finished. The old house demanded new life.

And there was Foster. Edward. Aunt Ada.

She had stepped into Jemma O'Hurley's life and out of her own. All she had ever dreamed of was so close, and yet so far. Given time she might have been able to convince her husband that there was room in his heart for love. For her.

But time had run out.


Cradling Celine in his arms, Cord tore across the veranda, kicked open the door and started up the stairs. Ada met him at the top of the stairs and led the way to Celine's room.

"We'll need hot water, Aunt," he shouted over his shoulder as he headed down the hall.

"Foster and Edward have everything ready. They heard you yelling up the drive. I'm certain the entire island heard you—"

"Pull the spread and sheet back." He hovered in the doorway with Celine in his arms, anxious to make her more comfortable, to wash the mud off her and do what he could to fight the fever raging through her. As he gently laid her in the center of the bed, Foster and Edward arrived with pitchers of hot water and clean rags.

Cord set to work, directing Ada and the others, admonishing his aunt when her trembling fingers were not moving fast enough to suit him. Instead of falling apart, Ada proved far more capable than he would have guessed. She sent the servants from the room and helped Cord strip off Celine's ruined clothing.

"Damn it," Cord swore when he saw the welts covering Celine's skin. He wanted to weep for her, but there was no time. She was burning up with fever.

Together he and Ada sponged the mud and dirt off Celine, who remained unconscious throughout their ministrations. As Cord lifted her bare arm, as he ran one damp rag after another over her lifeless limbs, he swore under his breath. He was cursed, he decided. Anyone who dared to care for him was doomed. His mother. Alex. His father. And now Celine stood at death's door, with one hand on the knocker.

"Cordero, dear, you really must do something about your language. What would Celine do if she were to awaken and hear such a vulgar tirade?"

*She would still love me.*

The words had come unbidden to his mind. Cord did not bother to answer. He continued to swab Celine's skin, making note of each red welt on her body. "We need camphor oil for these bites, Aunt."

"Quinine," Ada said. "A dose of quinine for the swamp fever. And ammonia. Ammonia mixed with sulfuric ether. We must bathe her scalp." Ada stepped back, crossed her arms over her waist and shook her head. "All that beautiful hair. It will have to go."

Cord closed his eyes and took a deep breath.

"Aunt, go find Foster. Give him the medications you've mentioned and send him up." Foster would work in silence, Cord thought; Foster would never dare suggest cutting Celine's hair.

At the mention of his name, Foster stepped into the room.

"Are you a permanent fixture outside my wife's door?" Cord did not bother to turn around.

"No, sir. Just when the occasion warrants."

Both men remained silent until Ada left to find the medications. Cord had discarded the dirty rags, wrapped Celine in a clean sheet and spread her hair out on the pillows. She was as pale as moonlight.

"Poor miss." Foster sighed.

"She's going to live, Foster." Cord clung to her hand.

"I've no doubt of that, sir."

"You don't look it. I'll not have any long faces at her bedside."

"Speaking of bedsides, might I suggest you move her into *your* suite, sir? It's more fittin'. The ventilation's better and the furnishin's more comfortable. That way, should you wish to stay with her—"

"I *am* staying with her."

"—there will be ample room for you to stretch out on the bed and rest without bothering her."

Foster waited for Cord to make a decision. It took all of half a second. Celine was once more nestled in the crook of his arm as Cord gently carried her into the master suite.

Cord sat beside her throughout the night and long into the next day while the others came and went on silent feet. Ada left covered dishes and took them away again untouched. At one point she drew the draperies tight, insisting dim light was best; Foster appeared an hour later, opened the draperies and threw the windows wide, declaring that Miss Celine needed healing ventilation and a sea breeze.

Because all he did was sob, Edward was not allowed in the room.

And so Cord sat alone with Celine hour upon hour. Sat alone and dealt with all his anxieties. Sat alone with his memories of the past and his fears of the bleak, endless stretch of tomorrows he would face if Celine were to die. He clung to her hand as if his will alone would save her; clung to her as he would have to Alex, had he been able to; clung to her as he might have to his mother on the night of the carriage accident, had he only known.

He ached with the ache of a man whose love had been locked inside for so long that the pain of letting it out was as great as having a limb torn off. He ached and he swore and he cursed and then out of fear he even begged God's forgiveness and made a chain of promises a saint would not have been able to keep, if only Celine's life might be spared.

It had been years since he had entered a church, aeons since he had recited the prayers his grandfather and the priest had insisted he memorize. They came back to him as he sat alone in the dark with his head in his hands. Every word of every prayer, a litany of supplication and penance.

Celine had asked nothing of him, and yet she had offered him a gift beyond the price of a rich merchant's dowry. She offered him a lifetime of commitment and a love he had been too stubborn to even acknowledge, let alone accept.

It would be his privilege to have it now, he decided. And to return it. In a hushed, broken whisper he promised her he would try to return that love, pledged that if she gave him the chance he would do everything in his power to learn to love again.

She began to toss and turn again, tearing at the bedclothes, mumbling in her delirium. He left his chair, brushed aside the mosquito net and sat beside her. He clasped both her hands tight and held on.

"Celine, can you hear me?"

"Persa's dead," she whispered. Her head thrashed back and forth against the pillow. "Sorry. Should have known. Should have tried to save. . . . Had to run. Run."

"Shh." Cord brushed the damp tendrils of hair off her forehead. "Wake up, Celine. You're safe. You're on St. Stephen."

"Cord . . ." She began to shake with the chills again. "Hates me. Doesn't want a wife. No wife. The wrong one. I lied . . . Thinks I . . . stole his memories."

Too well he understood her rambling delirium, and it broke his heart, the heart he'd thought no longer existed, until Celine.

"Celine. Shh. You are the one. The right one. The only one. Please, forgive me. Forget what I said. Take my memories, you can have them. Help me make new ones. Just don't leave me."

He took her in his arms and stretched out beside her. Her teeth were chattering.

"Cord . . ." Her voice carried to him on barely a whisper.

"I'm right here." He could barely utter the words. His throat was closing up, welling with sorrow. She was leaving him. Like Alex. Like his mother and father. Abandoning him.

He hugged her close, pressed his face against her hair and let go all the tears he'd held back for so long. His shoulders shook with the force of his sobs.

And still he held her.

# Eighteen

The air was close and stuffy, the light dim. Celine gazed around the room, disoriented. She had expected to awaken in the cottage shop in New Orleans, but everything in the room surrounding her was unfamiliar. Filmy mosquito net enveloped the bed like an ecru fog. Rain pelted the roof.

She stared up at the hook that held the gathered net and tried to bring to mind memory of how she came to be lying here in this strange bed. She tried to sit up, only to discover she did not have the strength to do more than turn her head.

The instant she laid eyes on the man at her bedside, her heart fluttered and memory came flooding back.

Cordero:

He was still alive and apparently, so was she.

He was half draped across the edge of the bed, his head cradled on his folded arms. She could tell by the even rise and fall of his back that he was sound asleep.

She managed to raise her hand and reached out to touch him. She let her fingertips trail down the gauzy mosquito net and sighed. They were separated by far more than the lacy web.

As if aware of her return to consciousness, Cord lifted his head. He found Celine staring back at him, her huge eyes luminous in her pale face.

Relief welled up from the depth of his soul. His heart sang with exultation. There was so much he had to say, so many places to begin, but when he finally collected himself enough to speak, all he could manage was, "You're alive."

"So are you." Her voice was no more than a whisper. "Where am I?"

"In my room."

He smiled, then found the overlapping edges of the net and brushed it aside, reached in and took one of her hands in both of his. She closed her eyes and absorbed his warmth, let his strength radiate through her.

"I thought I was dying."

"I thought you might."

"You look terrible," she said, taking in the shadowed growth that covered his jaw. "Almost as bad as I feel."

She wondered at the changes in him. His face looked gaunt. Deep shadows and new lines were etched beneath his eyes. There was a puffiness she had not seen there before, even after he had been drinking heavily. He acted afraid to take his eyes off her.

She did not mind, for in his gaze she saw a vibrant warmth and newly kindled light.

Cord needed more than to touch her hand. He left his

chair to sit beside her. The bed ropes creaked with his additional weight. Fighting the urge to gather her in his arms and hold her, as he had done for so many hours over the past four days, he contented himself with reaching out to brush some hair off her forehead.

"How did you find me?" Needing to touch him, she reached for his hands, found them both.

"Ada, Foster and Edward set up a hue and cry. Bobo got the boy, Philip, to confess that he helped lure you away."

"The obeah man—"

"Has disappeared. He and Gunnie have slipped off into the interior of the island. They can't hope to hide forever, but I want you to rest assured, you'll be safe, Celine."

"Gunnie came to me with one of your coats. It was covered with blood. I should have never gone with her, but I thought—"

"You believed exactly what they wanted you to believe . . . that I was hurt."

"That you were dying."

He looked away. She watched him take a deep breath, saw his jaw tighten, his dark winged brows draw toward each other. He was struggling with far more than words. Her heart began to pound.

"Cord?" She squeezed his hands, willing him to speak with all the strength she could muster.

He swallowed hard. Her grip felt painfully weak, but he knew the depth of her stubborn will. She was waiting for him to say something, anything. He'd had four long days and nights to think about all the things he would tell her if given one more chance, and now that he'd been given that chance, the words were lodged in his throat.

"It's stuffy in here," he finally said. Cord let go of her hands and stood up. He saw the disappointment in her eyes, and still he couldn't speak. He had faced his fears, but was still a coward when it came to putting his feelings into words.

He raked his fingers through his hair and walked over to the windows. Ada had been the last one in to monitor the state of the room. It was dim and still. He opened the curtains and then the veranda doors. Mist from the falling rain eddied in on a draft. He stared out at the rain that streamed in crystal threads from the roofline until he had control of his emotions again.

A pitcher of tepid water sat on the chest of drawers near the bed. He filled a glass and gave it to her. Her hand trembled so that he sat down beside her again and held the rim to her lips.

"Are you hungry?" he asked, watching her slowly sip the water. Her eyes were huge.

When she finished, she nodded. "A little."

"I'll tell Foster to send something up. He's either lurking just behind the door or seeing to Edward."

"Nothing's happened to Edward, has it?"

"He's been unable to cope ever since your disappearance. Ada has thrown herself into training a new cook—that and crying on Howard Wells's shoulder. There has been a steady stream of trays coming and going and all manner of reading material is piled up for you to read while you recover."

"You don't look as if you've eaten much."

He didn't comment. Instead he opened the door, expecting to find Foster there, but for once the long hallway was deserted. There was usually more than one member of the household hovering just outside for word of Celine's progress.

Cord yanked the bellpull three times and then scratched the stubble on his jaw as he walked back to the bed. Celine's eyes were closed. Beneath the bedclothes her breasts rose and fell in a rhythmic, even motion. Sleep would heal her more than anything else, he knew. The relief he'd experienced when she awakened had left him staggered. Cord wanted nothing more than to crawl into bed beside his wife and sleep the first real sleep he would have had in days.

Instead, he carefully drew the edges of the mosquito net together and sat down on the chair beside the bed. He stretched out his legs and closed his eyes.

He didn't know if he'd slept for a few moments or an hour, but when he awoke to find Foster standing over him, the rain had finally stopped.

"Has she . . . Is she . . ." Foster was staring down at Celine.

"She was awake a few minutes ago. Maybe you can get my aunt to make some soup—nothing heavy; nothing too spicy."

"I'll try."

Cord expected Foster to rush off, but he lingered near Celine's bedside, fidgeting with the top button of his vest.

"She's going to be fine, Foster," Cord tried to reassure him, but the servant's gaze darted about the room like a sparrow afraid to land.

"Is there something wrong?" Cord asked him.

Foster opened his mouth and closed it again. He tugged on his cuffs, first one and then the other. He stared at his feet and lined the toes of his shoes even with one another. He cleared his throat.

"Celine could starve waiting for the soup," Cord

said. Foster had definitely paled. "What in the hell is going on?"

"I don't know how to tell you this, sir, but—" Foster's frenetic gaze snapped to the open door.

Cord followed his servant's gaze. His breath caught in his throat when he saw his father framed in the doorway. For a split second he thought he had developed Ada's ability to see ghosts, but as Auguste Moreau stepped into the room, Cord knew this was no ghost, but the man he thought had died fifteen years ago. The man who had not wanted him around.

Cord shot to his feet.

"Get out!" Fury whipped through him. He would have recognized his father anywhere. Except for a few silver hairs threaded through the glossy ebony at his temples and creases around his mouth and eye, the man was unchanged. Still tall and straight, impeccably dressed in black and white, he was a commanding figure with the ability to fill a room with his very presence. The leather eye patch did not detract from his appearance, but rather added a touch of drama to it.

"I'm not leaving until I've had my say."

Auguste glanced over at the bed. Cord watched his father's face soften as without pause he walked to Celine's bedside. It was another shock to stand idly by and watch his wife smile up at his father as Auguste reached out, took Celine's hand and kissed it.

"I'm so thankful to find you recovering," Auguste told her.

"Thank you," Celine said softly.

"Get away from my wife. Get out!" Cord exploded.

"Cord . . . ," Celine whispered.

She tried to appeal to him, but he refused to listen. It had been enough of a shock to see his father alive without discovering his wife was already acquainted with the man.

"I have nothing to say to you. Before you walked through that door you were dead to me. I'd like to keep it that way," Cord told Auguste.

"I can understand your feelings. It wasn't easy to come here today, but concern for your lovely wife, as well as the need to say what should have been said long ago, has brought me here."

"Do you think I care how hard this is on you? I don't want to hear anything you have to say—"

"Cord, please listen to him." Celine was barely audible over the loud exchange.

"Gentlemen," Foster put in, "might I suggest you take yourselves out o' here? Miss Celine ain't up to this."

"I will wait for you downstairs, Cordero." Auguste bowed once more to Celine, nodded at his son and then left the room, with Foster dogging his heels.

Concern for Celine's fragile health overrode Cord's anger for the moment. As pale as the lace-edged pillowcase, she had closed her eyes again. When he stepped up to the bedside, she opened them slowly and stared up at him.

"How long have you known him?" he demanded.

"How long have I been ill?"

"Four days."

"I met him the day I was kidnapped. He came to me in the garden."

"I thought there were to be no more secrets . . ."

"I tried to convince him to go directly to see you. He said no, and when I told him I was going to tell you about him, he made me promise to wait three days.

Cord, I gave him my word, but I swear I would have told you.''

"We'll never know now, will we?''

He could see she was exhausted. The long battle she'd waged against death had been hard won. He would not argue with her now, would not risk her life again.

"Foster is getting you something to eat. It shouldn't take long.'' As he drew the chair close to the bed, he hoped his aunt was not experimenting with the broth.

"Go see your father, Cordero. He's waiting. Ada can sit with me. I would love to wash my face and comb my hair, and she can help.''

He didn't move.

"Please. Go to him. Hear him out at least.''

"Why should I?''

"Because your heart will never heal until you do.''

He stared down at her long and hard and weighed the truth of her words. Over four days, while she lay feverish, he had battled his demons. He had hoped the hurt and anger was behind him, but when he'd had the opportunity to tell her that he had found the courage to admit he'd fallen in love with her, he could not find the words. The appearance of his father and his reaction to it had proved that his heart was still bleeding from an old wound.

*Your heart will never heal until you do.*

"Go, Cord,'' she urged. "Hear him out.''

He did it for her.

He left Celine in Ada's care, although his aunt had apparently been so shocked by Auguste's appearance that Cord wondered who would be caring for whom.

His father waited in the parlor, seated on a settee upholstered in gold brocade now worn threadbare on the seat. When Cord joined him, Auguste was already holding a crystal snifter of brandy, lost in thought. Foster stood beside a tea cart crowded with decanters. He poured Cord a liberal amount of brandy.

"Nothing for me, thank you, Foster. You may leave."

Cord had made many promises the night he almost lost Celine, and now was not the time to go back on them. Once he refused the drink, it did not seem much of a sacrifice. After all, he never had drank because he needed to, but because he wanted to.

He walked over to the portrait of his mother above the mantel and stood beneath it. Captured in oil on canvas, Alyce's likeness was forever suspended in time, a one-dimensional memory of a vibrant, lovely young woman. When Cord finally summoned the courage to face his father, he found Auguste staring up at the likeness.

"She was a beautiful woman," Auguste said.

Cord remained silent. His father had demanded this meeting, he said to himself; let him talk.

Auguste took another drink. "As beautiful as your wife, but fair instead of dark. How is Celine?"

"Resting. She's no concern of yours."

"She is the reason I am here. When we met, she begged me to see you, to break my silence."

"She is quite the nag." Cord almost smiled at the old jest, so very thankful that he could make it again. But the moment was far too serious for more than half a smile.

"How is your grandfather?" Auguste asked.

"Heartless, when I saw him last."

"He had a heart years ago, when I was a boy. I suppose I broke it when I didn't live up to his expectations."

"I was forced to suffer for that." Cord leaned his shoulder into the mantel.

"That is what Celine told me. Cordero, if I had even suspected that he would take out his hatred for me on you, I would have never sent you to Louisiana," Auguste said.

"He tried to make certain I didn't turn out like you—a wastrel, a ne'er-do-well . . . a drunkard. He said he was ashamed of you, a man with no more ambition than to live on a paltry plot of worthless land you gained through marriage."

He could still hear his grandfather's voice as he berated Auguste over and over, a repetitive chant that never ceased.

"There was no way he would have ever turned the responsibility of the family plantation over to me while he was alive. I knew if I was to survive at all, I had to leave. I ended up here on St. Stephen and fell in love with your mother," Auguste said.

"And killed her with your drinking."

"Believe me, I hated myself as much as you did after the accident."

Cord walked over to the settee. He stood there staring down at Auguste, fists clenched, throat working as he tried to voice his thoughts. Finally he took a deep breath and everything he had stored in his heart and mind for years rushed out. The words came fast and furious. He felt as if he were about to shatter into shards and fly apart, but he could not stop.

"I didn't hate you then. I needed you. I had just lost my mother, damn you, and needed a father—it didn't matter that you were a drunkard. It didn't matter what you were. *I needed you.* And you sent me away.

"You sent me off to live with a coldhearted bastard

who thought nothing of having me whipped with a switch for the slightest infraction. He tried to humiliate me by having a slave perform the task—''

''Cordero, I couldn't have known—''

''You didn't try to find out, either. You shipped me off and never looked back.''

''I never forgot you. Not for one moment.'' Auguste raised both hands, pleading with Cord to understand. ''When your mother was lost to me, I wanted to die. I tried to kill myself . . .''

''Perhaps you should have tried harder.''

''I waited until you were gone. I left the island in that little sailboat you and your mother enjoyed so. I took no food, no water. When I was out to sea I shredded the sail. I was ready to die, and almost did, but through a twist of fate I was rescued by an old pirate. I changed my name to Roger Reynolds and became a privateer. From then on, Auguste Moreau ceased to exist. I put myself in danger, day after day. During the war, I worked for both sides. I thought surely death would be kind and I would be blown apart on one of my ships, but still I survived.''

''I'm your son, and you even let *me* believe you were dead.'' Cord pinned him with a cold stare. He had cried too many tears as a child to shed even one now.

''I wanted you to inherit my portion of the Moreau Plantation. Along with your mother's holdings here, it would have made you a very wealthy man.''

Cord laughed. ''The price was too high. I'm afraid that I have fulfilled grandfather's expectation. Much like you, I walked out on the Moreau inheritance.''

''So my brother's son, Alexandre, will inherit it all?''

''Alex is dead.''

''Dead? He was not much older than you.'' His shock

was evident. Auguste set the snifter aside and rose.

"Alex died for me. In my stead." Cord turned around so that his father would not see the swift stab of pain that had hit him.

"I was intent upon carrying on your reputation. One night I was too drunk to fulfill a challenge I had accepted. Alex went to the duel in my place. He had become like a brother to me. And he died for me."

"I only wanted what was best for you—"

"But you didn't want *me*!" Cord's voice faltered.

There was no sound in the room except for that of the rain falling outside and the whisper of wind through the palm fronds. Cord stood with his back to his father, stiffly staring out the window, wishing away the moment, longing to get back to Celine. Unable to move.

"Cordero."

There was no command, no demand in Auguste's tone, and yet Cord felt compelled to turn around and look at his father.

What he saw was what he had never thought to see again in this life. Auguste stood with his arms open and welcoming, ready to take Cord into them again, to hold him as he had done so long ago.

Cord looked across the room at his father. He did not want to forgive. He did not want to give in to the driving need for his father's embrace. But something stronger than hatred compelled him to take the first step. Something greater than injustices suffered at the hands of a hateful old man made him take the second.

Something he'd learned from Celine had made him start to close the distance between them.

Auguste met him halfway. Cord stepped into his father's arms. He stood there stiffly, hands clinched into fists, arms at his sides, unfamiliar and not quite sure how he'd even come to be there. Auguste held him tight.

Cord slowly opened his hands, raised his arms and hugged him back.

# Nineteen

"**I** think it's cut too low."

Celine stood poised in the middle of the master suite modeling an aquamarine ball gown with a scooped neckline. She felt was far too revealing, but Foster had declared it perfection. Her breasts were even further emphasized by the fashionable high waist set off with a matching satin ribbon.

"I think it's perfect," Edward said. "She's still too thin, but 'er color is better, don't you think, Fos?"

"Much better," said Foster. "She ain't that hideous yellow shade anymore."

"Let's not speak of that. I can't take it." Edward pressed his fingers to the bridge of his nose and made Foster promise not to mention Celine's illness ever again.

"Is everything ready downstairs?" Celine was more than uncomfortable with the attention.

"Very," Foster said. "Miss Ada has seen to it the new cook has everything in hand in the kitchen."

Edward commenced grumbling. "Don't see 'ow Miss Ada has time to do anything with Mr. Wells hangin' on her every word an' doggin' her steps like a 'omeless puppy."

"Lovesick is what he is." Foster reached out to tweak Celine's silk sleeve. "I still think we should've added some seed pearls 'ere and there."

"Trust me," Edward told him.

"When can I go downstairs? I don't think it's fair to make me wait any longer." Celine shifted from foot to foot, bursting with anticipation.

In honor of her recovery and to celebrate the end of planting season, Ada had insisted the occupants of Dunstain Place hold a gala soiree. Much to Celine's surprise, even Cord had agreed to the festivities—which included dinner and dancing—so long as Celine took no part in the preparations.

Aside from listening while Ada recited recipe after recipe for the menu, then agreeing to a fitting so that Jemma O'Hurley's formal gown could be altered, Celine did nothing but read, rest and recover.

Now, nearly four weeks to the day of her kidnapping, the evening of the celebration was at hand.

"It won't be but a few moments longer. Will it, Edward?" Foster nudged his fellow servant and the two exchanged knowing looks.

"What are you up to?" Celine asked.

Foster's glance shot to Edward. Both men shrugged.

"You look just like a princess," Edward said. "That's all you need to know, miss."

With a thank-you and a smile she couldn't hide, Celine watched them exit. Once the door closed behind them, curiosity got the best of her and she walked over to the oval mirror on a stand in the corner. As she gazed at the image in the simple but elegant dress the color of the Caribbean sea, she felt almost as if she were staring at a stranger.

For the past few weeks, she had been living her dream—or so it would have seemed to anyone who didn't know the most intimate details of her life. Cord had been attentive and solicitous all through her recovery, and had seen to it that the others pampered her as well, until she felt as fragile as a bisque doll.

Giving her the master bedroom, he had moved into her former room next door so that she could—as he'd put it with a smile—recover without his making a nuisance of himself. Although they did not occupy the same room, he sat at her bedside each morning and outlined his plans for the day. In the evenings they shared meals in private while he kept up a steady stream of conversation and told her all he had accomplished.

He spoke of fallow fields and sugarcane, of terracing hillsides so that they might increase the amount of sugar planted next season. He told her about the antics of the children in the village and praised Bobo's many skills. He was aware now of the part his father's man had played in keeping Dunstain Place running and admired Bobo's unfailing loyalty to Auguste Moreau.

Cord even related to her a few details of his somewhat tentative reconciliation with his father. He drank moderately, just a glass or two of wine with dinner. He talked of everything and nothing to keep her entertained. He smiled. On occasion he even laughed.

And he did not touch her intimately at all.

Celine sighed and turned away from the woman in the mirror, a woman who, on the surface, appeared to be young, carefree and happily married. No one would have guessed that she had spent the last few weeks yearning for the feel of her husband's strong arms around her, longing to have him make love to her again.

In subtle and not so subtle ways she had tried to hint that she was fully recovered from the swamp fever, but he'd ignored her every cue. Tonight she was determined to do more than play hostess to the few planters and their wives who lived near Dunstain Place and had accepted the invitation to celebrate. She was determined to change things between her and Cord.

A swift knock at the door pulled her away from her thoughts. She smoothed the soft drapes of her skirt.

"Come in," she called out, half expecting Ada. She was surprised to see Cord walk in and shut the door behind him.

He was so tall, so handsome, so elegantly attired in a black coat and trousers with a froth of lace down the front of his shirt, that the sight of him nearly took her breath away. For a moment she was light-headed and her heart began to race.

"Are you all right? Do you need to sit down?" Cord had taken her by the arm and had her halfway to a cozy sitting area near the long windows before she could convince him that she was fine.

"What is it then?" His forehead was creased by a deep frown.

"You look . . . stunning," she told him.

"Stunning?" At a loss for words, he blinked twice.

"Yes. Very." She reached up to arrange the starched lace ruffles that somehow made him look all the more masculine, and caught him smiling down at her.

"Stunning." He sounded as if he thought the idea absurd.

"Would you like me to say it again?"

"Not unless you are fishing for compliments yourself and want me to feel obliged to give one."

She could tell he was teasing. It was a whole new side of her husband she had come to treasure.

"I am not fishing for a compliment and you know it."

"I forgot. Your forte is nagging."

"In that case, what do you think?" She twirled around so that he could see her gown from all sides.

"You'll do." He shoved his hand into his coat pocket.

"I'll *do*?"

"You'll do quite well. In fact, you don't even need these to make you more beautiful, but I was told to give them to you." Slowly, inch by inch, he drew a string of fat, lustrous, evenly matched pearls out of his pocket and dangled them before her eyes.

"Where did you get them?" She had never seen, let alone imagined ever owning, anything so elegant.

"My father sent them over. He had given all my mother's jewelry to the solicitor for safekeeping and had these delivered. He said to tell you that since he couldn't be here tonight, he wanted you to have these with his sincere best wishes and apologies for having to miss the celebration. Playing dead has its limitations."

He stepped behind her and placed the pearls around her neck. Celine closed her eyes, tempted to lean back against him as he worked the clasp. When he finished, she felt his palms rest on her bare shoulders for a few, too brief seconds before he lifted his hands and moved away.

She reached up to finger the pearls. When their eyes

met and held, she instantly recognized the spark of longing in his. Certain he was about to kiss her, she leaned toward him, then felt him begin to ease toward her.

The door opened with such force it banged against the wall. Edward and Foster toppled into the room and landed in a heap of linen and a tangle of arms and legs.

''I told you not to lean on me so hard,'' Foster said, scrambling up and offering Edward a hand.

''I thought you'd 'ave the good sense to see that the door was closed right an' tight,'' Edward complained.

Cord cleared his throat and the two men suddenly remembered where they were.

''We're sorry, sir. Just wanted to see if she liked the pearls.'' Foster had the good grace to look sheepish.

''Next time just knock.'' Cord turned to Celine. ''It would be nice to have a little privacy around here.''

The servants couldn't clear out fast enough. They stumbled over each other trying to get through the bedroom door, in their haste leaving it wide open.

''I suppose we should go down. The guests will be arriving anytime now.'' Cord offered her his arm.

''I must thank your father for the pearls,'' she said as she slipped her hand into the crook of his arm. She gave him a squeeze and smiled up at him, knowing her heart was in her eyes. She hoped he saw it there.

As Cord looked down into his wife's radiant, upturned face, he was tempted to slam the door shut, lock it and throw away the key. He had grown hard and as randy as a billy goat just looking into her eyes. Beneath the milky strand of pearls that glowed like moonlit orbs, her firm, tempting breasts rose and fell with her every breath. He would have kissed her then and there, but he knew that if he did he would never want to go downstairs to the party.

In that instant he decided that tonight he would move back into his own room and give up sleeping alone, even if she was not up to doing anything but having him hold her through the night.

They left the room and headed down the hall, the heels of their dress shoes tapping out a lively cadence as they walked briskly along. When they started down the long staircase, Cord took a deep breath. His heart was hammering like a carpenter gone mad. He leaned toward her until he was close enough to brush her ear with his lips.

"I love you, Celine."

The words were out before he realized he was even going to say them.

She was so startled by his admission that she missed a step and would have tumbled down the stairs if he hadn't grabbed her. He brought her up full against him. They were poised in the middle of the open staircase.

"Say it again," she whispered against the lips that hovered so close to her own.

"Nag." He hesitated but a moment more before he repeated the words she had waited so long to hear. "I love you."

"Kiss me." She stood on tiptoe, balancing precariously, knowing he would never let her fall.

"You nag me incessantly, wife."

"Then do it, husband."

He did, with all the enthusiasm and demand of a man in great need of release. Cord drank in the taste of her, the feel of her, the scent of jasmine in her hair. He kissed her without reservation, without any fear that she might violate his trust and sneak a glimpse of his memories.

She kissed him with a light heart, ecstatic that he had finally accepted the love she had to offer and had even gone so far as to present her with the precious gift of his own.

When Cord raised his head, he stole one more quick kiss on her lips and then placed another on her cheek. A round of applause and laughter swelled in the stairwell, and Celine buried her face against his ruffled shirtfront. Cord kept an arm around her as he saluted the small gathering at the foot of the stairs.

Ada and Howard Wells stood beside one another like two mismatched bookends, one plump as a muffin and the other thin as a string bean. The two couples who had arrived did not seem at all offended that their host and hostess had chosen to put on such a display. Edward and Foster held trays of champagne and at the same time beamed up at them as if the entire episode had been their idea.

"We have to go down and face the music," Cord said, prying Celine away from him.

She groaned audibly. "You made me forget myself."

"Obviously you have succeeded in making me forget everything but what matters most, Celine."

"If I have done that, then I am happy." Celine smiled to herself. Persa had always said that to teach one to love is the greatest of gifts.

By the time they reached the foot of the stairs, everyone had gathered around. Cord took a glass of champagne off the tray and handed it to Celine, then took one for himself.

"To my wife," he said, raising his glass in salute.

"To my husband," she echoed, watching him over the rim of her glass.

"To us all!" Ada shouted with champagne-inspired enthusiasm. She lifted her glass so high that one of the gussets under her sleeve ripped.

Before anyone could finish off the first glass of champagne, Bobo came striding through the front door. A hush fell over the crowd. Cord handed Foster his glass and stepped past Celine. He could tell by the look on his manager's face that the tidings were grim. They went outside to speak in private.

Celine was determined not to be left out. She, too, handed her glass to Foster, then apologized to the waiting guests, picked up her skirt and hurried after the two men. By the time she reached the side veranda, she could hear Cord speaking in hushed tones.

"Where are they?" she heard Cord ask Bobo.

"What is it?" Celine moved up behind him and reached for his hand.

"Nothing that concerns you. Why don't you go back inside and meet our guests. I'll be in shortly." He tried to let go of her hand, but she held on tight.

Celine looked to Bobo for answers.

"What's going on here?"

Bobo deferred to Cord. Celine felt a chill go up her spine and immediately suspected that Cord was trying to protect her from the truth.

"I'm not going inside until you tell me, Cordero."

She felt him stiffen. He was about to refuse.

"I mean it. You may as well tell me and save me the trouble of hounding you all evening. You know very well what a nag I can be—you've said so often enough yourself."

His voice was stern, his mouth set in a firm line. "The obeah man and Gunnie have been caught. They've been delivered back here. Bobo has them under guard at the mill."

"What are you going to do with them?"

Cord didn't hesitate to pronounce sentence. "The

punishment for what they have done is death.''

"But . . .'' She was stunned.

Cord and Bobo were walking away before she could finish. Celine paused to glance back at the open front door. The bright candlelight beckoned. She heard a burst of laughter and recognized Ada's voice above the others. Everyone seemed to be carrying on without them.

She picked up her skirt and left the veranda, following Cord and Bobo through the twilight to the slave village.

Bobo led Cordero to the center of the village, where the obeah man and Gunnie were bound and tied to uprights that supported the potter's shed. Night had fallen and a fire had been lit close by. Firelight danced and flickered over the features of the two prisoners.

It was all Cord could do to keep himself from lunging at the obeah man and wrapping his hands around the old man's throat. The venom and hatred that spewed from the ancient African's eyes attested to a defiant spirit that would never die as long as there was a breath left in his twisted body.

Gunnie was sobbing. Cord ignored her. He knew who had conceived of the kidnapping and murder attempt on his wife. He moved closer until, his fists planted on his hips, he stood over the obeah man.

An uneasy tension filled the air in the village. Although there were not more than a few men brave enough to loiter in front of the shacks, the eyes of all of the village occupants were watching them.

Disheveled and winded, Celine ran into the circle of firelight and paused beside Cord. He cursed under his breath.

"I don't want you here,'' he told her. "Bobo, take her back to the house.''

"Sorry, miss," Bobo said, waiting for her to follow orders.

"You can't do this, Cord. Please. Don't for God's sake think you are doing this for me—"

"They have to pay, Celine."

"But you can't play God, Cord. Not with these people's lives. I won't let you."

"I can't let something like this happen again, and it will as long as this man is capable of—"

"But surely there is some other way."

Somewhere in the forest a monkey shrieked and badgered a neighbor. Bullfrogs kept up a deep, hypnotic chorus. The soil was damp, soaked from recent rains. The close tropical air smelled of decay and the sticky-sweet scent of night-blooming jasmine.

Cord's eyes scanned the darkness beyond the firelight. Celine had recovered. Although they were still feeling one another out, his father was a part of his life again. Everything seemed to be in order, and yet he couldn't shake the feeling of impending doom.

He turned his attention back to the obeah man and a solution suddenly came to him. Cord turned to Bobo.

"Don't wait until daylight. Take as many trusted men as you need, keep these two bound and gagged and transport them to Baytowne. I want them sold and shipped out on the very next boat to leave the harbor."

Bobo nodded.

"You're selling them?" Celine's glance shot over to Gunnie. The girl refused to meet her eyes. "But—"

"Anyone else would have them drawn and quartered. Don't argue with me on this, Celine. He must be punished, and moving the obeah man away from the graves of his kin is a terrible sentence."

"What do you mean?"

"Superstitious attachments are formed to a place through the kin buried there. Even by the time I was old enough to understand, it had become unprofitable to buy slaves who had been uprooted from other plantations."

"Why? It's done in Louisiana all the time."

"Here in the islands, uprooted slaves lose the will to live. They languish and die, for no apparent medical reason. Maybe the ties to the old beliefs are stronger here, who knows."

"The mind is the most powerful of magicians," Celine said. It was something she understood very clearly.

"You of all people should understand," Cord said. He was watching her closely. "The obeah man's strength lies in his ability to make the others think he is all-powerful. His believing that you are stronger than him is a death sentence for you as long as he is here, so he has to go. I know I sound harsh, but I won't argue this."

He could see what running after him all the way from the house had cost her. She appeared tired. The bright smile she had worn earlier had faded, replaced by an expression of concern for the very man who had wanted her dead. Cord doubted he would ever have that depth of love.

"Let's get back to the guests," Cord said as he slipped his arm around her shoulders. As they started back up the hill he looked over at Bobo. The giant nodded. Cord was confident his orders would be carried out.

Celine tried to shake off the solemn mood that had settled over her as they left the village. The shimmering promise of contentment had been tarnished. She knew Cord had been more than fair in his decision to send the obeah man and Gunnie away. They had to be punished lest they try again, but the knowledge did little to rid her of the unsettled feeling that had set her nerves on edge.

She glanced around the sitting room, where they had all gathered after dinner, and found Cord standing near the open windows talking to three gentlemen. As if he felt her gaze, he made a half-turn and smiled over at her. Her heart skipped a beat. The sudden flush of her cheeks prompted her to snap open the delicate ivory fan Ada had loaned her and look around to see if anyone had noticed her reaction.

The other planters' wives all knew each other and had fallen into comfortable chatter. Celine wished she was better at engaging in polite conversation. She had tried earlier at dinner, but had found herself lacking when it came to being able to discuss the latest styles, and so she had grown quiet. What did she know of fashion? Since money had always been scarce, she and Persa had learned to make do with very few items in their wardrobes.

"When will your new furnishings arrive?"

Celine started and nearly dropped the fan. Cassandra Smythe-Whipple, a pert blond with heavy powder and rouged lips, had recently married a man two and a half times her age. She was leaning over to address Celine from the other end of the settee.

"New furnishings?" If new furnishings were on the way, Celine knew nothing about them.

"I think it was quite brave of you to have come here before everything was in perfect order. Mind you, it's none of my business, but I would have sent my husband on ahead to get things settled."

"We left just after—"

"I don't doubt that this depressingly dismal decor is

one of the reasons why you suffered so from the fever. Newcomers often contract it—that's why it's best to go outside as little as possible,'' the new Mrs. Smythe-Whipple warned.

''I was never sick a day in my life before—''

''I'm sure you miss the city. *Anywhere* would be better than here. I told Harry that if he didn't take me to visit England soon I would surely perish.'' Cassandra rolled her eyes and paused to take a breath.

''I don't really miss New Orleans; in fact, I find I like it here—''

''Yes, you must be devastated. No wonder you had your decline. Everyone says this place is haunted, you know. I think it was supposed to be the ghost of some woman who threw herself off a balcony or over a cliff or down the stairs. She went over something, anyway. Who knows. Dreadful, but I can see how suicide happens—the heat and all. And the rain this time of year! Dismal.''

Celine wondered if Alyce's elusive spirit was in attendance tonight. If so, she thought with some amusement, perhaps she could be persuaded to haunt the talkative Mrs. Smythe-Whipple. Not only did Celine stop trying to respond, but she stopped listening entirely while Cassandra went on and on and on.

Within ten minutes she was wondering if anyone would miss her if she slipped upstairs and took a nap.

''Celine?''

At the sound of Cord's voice, Celine looked up from folding and unfolding the fan in her lap. He was standing over her.

''The musicians are about to play,'' he said softly. ''Would you join me in starting off the dance?''

"Of course, although I haven't had much occasion to learn."

"Then I'll have to teach you." He held out his hand.

Together they crossed the veranda and stepped onto the terrace. Torches had been scattered at random around the garden and bordered the paving stones of the terrace floor. The flames cast the open-air dance floor in a shimmering light that gave the garden a primitive, exotic atmosphere. The guests had assembled along the veranda and at the edge of the terrace, ready to join in the dance as soon as Celine and Cord led the way. Celine saw Ada nearby, staring longingly over at Howard Wells as if he were a huge confection she could hardly keep from tasting.

Cord slipped his arm around her waist and leaned close.

"You look exhausted already. If you aren't up to this, I'm sure Aunt Ada wouldn't mind leading off the dance."

Celine shook her head. "I think I was just tired of sitting. If you'll show me what to do, I'll try my best."

He nodded over at the trio of musicians set up at the nearest corner of the veranda. They began to play a slow, lilting waltz. Cord left his arm around Celine's waist and took her hand in his. Confident and accomplished, he slowly led her through the steps of the waltz with the finesse of a master.

When she felt sure of herself, she tilted her head back to look up at him, and became entranced. His dark lashes were thick and lush, enough to make any woman jealous. He was watching her so closely, and with such an intense hunger in his eyes, that she felt a surge of her own desire. Her hand tightened in his.

Ada and Howard joined them. The jovial bookseller

appeared to be having the time of his life as he maneuvered Ada's bulky frame around the dance floor. Cord glanced irritably at the gathered guests.

"Whose idea was it to hold this affair?" he asked Celine.

"You can't blame me. I was instructed to do nothing but appear."

"That's right," he said. "I can't fault you."

"No indeed."

"I didn't inherit my father's love of parties. Are you as bored as I?"

"I was until now." She smiled up at him.

"I suppose it would be rude to disappear," he said.

Together they cast sly glances at their company. Cassandra had cornered one of her neighbors. The women had their heads together behind their fans, watching Ada and Howard Wells closely as they waltzed past. Two men were in the corner boisterously arguing the price of imported versus island-made barrel staves. Foster and Edward moved around the edge of the crowd with trays of confections and more champagne.

Cord began a series of steps and twirls that soon had them across the terrace, near the stairs that led to the beach walk.

He leaned close to Celine and whispered, "I'd like to take you down to the cove."

"I've already seen it," she said.

"Not by moonlight."

"No, not by moonlight."

She held tight to his hand, trusting him to lead her through the shadows to the crescent strip of silvered sand below that even now reflected the blue-white light of the moon.

Instead of starting down the path, Cord pulled her into his arms and held her close.

"I want you, Celine." he whispered against her lips before he plundered them with his own.

The taste of him was heady and decadent, like champagne and chocolate. She couldn't get close enough, couldn't get enough of him and wished away their clothes, the crowd, the time it would take them to maneuver the dark path to the beach. She felt his palms through the silk of her gown, warm and seeking as they slipped along her ribs. His tongue, hot and searching, delved into her mouth, toyed with her, tempted and teased her.

He turned his back to the other dancers so that she was hidden by him. Celine was unable to stifle the moan that escaped her when he cupped her breast, molded and massaged her with his hand and then traced his thumb back and forth over the tightly budded nipple that thrust beneath the fabric.

Finally, when she had been so thoroughly kissed that she felt as warm and pliant as honey, Cord raised his head.

"And you, Celine?"

She slipped her hand between his legs, tenderly cupped him and then drew her hand up along the hard ridge of his erection.

"I want you, too."

"I'm not one to deny a lady her wishes. Let's go." Cord started down the path to the beach. Suddenly, a man's voice shouted over the music, drawing them up short.

"I'd stop right there if I were you!"

One by one, the musicians stopped playing. The last sound to die on the tropical night breeze was the sad, low whine of a violin. Cord and Celine turned as one. His arms wrapped around her, she stood with her back pressed against him as they faced the crowd.

Across the terrace, near the entrance to the garden, stood Collin Ray. Beside him was a shorter but heftier man in a tall beaver hat.

"What do you want, Ray? I thought we had this out long ago," Cord challenged the man from across the terrace.

The exchange caught everyone's attention. Foster and Edward set down their trays and wove their way through the guests toward Ray and the stranger standing alongside him.

"You weren't invited, Ray," Cord said. He let go of Celine and began moving across the terrace.

"I'm here in an official capacity this time."

"And what would that be?" Cord demanded.

Celine caught her breath. She concentrated on the stranger who stood silent beside Ray. For the first time she noticed he was holding a piece of paper in his hand. Content to let the magistrate's brother speak for him, the man had not said a word.

She had known what he wanted the moment she'd laid eyes on him. Celine started to run across the terrace, hoping to get to Cord before Collin Ray had a chance to speak. Each step she took was harder than the last.

"I think we should go inside, Moreau," Ray urged.

"Whatever you have to say to me can be said right here, right now."

"Cord, no!" Celine stepped up beside her husband and took his hand. She held on to him so tight that he shot her a hard, questioning glance before he turned to face Ray again.

"You are upsetting my wife. I'd like you out of

here.'' Cord still had enough command of his temper to lower his voice, but his control was slipping.

''I would imagine I'm about to upset her even more,'' Ray said.

''What in the hell are you talking about?''

''Cord!'' Celine knew there was nothing she could do or say to forestall the inevitable. If only she could tell him herself, in private. If only . . .

''Your wife is wanted for murder.''

A collective gasp went up from the shocked guests on the terrace.

''What did he say? What does Celine want?'' Ada was quickly hushed by Howard Wells.

Celine felt her knees begin to tremble.

''I swear if you don't shut the hell up and get out of here I'm going to kill you, Ray.'' Cord took a threatening step toward Collin Ray, who merely laughed in his face and grabbed the paper out of his companion's hand.

''Fine. Perhaps you and the lady can swing together. This,'' he said, producing the page and waving it in Cord's face, ''is a document from Louisiana delivered by this gentleman, Mr. Jonathan Hargraves, an agent acting for the Perot family of New Orleans. It states that your wife, formerly Celine Winters, is wanted for not one but two murders. I, as my brother's deputy, am to see that she is convinced that it would be in her best interest to return to New Orleans to stand trial.''

When Cord shook off her hand and snatched the page from Ray, Celine's knees turned to water and her head began to swim. If not for Foster and Edward, who had moved up beside her, she would have crumpled to the ground.

Cord tilted the page so that he could read it by the

flickering torchlight. The meaning of the words seared its way into his mind. His eyes scanned the warrant and as he read, his heart went stone cold. It had been a lie. All of it.

*Is there anything else you have to tell me?*

*Do you possess any more little secrets or hidden talents that I should know of?*

He had asked for the whole truth that day on the beach.

She had persuaded him to trust her.

She had worked her way into his heart and mind until he had become such a besotted fool that he had even told her he loved her.

He thrust the warrant back into Ray's hands, so angry that he could hardly focus. Foster and Edward were holding Celine, flanking her, offering the support Cord could not give. Ada began to sob.

He wanted to go to Celine, take her in his arms and tell her not to worry, that they would straighten this mistake out together.

But this was no mistake. He knew with a sudden, awful clarity that it was the most horrible of truths.

# Twenty

Through a red haze of anger, he stared at the faces of his guests and household. Some watched in horror, others turned away. The women speculated in hushed tones behind their fans. He could not bring himself to look at Celine. He did not dare. Somehow he found the strength to address the small gathering.

"That's all the entertainment we have for you this evening." He did not make eye contact with a soul until he turned to Edward.

"Have the carriages brought to the door." That said, he turned his back on all of them. Before he left the terrace he snapped an order at Collin Ray. "Bring her into the library."

"Cord, wait!" Celine cried out, frantically reaching for him, but he didn't so much as break stride.

As the magistrate's brother stepped toward her, she gathered her strength and shook off Edward and Foster. She had to pull herself together. She would walk on her own two feet, not be led like a lamb to the slaughter. Somehow, someway she had to convince Cord that no matter what else he thought of her, her love for him was real and true and lasting.

It would last, if necessary, beyond the gallows.

She didn't think she would make it up the low stairs and into the house, but she did. As if they thought she was going to try to escape, Collin Ray and Hargraves were dogging her heels. It was a ridiculous notion. She barely had the strength to walk under her own power.

Candlelight bathed the rooms in a rich caramel tone. In the muted gold wash, the shabby interior appeared almost luxurious, the way she'd always imagined it could be. She would miss this house that had almost become a home.

By the time she reached the library, she was beset with chills and near a state of collapse. Every joint in her body was screaming with pain. She stepped into the small room lined with bookshelves and saw that Howard Wells had actually been sorting and categorizing the volumes when he was not courting Ada. There were stacks of books on the floor in front of the shelves.

Celine stepped aside so that Ray and Hargraves could enter. With her hands behind her for support, she leaned back against the bookshelf, dreading the moment Cord, who was standing before his desk, would turn around.

He stood with his back to them, his broad shoulders rigid, his hands wrapped around a crystal tumbler as if it were a lifeline. She watched him toss back a glassful of rum and then deftly poured himself another from the decanter on the desk.

"Close the door," he demanded without turning around.

Hargraves obliged.

After three heavy shots, Cord felt calm enough to face them, the urge to kill someone having been numbed. His gaze flicked over Hargraves, a nondescript, slightly stooped, hawk-nosed little man. Why kill the messenger?

Collin Ray, a perfect candidate, was staring back at him, watching him with a snide, smug smile. He had won after all. He would be taking Celine away.

Finally Cord's gaze came to rest on his wife. His deceitful little wife, who had lied to him from the moment he'd first laid eyes on her. She had lost all color and was as white as the delicate frangipani blossom. He could see her shivering and would have believed her a consummate actress if he didn't know that that glazed look in her eye meant the fever was on her again.

To keep from going to her aid, he spun around and poured himself a fourth drink. The decanter hit the rim of the tumbler, crystal on crystal, but neither cracked. The sparkling glass was stronger than it looked.

"I would offer you gentlemen a drink, but I'm afraid there wouldn't be enough left. As it is, I'll have to send for a few more bottles before dawn . . ."

"Don't, Cord." Celine's voice broke on his name.

He walked toward her and did not stop until they were toe to toe. He lowered his voice.

"It would have been so very easy for you to tell me before tonight, Celine. Anytime would have done. You had every opportunity. In my stupid lust I might even have tried to protect you, to lie for you, to lie *like* you."

"I tried . . ."

"When? When did you try, Celine? When did you

ever try to tell me something until after the fact? You begged me to trust you, and I was stupid enough to agree. I was even stupid enough to fall in love with you.''

''I do love you, Cord. No matter what, I—''

''This is all very charming, but we need to get back to Baytowne before Mr. Hargraves's ship sails on the morning tide,'' Ray said.

Cord went back to the desk and the decanter.

Collin Ray took a step toward Celine, but she balked and tried to skirt away from him along the bookcase.

''I killed Jean Perot in self-defense,'' she told them. ''He attacked me. Tried to strangle me. Earlier I touched him and saw that he had killed Persa. I was a threat to him because I knew what he had done. He had to get rid of me, tried to strangle me in his courtyard. I stabbed him to save myself.''

Cord laughed and threw back another drink. ''She's good, isn't she?''

''If that's true, why did you run?'' Ray asked.

''And why bash his face into an unrecognizable pulp?'' Hargraves could not hide his disgust.

''I did no such thing! I stabbed him. When he fell to the ground, I ran. I went back to the house and found Persa's body lying in the middle of the floor. The scene was just as I had seen it when I touched Jean Perot.''

Ray frowned. ''What do you mean, just as you had 'seen' it?''

''She has visions. My incredibly talented little murderess is also a thief.'' Cord walked up to Ray and stared him in the eye. ''Be careful or she'll surely steal into your mind, too, if she hasn't already.''

''Why would Perot want the old lady dead?'' Hargraves wanted to know, ignoring Cord.

"Persa was a fortune-teller. Jean killed her because she must have known something about him. I was going to the police when I heard them about to enter the house. I was sure they were already looking for me, blaming me for the murder. I knew how wealthy the Perots were and knew they had the money to have me convicted. They would never have believed that their precious son was capable of murder. I panicked and ran."

"You were right about the Perots," Hargraves said. "They have spared no expense to hire me to track you down. For two months we had no clues as to how you escaped the city—that is, until a man named Thomas O'Hurley went to the police demanding they search for his daughter. It seems he had missed the wedding because of a family emergency and had then gone out to the Moreau Plantation to visit his daughter. Once there, he learned that the woman who married Cordero Moreau did not fit his girl's description at all. When everyone was questioned and the description of the mysterious bride matched Celine Winters's, we could only hope that she was still on St. Stephen."

"Technically she is outside of your jurisdiction, is she not?" Cord set the tumbler down beside him on the desk.

A glimmer of hope flickered through Celine.

"I was hoping she would give herself up without argument, but as her husband, you can simply turn her over to us. I appeal to you to do so. I wouldn't think you would want to knowingly house a murderess under your roof."

Celine held her breath. Cord was her only hope—yet one look into his dark eyes told her that was no hope at all.

"Take her if you want. I don't care one way or another."

Her pain could not have been any greater had he ripped out her heart and danced on it.

Hargraves was speaking to her again. Celine forced herself to try to concentrate on his words.

"If you come back willingly, things will go easier for you. You can plead self-defense."

"Just think, they can only hang you for two murders, since the other body has yet to be found." Collin Ray crossed his arms and rocked back on his heels with a satisfied smile.

"What other body?" Celine was certain the fever had dulled her mind.

"You are under suspicion of murder in the disappearance of Jemma O'Hurley."

"What?" Celine was staggered. "The last I saw of Jemma O'Hurley, she was hiding in St. Louis Cathedral."

Hargraves turned to Cordero. "I cannot believe you never even realized you were marrying the wrong woman."

"None of us had ever laid eyes on Jemma O'Hurley. My grandfather was warned the marriage wasn't her idea and that she would say or do anything to get out of it, so when she said she was not Jemma O'Hurley, no one believed her." Cord looked over at Celine. "She obviously didn't try hard enough to convince anyone, nor did she tell me her name until it was too late."

She held out her hand, pleading. "I tried to tell them I was only there seeking employment. I told you my name almost as soon as we went aboard the *Adelaide*."

"But not until we were conveniently out of Louisiana and headed for St. Stephen, as I recall—"

"We could argue this all night," Ray interrupted. He grabbed Celine by the arm. "Are you willing to surrender to us, or do we have to put you in chains?"

When Collin Ray touched Celine, Cord almost grabbed him by the throat, but quickly reminded himself that she was no longer his concern, that he did not care what happened to her as long as he never had to lay eyes on her again.

"Let her go, Ray. She must come of her own volition," Hargraves said, and Collin Ray released her.

Celine bit her bottom lip to keep it from trembling. Cord refused to meet her eyes and concentrated on pouring himself another drink. She was shaking as hard as a cane tassel in a high wind.

"I'll go," she whispered to Hargraves.

Her life was over now anyway. What did it matter how it ended?

Jonathan Hargraves had started to guide her out of the room when Celine said, "One moment, please."

She reached up and fumbled with the clasp on the pearls. After two tries it opened, and she drew them off her throat and held them in the palm of her hand, then walked over to Cord.

"Here," she said, offering him his mother's necklace.

His eyes flicked over the pearls in her hand and then back up to her eyes. The distance in his ice blue gaze chilled her to her soul.

"Put them on the desk," he said, turning away from her.

Humiliated, she laid the strand of pearls on the desk and let Hargraves and Collin Ray lead her out.

Cord thought they were gone, turned too soon and caught sight of Celine dwarfed between the two men. She walked away as regal as a queen, her shoulders straight and proud, her hands fisted at her sides.

Crowded in the hallway, unabashedly watching the unfolding drama, stood Edward and Foster, his aunt and Howard Wells.

"Cordero! Alyce wants you to stop them. She's very, very upset," Ada cried, pleading with him.

"When are you going to start speaking for yourself, Aunt?" Cord glared at her from the doorway, sick to death of the ridiculous way she used his mother as an excuse to state her own mind.

Ada turned away and sobbed on the bookseller's shoulder. Unlike the others, who all expected Cord to save Celine, the cultured gentleman from Barbados could not even meet his eyes.

Cord spat out a venomous curse as he crossed the room and slammed the door in their faces with all the strength he could muster, rattling the house to its very foundation. But he could not shut out the image of their accusatory stares. He hurled the crystal tumbler at the door, and it shattered into countless glittering shards, beautiful but dangerous.

Like Celine.

He could not think about her. Would not allow himself to think of her. She was gone and he was alone again—alone with half a decanter of rum that would not even begin to dull the overwhelming ache lodged in his newly resurrected heart.

On an island, good new travels fast, scandal even faster. The populace of Baytowne turned out at the wharf to witness the public humiliation of the newly arrived planter's wife—an alleged witch—as she was taken aboard the ship that would transport her to America. There she would stand trial for not one, but two murders. Rumors circulated that they still burned witches in Louisiana.

Celine had not slept at all during the night. By the time her jailers came for her she didn't care whether she lived or died. Did it matter if by some miracle she could clear her name despite what Hargraves kept referring to as "overwhelming" evidence? She had been a fool to have run in the first place. Would it matter now if she had never met Cordero?

Yes, her heart answered. It mattered. She refused to take back one moment. The only thing she regretted was hurting him so much, when all she'd really wanted to do was heal him with her love.

They had locked her in a filthy cell in a jail not fit for the rats who went hungry there. Upon seeing the crowd gathered along the way to the docks, Collin Ray had insisted she be shackled, arguing that someone might make a melodramatic attempt to rescue her. Hargraves insisted her ankles be left free or it would take her too long to walk up the gangway.

Celine, still fighting recurring bouts of fever, remained mute. She concentrated on the world beyond the rock-walled jail, tried to picture the white sand that shimmered with heat and the rolling surf that dissolved into frothing foam as it broke against the shore. She thought of Cordero as she had first seen him, drunk as sin at their wedding. Cordero kneeling on the floor as he embraced Alex's children and told them good-bye. Cordero the night he held her through the storm. Cordero holding Bobo's child, rejoicing when he was found. Cordero swimming naked through the waves.

Cordero over her. Cordero inside her. Cordero announcing his love for her before the household.

*Cordero. Cordero. Cordero.* She squeezed her eyes

closed and held her hands over her ears, trying to shut out the echo of his name.

"Let's not have any theatrics," Collin Ray warned as he locked the heavy iron shackles around her wrists. "Hargraves, are you ready?"

The Perots' hired man nodded and opened the jail-house door.

Suffering the chills, her mouth dry, her joints screaming with pain, Celine left the building, the heavy wrist cuffs and chains weighing her down. Although she did not look directly at anyone, she was aware of the crowd gathered on the street as she crossed the cobblestone wharf. Frilly parasols bobbed like huge, colorful blossoms against a backdrop of ladies and gents, vendors and merchants, planters and slaves who had stopped what they were doing to gawk. Her humiliation was complete.

A gang of slaves chained together were being herded toward a ship docked alongside the one she would board. The clink and rattle of their chains drew her attention. Celine looked over at the lines of blacks and found that they were all stone-faced and silent. When one of the women among them glanced her way, Celine realized it was Gunnie. She quickly searched for a glimpse of the obeah man and found him near the rear of the line.

Their eyes met across the wharf. Nothing about the old man showed any sign of the defeat so evident in his fellow prisoners. He was bent with age, but not broken. In his eyes burned a fire that would not be extinguished until he drew his last breath.

She tried to turn away, but was powerless. His sharp eyes took in her disheveled state, the shackles on her wrists, the men who watched her so closely. When their gazes locked again, he smiled, a slow, toothless, triumphant smile. The obeah man was still smiling when he and his companions in misery were led aboard a ship bound for Jamaica.

By the time she reached the end of the gangway, the iron shackles had already cut into the soft flesh of her wrist. The toe of her muddy slipper caught in the hem of her gown. She lurched forward and would have gone down face-first and pitched over the side of the gangway into the water if not for Hargraves's swift move. He caught her arm and jerked her to her feet again.

"The Perots are paying me good money for your return, so don't think you can drown yourself when I'm not looking. I'll be watching you every minute."

"Thank you for the suggestion," she told the agent, "but I am innocent. I'm not afraid."

Although she longed to be rid of him, Collin Ray had accompanied them. He found a moment to speak with her alone as Hargraves spoke to the ship's mate about accommodations.

Ray reached out and cupped her cheek with his hand and then rubbed it with the pad of his thumb. She tried to turn her face aside, but he had imprisoned her jaw between his thumb and forefinger.

"You should have taken me up on my offer, Celine. If you were mine, I would have never turned you in when Hargraves came to the magistrate looking for you." He let go of her chin, then shrugged and brushed his hands together, as if touching her had soiled him. "But as it is, since you chose your mongrel husband over me, there was nothing else for me to do."

"I wouldn't have you if you stood beneath the gallows willing to cut the noose." She spat in his face.

Before she knew what was coming, Ray pulled back

his hand and slapped her full across the cheek just below her right eye. Celine reeled back with the force of the blow and slammed into the rail. She gasped as pain shot through her lower back below the ribs.

Jonathan Hargraves was beside her in an instant.

"Keep your hands off her, Ray. I don't want to take back damaged goods. You can take your leave now that you've seen us aboard."

Ray departed without another word to Hargraves, but eloquently executed a bow to Celine in imitation of the one he had given her on the day she'd first arrived on the island.

As the ship weighed anchor, Celine couldn't bear watching the emerald fields of sugar or the thick mountain jungle gradually fade from view. Nor did she dare catch one last glimpse of Dunstain Place perched high on the hillside above the sea.

She turned her back on St. Stephen and on her shattered dreams of what might have been.


Foster stood in the butler's pantry preparing tea as Edward perched on a tall-legged stool rubbing his hands on the knees of his breeches.

"This is the worst I've ever seen him," Foster said.

He chatted as he concentrated on carefully arranging fanned lemon slices on a butter plate. When he was satisfied with the presentation, he placed the plate on a huge tray beside a pot of tea, matching cups and saucers and pineapple tea cake.

"Drunk for two and a half days." Edward shook his head in dismay and drew a ragged, shuddering breath. "What's to become of 'im? 'E's takin' this far worse than when Alex died."

"Of course he is. He wasn't married to Alex. Can

you carry this into the sitting room? Miss Ada and Mr. Wells are waiting for their tea." Foster busied himself folding napkins in the shape of giant bird-of-paradise blooms.

Edward sighed. "I can't. I'm too upset to do anything but worry. Besides, if I see Miss Ada cryin', I'll burst into tears, too. You know 'ow I am, Foster. I can't 'elp it."

Foster added the napkins and grabbed the handles of the tray. He lifted it, then set it down again. The fact that he and Edward had tried to make Cord's marriage work haunted him.

"We should 'ave believed Miss Celine that first night when she tried to tell us she weren't Jemma O'Hurley. Maybe none of this would 'ave happened if Cordero 'ad married the right woman," Foster said.

"We should 'ave known when none of the clothes and shoes in 'er trunk fit that somethin' was up."

"I'll never believe she's a murderer, though. Never. Miss Celine don't 'ave a mean bone in 'er body," Foster said.

"I wish there was somethin' we could do. I wish Cordero would pull 'imself together."

"If wishes were horses, beggars might ride, Eddie." Foster hefted the tray again. Edward rose wearily from the stool and held the door, then followed him into the sitting room.

Foster walked over to a side table and set down the tray.

"A spot of tea will do you good, Miss Ada," he said, pouring her a cup without waiting for her to agree.

She had taken up permanent residence in the corner of the settee, and nothing Howard Wells or anyone else said or did could cheer her. Her eyes were red and puffy, her face was blotched. Foster wanted to tell her that her coloring didn't lend itself to such crying.

Ada reached for the cup of tea. Her hands were shaking so hard that it would have sloshed over the rim and onto the saucer if Foster hadn't steadied the cup. He was fast running out of patience with the lot of them.

"What are we going to do, Foster?" Ada stared up at him pitifully. Her eyelids were almost swollen shut. "Even Alyce is so very upset."

"If you ask me, Miss Ada, I think we should all pull ourselves together." He looked meaningfully at Edward. "We ain't a bit o' good to anyone in this condition."

Wells reached for a cup of steaming tea and poured milk in it until it was white. "Whenever I think of poor Celine alone and incarcerated in the bowels of a ship, or worse yet, if she is convicted—"

Ada let out a wail. Foster dove for her teacup and rescued it before it tipped off her lap.

"There's always hope," he said.

"We'll never see 'er alive again!" Edward began to run from the room and collided with Auguste Moreau.

"Damn it, Lang," Auguste said as he grabbed Edward by the shoulders, set him aside and strode into the room. He took one look at Ada and Howard Wells and ignored them both as he addressed Foster.

"Where is my son?"

Foster almost sagged with relief. "He's in the library. The most terrible thing has happened . . ."

"I know. It's all over the island." Auguste was already out of the sitting room, headed down the hall. "I came as soon as I heard. What is Cord planning to do?"

"Nothing, I'm afraid," Foster said with a disgusted sigh. When Auguste halted abruptly and turned on him, Foster fell back a step.

"What do you mean *nothing*?"

"Cordero's dead drunk. Been that way since they took Miss Celine away."

Death is kinder than too much rum.

Cord's head was pounding so hard that he could barely open his eyes. His tongue was too big for his head, his teeth tasted as if they were wrapped in individual wool shawls. He was slumped in a chair, unwilling to move because his heart would pound like a smithy's hammer every time he attempted to sit up.

He tried and failed to curse whoever was insisting on beating down the library door. He had locked it for a reason, damn them, after the first time Foster had tried to get him to eat.

"Go away," he managed weakly, just seconds before the frame splintered and the door crashed open.

Cord opened one eye. His father was framed in the doorway, looking every inch a retired gentleman pirate in a crisp white shirt, black pants and coat and a black leather eye patch.

"I said get out," Cord slurred.

Ignoring the demand, Auguste crossed the room and picked up the vase of flowers that sat off to one side of Cordero's desk.

"What are you doing?" When Cord sat up a little straighter, the room started to whirl. He closed his eyes and pressed his fingers against his temples.

"I'm doing what someone should have done for me years ago. If they had, I might not have sent you away and made the biggest mistake of my life," Auguste said.

The next thing Cord knew, a shower of long-stemmed blossoms and stagnant water came raining down on him.

"Shit!" Wiping his eyes, he shot to his feet and

lunged for his father. Auguste easily sidestepped the attack, further infuriating him.

"You have no right to barge in here!"

"I have every right to keep you from letting your life go to hell in a handbasket. What are you going to do to save your wife?" his father asked.

"Nothing." Water that smelled of rotted flower stems dripped from his hair.

Auguste slammed the palm of his hand on the desktop. "Damn it, Cordero! Why the hell not?"

"Why should I?"

"Because you love her."

"She lied to me from the day I first laid eyes on her. Lied by omission."

"You're angry because you see this as another desertion. You aren't thinking of Celine, Cordero, but of yourself."

"I thought I could finally trust her." Cord longed to return to his mind-numbing drunken state. He'd have preferred anything to this torture.

"Trust her to stay?"

"To trust me enough to tell me the whole truth, but she didn't . . ."

"You expected her to tell you she was guilty of murder and take the chance of losing you? If you didn't love her, you wouldn't be doing this to yourself; you would be about your business as if nothing had happened. But something terrible *has* happened, and now you can't face it, or won't. I know. I've been there. Admit it. You love her so much this is killing you."

Cord sat back down, hunched over with his elbows on his knees, and propped his head in his hands. His gut churned.

"I tried so hard not to," he whispered. "I swore I

would never love anyone ever again.''

Auguste's voice came to him from across the room. ''Why?''

Cord's throat was so tight with emotion that the words wouldn't come. He swallowed, bit his lips and stared at the floor between his feet.

''Because it hurts so bad when they leave,'' he admitted.

Auguste knelt beside the chair and slipped his arm around Cord's shoulders. Cord pressed his hands against his eyes, willing himself not to break down. The only way he'd been able to keep Celine out of his mind had been to stay drunk. Now he was forced to face the fact that she was at sea, no doubt sick, frightened and alone, all because of his blinding anger and his unwillingness to trust and believe in her.

The facts plagued him. He knew Celine loved the old woman who raised her; Persa's death at Celine's hands was out of the question. But what of Perot? Had she really killed him in self-defense, as she'd said? And what of Jemma O'Hurley? Where had the girl disappeared to?

Without proof of her innocence, Celine would hang. But how would she be able to obtain proof locked behind bars? She had no family or money to aid her cause. No one to stand up for her—no one but a husband who had turned his back on her.

''I've been a fool,'' he whispered. ''Such a damned fool.''

''I did you a great injustice when I sent you away. I was thinking only of myself and my hurt,'' Auguste said. ''God help you if you do the same and lose Celine.''

''How long ago did they sail?'' Cord rubbed his hands

through his hair, wondering how much time he had squandered on self-pity.

"Two days. Cordero, I'm willing to do everything I can to help. My ship and crew is hidden in a cove six miles away. We can set sail for New Orleans by night-fall."

"Then let's go. First, though, have Foster brew plenty of hot coffee and tell Edward to lay out a change of clothes."

As soon as the words were issued, Foster stuck his head and shoulders around the shattered door frame. "The coffee will be ready in a moment. Edward is already off to see to the packing."

# Twenty-one

*H*er long journey ended where it began.

The Cabildo, which housed the underbelly of Louisiana society, stood across from St. Louis Cathedral, where she had stepped out of her old life and into Jemma O'Hurley's carriage.

Celine thought of the irony of having come full circle as she lay naked beneath a filthy, tattered blanket on a cot in her cell. The thin wool provided scant relief from the cold and damp, but the guards had taken her clothes to discourage any notion she might have of escaping.

She smiled in the dim light that dribbled through the window high on the wall. The authorities were fools. There was no one who would shelter her even if she did find the strength to somehow manage to flee the old fortress. She was alone. She had faced that bleak truth from the moment she stood on the deck of the ship and turned her back on St. Stephen.

The voyage was a blur of endless days and nights that melded one into another. Through hours of illness, her body had been tortured by a combination of recurrent swamp fever and the accursed seasickness. Chained to the wall, she had been housed belowdecks, too weak to take the air, to watch the stars above the night sea, to feel the salt air on her face. There was no one to tend her save Jonathan Hargraves. When she had refused to eat, he'd force-fed her.

*"The Perots don't want me to deliver a corpse. They want you alive for the hanging."*

When the hideous voyage had ended she was imprisoned in the Cabildo with the other accused awaiting trials. Presided over by a newly arrived American judge named Bennett, hers was one of the shortest waits and trials in New Orleans's history. The Durels, the young couple out walking the night of the murder, admitted they had seen her with Jean Perot a scant two hours before his body was found.

Perot's housekeeper attested to serving Celine hot cocoa. His entire house staff related in bloody detail how they had returned after dark and found their employer's mutilated body in the courtyard.

Celine's neighbors could shed no light on her whereabouts the afternoon and evening of the murders. They had not seen her, nor had they seen Persa at all the day of her death.

*"She's a strange one, that girl. Different,"* said a woman who had lived behind them for years.

*"Never trusted her. I always knew she was odd. It was the eyes, you see. She has strange eyes,"* said a

man Celine remembered seeing only once or twice in her life.

Throughout the trial Jean Perot's mother and father sat in the front row, hungry for revenge as they watched her with hard, venomous stares. Who could blame them? Their son was dead.

A heavyset gentleman who identified himself as Thomas O'Hurley spoke with her before the trial. He pleaded with her to confess what she had done to his daughter. O'Hurley begged her to tell him where she had hidden Jemma's body.

*"All I want is to give my little princess a decent burial,"* he cried.

Celine told him in great detail, over and over again, what had taken place that rainy night in the shadows of the cathedral. She swore to O'Hurley that she had no notion of where his Jemma had disappeared to. He attended the trial, stymied yet hopeful that she would break down and confess to his daughter's murder. Who could blame him? His precious angelic girl had disappeared without a trace.

With no one on the outside to prove her innocence, she was found guilty of two counts of murder after a day and a half of testimony. No one, least of all her, had been surprised when she was sentenced to hang.

The judge gave her the opportunity to speak in her own behalf after she was sentenced. Even now, as she languished in her cell, she thought of the pitiful picture she must have made there in the courtroom. She had lost so much weight that her filthy aquamarine ball gown hung from her shoulders. Her hair was matted and dirty, her skin was sallow, her eyes were sunken. She recalled how she had barely been able to raise her voice above a whisper.

*"I stabbed Jean Perot in self-defense . . . I did not leave him the way he was found . . . I could not have killed Persa . . . She was like a mother to me . . . I loved her too much . . . I do not fear death, for I know I am innocent."*

"Wake up, girl. You have a visitor."

The jailer's voice roused her, shaking her out of her reverie. Celine pushed up off the thin moss-filled mattress with one hand. She waited for her head to stop spinning before she turned toward her jailer's face framed in the barred window of the heavy door. Today it was the fat one who reeked of wine. His ruddy cheeks were webbed with broken lines of spider veins.

She licked her dry lips. "Are you talking to me?"

"I am. Pull yourself together, girl. There's a gentleman here to see you. No tricks now and I'll show him in." His face disappeared.

Over the past few days she had actually grown sorry for her jailers, for day after day they too had to endure the dank, mildewed walls, the stench of overflowing slop buckets, the overcrowding. She drew the blanket tight around herself and swung her feet over the side of the bunk, steeling herself against the shock of the chilly, filthy floor.

As she shoved her hair back off her face, Celine wondered who might have come to see her. She knew no gentlemen—and certainly none who would come here—except perhaps Cordero, and she had better sense than to hope that he would come.

Outside the cell, the sound of approaching footsteps echoed against the stone floor. Her head had stopped spinning, but her hands shook. She prayed for the strength to stand. Someone in another cell screamed, the sound quickly swallowed by the usual shouting and curses that ensued whenever the guards demanded order. The Cabildo had already been the site of more than one inmate riot, and its guards were overzealous. Murderers, criminals and slaves, some insane, some diseased, were pinched together like toes in painfully tight shoes. She was lucky: The condemned were held in solitary confinement.

Celine closed her eyes and rocked back and forth, grasping the edge of the bunk. Unbidden, a vision of Cord came to mind. He was riding along the shoreline against a backdrop of glistening sand and foaming waves, tall and proud in the saddle, sunlight reflecting in the flashing highlights of his hair. On the hill beside him, lush green cane tassels undulated on the tangy breeze.

As she tucked the picture away in a corner of her heart, she couldn't help but wonder: *Does he ever think of me*?

The guard's face appeared in the window again. Keys clanged on a ring. One scraped in the keyhole before the heavy cypress door swung open.

Celine clasped the edges of the blanket together and remained seated on the edge of the bunk as the bulbous-nosed guard led Thomas O'Hurley into the cell. The heavyset middle-aged merchant wore an expensively tailored serge frock coat that was as out of place in the dingy cell as a silk slipper in a bayou. The room suddenly became dwarfed by the presence of the two big men. Her visitor cleared his throat repeatedly as he glanced around the cell.

Celine made no move to speak to him or put him at ease. She merely waited. He had no doubt come to beg her one last time for information as to his daughter's whereabouts.

When O'Hurley finally spoke, it was to the guard, not her.

"Can you leave us alone?" he asked.

The guard stared at Celine for a moment. "Don't give him any trouble."

The warning didn't deserve an answer. He knew very well she barely had the strength to swat a fly. The guard left the cell, but even after the key turned in the lock, she could tell he was waiting outside the door.

Celine turned her attention to Thomas O'Hurley. Something had changed since she had seen him in court. There was an air of bold confidence about him. His shoulders were no longer hunched in defeat, his eyes no longer haunted by shadows of despair. He withdrew a folded paper from his pocket and carefully opened it as if it were made of thin, pressed gold.

"I've heard from Jemma," he said softly, staring at the page with something akin to reverence. "She's alive."

Celine felt a rush of relief, not only because the missive cleared her name of suspicion, but also because she was sincerely thankful no harm had come to the smiling blond girl who'd traded lives with her.

"Is she in a convent?"

"Jemma? Of course not." O'Hurley laughed.

"She told me she wanted to be a nun." Celine had said the same thing when he'd questioned her before. He had not believed her then, either.

"She doesn't say where she is exactly, just that she is safe and happy and well taken care of. She writes that when she's good and ready, she'll come home, but she wants to wait long enough for me to get over the notion that I have the right to choose a husband for her." He smiled at Celine. "You can believe me, I'll never try that again."

He continued to stare down at the words his daughter had penned. "She goes on to say that on the night of the wedding, she changed places with a young woman about her height with dark hair. It's all here, just the way you explained it. I showed the letter to the authorities and they've called off the search for her. I wanted to tell you myself, and had to say that I hope you can forgive me for doubting your word, but you must understand how distraught I was . . ."

"I do understand. But I'm afraid there is not much left of her dowry money. A great portion of it went to Alexandre's illegitimate children. I'm sorry . . ."

He waved away her apology. "I've got more money than I can count. I'm just glad Jemma is alive. Celine, is there anything I can do?"

"There is nothing anyone can do without proof that I didn't murder the others, and there is no time to prove anything now anyway."

He paced to the high window and looked at the wedge of sunlight that angled across the wall.

"Do you have anyone who will be with you when . . . when they . . . ?"

"When they hang me? No. There is no one."

"How can you sit there so calmly, knowing that in two days you are going to your death?"

"I have done nothing wrong. I may be afraid to die, Mr. O'Hurley, but believe me, I am not afraid to face God."

He swallowed hard and ran his hand over his face.

"I wouldn't want my Jemma alone at a time like this."

O'Hurley was talking to himself, mulling over an idea. Abruptly, he turned and walked back over to Celine. He paused beside her bunk.

"I'll be here next Friday, Celine. I will walk with you to the gallows."

Celine sighed with relief. He was a stranger, another girl's father, but thanks to him she would not have to face the end alone. Celine felt her eyes sting with tears.

She bowed her head. Hot tears dropped onto the back of her hands. It was a moment before she could gather the self-control to speak.

"Thank you, Mr. O'Hurley. I cannot ask for more than that."


"Where in the hell are we?" Cord demanded of Auguste.

He stood beside his father on the deck of Auguste's *Lady Fair*, staring at the labyrinth of murky waterways that trailed off into tangled Louisiana swampland. The air was dense with the fecund scent of rich, muddy topsoil that the centuries had deposited. Moss-blanketed cypress trees stood silent and ghostly, mute keepers of countless dark secrets. It was a world that had always existed on the edges of the Moreau Plantation, a world into which he had never had occasion to venture deeply.

Auguste smiled, apparently at home as he personally guided the helmsman through the inland channel.

"This is Barataria Bay. Believe it or not, as the crow flies, we're only a few miles from New Orleans. Many's the time I sailed these waters under the flag of Cartagena. Many's the time I gave a portion of captured booty to Jean Lafitte for the right to hide here."

Startled, Cord looked at his father. Auguste was watching the channel intently. A tentative, uncomfortable truce had existed between them on the voyage. For a few hours during a hurricane, while his father's seaworthy craft was being tossed about like a cork, he'd thought that his father's old wish to die at sea had been granted, and that he was taking his son with him.

"So you were this close to Moreau Plantation and never once came to see me?" Cord felt the old bitterness rise up like bile.

Auguste shrugged. "And say what? That I was a pirate? Admit that I had given up my past, and you with it? Let me ask you: Do you plan to contact Henre while we are here?"

"I see your point. No, I won't be seeing Henre if I can help it," Cord said.

The hatred of his grandfather ran too deep. He gripped the rail so hard his knuckles whitened. This was no time to let anger blind him in carrying out his mission. The past was over. What was important now was the future, and Celine.

"I thought we were going directly to New Orleans. If we don't get there in time—"

"Don't even think it." Auguste signaled his helmsman with a wave of the arm. "The only ones who know these waters well are shrimpers and pirates. Here we can escape the authorities if necessary."

"Is there a price on your head?"

"Not as Auguste Moreau. Roger Reynolds, on the other hand, has committed more than a few petty indiscretions. But that isn't the only reason I wanted to leave the ship hidden in the bayou and slip into the city."

Cord squinted when the sun appeared from behind low, dark clouds. "I told you I'm willing to do anything to save my wife. Were you thinking we might have to escape quickly?"

"Exactly." Auguste turned away from the rail. "I'm glad to note we are thinking along the same lines. But there is no price on your head, and no reason there should ever be, Cordero. My crew and I have had experience in similar situations. We can handle this."

"While I do what? Sit here in the mud and wait?" Adamant, Cord shook his head. "Celine is my wife. I've done little enough to deserve her as it is. I will see her safely out of this—one way or another."

"Are you willing to spend the rest of your life on the run? Always looking over your shoulder? Never able to put down roots?"

"To save Celine? Most definitely."

"We will be in the city by nightfall," Auguste assured him.

The fetid smell of unwashed bodies, feces, and fear swilled around Cordero as he followed a jailer down a narrow hall lined with identical cell doors. Picturing Celine existing within these walls, he fought down the urge to retch and forced himself to keep moving. Outside, rain poured down upon New Orleans, turning the streets into ribbons of rich mud churned by cart and carriage wheels into thick goo. Steel clouds stained the sky a deep, depressing gray.

Suddenly, the guard stopped outside a door that looked like all the rest and unlocked it. Not a sound issued from inside.

"She's in here." The guard's contemptuous gaze flicked over Cord and then dismissed him.

When Cord stepped into the dimly lit cell, he thought for a moment the guard had been mistaken. The room appeared empty. A slop bucket stood in a corner. A forgotten pan of food lay on the filthy floor near the door.

He turned around, ready to exit the cell, when the door closed behind him with a loud thud and the key scraped in the lock.

A shape moved beneath a foul blanket on the narrow bunk. Cord watched, stunned with disbelief, as Celine's head and shoulders appeared over the edge of the utilitarian wool. Her hair was matted and filthy, her cheeks were sunken, her skin was sallow. When she stared back at him without a hint of recognition in her eyes, a cold finger of fear raked down his spine.

"Celine?"

What hell had she suffered? What might he have spared her with a word?

She did not move. The blanket slipped lower, exposing the swell of her breasts. She shivered, but did not speak.

He went to her side and knelt on one knee in the filth, then reached for her and drew her into his arms. She lay limp in his embrace as he held her close and rocked her slowly.

"I'm sorry, Celine. So sorry. Please forgive me," he murmured again and again.

Slowly he lowered her to the thin, stained mattress. He tried to brush her hair off her face, unable to miss the dried tearstains that made tracks down the dirt on her cheeks. He took her hands, then rubbed them between his, willing her to come back to him.

"Celine, speak to me." He cast his gaze about the room and then back to her again. "Please," he whispered.

"Am I dreaming again?" she whispered so low that he had to lean closer to hear. "I've imagined you here so many times . . ."

"We sailed two days after you left; it took me that

long to sober up and come to my senses. I've been in the city two days trying to get in to see you. The authorities finally agreed.''

The slight tilt of her lips cut through him as swiftly as a hot blade. He traced the corner of her mouth. Her smile faded.

''Forgive me, Celine.''

''It's too late,'' she whispered before she closed her eyes.

His heart felt as if a stone had lodged there.

''I don't blame you for hating me, Celine. Not after I told you I loved you and then let them take you like that. I should have never turned you over to Hargraves: I should have fought to defend you. Please, don't say it's too late for us.''

''I don't blame you, Cord. How could I? Our love was too new, too fragile. What a chance you took that night, to tell me you loved me . . . and then to have those men show up like that, to be slapped in the face with the truth.'' She sighed, all the sadness of the world reflected in her eyes. ''It is too late for me, Cord. I hang tomorrow.''

''We're going to get you out of here and out of New Orleans.''

''I tried running once. It didn't work. Tomorrow I am to hang. I have to atone for killing Jean—''

''Listen to me!'' Frightened by the resignation in her voice, he grabbed both her hands and held them tight. ''I didn't lose you to the swamp, and I'll be damned if I'll lose you to the hangman. My father and his men are here in New Orleans. So are Foster and Edward. They have been prowling the streets and skulking in every coffeehouse, tavern and market stalls, and along the wharf, questioning, listening, searching for any scrap of proof to clear your name.

"We have already learned that Perot was gambling heavily, that he was in debt to a cousin who disappeared the very day Perot was killed. This cousin might have come upon Jean Perot's body and smashed his head in just to be certain he was dead. But Jean may have still been alive. You might not have killed him at all."

Her gaze strayed to the wall. "I don't want you there tomorrow," she whispered. "Please, leave me some dignity."

"Celine—"

"It's my hanging. You are not invited, Cord."

Cord pinched his eyes shut to ease the sting behind them.

"I am not going to let you hang, Celine."

She raised herself up on an elbow and planted a finger against his breastbone. "I am happy that you and your father have reconciled, but I can't allow you to do anything stupid, Cord. You're not to put yourself, your father or the others in jeopardy."

"Nag." He bent to kiss her, but she turned her face away.

"I'm filthy," she whispered. "Don't humiliate me."

"Clean or filthy, you are mine and I love you. You have been mine since the night you came to me out of the storm . . ." He took her chin in his hand and forced her to look at him.

"Cord, please don't."

She hadn't any more strength to hold him off. Sensing this, Cord kissed her long and thoroughly. When he lifted his head, she sighed and lay back down.

"Tell me you believe in me. Tell me you will give

me a lifetime to prove my love and make this up to you,'' he begged.

A tear slipped down her cheek. Cord kissed it away.

''If I had a lifetime to give, it would be yours. Tomorrow at dawn they will bring me fresh clothing and I will be allowed to bathe. I've ordered gumbo with shrimp and plenty of okra.''

A tight knot of fear twisted his insides. He tried to uncoil it by running the back of his knuckles along her cheek.

''I have heard they will bring a bottle of whiskey to calm you. If they do, don't drink it, Celine.''

''*You* are telling *me* not to drink?''

''I want you to have your wits about you tomorrow.'' He took her hand again.

''If I knew how to keep my wits about me, I wouldn't have ended up here.'' She smiled again, and it broke his heart.

''Promise me,'' he begged.

''You're crushing my hand.''

''Say it.''

''I promise,'' she whispered. ''For you, I'll go to the gallows as sober as a judge.''

# Twenty-two

$\mathcal{N}$oon was the appointed hour for hangings.

With a quarter hour to go, the crowd packed into the Place d'Armes, hungry for Celine's death. She encountered the boisterous mob as her nervous jailers led her out into the light of a bright, cloudless day. Freshly bathed, outfitted in a starched white cap, white shirt and pantaloons, and fortified by a meal of gumbo and shrimp, she felt stronger than she had in weeks.

Thomas O'Hurley had arrived earlier, as promised, but the man needed more support than she did, so Celine told him to go home and pray for her. And because she had given Cord her word, she did not touch the bottle of whiskey they had offered her.

She wished now that she had drained it.

The guards were jittery. None of them, not even the

familiar fat one or the one she called Hawk-nose, would meet her gaze. To a man, they kept a constant eye on the crowd. Surrounding her, they moved as a tightly packed unit, forced to keep a slow pace because of the shackles around her ankles.

She scanned the route they would take and saw the gallows erected across the square. She focused on it rather than on the faces that swarmed around her. Unwashed, slovenly derelicts and undisciplined youths were the cruelest. They leered and jeered, pushed and shoved, threatening her with their upraised fists. The others, who stood back in silence or muttered to one another, were merely curious.

''Celine!''

She had not taken half a dozen steps outside before Cord had shoved his way between the onlookers and shouted her name. He was as near as the guards would possibly allow. The instant she saw him, she forgot that her wrists were shackled and raised her hands, trying to reach him. Bleak despair whipped through her when she realized she would never touch him again. She tried to smile at him, but could only manage a tremulous, wavering imitation.

She focused on the gallows, blinking furiously.

Cordero's heart had lurched when he'd seen her step out of the Cabildo surrounded by a phalanx of guards. Doubt assaulted him, and he knew a moment of terror, even though his father and most of his crew were scattered throughout the crowd, ready to divert attention away from her so that he and Bobo, along with two of Auguste's most trusted men, could spirit her away.

Last night, confidence had run high when Auguste had been able to bribe one of the Cabildo guards into outlining the details of the execution ahead of time—but it was one thing to go over and over the plan and escape routes and quite another to see Celine shackled and surrounded by guards only a few yards from the gallows.

He glanced around the horde jammed into the square and marveled at the way his father's men blended into the crowd. All hands were present and accounted for except Foster and Edward, as the latter's nerves had gotten the better of him. Terrified that something would go wrong and he would be forced to watch Celine hang, Edward was so hysterical that Foster suggested they wait along the escape route near the edge of the swamp.

Cord watched the guards walk his wife through the crowd and tasted his fear. Failure, he knew, would mean all of their deaths.

"Celine!" he called out again, demanding her attention.

He could only catch a glimpse of her between the burly guards. She turned her gaze his way, stunning him with the love in her eyes. Even now, he could see, she loved him.

"Trust me," Cord shouted.

Celine watched him shove a man back in order to keep stride with her jailers. Suddenly, Cord's eyes became wild and his gaze went everywhere and nowhere. She saw his brows meet and his jaw set. She glanced around, searching for the cause of his anger.

She spotted Henre Moreau ahead of them, head and shoulders taller than those around him. Two slaves stood beside him, flanking him like burly watchdogs. He had seen Cord, and the two were staring daggers at each other.

Then she saw Auguste, his leather eye patch making him easily recognizable to her despite the oversized hat he wore. As the crowed shifted to allow the guards to pass, Henre and Auguste recognized each other over the crowd.

Henre visibly blanched as he realized his youngest son was still alive. The old man stared for a moment longer, then briefly said something to one of the blacks. An instant later, he turned his back on Auguste and Cordero as his escorts began to clear a path through the crowd. By the time she had taken two more shuffling steps, all signs of Henre Moreau had been swallowed up by the throng.

Cord knew a moment of release as he watched his grandfather walk out of their lives. He took it as a sign that the past was indeed behind him, that it was time to focus on the present.

He kept his eyes on Celine. The closer they moved to the gallows, the less he could afford to be diverted. He saw her pause, then shake her head and stumble. A guard reached out and broke her fall. When she straightened, she had a bewildered look on her face. He saw her lips move and was almost certain she had mouthed the word *Perot*.

She halted abruptly and before the guards could make her move forward again, her gaze swung back to him. Her amethyst eyes were narrowed in confusion.

"What is it?" he shouted. They were nearing Auguste's position now. The escape plan was about to be put into motion. There was no time for her to balk, no time for anything that veered from the carefully laid plan.

"I think I saw Jean Perot!" she called out to Cord. One of the guards had taken her arm, and she tried to shrug him off.

"Where?"

"I saw him through there!" she said, nodding toward the Mississippi side of the square.

"None of this, now, you hear?" The fat guard with his hand clamped above her elbow shook her. "Keep moving."

Celine thought for a second that she had been hallucinating, and then she saw him again. The sight of the glassy-eyed man on the edge of the crowd caused her to lose her footing and stumble again. Her heart was pounding, her breath short. She knew without a doubt she was seeing either Jean Perot or his ghost.

"It's him. He's here, Cordero. Perot is *here*!"

The crowd sensed her panic. Those nearest her easily understood what she had said, and a cry went up. The name *Perot* began to be murmured, first by a few and then by many. The word spread through the mass of people like wildfire.

Cord understood, but was hesitant to leave her side. He didn't intend to get very far away, in case she was mistaken. Agitated, he scanned the nearest faces in the crowd.

Auguste had moved into position on the other side of the guards and had seen what was happening. "Go!" he hollered to Cord, the meaning of their exchange lost on the surging tide of humanity around them. "Find him! If you fail, we'll meet as planned."

Cord stared at his father, unwilling to relinquish Celine's life to the man who had walked out on him so long ago. Their gazes met and held across the huddle of guards, was momentarily cut off and then was reestablished as the blue-coated men shuffled slowly by.

His father was pinned on the far side of the crowd, away from the river. There was no way Auguste could follow Perot. If one of them was going to get to the man, it would have to be him.

"There!" Celine shouted again, trying to point. "With the beard, in the brown coat!"

The man she indicated was being jostled by the crowd. He was hunched over on his left side, his skin was pale and his eyes were bright but glassy, as if he were drugged. Some in the throng were still murmuring Perot's name. The man's gaze was darting wildly. Hemmed in as he was, there was no escaping the crowd.

The guards had almost reached the gallows. Cord lunged ahead of them. He nearly pushed over a toothless old woman with a chignon tied around her head and lost precious time as he made a grab for her and stood her on her feet before he shoved on. After nearly coming to blows with a burly Kaintuck, Cord finally reached the man Celine claimed was Jean Perot.

From two feet away, the man's body odor was merciless. Cord ignored the stench as he clamped a hand on the padded shoulder of what had once been a well-tailored cutaway coat. The slight, dark-eyed Creole tried to pull away but lacked the strength to do more than lean back.

"Who are you?" Cord asked, giving the man a vicious shake.

"Let me go! Let me go, I say!"

Up close, Cord could see that the man was more slovenly and disgusting than he had first thought. He was also quite young. It wasn't until the brown coat opened to reveal a dark stain low on the man's shirtfront that Cord felt certain Celine had correctly identified Jean Perot.

Cord put one hand around the back of Perot's neck. His captive winced and whimpered, favoring his left side, but could not escape.

"Please, let me go. I've done you no harm . . ."

"You think not?" Cord glared down at Perot as he

dragged him toward the gallows. "That's my wife they're about to hang."

"It's Perot!" a hardy, suntanned youth beside Cord began shouting. The note of urgent hysteria carried above the din. "He says he's got Perot. Stop the hanging!"

It took Cord an instant to recognize the youth as the cabin boy from the *Lady Fair*. Like the others in the ship's crew, the boy had donned nondescript clothing and a wide-brimmed panama hat.

"Keep it up, Raymond," Cord mumbled to the youth. "This is a far better diversion than we could have ever hoped for." He shoved Perot toward the gallows through the onlookers surrounding them.

Cord reached the base of the wooden platform at the moment Celine's guards arrived at the steps. He saw Auguste at the stairs, standing but a few feet away from Celine. She was scanning the crowd, searching for him, so Cord called her name. When she saw him with Perot, a tremulous smile of hope lit her face.

Dignitaries from the Cabildo were in attendance, assembled in a roped-off area fronting the gallows. Cord pushed Perot up against the gallows platform and held him there while he called out to the men and the few women in the official viewing area. The uniformed police had begun to take notice of the disturbance behind them.

"Governor! Stop the hanging!" Cord shouted, thrusting Perot forward.

"Jean! Oh, my God, my son! My son . . ."

A frantic woman disengaged herself from the viewing area, arms outstretched, hands grasping for the creature Cord held like a bedraggled cat.

Celine was prodded up the steps of the platform until

she stood directly below a thick rope fashioned into a noose. An ominous figured stood to one side of the platform. With his arms crossed over his chest, he stood as silent as death. A black velvet bag, unrelieved but for two small eyeholes, was draped over his head. Celine shivered as she exchanged a glance with the cold, dark eyes staring out at her from the shadowed interior of the hangman's hood.

From her vantage point above the crowd she saw Cord refuse to relinquish Jean Perot to his babbling mother and his father, who now stood on both sides of their son. As the astounded officials looked on, the mob, led by Auguste's crew, was chanting in unison. Cries of "Stop the hanging! Stop the hanging!" shook the square. The guards were milling about uneasily on the platform.

The governor himself raised both hands in the air and tried to quiet the crowd. Silence fanned out like ripples on water from the officials' section toward the edges of the mob. There was a press to move forward, a collective strain to hear what was being said by the tight knot of officials near the base of the gallows.

Throughout the crowd the citizens of New Orleans began to speculate. Who had come forward to save the penniless fortune-teller's ward? Were the rumors true—could she truly work black magic? Was she in league with some voodoo priest or priestess? Was that really Jean Perot or a zombie groveling beneath the gallows built to hang his murderess?

Celine recognized Jean Perot's mother. Her be-ringed hands clutched her son to her breast, smoothed his oily hair, patted his back. If it had not been for Perot's coloring and height, or for the fact that the frantic gaze in his eyes today was the same one she'd seen the night he'd tried to kill her, Celine would have never recognized him.

She was about to see Jean firsthand, for the governor and his deputies had persuaded Cord to relinquish the man to them and were now leading Perot and his family toward the Cabildo. Cord disengaged himself from the group and came bounding up the stairs.

Behind them, at a slower, more sedate pace, came Judge Bennett, who had presided over her hearing.

"Cordero." She reached for him, but once more the shackles prevented her from raising her hands. Then she noticed Auguste standing beside Cord.

"Auguste, go!" she whispered. "Someone might recognize you."

The distracted guards gave Auguste a quick once-over and said nothing. Like the rest of his crew, he had donned a panama hat, and kept it pulled low. With his head tipped down, the wide brim cast a shadow that partially shielded his face from the crowd.

"The only one who might remember me left the moment he saw me," Auguste whispered back to Celine.

"Henre?" she asked.

"You are quite perceptive, dear Celine."

Cord grabbed her wrist shackles. "Get these off her," he said to one of the guards, who ignored him. When Judge Bennett issued orders for the men to escort Celine back to the Cabildo, Cord turned on him.

"I want these shackles off my wife."

"Young man," Bennett said, peering up at him over his gold-rimmed spectacles, "it will do you no good whatsoever to yell at me."

"But Perot's been found. This is ridiculous."

"As ridiculous as it may seem, she was found guilty of two murders. One is still outstanding. I will have her unshackled when and if she is proven entirely innocent or I am good and ready. Now, might I suggest you go with your wife and these gentlemen here while I break the news to this mob that they are going to have to disperse without their afternoon's entertainment?''

Jean Perot smelled even worse in the close confines of the judge's chambers.

Sitting beside Celine, Cord wouldn't have cared if the man reeked like a very dead horse. Her shackles had been removed after they were all closeted with Judge Bennett, the Perots, Jean and four of the police guards. At Celine's insistence, Auguste had left them at the door of the Cabildo and disappeared into the crowd, though not before he'd kissed her on the cheek.

Cord, Celine and the three Perots sat like penitents on hard-bottomed chairs, waiting for the judge to speak. Cord removed his coat and slipped it over Celine's shoulders. She smiled up at him as she pulled the edges of the wide lapels close.

''Mrs. Moreau, it is obvious you did not murder Jean Perot, for here he stands. Sort of.'' Bennett wrinkled his nose as he looked Jean up and down. ''It still remains to be seen just who you did kill.''

''No one, sir,'' she said softly.

''Ask *him*,'' Cord said, leaping to his feet. He was barely able to refrain from strangling Perot.

''I was just getting to that,'' the judge said. ''Sit down, Moreau.''

Cord sat beside Celine again. When she slipped her hand into the crook of his arm, he covered it with his own.

Judge Bennett turned to Jean, who sat beside his parents, hunched over on his left side as if he were ninety, not nineteen years old.

"Young man, it would behoove you to tell me the truth, and all of it. Now. If we have to drag it out of you with a long, lengthy trial, things will not go as well for you."

Before Jean could utter a word, the elder Perot jumped to his feet. "I have money. I want the best lawyer available for my son. I want—"

"I want you to sit down, sir," Bennett barked.

Cord smiled until Jean began in a weak, singsong tone that demanded everyone strain to hear him. He raised a filthy hand and pointed it at Celine.

"She tried to kill me. I had to disappear. I knew she would not give up until I was dead. She cursed me, just as the old woman did. I am ill," he said, imploring the judge with outstretched arms. His coat gaped open to reveal the bloody stain at his midriff.

"I have been ill since that night when she stabbed me," he went on, his gaze darting from one person to the next. "I was . . . delirious, wandering the . . . the city. I . . . don't know what happened. I . . . lost all track of time, of days . . . weeks . . . until today, when I saw the crowd. That's all I know . . ." His voice trailed off.

Without taking his eyes off Jean, Judge Bennett leaned across his desk.

"There is a little matter of the body found in your courtyard, Perot, the one everyone assumed to be you. Someone of the same height, the same build, wearing your clothing. How do you explain that?"

"She did it," Jean said quickly, pointing at Celine. "She killed the old woman, too."

"You'll have to do better than that," Bennett told him.

"*I* can do better than *that*." Cord started to get to his feet again.

"Your Honor?" Celine said, pulling Cord down beside her. She closed her eyes for a second to collect her thoughts. The judge seemed willing to listen and waited for her to go on.

There was not a sound in the small chamber when she began.

"My husband has recently learned that Jean's cousin has been missing since the night of Persa's murder. I had met this cousin on only one occasion, when he came with Jean to my guardian's shop. Dressed in Jean's clothing, this young man might have easily been mistaken for Jean. With his face—"

When she pictured the laughing, dark-eyed, devil-may-care youth who had encouraged Jean to have his fortune read, she could not continue.

"What you're trying to say is that with his face bashed in, the fellow might have been mistaken for Jean here?" Bennett finished for her.

"Yes, sir. I believe Jean killed Persa, then went looking for me, certain I would sense the truth. When he tried to kill me to keep me quiet, I stabbed him and ran, thinking he was dead. I don't know when or how he killed his cousin, but he must have."

"That's a lie!" Jean cried.

Madam Perot appealed to Bennett. "My son needs medical attention. His wound, the wound that woman inflicted upon him months ago, is seeping. It is infected. Surely you can see that he is burning up with fever and crippled with pain—"

Cord jumped up again before Celine could stop him.

"Your Honor, I know how we could get to the truth once and for all. It's a bit unconventional—"

"Everything about this place is unconventional," Bennett cut in. "Had I known what was in store for me before I came to New Orleans, I would have stayed in Boston." He sighed. "What is your idea, Mr. Moreau?"

"As you know, my wife was raised by a fortune-teller. Perhaps as a result, she herself has a somewhat unique talent."

He looked down at Celine. She shook her head, trying to get him to stop, but Cord went on.

"Let her lay her hand on Perot and you'll have your answers," he urged Bennett.

"No!" Jean Perot screamed like a stuck pig and began thrashing in his seat, his wild eyes locked on Celine. "Don't let her touch me. Don't let her even come near me. I've been in hell since that night she touched my hand!"

Madam Perot started wailing and crossing herself to ward off evil. Cord held out his hand to Celine, urging her to stand and walk with him over to Jean.

Bennett frowned. "Is this some of that voodoo you people down here are so fond of?"

"You're thinking of gumbo," Cord said as he led Celine across the room. They stopped before Jean Perot and his mother.

"With Your Honor's permission?" Cord asked Bennett.

"I wouldn't miss this for the world," the judge said. He stood and spread his palms on the desktop, leaning forward to get a better view.

"Touch him, Celine." Over the protests of both elder Perots, Cord pinned Jean in his chair.

"No! Don't!" Jean cried out, writhing, as Celine reached for him.

She nearly balked, then closed her eyes and touched

his hand. Almost immediately she whispered, "I see it. I see it all," and then let quickly go. Cord was watching her closely, with a curious stare.

As Celine stared down at Jean Perot, the man who'd killed Persa, the man who'd sent her running headlong into the night, she could only feel sorry for the pitiful creature he had become.

She turned to Judge Bennett.

"Well, young woman?"

"It happened just as we suspected." But Celine knew it was only her word against Perot's, that her visions would probably count for naught. She was about to warn Cord not to be disappointed when Jean started babbling.

"She sees true. I killed him! I killed my cousin Renard and hid his body in the stable. Then I went to the old woman, because I needed to know what would become of me. She knew right away, said there was evil upon me, said I would die very shortly for what I had done."

His fingers kept scratching at the fabric of his trousers as he stared off into space reciting his crimes, while his mother wept copious tears into her palms.

"I had to kill Persa, too, you see? She knew too much. And then, as I was leaving the shop, I remembered Celine. She could see everything, just like the other one. She would surely know I'd killed Renard and old Persa. So she had to die, too." He looked over at the judge. "It's a pity that others had to die just because I owed so much money to Renard. He was going to tell Papa, you see."

"I'm afraid I do see," Judge Bennett said slowly. "I'm afraid I see all too well. Officers"—he turned to the policemen, who had managed to blend into the far corners of the chambers—"see that young Mr. Perot here is treated to our fine accommodations.''

After Jean was led sobbing from the room and his parents filed out in shock, Judge Bennett came around the desk. He stood before Cord and Celine, took her hand and shook it.

''Mrs. Moreau, I have never known anyone who stood beneath a hangman's noose and lived to tell about it. I'm certainly glad your husband saw fit to arrive in time.''

Celine looked up at Cord. She could see that he was more than a little distressed at the reminder that he'd almost let her down. She slipped her hand around his waist and leaned against him.

''So am I, Your Honor, but anyone who knows Cordero as well as I do knows that in the end, he always does the honorable thing.''

# Twenty-three

## DUNSTAIN PLACE
## ST. STEPHEN ISLAND

"Most men think one wedding a lifetime is more than enough," Auguste said with a laugh as he handed Cordero a double-breasted black jacket. "If I didn't know Celine I would think you were a glutton for punishment, but if she were my wife I would also want to contrive as many honeymoons as I possibly could."

Closeted in one of the spare rooms at Dunstain Place, the two talked as Cord slipped on the jacket and buttoned it up.

"Let's just say our first wedding was not the stuff a girl's dreams are made of." Cord grinned at his father, unable to keep the embarrassment out of his tone. "I wasn't even sober."

"Do you think you should have kept this a surprise?

What if she doesn't want to marry you again?''

"After last night, I think that's highly unlikely,'' Cord said, bending down to concentrate on his image in the mirror above a dressing table.

"So things are going well? Might I be expecting a grandson soon?''

"Things are going well. I hope before long you'll get your wish—and we ours. I'm certainly doing my part.'' Cord paused with his hand on his high shirt collar, after having made certain it was adjusted just so. He wanted everything to be perfect for the ceremony he had planned for sunset.

"Can you believe I'm actually nervous?'' he asked his father after he realized his hand was shaking.

"As nervous as we were when we escorted Celine to the gallows?''

Cord's smile instantly faded. "I'd rather not ever be reminded of that day again.''

"I'm sorry. Since all went well, I felt it safe to jest. Now,'' Auguste said, brushing off the cuff of his coat sleeve and standing at attention, "what would you have me do to help? Should I give the bride away?''

"I've already asked Howard Wells to do that. Since he seems to be a fixture around here, he should at least earn his keep.'' When Auguste's face mirrored his disappointment, Cord quickly added, "I had thought to ask you to stand as best man for me.''

The man was speechless for nearly a minute and then, grinning broadly, he took Cord's hand in his and said, "There is nothing I'd rather do.''

"I'll see you in a quarter of an hour then,'' Cord said, grabbing his hat from the bed. "I'm off to collect the bride.''

"At least you don't have far to go.''

"No, she's just down the hall."

Celine had just stepped out of her bath when a knock sounded on the bedroom door. She smiled as she tossed aside her towel, slipped on her dressing gown and tied the sash. After more than one very embarrassing episode, Cord had finally convinced Foster and Edward that at the very least, they should knock before entering the master suite.

"Come in," she called as she shook her damp hair out and began to comb her fingers through the wet mass. When she saw her husband walk in instead of one of his servants, she couldn't contain her joy. She ran across the room and into his waiting arms, unmindful of the flowered silk fabric draped over his arm.

"Cordero! What are you doing home from the fields so early?"

"Would you like me to go back?"

She wrapped her arms around his neck and pressed a long, slow kiss on his lips. It didn't take much encouragement for him to kiss her back with gusto. Finally, out of breath, her heart racing, she pulled away.

"You're all dressed up. I've never even seen this jacket before." She frowned. Life had been one long blissful reunion since they had left the nightmare of New Orleans behind and sailed home. "You're not going away, are you?"

"My father had the jacket made for me in Jamaica last time he was there and no, I'm not going away. I brought you this." He managed to extract himself from her embrace to present her with the flowered silk gown, which was not, thankfully, very wrinkled from having been smashed between them.

"What's this?"

"A gown. I must request that you put it on right now,

because if you don't, we're going to be late."

Puzzled, she frowned, unable to recall any pressing engagement they might have made with anyone. She reached up to push a stray lock of hair off his forehead, thrilled with the simple act of touching him. "Late for what?"

"For the surprise," he said.

"What surprise?"

"If I tell you, it won't be a surprise. Get dressed and you'll see." He walked over to the bed, shoved back the mosquito net and stretched out, propped against the headboard, his ankles crossed and his boots dangling off the edge.

"Will you help me?" She held up the silk gown and smiled over her shoulder.

In the mood to tease, Celine lay the silk gown across the footboard and stood at the end of the bed, staring at Cord through lowered lashes. Slowly, provocatively, she untied the sash at her waist and opened the dressing gown. Inch by inch, by slow, seductive degrees, she opened the robe, exposing her nakedness to Cordero.

She let the robe slip down her shoulders, to her waist and then onto the ground, where it pooled around her feet. Running her hands over her waist and down to her hips, she kept her eyes locked on Cord's smoldering stare.

"You're playing with fire, Celine." His voice was thick with passion.

"I know it. That's what makes this so exciting." She walked naked around the foot of the bed until she stood before him.

Celine reached out and nudged his boot up so that his ankles uncrossed. She ran her hands up his pant legs to his thighs. With her fingertips, she teased the telltale bulge beneath the fine serge of his trousers. Moving up to the side of the bed, she cupped his arousal with one hand as she reached out and slipped the fingers of her other hand through his hair and brought his mouth down to her breasts.

When his mouth closed over a tightly budded nipple, she pressed him close until he suckled. She arched back, savoring the heat that spiraled through her, melting her, starting a deep throb in the sensitive nub at the apex of her thighs. He teased her nipple, toyed with her as he nipped her with his teeth. She nearly came undone when she felt his hand slide between her thighs and slip inside her.

"You're melting for me," he whispered at her breast.

"Yes," she whispered back, and pressed against his hand, silently urging him to delve deeper. "Only for you."

"We have to hurry," he said, increasing the friction as he stroked her faster.

"Yes," she sighed, bringing her lips to his mouth and her hands to the buttons of his coat. "Hurry."

His coat hit the floor a second later. As he pushed her to the brink of climax, she whimpered and fumbled with his shirttails, trying to extricate them from his trousers.

"Help," she urged. "Get them . . . off!"

"You want me, Celine?"

"Yes, and I want you naked."

Without letting her go, he lifted and shrugged, rolled, kicked and adjusted until she had divested him of his shirt, his pants, his boots and even his stockings, and he was as naked as she.

As her fingers explored him, as she ran them over his suntanned upper body, over the corded muscles in his arms, over his ribs and the tight ripples of his abdomen, he pulled her close and kissed her deeply, teasing her mouth with his teeth and tongue until she was begging him to take her.

In one swift move he rolled her beneath him and they lay crosswise on the bed, entangled in clothes, mosquito netting and her still damp hair. He did not tease her any longer, because he could not wait. Cord thrust himself inside her ready, willing body, gathered her close and began to slowly slide along her soft inner core until she was writhing beneath him, clutching the bedclothes, her head thrown back in passion. He was burning to take her, longing for the sweet agony to end and wondering how he could make it go on forever when she grasped his hips and raised up to meet him.

"Oh, sweet heaven, *now*, Cordero," she cried as she felt herself about to splinter into a thousand throbbing pulse points. "Come with me *now*."

"Celine." Her name was a prayer on his lips as he shattered and drove into her for a final thrust. He spilled his seed into her womb and thanked God that she was alive and in his arms.

"You should have told me you were serious about this surprise. I would have never distracted you," Celine said as she pulled her new, very wrinkled gown down over her breasts and began tying the forest green ribbon beneath the bodice.

"Which is exactly why I didn't tell you I was serious." Cord shoved his shirttails back into his trousers and then bent to pull the stirrups over his boots before tugging his pants all the way up.

"Where are my shoes?" She was on her hands and knees, looking under the bed. "The dark green ones."

"The closet?"

"I think I kicked them off just before I got into the tub."

He got down on his hands and knees beside her, searching the floor for her missing shoes.

"Don't you have another pair?"

"They match the dress."

"Does it matter?"

"That depends on the surprise. Is this important, or is this one of those evenings Ada has decided to try out a new recipe and we all have to dress for dinner?"

He pulled her to him.

"It's more important than that," Cord said softly, holding her upper arms, massaging them with his thumbs as he stared down into her eyes.

"What is it, Cord?"

"Will you marry me, Celine?"

She laughed, and the sound filled his heart with joy.

"It's a little late for that, don't you think? Were you out in the sun without a hat a little too long today?"

"I'm serious." He let go of her arms and took both her hands in his. "Would you marry me again if you had a choice?"

"Oh, Cord," she whispered, clinging to his hands. "I would marry you again and again and again. I wouldn't change a minute of it . . ." She stopped and tipped her head, as if thinking it over. "Well, maybe I would want to forget the trial and the day of the hanging but . . . nothing else."

He stood up and pulled her to her feet. "We're getting married at sunset. Actually, thanks to that pleasant little interlude, we're almost too late for sunset."

"What are you talking about?"

"The surprise. We're getting married all over again. This time with flowers and guests and a grand reception, just the way it should have been before. Only this time we will marry for love.''

"Where? When?'' She was too astounded to phrase a coherent thought.

"Out in the garden, as soon as we find your damn shoes.''

The house was silent and empty, a far cry from the usual afternoon activity in and around the place. Celine felt a flutter of anticipation, wondering when Cord had had the time to plan this second "wedding'' and how he'd been enable to enlist everyone's help without her knowledge. He quite formally escorted her down the stairs, insisting she tuck her hand into his elbow and hold her head high. When they reached the first floor, he stopped long enough to tuck a strand of hair behind her ear and smile down at her, then walked to a side table near the front door and collected a bouquet of hibiscus and crepe myrtle.

"You look radiant, Celine. You're the most beautiful bride I ever saw." He handed her the bouquet and kissed her—briefly this time, afraid as he was to get carried away again.

She clutched the flowers in one hand and fingered the thick strand of pearls at her neck. "I wish Auguste could be here.''

Cord only smiled. When he walked her out onto the veranda overlooking the terrace, Celine gasped in shocked surprise as a cheer went up. Gathered there on the terrace were not only their immediate household—Ada, Howard Wells, Foster and Edward—but Auguste, looking every bit as handsome as Cordero: Auguste's solicitor, Timothy Tinsdale, recently returned from England; all of the newly freed Dunstain Place slaves, from the oldest down to the squirming, wriggling youngest in their mothers' arms; and the entire crew of Auguste's ship, the *Lady Fair*.

"Nothing too large," Cord smiled. "Just family." He gave her hand a reassuring squeeze and nodded to Howard Wells, who hurried up onto the veranda to take his place at her side.

"Howard will give you away, Celine," Cord told her, slipping her hand into the crook of the bookseller's arm.

Auguste walked up to the veranda next and stood beside Cordero. Celine waited to see who would officiate, wondering what manner of minister would conduct a marriage ceremony for the already married. She glanced down at the assembly and realized there was no one there she did not recognize. Edward and Ada stood side by side, each of them smiling through the copious tears they were shedding, their noses pressed into lace-edged handkerchiefs.

Foster looked as proud as a peacock and gazed up at the two of them as if the success of their marriage had been entirely his doing. Bobo also had a place of honor in front of the crowd. He stood beside his wife, his son riding high on his shoulders.

Beyond them all, the sea shimmered silver-blue beneath the tropical sun riding just above the horizon. The trade winds scattered the scent of frangipani through the garden. Torches flickered against the sunset sky.

At some silent cue, Howard Wells turned Celine so that they stood facing Cord and Auguste. The kindly, soft-spoken bookseller cleared his throat and announced, "I am here to give the bride to the bridegroom and to stand witness for her. Before I do, I would like to say that if I ever had a daughter, I would be proud to have one exactly like you, Celine." He smiled down at her and then turned to give a slight bow to the assembly.

"So beautiful," Ada murmured as she sobbed on Edward's shoulder. Celine wondered if the two of them might have to be led away before the ceremony ended. She turned back to Cord to see what was next in store.

"I stand witness for this man, my son, Cordero Moreau," Auguste said, his voice well able to carry to the back row of the crowd. "He would now like to recite his vows."

The crowd hushed. The children, sensing the solemnity of the occasion, all quieted. When Cord reached for her hand, Celine forgot that there were over two hundred people crowded together on the veranda and terrace overlooking the sea. She had eyes only for her husband as she handed Howard Wells her bouquet.

The only sign of Cord's nervousness was in the way he held her hands so tight as he began to speak.

"I, Cordero Moreau, take you, Celine Winters Moreau, to have and to hold from this day forward as my lover, my wife, my other half. I promise that I will never betray your trust, nor will I ever take your love, which you shower on me so abundantly, for granted. I will honor you, defend you, protect and cherish you for as long as we both shall live. I will seal my pledge with this ring as a token of my love."

He reached into his pocket and withdrew a sparkling amethyst and slipped it on her finger. Then Cord reached out and gently wiped the tears from her cheeks, cupped her face in his hands and kissed her. Another rousing cheer went up from the crowd.

When it was quiet again, Howard leaned close and whispered to Celine, "If you wish to say anything to Cordero, you may do so now."

Celine took a deep breath and held tight to Cord's

hands. Unlike him, she'd had no time to rehearse what she would say to him, what vow she would make, so she trusted in herself and her feelings for him, opened her mouth and hoped the right words came out.

"I, Celine Winters Moreau, take you, Cordero Moreau, from this day forward, to have and to hold, as lover, as husband, as friend. I will accept your love and give you my own. I will trust you with my life and never betray the trust and love you give to me. I give my heart into your safekeeping, just as you have given me yours—a gift beyond measure and a responsibility I will never take lightly."

She paused, gathering her thoughts. "I have no ring to exchange as an outward sign of my love—"

"Celine, it doesn't matter," he said softly.

She shook her head, and then, in a voice that carried to the crowd, added, "But if you are willing to wait a few months, I will present you with our first child." Celine smiled in triumph. "You see? I just happened to have a little surprise of my own, husband."

"I love you, Celine," he whispered.

She stared up into eyes as blue as the Caribbean, eyes filled with love, and softly told him, "I thank God every day that I was able to change places with Jemma O'Hurley. I only hope that wherever she is, she is one tenth as happy as I am today."

He smiled, a slow, secret smile. "For bringing me you, so do I." He kissed her to seal the vows and then turned to face the crowd. "I want to thank you all for coming to hear us exchange our vows again and I invite you all to enjoy a wedding feast to celebrate this day. Since everyone helped, you know there will be plenty of music and food for all, so just follow the path through the garden to the mill, where everything is ready."

Cord slipped his arm around Celine's shoulders as they watched the assembled guests begin to head for the mill. The torches were glowing brighter now that the sun had gone down. In a few moments, they were alone with Foster and Edward, Ada, Howard and Auguste. Everyone wanted to talk at once.

"Celine, a baby!" Ada clasped her hands at her bosom, her eyes twinkling. "Just think! We'll have to prepare the nursery, and it will need so much care, so many things to eat, porridge and mashed fruit . . ."

"Congratulations, Cordero. Celine, you have made an old man very happy." Auguste kissed her on the cheek. When he pulled away, she noticed a tear glittering in his eye.

"Forty is not that old," Celine said. "You could still marry and give our child an aunt or an uncle of nearly the same age."

"I'll leave the baby making to you two," he said, laughing. "Shall we get a head start on that food, Howard?" Auguste and Howard left, with Ada between them.

"The perfect ending." Foster nodded up at them from below the veranda steps. "Just as I always knew it would be, though it took some doing."

"Yes, a 'appy ending. Just as it should be." Edward sniffed into his hankie. "The 'appiest ever."

"Before you turn into a bucket o' tears, I say we get ourselves down to the celebration and see that all's goin' right before the bride and groom arrive." Foster took Edward by the arm and led him toward the mill.

Cord turned to Celine just as the sun slipped entirely below the horizon and the sky blazed pink and gold. "It truly is a happy ending, isn't it?" He no longer wondered how and why he'd come to deserve her love, but simply reveled in the joy of it. "When I'm old and you decide to wander through my memories, you'll find this one tucked safely away," he told her.

She looked away, out across the sea, debating how to tell him something she had been wrestling with since they'd left New Orleans.

"What is it, Celine? What's brought that worried look to your eyes on such a happy day?" He hugged her close, teased her by rubbing his nose against hers. "Tell me."

"It's gone," she said.

"What's gone?"

"My gift. I can't see anyone's memories anymore—not yours, not anyone's. I don't know what happened . . ."

"Do you think it's because of the baby? Maybe this is only temporary?"

She shook her head, having lived with this last secret long enough to know that her gift would never return.

"No. It happened before the baby, perhaps long before. I think the fever may have had something to do with it. All I know is, that day in Judge Bennett's chambers, when you had me touch Jean Perot, I saw nothing, felt nothing at all. Thank God Jean broke down and confessed, for when I touched him, I was filled with my own thoughts, and nothing more."

"I wondered why you spoke so quickly. You had barely touched him, and you didn't seem to take on that faraway look or to go all pale and vacant as you always did. I can tell you now, the whole thing always scared the hell out of me."

"Are you pleased, then?" she asked.

"In a way. I would have always been afraid for you, afraid that if word got out, you would feel compelled to use your gift to help others who came to you in need. I saw what a physical toll using the gift took on you, Celine. Too many demands would have been too much for you." He looked out across the horizon. "No, I can't say as I'm upset that it's gone. Are you?"

"I might be, if I wasn't so happy with my life here with you, and with the child to come."

"And who knows—maybe she'll have a gift," Cord mused. "Or maybe she'll just be a little nag."

"Maybe *he* will be exceedingly handsome and as incorrigible as you."

"We could have one of each." He smiled down into her eyes, held her hand and rubbed his thumb over the surface of the amethyst ring.

She kissed him and then said, "You know, we *could* take advantage of the empty house and get started on—"

Before she could finish the thought, Cord grabbed her hand and led her back inside.